Lady Standon gaped at him. "Whatever are you doing?"

"Taking your advice." Flinging his jacket in one direction, he plucked off his cravat with one hand, while the other flipped open the buttons on his waistcoat.

She eyed him with open horror. "You're mad! I never told you to disrobe!"

Having added his cravat and waistcoat to the pile, he opened up his shirt a bit and stalked across the room, catching her in his arms. "No, you didn't."

She struggled, her fists pounding at his chest. "I certainly didn't tell you to accost me, either!"

"No, madame, you didn't."

"Then whatever are you doing?" she gasped.

"Exactly what you told me to do. Taking a wife."

And as the door crashed open, he sealed his proposal with a kiss.

By Elizabeth Boyle

LORD LANGLEY IS BACK IN TOWN
MAD ABOUT THE DUKE
HOW I MET MY COUNTESS
MEMOIRS OF A SCANDALOUS RED DRESS
CONFESSIONS OF A LITTLE BLACK GOWN
TEMPTED BY THE NIGHT
LOVE LETTERS FROM A DUKE
HIS MISTRESS BY MORNING
THIS RAKE OF MINE
SOMETHING ABOUT EMMALINE
IT TAKES A HERO
STEALING THE BRIDE
ONE NIGHT OF PASSION
ONCE TEMPTED
NO MARRIAGE OF CONVENIENCE

ELIZABETH BOYLE

Lord Langley
Is Back in Town

AVON

An Imprint of HarperCollinsPublishers

AVON BOOKS
An Imprint of HarperCollins*Publishers*
10 East 53rd Street
New York, New York 10022-5299

Copyright © 2011 by Elizabeth Boyle
Excerpts from *How I Met My Countess* and *Mad About the Duke*
copyright © 2010 by Elizabeth Boyle
ISBN 978-0-06-178351-7
www.avonromance.com

First Avon Books mass market printing: June 2011

Avon Trademark Reg. U.S. Pat. Off. and in Other Countries, Marca Registrada, Hecho en U.S.A.
HarperCollins® is a registered trademark of HarperCollins Publishers.

Printed in the U.S.A.

10 9 8 7 6 5 4 3 2 1

To Louise Pledge,
whose generous spirit and kindness
deserves this heartfelt recognition,
and for her dedication to readers all over the world,
including those who love her library in Saudi Arabia.

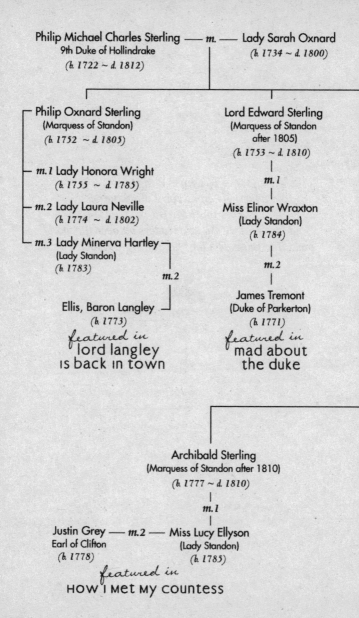

Philip Michael Charles Sterling — m. — Lady Sarah Oxnard
9th Duke of Hollindrake
(b. 1722 ~ d. 1812)

(b. 1734 ~ d. 1800)

Philip Oxnard Sterling
(Marquess of Standon)
(b. 1752 ~ d. 1805)

— m.1 Lady Honora Wright
(b. 1755 ~ d. 1785)

— m.2 Lady Laura Neville
(b. 1774 ~ d. 1802)

— m.3 Lady Minerva Hartley
(Lady Standon)
(b. 1783)

m.2

Ellis, Baron Langley
(b. 1773)

featured in
lord langley
is back in town

Lord Edward Sterling
(Marquess of Standon
after 1805)
(b. 1753 ~ d. 1810)

m.1

Miss Elinor Wraxton
(Lady Standon)
(b. 1784)

m.2

James Tremont
(Duke of Parkerton)
(b. 1771)

featured in
mad about
the duke

Archibald Sterling
(Marquess of Standon after 1810)
(b. 1777 ~ d. 1810)

m.1

Justin Grey — m.2 — Miss Lucy Ellyson
Earl of Clifton   (Lady Standon)
(b. 1778)   (b. 1785)

featured in
HOW I MET MY COUNTESS

the BACHELOR CHRONICLES 💜 💜
sterling family tree

Lady Mary Sterling
(b. 1755 ~ d. 1759)

Lord George Sterling
(b. 1758 ~ d. 1761)

Lady Geneva Sterling
(b. 1770)

m.

Mr. Robert Pensford
(b. 1765)

Lord Charles Sterling — *m.* — **Lady Rosebel Redford**
(b. 1757 ~ d. 1801) · · · · · · · · · · · · · · · · *(b. 1760)*

Aldus Sterling
(b. 1778 ~ d. 1806)

Aubrey Sterling
aka Captain Thatcher
(Marquess of Standon after 1810,
Duke of Hollindrake after 1812)
(b. 1780)

m.

Miss Felicity Langley
(b. 1793)

featured in
love letters from a duke

💜 For more of the Bachelor
Chronicles Family Tree,
please visit ElizabethBoyle.com

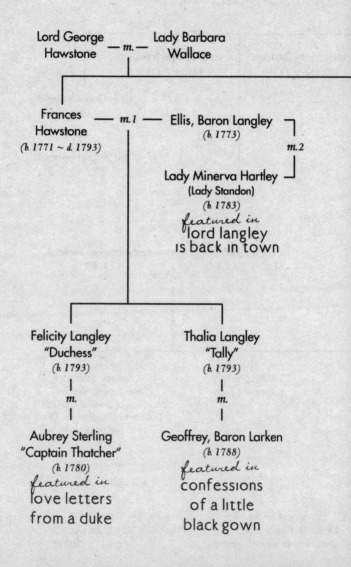

Lord George Hawstone — *m.* — Lady Barbara Wallace

Frances Hawstone
(b. 1771 ~ d. 1793)
— *m.1* — Ellis, Baron Langley
(b. 1773)

m.2

Lady Minerva Hartley
(Lady Standon)
(b. 1783)
featured in
lord langley
is back in town

Felicity Langley
"Duchess"
(b. 1793)

m.

Aubrey Sterling
"Captain Thatcher"
(b. 1780)
featured in
love letters
from a duke

Thalia Langley
"Tally"
(b. 1793)

m.

Geoffrey, Baron Larken
(b. 1788)
featured in
confessions
of a little
black gown

the
BACHELOR
CHRONICLES *family tree*

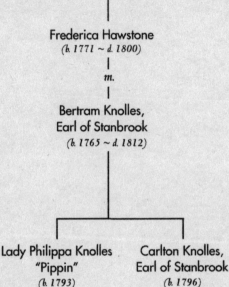

Frederica Hawstone
(b. 1771 ~ d. 1800)

m.

Bertram Knolles,
Earl of Stanbrook
(b. 1765 ~ d. 1812)

Lady Philippa Knolles
"Pippin"
(b. 1793)

Carlton Knolles,
Earl of Stanbrook
(b. 1796)

m.

Captain Thomas Dashwell
"Dash"
(b. 1788)
featured in
memoirs of a
scandalous red dress

♥ For more of the
Bachelor Chronicles
Family Tree, please
visit ElizabethBoyle.com

Cast of Characters

Ellis, Baron Langley. Our hero. Father of Felicity and Thalia Langley.

Minerva Hartley Sterling, Lady Standon. Our heroine.

Philip Oxnard Sterling, Marquess of Standon. Minerva's first husband. Most decidedly not a hero.

Lucy Ellyson Sterling, now the Countess of Clifton. The first Lady Standon who ventured back into marriage.

Elinor Knolles Sterling, now the Duchess of Parkerton. The other Lady Standon, who not only found a husband, but a ducal one at that.

Aunt Bedelia, Lady Chudley. Minerva's aunt and an expert on marriage, having snared two marquesses, an earl, a baron, and now a viscount.

Captain Gerald Adlington. A terrible villain.

Thomas-William. The loyal servant of George Ellyson.

Mrs. Hutchinson. The drunken and wretched house-keeper at Brook Street. But she bakes a mean scone, which makes her indispensable to this story.

Sir Basil Brownett. With a name like Basil, of course he's a villain.

Lord Andrew Stowe. A young nobleman said to be related to the infamous Robin Hood. Has future hero written all over him.

And of course, the Nannies:

Nanny Brigid, the Contessa von Frisch, late of Vienna. Ranks her lovers by the breed of dog they remind her of, from terriers to Great Danes.

Nanny Jamilla, once the Duchesse de Fraine, most recently Princess Jamilla Kounellas. Suspected of sending her last husband to an early grave.

Nanny Lucia, the Duchessa di Oristano of Naples. A Borgia by blood, and a Borgia through and through.

Nanny Tasha, the Princess Natasha, a distant cousin of the tsar. Keeps her own Cossack ~~lover~~ guard ever at the ready.

Nanny Helga, Wilhelmenia Charlotte Louise, Margravine of Ansbach. No man turns his back on the margravine. Not unless he knows how to remove a halberd from his spine.

Prologue

A lady's best advantage in Society is to keep informed of all the comings and goings around her. How else can one keep a rival from the best candidates for a new ~~lover~~ husband?

Advice to Felicity Langley from her Nanny Tasha

March, 1815
Her Grace the Duchess of Hollindrake
Hollindrake House
Surrey

Dearest Felicity,

I must say your idea to put all those bothersome and scandalous Standon widows together under one roof was truly inspired. I wish I could take credit for the entire scheme, for who would ever have believed that Lucy Sterling would marry the Earl of Clifton or that Elinor Sterling would marry the Duke of Parkerton? Parkerton, indeed!

But I write you not over your matchmaking successes—which, my dear girl, have made you the envy of all—or the removal of those ladies from your husband's familial obligations, but with regards to Minerva Sterling, the last remaining Lady Standon.

I would have hardly believed it, if I had not heard the news from Lady Kingsbury who had it from Lady Ratcliffe who claims Minerva Sterling is betrothed.

While that is remarkable in itself, I am sending this letter directly by private courier because of the gentleman to whom Minerva is rumored to be married.

My dear Felicity, I think you should brace yourself . . .

—An excerpt from a letter written with great
   urgency by Lady Finch

Chapter 1

Marriage is the goal of all illustrious women, but widowhood, a well-endowed one, is to be the most coveted of all.

Advice to Felicity Langley from her Nanny Helga

London
One week earlier

I won't. I will not. I will never," Minerva Sterling, the dowager Marchioness of Standon, declared. "Aunt Bedelia, you can save your breath and your time—and your shoe leather as well—for there is no need to trot over here every day and try to cajole me into seeking another husband. I have no interest in marriage. None. So you can just forget any notion of me attending Lady Veare's soiree with you."

That should have been enough to deter anyone, but this was Aunt Bedelia. And as such, Minerva's adamant assertion did nothing to deter the lady.

"My dear girl, never worry about my shoes. Chudley is as rich as Midas. I can have as many pairs as it takes to make you gain some sense. That is the advantage of having a husband," Lady Chudley, the aforementioned Aunt Bedelia, said, waving off her niece's protests as one might the stale cakes at Almack's. "Just look at what I did for Lucy and Elinor! Imagine, Lucy Sterling a countess—that alone should make me the most successful matchmaker in London. But now! Why, not even a month later, and here is our dear, dear Elinor married to the Duke of Parkerton, just as I planned. How could I fail to do anything less for my own niece?"

Minerva pressed her fingers to her forehead, feigning the beginnings of a megrim, while she resisted the urge to point out that for her to do better in marriage, her aunt would have to find her a prince.

Not that she was looking. For she wasn't.

But that didn't mean she wasn't slightly envious of her friends' happy situations.

Friends! With Lucy and Elinor, no less. Why, a month ago Minerva would have scoffed at such a thing.

Having summoned them to London, the Duchess of Hollindrake had banished the lot of them to this house and given them a choice—live together under the same roof or get married.

Oh, the first few days had been a horror, but then something amazing happened: Minerva, Elinor, and Lucy established an uneasy truce. Then, unbelievable as it was, discovered they could be friends. And finally, had joined forces to help each other.

Now, best of all for Minerva, with Lucy and Elinor's marriages, she could live in the house on Brook Street to the end of her days in relative comfort. Alone. Without a husband. Doing exactly as she saw fit.

That thought, while a welcome notion a month ago, now yawned before her. Like this evening, which Aunt Bedelia had interrupted by arriving and announcing that she was taking her to Lady Veare's soiree. Not that her planned entertainment of attempting the latest embroidery pattern from the new issue of the *Lady's Magazine* had been all that inviting.

For if she was inclined to be honest, life with Lucy and Elinor—though initially repugnant—had turned out to be full of adventure, especially when her two fellow dowagers had discovered love and their own perfect happy endings.

Minerva's heart skipped a beat as she considered her own hand in both matches . . . and just as quickly she stopped herself.

Oh, gammon! She was turning into Aunt Bedelia if she was taking credit for such things. Heavens, what would she be like in a few years, if after only a few days alone she was already making such assumptions?

Minerva stole a glance at her aunt, who was pouring herself another glass of wine from the decanter—never a good sign, for it meant the old girl was deep into a plot. Most likely how to foist some unsuspecting lord into her niece's path. And as it turned out, she wasn't too far off on that suspicion.

"Dear girl, there is nothing wrong with seeking a husband," the lady began, settling deeper into the settee, which was as bad a sign as the wineglass filled nearly to the brim. "I would be delighted even if you were able to secure a mere baron. I was married to one once. Lord Taunton." She sighed dreamily, as if she were once again a debutante of seventeen. "Taunton was a wicked man if ever there was one. Barons do seem to be inclined toward a wildness that is unmatched. Why I remember once, we were at the Grassby ball, and he suggested we go upstairs in the middle of a cotillion and—"

"Aunt Bedelia!" Minerva protested. She should never have brought out that bottle of Madeira. "Honestly! Are such details necessary?"

"Apparently so," the lady insisted. "There are advantages to having a man in your life—advantages you seem to have forgotten."

"Might I remind you I was married to Philip Sterling?" Minerva shuddered, as she usually did when she remembered her short and very unhappy marriage to the Marquess of Standon. He'd lived a long, ruinous life before she'd been hauled to the altar and forced to marry him—the third such unhappy bride to pledge her troth to the spoiled, drunken Hollindrake heir.

Aunt Bedelia took a long sip from her wineglass. "I doubt Standon could even do his duty, given the dissolute life he led. Why no wonder you are so averse to marriage, dear girl. You haven't been properly tupped, have you?"

Minerva opened her mouth to protest, but what

could she say? First of all, she was mortified beyond words to be having this discussion with her elderly relation, and secondly, her aunt was utterly correct.

Philip Sterling's licentious life had left his manhood as flaccid as his protruding belly.

So there it was, she'd never been properly "tupped." Not even close.

"Never mind, my dear," Aunt Bedelia said. "That is what your collection of French novels are for. At least for the time being. We just need to find the right man for you so you can put your reading days behind you. Then you can forget all about that loathsome Standon. He certainly wasn't a fit example of matrimony."

"Truly?" Minerva remarked with every bit of sarcasm she possessed.

A note her aunt did not miss. "I will say it again, my dear, if I had known what your father intended back then, I would have come to your defense. I would never have stood for—"

"Yes, I know," Minerva said hastily, for she didn't like dwelling on her father's deception. His machinations back then haunted her still. And for a few moments an awkward silence sat between them.

Not that this uncomfortable pause would give her indomitable aunt a moment's hesitation at continuing to press her suit. Especially fortified as she was with not one, but two glasses of Madeira.

"Shall we just agree that you were married to the wrong man?" her aunt offered. "However, Minerva, I tell you as one who knows, the right husband will put a spark in your eyes and a spring in your step."

Now it could be argued that Bedelia knew more on the subject of marriage than anyone else could profess to, for the lady had managed to walk down the aisle no less than five times. And as further proof, there was no disputing that her aunt had been blushing like a schoolgirl ever since she'd married Lord Chudley.

Good heavens, her aunt and Chudley . . . together? Minerva shuddered again. For certainly they were too old for such antics . . . weren't they?

She glanced over at her aunt, only to spy the tell-tale hint of pink on her aunt's cheeks and a sly grin that suggested a secret satisfaction with life—not unlike the expressions Lucy and Elinor had been sporting of late. Why, Elinor had positively glowed yesterday when she'd come by to fetch her sister Tia, as well as her dogs and the litter of pups that had taken up residence in the second floor linen closet.

With all of them gone, the house had been uncharacteristically quiet last night—something Minerva hadn't considered. Without the dogs, Tia's youthful chatter, Lucy's nephew Mickey bounding up and down the stairs, why it was rather like a mausoleum around here.

"Minerva—" her aunt began, and as if she could read minds, picked up that very thread and marched forward with it. "You cannot tell me that you will be happy living alone in this drafty, wretched house for the rest of your days?"

Minerva ruffled a bit. For indeed the house on Brook Street was hardly a fine mansion, but now that it was hers, she took offense to having its deficiencies pointed out. "Whatever is wrong with this house? The address is most sought after"—which was the truth, for it sat only a few steps away from Grosvenor Square, one of Mayfair's finest—"and I have already been given permission by His Grace to make the necessary repairs—at his expense."

Since the house was the property of the current Duke of Hollindrake, Philip's nephew, Minerva had applied to him for the funds for her renovations. And to her surprise and delight, he'd written back in his usual direct and informal manner: *Do whatever you want to make that wreck a home. Just don't tell Her Grace.*

For there it was, for all his military accolades and lofty title, the Duke of Hollindrake was a good man at heart. And he knew his wife's shortcomings as well as her virtues.

Aunt Bedelia let out a sniff at this news—most likely in disapproval, for if Minerva was back in the duke's good graces, that would make all her arguments about her niece finding a new husband utterly moot.

"I've had the house scrubbed from top to bottom," Minerva pointed out—having borrowed a legion of scullery maids from the duke's London residence. Unfortunately, the cleaning had only served to reveal all the more that needed to be fixed, not that she was going to tell her aunt this. "The painter, the plasterer, and a man recommended by Lady Geneva for the wallpapers have all called on me and are scheduled to begin in a fortnight. With the house nearly empty, save for me, Agnes, and—"

"The rest of your riffraff!" her aunt rushed to add. "However can you live in this house with such a collection of servants? Why you might wake up to find your throat slit *and* the silver missing."

Minerva wasn't about to ask which was the worse scenario. Still . . . "Yes, yes, the staff is hardly up to snuff," she agreed. For they too had come with the house. Mrs. Hutchinson, a rather drunken surly housekeeper/cook; the lady's dim daughter, Mary; Mr. Mudgett, their nearly nonexistent butler; and Thomas-William, Lucy's father's former servant.

None of them were proper, respectable employees, but the household was hers, and that counted for something.

Minerva sat up straight and gazed directly at her aunt. "In a few months this house will be as comfortable and fashionable as any on the block. And I will be happily situated. You should be pleased for me, not trying to drag me off to Lady Veare's soiree—which will boast nothing more than a collection of mushrooms and *cits,* given her poor connections. Now leave me in peace, Auntie, or I will set Thomas-William after you."

"Well, perhaps you are correct about Lady Veare's, but my darling girl, you cannot prefer to remain alone—"

"But I do!" she said, cutting her aunt off. "The quiet and solitude suits me perfectly. In no time I shall be the envy of all."

Or so the last remaining Standon dowager claimed. That is, until the doorbell jangled and she made the mistake of opening it.

Sir Basil Brownett got into his carriage in front of Whitehall and tapped on the roof once he was settled into his seat. In twenty minutes he'd be home, and he hoped his wife was ready and waiting to leave for their evening at the Prime Minister's.

Dining with the Prime Minister.

He straightened a bit. Yes, his career was on the

rise. Quite the accomplishment for an ordinary fellow from Buxton. In an hour or so he'd be offering advice on the French reconstruction using information he'd gleaned from recent reports, adding a few suggestions for new (and profitable) trading partners along the African coast, and ending the evening with a few *on dits* about one of the PM's rivals.

Yes, yes, the perfect evening, he mused, silently practicing his delivery of a particularly interesting bit as his carriage rolled right on schedule past the government buildings lining Whitehall, and then into the darkening streets of London.

Sir Basil only hoped Anthea would be dressed and ready to leave on time. Good heavens, whatever took the woman so long to get ready? Anthea did love to have every detail perfect, but this was the Prime Minister, as he'd admonished her this morning—it wouldn't do to keep the man's meal waiting all because she couldn't decide which ear bobs to wear.

But his wife's jewels became the least of his worries when, as his carriage slowed to round a corner, the door suddenly opened and a masked man slipped inside. Before the baronet could even utter a peep, raise his cane to pound the roof in alarm, the intruder had a pistol thrust at his forehead and had issued a single warning.

"Don't say a word or it will be your last, Brownie."

Sir Basil hadn't made it up through the steep ranks of the Foreign Office for nothing. "Do you realize who I am? This is treason, you blackguard! I'll see you hanged!"

The fellow took the seat opposite him and laughed, his amusement belied by the fact that the pistol in his steady grasp remained pointed determinedly at Sir Basil. "Still blustering your way through life, I see. Never were one for fieldwork, or you would know not to take the same route home every night. Such regularity will get you killed."

"Get out of my carriage," Sir Basil ordered, determined not to show the fear that was even now wriggling its way down his spine. For one didn't get to the top of the Foreign Office without making a few enemies. Passing along a few scurrilous and damaging morsels at one dinner party or another . . . and he had no idea who this man was—though his voice . . . well, it was utterly familiar, and yet . . .

"Take my wallet and be gone, if that is all you want," he said, starting to reach inside his coat.

The pistol wagged in warning, like a nanny's finger. "*Tsk tsk tsk.* Keep your hands where I can see them, so I don't have to put a hole in that jacket. It looks well cut—which suggests you've discovered a better tailor in my absence . . . and the means to pay him."

"Who the devil are you?" Sir Basil blustered anew, keeping his hands fisted at his sides. For this blackguard was right, it was a very expensive jacket. One he could have ill-afforded a few years back, but now . . .

"If you must know, I'm the one with your life in my hands. So cease your bombastic posturing, for I am not one of your minions to be browbeaten and frightened by your meaningless threats." He paused and leaned back into the cushions. "For I remember when you were merely Basil Brownett, the Brownie from Buxton. Though I must say, for all your finery, you've managed to still cling to most of your old manners—always were a bit of a rat—knowing when to jump ship and how to find the richest pickings, weren't you?"

A shiver ran down the baronet's spine. For no one had spoken to him thusly, called him by that hideous nickname in some time. Not since he'd been naught but a lad at Eton, and the other boys—those with loftier connections and noble relations—had teased him over his humble origins and country clothes.

And it was more than this whisper from the past, but the voice. The deep, steely voice pierced him. For it couldn't be . . .

No, it was too ridiculous to consider.

For it meant he was in far more danger than he'd suspected.

"How dare you address me so. You'll hang for this effrontery," the baronet said with far more bravado than he actually possessed, for he wasn't about to believe that this man before him, this shadow from his past could really, truly be . . .

"Hang the dead often, Brownie? You arranged for my death once before, so what makes you think this time you'll actually manage to get the deed done?"

If there was ever a moment in a man's life where he looks back upon his actions and sees the long, rippling line of consequences with all the clarity of a Cassandra, this was Sir Basil's. His heart stilled as if it was going to stop, and he tried to breathe, but the air rushed from his lungs.

"Dear God, no," he wheezed. "You're supposed to be dead."

His adversary leaned closer, the nose of his pistol sitting a hairsbreadth from Sir Basil's temple, a pair of blue eyes glittering dangerously above the scarf that masked the rest of his features. "Sorry to disappoint you, you double-dealing upstart bastard. It's me. I'm back in Town."

"Where is he?"

"I know he is here! Show me to him at once!"

"To you? Whyever would my *liebling* want one such as you?"

"Your *liebling*?" This derisive snort was followed by a catty laugh. "I doubt as much."

This let loose a cacophony of insults and taunts in no less than four languages—German, Russian, French, and Italian. Slurs, retorts, and what Minerva Sterling suspected was outright profanity, flew about the room without any hint of decorum.

In all four directions of her previously quiet parlor stood a lady who had arrived at the house on Brook Street in the past half hour all demanding one thing: to know the whereabouts of Lord Langley, the Duchess of Hollindrake's infamous father. And in between this collection of Continental nobility was a landscape littered with luggage, trunks, hat boxes, valises, cases, and even a traveling desk. An equal number of colorful servants and maids stood at attention in the foyer.

"Who did you say they are?" Aunt Bedelia asked over the continuing argument.

"The nannies," she replied, diplomatically. "The duchess's former nannies."

Truly, Minerva would have confessed it was impossible to think of these ladies by any other title than "Nanny," for that was how the duchess had always referred to them.

"Nannies, my old reticule!" Aunt Bedelia snorted. "They are Lord Langley's Continental collection of doxies."

Yes, they were that as well. For the Duchess of Hollindrake, for all her airs, had been raised—alongside her twin sister Thalia—by her widowed father's mistresses. Felicity constantly quoted her beloved "nannies" as if their outrageous and often questionably moral advice had been engraved in gold, and now they were here . . . in Minerva's salon.

The lady who sought her "liebling," the Contessa von Frisch, or rather Nanny Brigid, stood at attention with a small black dog seated at her feet. The black, monkey-faced little devil, which she called her "Knuddels," looked alarmingly like Thalia Langley's wretched dog Brutus—the one who had chewed nearly every shoe and footman's ankle at Hollindrake House. No less than three of the duke's underfootmen and half a dozen maids had quit rather than continue with that "French devil of a dog" nipping at their heels.

And now there was another of these vermin masquerading as a hound in England.

"Whoever are you to question me?" Nanny Brigid was saying, directing her scathing tone at the far corner, where the Princess Natasha, late of St. Petersburg, and known as Nanny Tasha, stood in regal elegance, though she had just referred to the Austrian noblewoman as a "mewling heifer," if Minerva's French was correct.

"When my *liebling* arrives," the contessa declared, "he will send the lot of you back to the gutters from whence you came."

This only inflamed her rivals, who flung back

equally insulting comments about Nanny Brigid's apparently infamous reputation in diplomatic circles.

Minerva heaved a sigh and sent an imploring glance at Aunt Bedelia. *Do something!*

Aunt Bedelia glanced around the room and just shrugged. *Whyever would I?* The old girl sat happily ensconced on the settee, having stayed for the proceedings like an eager theatergoer.

For certainly not even a Haymarket playwright could have envisioned such a scene.

"Ladies, please!" Minerva said, pushing her way into the middle of the room. "I will not stand for such behavior in my house!"

There was a sniff from one of the corners.

Apparently being designated as merely a lady was not enough for her highbrowed company. So Minerva tried a more diplomatic approach. "Your Grace, Your Highness, Contessa, Margravine, please, all of you, I implore you to listen to me. Lord Langley is not here. You have made a terrible mistake, and I would ask for you to leave my—"

"Not here! Impossible!"

"Of course he is here! I had it from a very reliable source—" the Duchessa di Oristano, the onetime Nanny Lucia, said, waving a letter she'd plucked from inside her pelisse at Minerva.

"You think you can keep him to yourself? You? What could you be to such as him?" This remark came from the formidable Wilhelmenia Charlotte Louise, Margravine of Ansbach, or simply, Nanny Helga, the fourth and last lady of this unwelcome party. The margravine and her rivals all cast scathing glances that ran from the top of Minerva's head down to her shoes.

Good heavens, what an insufferable woman! And while Minerva hadn't even the slightest idea how one properly addressed a margravine, right now she thought it more preferable to discover how to get rid of one.

Nanny Lucia chimed in right behind the margravine. "Yes, Lady Standon, if you think you can satisfy my Langley—"

"Cease this instant!" Minerva said, adding a stamp of her foot as an exclamation point to her annoyance. "I will call the watch and have all of you arrested if you are not silent."

There followed some general sniffs of displeasure and a few muttered complaints about English hospitality, but the nannies came to an uneasy peace accord, their hostilities held in check.

At least for the moment.

"Now once again, Lord Langley is not here—" Minerva began.

"Of course he is!"

"I have conclusive information that says he has been seen—"

"Why do you keep insisting that he is not here, when the evidence—"

"Enough!" Minerva bellowed, forgetting every bit of decorum she possessed. "If, and that is a very big if, he were here—"

"But he is, and I insist—" Nanny Helga started to say, but as quickly stopped when Minerva turned her most quelling look on the lady.

She might not have these ladies' flair for fashion,

she may not have their natural beauty, but she was an Englishwoman through and through, and that, in Minerva's estimation, counted for much.

And as a marchioness she had to guess she outranked a mere margravine. At least she hoped she did.

It was at this point that Aunt Bedelia finally decided to wade into the fray.

About demmed time, Minerva would have said aloud if she were inclined. Another half an hour in this company and she'd probably be inclined to say much more.

"Please, ladies, my niece is a respectable widow," Aunt Bedelia told them. "She lives here only with her servants. Alone. Unmarried. Without even a suitor or any hope of—"

"Auntie!" Minerva blurted out. "Your point?"

Aunt Bedelia blinked and then shook her head. "Oh, yes, my point is that your search for any gentleman—here of all places—is for naught." Minerva groaned, but her aunt continued, undeterred. "As for Lord Langley, he is not here for one simple reason: He is not alive. I myself know that the man was lost in the war. My former husband—God rest his soul—was with the Foreign Office when the baron was lost. He's been dead for some time, so I fear your travels here have been in vain. Lord Langley is lost."

"Bah!" Nanny Tasha snorted. "You do not know the man. He could never be, how did you say, 'lost'! Why, it is a preposterous suggestion. Langley has simply been indisposed. And now he has come home."

The others nodded emphatically.

"It is how she said," Nanny Brigid agreed, gathering her dog to her ample bosom. "Langley is in London and I have it on the best authority."

Another round of agreement circled the room, and Minerva was at a loss as to how to argue with them in the face of their conviction that the Duchess of Hollindrake's father was not only alive, but here in London.

In her house.

It was all so ridiculous. Too fabulous to believe. For if indeed Lord Langley was alive, wouldn't his daughter, Felicity, be the best person to answer their questions?

And more to the point, house them?

"I would suggest," Minerva began, waving a gracious hand toward the door, "that if you do indeed think Lord Langley is here in London, you seek him in the most likely of places, his daughter's house. I am certain the Duchess of Hollindrake would be more than happy to accommodate your needs as well as discover the truth to this most vexing mystery." She managed to say all this with a concerned air and a placid smile on her face, as if coaxing four madwomen off London Bridge. "I can even call a carriage to take you all—"

"I will not be tossed out again just because you want to keep him to yourself!"

"This is an outrage! I am cousin to the tsar! I will not be sent begging like some peasant!"

"Nor I! This is an affront to my country!" Nanny Helga stomped her boot to the floor with a sharp resounding *thud*. Apparently the margrave hadn't the lofty relations to fling about, but Minerva knew she didn't want to be the catalyst of some foreign debacle that drew England into a war with a minor principality that most likely could only muster a single regiment.

Then again, war could hardly be imminent. It would probably take the English army some time and effort to find Nanny Helga's outraged populace.

Minerva stole a glance over at her aunt. *Really, now would be the time to help.*

Bedelia's gaze rolled upward and her hands went up in defeat. *There is no talking sense with these sorts.*

But Minerva wasn't about to give in so easily. "I am simply asking you to go to Hollindrake House and—"

"Whyever would we go back there?" Nanny Brigid asked.

Nanny Tasha shook her head with an imperious air. "I will not be so insulted again. That awful man at the door"—Staines, the duke's imperious butler, Minerva guessed—"refused me entrance. He said that the little duchess had gone into the country and would not return for a fortnight."

Minerva tamped down the desire to go over and strangle Staines. Wretched man!

"But of course, Langley would come here," Nanny Helga added.

"Whyever would he come here?" Minerva dared to ask. For if she had been feigning a megrim before, one was really coming on now.

Nanny Lucia snapped her fingers and one of her servants who had been hovering in the foyer came bustling in. The duchessa issued her order in brisk Italian, and the young man reached inside his coat and produced a packet of letters for his mistress. Nanny Tasha and Nanny Brigid did much the same, bringing out packets of letters, some tied with ribbons, others just a loose collection of missives. Each lady sorted through her papers and came up with a single letter, which they handed to their servants, who passed them on to Minerva.

"You will find your answer there on the second page," Nanny Lucia instructed, wiggling her fingers at the document.

Minerva glanced down at the letters in her hand, all composed in the Duchess of Hollindrake's familiar hand and written about a year earlier. She scanned the lines—bits of gossip, questions about fashions, and finally came to the one that stood out.

That answered that very important question.

Why this address?

I would be ever so grateful that if you hear word of my father, to direct him to return to London. And when he does, to take refuge in my house on Brook Street. Number 7. Despite rumors to the contrary, I am most assured he is alive.

Minerva glanced up at the ladies, who all smiled like cats who'd discovered the cream uncovered. And then she sank into her seat. Alive? The man was alive?

But still, this was hardly proof that the missing baron was in her house. Certainly she would know if she had an uninvited guest living under her roof.

That is, if her house was run like most houses in London. By regular servants. Not the hodgepodge collection of Seven Dials thieves and miscreants that Felicity Langley had hired when she hadn't two shillings to rub together and, if rumors were true, had moved into this house without actually renting it.

"I shall not leave without him!" Nanny Lucia declared. "I will not." She then took over the corner of the sofa opposite Aunt Bedelia.

"Nor I," Nanny Helga said, boot heels clicking together and her hand coming to rest on the desk beside her as if she were claiming that corner for her homeland of Ansbach.

Not to be outdone, Nanny Tasha flounced down on the sole remaining chair, planting herself in Minerva's parlor with the same stubborn (and unwanted) presence of a deeply rooted dandelion in a rose garden.

That left only the Contessa von Frisch, Nanny Brigid, who glanced around the room like a general might with the battlefield before him. But instead of taking a firm stance, she set her dog down and marched to the door, Knuddles following at her heels like an anxious sergeant-at-arms.

For a moment Minerva held a small hope that the lady, having taken the lay of the land, was going to beat a hasty retreat rather than stay and fight.

Little did she understand the lure of Lord Langley.

Instead, the lady spoke quickly in her own language, ordering her servants—a maid and a rather large footman—to gather her bags. While Minerva and Aunt Bedelia might not have a command of what the lady was saying, apparently the margravine did. Nanny Helga bounded to her feet and began hastily ordering her own servants to gather up her belongings, and then the two ladies began a race to the stairs.

That was enough to translate what had just transpired for not only Minerva, but for the nannies Lucia and Tasha. For in a matter of moments Minerva's empty house, the one she'd been extolling to her aunt not an hour or so earlier, was filled to overflowing with four unwanted guests as they jostled and vied to claim the empty rooms.

Minerva followed mutely, only to find herself routed and defeated in her own foyer as the cacophony of languages and insults echoed through the house, sharply punctuated by the tromping footfall of servants as they hurried bags and valises up the stairs—servants who, much to her chagrin, ignored her protests that Lord Langley was not to be found in her house and instead followed their mistress's exacting bidding as if this was their home.

"Do something," she sputtered to her aunt as the lady came to stand by her side.

But Aunt Bedelia only smiled. "Well, you did say you wanted to be the envy of all." She adjusted her pelisse and leaned over to peck her niece affectionately on the cheek. "You'll certainly be the talk of the Town with this collection in your house." The heavy *thump* of a trunk as it was dropped overhead rattled the walls. She glanced upward and shook her head. "Best get up there and make sure one of those Continental Cyprians hasn't laid claim to your bedchamber." With that, she sauntered over to the door, where she paused once again. "Oh, yes, and Minerva, I daresay that Nanny Helga looks as if her ancestors came across the continent with Attila the Hun. I've no doubt the margravine can ransack and pillage with the best of them. So if Lord Langley does arrive—best not get in the middle of it."

Ellis, Baron Langley, pulled down the scarf that had concealed his identity and looked his old school-mate dead in the eye.

So his checkered career with the Foreign Office had come to this. With his pistol shoved into Basil Brownett's quivering brow. How demmed lowering. But since no one other than Sir Basil had the authority to order him killed, it seemed the most logical place to start . . .

"How the devil . . . I mean to say . . ." Sir Basil stammered. "Egads, you're supposed to be dead!"

"Not from a lack of effort on your part," Langley pointed out.

"My part? I have no idea what you are talking about," Sir Basil said, but he colored slightly.

"Save your demmed speeches for your dinner tonight with the Prime Minister and his sycophants."

Sir Basil's eyes widened. "How did you know—"

"Brownie, I was the best agent Ellyson ever trained. I know *everything* about your dull life."

This time the baronet paled. Deadly so. "My good man, this is no time to be threatening me. I am unarmed. I would never have ordered—"

"Me killed? By having me bludgeoned from behind? Wouldn't you?"

The fellow across the carriage shook his head vehemently. "Demmit man, we all thought you'd gone over. Turned traitor."

"Traitor?"

"Yes, though it was never made official," Sir Basil said, looking all too disappointed over the fact.

"If you'd ever had the courage to venture out from behind that demmed desk of yours, you would have known that those reports were lies. That I was no—"

"We had it from the best sources," Sir Basil pressed, as if that made it all true. "You'd turned and could no longer be trusted." His brow furrowed to a hard line. "You of all people know procedure in these cases. The only difference is that your frog friends beat us to you—"

The French? Could this be true? Langley wondered. He'd turned and then been turned on? No. It couldn't have happened that way.

"Lies. You believed a pack of lies." Langley set his jaw, the pistol wavering in his grasp. He was tired and cold and hadn't eaten in some time, so he was ill-disposed to be patient with the likes of Basil Brownett.

"Apparently I also believed the lie that you were no longer living." Sir Basil sat back and looked overly disgusted at the entire ordeal, though his gaze remained fixed on the pistol still pointed at him.

Langley knew exactly what had Sir Basil in a fettle. Since he, Lord Langley, was indeed alive, there would most likely be an investigation, statements to be taken, records reviewed, and finally, dispatches to higher-ups . . . the sort of examination that could stall a promising career. The sort of thing that worried bothersome little toadies like Sir Basil, but were more akin to a gnat's bite to men like himself.

Then again, the baron had never held much concern for the niceties of procedure and paperwork. His unconventional methods, notorious goings-on, and disregard for protocol had made him from time to time—nay, most of the time—a giant headache for Whitehall bureaucrats like Sir Basil.

"My good man, do you mind?" Sir Basil nodded at the pistol.

Drawing it back, Langley slid the hammer slowly into place and set it down on the seat next to him. "Who sent in those reports, Brownie?"

The man cringed to be so addressed, for it probably stung to be reminded that his elevation had been so very recent. And that someone remembered where he had come from. "I don't recall."

"Don't or won't?" Langley asked smoothly, letting his hand rest on the butt of the pistol.

The man surprised him with his answer. "Won't."

"I have a right to know who wanted me dead, a chance to clear my name."

"Why someone wanted you dead?" Sir Basil laughed. "Good God, man! You weaseled secrets out of nearly every crowned head on the Continent, and if not from them, from their wives and mistresses. Not to mention left a rather wide swath of unhappy paramours in your wake, and now you have the impertinence to wonder why someone wanted you dead?"

Leave it to a plain fellow like Brownie to cut through the bluff and blunder of a matter. It was a sobering notion. Owning up to one's past. Something Langley really didn't want to do. Not until he got to the bottom of all this. Made up for his mistakes. Discovered the truth.

Most of all, cleared his name. He wasn't a traitor. He wasn't. That much he knew. That much he could trust.

Meanwhile, Sir Basil continued on, "Lord Langley, the war is over. Best you realize that."

"War is never over."

"Perhaps," the other man acknowledged. "But my advice—"

"Yes?"

"Stay dead."

"Stay dead?" Langley shook his head. "No. I've given the last twenty-five years of my life in the king's service and I want to come home. I want my name cleared." He picked up the pistol and looked Sir Basil directly in the eye. "All of it, sir. That is what I want."

"I don't see how you expect me to—"

He cocked the pistol. "I do. And you'll grant me access to the dispatches from Constantinople, Naples, Vienna, St. Petersburg, and Paris for the six months before I was struck down, and you'll—"

Sir Basil burst out laughing. "You're joking, surely?"

Langley raised the pistol.

"No, apparently not," the baronet muttered. "But you must see how completely out of the question such a request is. Those reports are confidential. I certainly cannot turn them over to a known—"

To the man's credit he stopped short of saying "traitor," which was probably why he had risen through the ranks.

"—to just anyone," he finished smoothly. Eyeing the pistol once again, he added slowly, "But, perhaps, I can assign an agent to look into this. See if there are any discrepancies that might have been missed then."

Hardly acceptable, but given that he was running out of time, Langley was forced to ask, "Who?"

Scratching his brow, Sir Basil considered his options. "Hedges, perhaps."

"Hedges? That demmed fool? Surprised he continues to find his way to Whitehall on a daily basis."

From the wry tip of the baronet's lips, it appeared he agreed with Langley's estimation of the fellow. "I suppose I could find someone else . . ."

They both paused as the carriage started to slow. Langley glanced out the window to gauge where they were—about to make the final turn onto the street where Sir Basil's house sat—which meant he was out of time.

At least for now.

"I want my life back," Langley repeated, pulling the scarf back up to mask his features. Dressed in black from head to toe, he was instantly a shadow, save for his distinctive blue eyes, which shone menacingly even in the darkness.

Shaking his head, Sir Basil heaved a sigh. "Impossible, my good man. You can't get back what you gave away. And besides, the entire office thinks you're a traitor. You'll have a devil of a time proving otherwise."

Slipping from the carriage as it moved through a dark spot between the gaslights, Lord Langley glanced over his shoulder and said, "We'll see about that."

Chapter 2

How a man enters a room says much about his character.

Advice to Felicity Langley from her Nanny Tasha

*N*ow long past midnight, a sharp biting wind whistled through the empty streets of London, and Lord Langley drew the collar of his coat up higher as he made his stealthy way down the alley behind the houses lining Brook Street. It was demmed cold outside, but he'd spent the last fortnight thusly, whiling away his evenings in the shadows until there was a sign from Thomas-William that it was safe for him to come in.

Certainly, he'd never envisioned his return to London in this manner. Hiding in byways and attics, remaining unseen so he could stay alive.

And tonight the lamp in the kitchen window wasn't lit, and a strange stillness fell over the mews. It had Langley on points, for something was

wrong—he knew it like he knew his own boots.
Even the kitchen door was locked.

Then he learned why.

"You've been discovered." From the shadows,
Thomas-William stepped forward, his French accented words a leftover from his childhood spent in
the service of a chevalier. That was before George
Ellyson, Thomas-William's former employer and the
spymaster who had taught Langley everything he
knew about the business, had bought the man off a
Paris auction block.

"Discovered? By whom?" Langley asked, glancing instinctively over his shoulder, even though he
knew no one was there.

Thomas-William was not the most loquacious of
fellows, and he answered with the same concise
turn of phrase that Ellyson had always favored.
"Your paramours."

"My what?" Langley asked, slightly confused and
stealing a glance at the house. He hadn't been with
a woman in ages, and his infamous conquests—the
ones that had given the *ton* and the European courts
enough fodder to keep the gossips happily chatter-
ing for years on end—had all taken place on the
Continent—not here in London.

Why, all his former mistresses were happily closeted away, from the turreted courts of St. Petersburg
to the minarets of Constantinople, and in a good
portion of the capitals in between.

Then he stole a glance at the house, which was
uncharacteristically lit from the ground floor to the
attics, as if it were filled with . . .

"Oh, good God, no!" he groaned. Lord Langley,
who'd managed to defy death on enough occasions

to frustrate even the devil, wavered with a fear that no man likes to consider. "They" implied more than one. As in several. And all under one roof.

It was a rake's worst nightmare.

"What the hell am I going to do now?" he muttered, plucking off his hat and raking his hand through his hair. "I've no place left to go."

Thomas-William glanced over his shoulder at the house and shuddered. "I agreed to stay here for Miss Lucy, but no more. Not with that lot."

It was then that Langley noticed the battered valise at the man's feet. "As bad as all that."

The fellow nodded. "Best you join me at Clifton's house in the country. I can hide you there."

"No," Langley said, shaking his head. This was getting to be an old argument between them. Thomas-William thought it best for the baron to stay hidden, out of sight as they worked through who might be to blame for his fall from grace. "I'm done with hiding."

"If you go out in the open, you'll only get yourself killed," Thomas-William said. More like repeated. "As long as no one truly knows you are here in London—"

"Well, I think it is rather too late now," Langley admitted.

"What did you do?"

"Went and saw an old friend tonight."

Thomas-William groaned. "Who?"

"Brownie."

The older man looked askance. "You did what?"

"Now before you start lamenting the moment you ever laid eyes on me, I think he knows more than he is letting on," Langley rushed to say. "He went rather pale when he realized I wasn't dead. Well, that and I shoved a pistol between his eyes."

"I think you will find that a common response," the man muttered.

"No, no, not like that. I think he was scared because he knows why I was betrayed."

Thomas-William studied him, then shook his head. "Too bad you don't, my lord. It would be better than baiting the lion in his own den."

This is exactly what George Ellyson would have said. For George had always gone on and on about not plunging into a situation without having a plan. Without knowing what you were after.

But it was rather hard to do that when you didn't remember anything. And that was the rub. When Langley had been struck in the head that fateful night in Paris, the injury had struck at his memory as well.

Why he'd been betrayed, who betrayed him, and what he'd been doing in Paris to begin with were all lost. Just fragments and scattered bits in his thoughts, flashes of images, none of which made sense.

"Have you considered that you just gave him time to see the original assignment finished?" Thomas-William said, arms folded over his chest. "Or simply the reason to have you openly declared a traitor and hung?"

"I can't sit around and wait."

Thomas-William looked as if he wished the baron would do just that. Wait. For by taking his cause—their cause, really—out into the open, it put them both at risk.

"What if it is true, Thomas-William? What if I am

a traitor and I just don't remember it?" He looked over at his old friend to see what the other man thought of that, for it was something that had been festering in the back of his mind for months. Years, really, ever since he'd woken up in a Paris prison.

"Then why did you come back to England?" he asked. "Why even bother?"

Langley stared at him. *Why bother?* "Because it is utter nonsense! I can't be a—"

Thomas-William laughed softly and then clapped him firmly on the back. "Exactly, my lord. You are no traitor. Ellyson trusted you. And I trust you as well."

"Thank you, sir," he said, bowing slightly.

"Enough of that," Thomas-William told him, looking embarrassed. "Now it is time for us to leave." He leaned over to retrieve his valise. "Not even for Miss Lucy will I stay in this house. Not if you intend to stand out in the open like a stag in the meadow." He smiled at his own joke.

"Come now, my old friend," Langley cajoled. "It isn't like you to pass up what might be a rout. You always did like a losing proposition."

The man looked over his shoulder at the house behind him and shook his head. "We had better odds playing cards with Miss Tia."

That bad, eh? Langley looked back at the house, the shadows of figures passing back and forth in front of the curtains like a regimental parade. Egads, how many of them could there be inside?

And as if he'd read his thoughts, Thomas-William told him. "Four."

"Four?" Langley's gaze narrowed. "Which ones?"

"A Russian—"

"Tasha?" he murmured.

Thomas-William nodded. "An Italian—"

"Lucia?" Langley glanced again at the house. His fiery Italian countess with his ruthless Russian mistress? Good God, he was shocked the house wasn't yet in flames and London burning down around them.

"A contessa with a dog—"

"Brigid," he said, a chill running down his spine. If anyone was capable of killing him, he might look no further than Brigid—for the lady was as beautiful as she was deadly.

"And a margravine with a temper," Thomas-William said.

"Wilhelmenia?" Langley couldn't even imagine the lady leaving her corner of Europe unless she was following her ancestors' tradition of conquest and pillaging. *Saint George, save them all, if that was the case.*

It had been difficult enough sneaking in and out when Elinor Sterling and her young sister Tia had been living in the house, but now? Why, it would be nigh on impossible.

For even with his careful planning, Tia had caught him a week into his residence. She'd snuck down to the kitchen in the middle of the night and discovered him and Thomas-William playing cards. They'd tried to fob her off with lies, but she'd coolly regarded the stranger at the table, declared him a gentleman and obviously a spy, and then anted into their game of *vingt-et-un*, soundly beating them both before she'd toddled off to bed again, declaring, "I care not if you are living in the attic, but best not let Minerva find out."

Luckily for Langley, the rest of the servants were much like Tia, and had taken little notice of Thomas-William's mysterious guest in the attic. For as long as there was no work associated with his care and upkeep—it was no matter to them.

But the baron suspected the sole remaining mistress of the house would not share their largesse.

Proper and strict, Minerva Sterling, from what Thomas-William had told him, would most likely set a pack of hounds on him. If she owned any. Luckily she didn't. But Thomas-William had muttered something about her stealing his pistol once, something he'd dismissed as a drunken blithering.

Still, Langley glanced over at her window, the one on the corner near the drainpipe. The chamber was dark and still, which said to him she had either sought her bed long before or was out for the evening.

"Why hasn't she cast them out?" he asked. From what Thomas-William had said about the lady, he couldn't imagine Minerva Sterling suffering a pack of fools gladly.

Thomas-William's answer was one upraised brow that said so very clearly that the lady had tried . . . and failed.

Langley nodded. "It would have probably taken a regiment of the king's finest Marines, a dedicated group of cannoneers, and a nearby sale on silks to get those four to quit their stronghold now that they've dug in."

"And they know you're about," the other man grumbled.

That was the worst of it. They knew he was alive. And that he was in London. So how was it that all four of them had discovered this, and discovered it early enough to journey all this way just to corner him? And what if they believed the rumors, the lies that he was guilty of treason . . . guilty of something he couldn't even remember . . .

Perhaps he should take a more a careful tack, listen to Thomas-William.

"Are you coming?" the man prodded.

Shivering in the cold, Langley muttered, "I must get my notes . . . my clothes . . ."

"Have you considered that one of them might be . . ." Thomas-William's words trailed off, but it didn't take much wit to finish his supposition.

The one who wanted to see him gain his just reward . . .

Oh, yes, that thought had run its wild course through his rattled senses.

"This complicates everything," he said, more to himself.

Thomas-William made a loud snort, as if to underline such a statement. "I have your things—at least your clothes. Come with me to the earl's estate. We'll catch the first tide."

Langley shook his head. "No, I stay in London. I'll never discover the truth, never clear my name, cowering in the countryside."

"Suit yourself. You might try the King's Barrel in Shoreditch. Ellyson favored it when he came to town. Mention him, and the landlady might extend you credit." This was Thomas-William's oh-so-subtle way of reminding him that he had no money. No money for lodgings, no money for bribes, all the things that would have made his task much easier.

That was the rub of it. He had no money—other than the handful of coins he'd stowed away in the attic. Nor was Thomas-William sporting plump pockets, not unless he'd finally found a way to win back his last six months of salary from that cheating little minx, Tia.

Since most everyone thought him dead anyway, his fortune had been divided between his daughters. There were no accounts to draw from, not unless he wanted to drag Felicity and Tally into his dangerous pursuit. And that was exactly why he'd deposited them in Miss Emery's school all those years ago. To keep them safe. Hidden away from his enemies.

Hiding.

God, he hated that word. It left him in alleyways, grasping at fleeting memories and chasing shadows. What if this was it? The rest of his life was to be spent thusly? At the edges of society, if only to avoid the scandal of treason, of his name—not to mention his carcass—being dragged through the streets and what that would mean to his daughters, their reputations.

Shivering anew, Langley lost patience with this half-life of his—even if it was only for a narrow bed and the faint warmth of Lady Standon's attics. By God, he needed to finish this. But to do that, he needed to retrieve his journal—for it held what little he did remember of Paris, along with his list of suspects, top of which sat one name: Sir Basil Brownett.

That was one of two things he'd recalled all this time. Sir Basil's name and a shadowy profile of the villain who'd struck him down in Paris.

A face so familiar he swore he knew who the fellow was, if only he could make out the man's features, remember where he'd seen him before.

No, there would be no clearing his name until he solved this mystery, so he started toward the house. That is, until Thomas-William caught him by the elbow, tugging him to a halt. "Are you mad? You can't go in there."

"I must have my notes. I've been collecting every bit I can remember from Paris, and I don't dare lose them." All he really had were his suspicions of Brownie scrawled in a journal full of nonsensical notes.

Yet when he started for the kitchen door again, Thomas-William shook his head. "You cannot go that way," he said, nodding toward the windows.

For between the kitchen and the attic stood five flights of stairs—any of which could be occupied by one of the visiting servants. While Mrs. Hutchinson didn't care about a stranger in their midst, Helga's maid or one of Tasha's footmen might not be so willing to look the other way.

After all, they'd come all this way for their mistresses to find her man.

Langley muttered a curse, to which Thomas-William chuckled and said, "Seems you have no other choice but to do as I advise. Come away with me. It is what Ellyson would do. It would hardly do for you to find yourself out in the open."

"I don't intend on being caught," Langley said. "Watch and learn something not even Ellyson would have tried."

Edging his way along the garden wall, for there was still a light on in the first floor parlor, Langley worked his way to the side of the house, where the drainpipe ran up all the way to the attic balcony. He glanced over his shoulder and smirked at Thomas-William. Now it was time to show the man how it was he'd managed to steal so many secrets from the courts of Europe. And contrary to popular opinion in the Foreign Office that it had been his prowess in seducing the wives and mistresses of the various princes, ministers of state, and high ranking nobles, it had more to do with the fact that he could prowl like a cat.

He glanced up the drainpipe and measured the distance, which was considerable, but then again Lord Langley had never been known for avoiding a bit of risk, and a few moments later he was climbing up the side of the house with the agility of one of Astley's rope walkers.

Grinning down at an astonished Thomas-William, he continued upward—silently and stealthily. Truly, if he hadn't become a spy, he might have done well as London's finest burglar. That is, until the old pipe groaned in complaint and began to shudder beneath his hands. A ripple of panic ran down his spine, and he cursed his own bravado as the cold metal began to waver and shudder in earnest.

He should have known. Most of this house was in ill-repair. Why should the drainpipe be any different?

Yet here he was, halfway up, having to weigh his options in a split second—and he did, making a scrambling leap onto the wide ledge of the nearest window just as the pipe gave way, clattering onto the ground below.

Clinging to the stonework, Langley held his breath, waiting for some sound of alarm. Below him,

Thomas-William had melded into the shadows, now unseen, as if he too were waiting to see what sort of aftermath would come of this.

But by some miracle of chance, the house remained silent, not a soul stirred. Thomas-William eased out of his hiding place and glanced up at Langley. Then he shook his head, as if the real calamity had yet to drop.

For indeed, Langley's refuge could hardly be called that. His only option now was to climb into the room the window led to.

Lady Standon's room, to be exact.

Glancing inside at the pitch-black bedchamber, Langley wondered if he wouldn't have been better off staying in Paris.

Without his title. Without his name.

No, that would never do. As he told Brownie, he'd never give up. So, he took a deep breath and let it out slowly before he slid the window open as quietly as he could and slipped into Lady Standon's room.

It wasn't like he could spend the night on her ledge.

He blinked, trying to discern anything in the room to gain his bearings, and took one tentative step toward where he hoped he would find the door.

Instead, he tripped over the bed and landed atop the lady herself.

Minerva had fallen into an uneasy sleep rife with dreams of her unwanted houseguests and their paramour, Lord Langley.

While the ladies were all as clear as day, and just as unwelcome in her dreams—Lord Langley remained in the shadows, a figure she couldn't quite see, a man who moved with catlike elegance, enticing her to come closer.

Minerva twisted fitfully from one side to another until her fanciful flight was interrupted by an equally shady figure falling over her.

The man's body—for there was no doubt it was a man—covered hers, pinning her down in the depths of her mattress. One of his hands had landed quite squarely over her breast.

"Aaaah," she began to cry out as she struggled to bolt upward, but he clapped a hard hand over her mouth, silencing her scream.

"No, no, no," he told her in a voice deep and rich. "I'm not here to harm you."

His reassurances did nothing to stop her from struggling, but it was to no avail, for her arms were trapped under the coverlet and he had her entirely pinned.

Covered with his long figure, the muscles that seemed to be . . . well, everywhere.

If only she could reach the nightstand . . . where earlier tonight she'd concealed one of Thomas-William's pistols.

After all, her house was filled with strangers, and now it seemed a thief as well . . .

"Truly, my lady, I will not harm you, you have to believe me," he continued, his hand still covering her mouth. There was a cultured air to his plea, tinging his words, as if it had been a long time since English had been his native tongue.

A long time since he'd been home . . .

Minerva's lashes blinked as she tried to discern in the darkness some hint of his features, spy something about this man that might soothe her panic.

Then the words on the duchessa's letter from Felicity echoed through her rattled senses.

I would be ever so grateful that if you hear word of my father, to direct him to return to London. And when he does, advise him to take refuge in my house on Brook Street. Number 7.

"I am no villain. But I must beg of you to be quiet."

Lord Langley?

Ridiculous! she told herself. Whatever would a respected—well, infamous might be a more apt description—English diplomat be doing sneaking into her bedchamber like a common thief?

She blinked again, and this time, in the dim moonlight, she could make out his face—the handsome Roman features, the cleft in his chin, and the rich curve of his lips. His aristocratic features shocked her, for she hardly expected to discover such a handsome man—and certainly not one in her bed.

Then out of the blue she heard the declaration she'd made the other day to Lucy and Elinor, words that now sounded something akin to prophecy.

A man will have to fall out of the sky and into my bedroom before I marry him . . .

How was she to know such a thing was possible? For there was her window, open, and here he was.

The sort of man she'd always dreamt of marrying. Long before her dreams of a happily-ever-after had been quashed by her father's plots and her forced marriage to Philip Sterling.

Oh, what utter rubbish! She was far too practical to believe that perfectly handsome husbands just tumbled out of the heavens.

No, it was better to hold onto her reason and realize that the only sorts who stole into a lady's bedchamber in the middle of the night had other thoughts on their mind.

Then again, whatever his reason, this fellow had yet to molest her, other than his initial landing and holding his hand over her mouth.

"Please, I don't want to cause a scandal—" he whispered.

Then whatever are you doing in my bedchamber, you wretched beast?

"—I merely came to get my belongings and then I'll be gone. If the door hadn't been locked . . ."

Get his things? As in, they were in her house?

"I know it might be hard to believe—"

Impossible would be more like it. Wouldn't she know if there was a man living in her house? Certainly one of the staff would have said something . . .

Well, perhaps a real staff, she conceded.

"Now I am going to take my hand off your mouth," he was saying, even as he was slowly easing his fingers away, "but only if you promise not to—"

There was such a seductive lull to his voice, so deep and enticing, that it almost had her believing he wasn't there to harm her. She even found herself nodding in agreement to his request like some dim-witted simpleton.

Whatever was she doing? Oh, this was all madness, and so was this fellow.

So the moment his hand slipped from her mouth, she screamed. Bloody murder.

And just as quickly her hand snaked out from beneath the covers and snatched Thomas-William's pistol from the nightstand.

Shoving it forward even as she scooted back, her knees tucked in front of her like a walled fortress, poor blockade that they were, they were enough for now.

Now that she'd gained the upper hand.

Taking a few gulps of air, she said in an unsteady voice, "Don't think I won't shoot."

"My lady, from what I know of you, I'm surprised you haven't already."

"I will shoot," Lady Standon averred, the pistol trembling traitorously in her hand. "See that I don't."

Langley reached out and with a single finger steadied the barrel. "If you must, make a good shot of it. All that wavering about is making me nervous."

All through the house he could hear the scrambling of feet—the curious and the wary—rummaging about as they tried to determine whether her round of screeching cries were worth their own life.

Apparently they were, for now the footsteps were on the stairs and in the hall, and a thread of light began to creep under the door as candles in the hall were lit and furtive search for the source of the alarm began.

"It was in her room!" he heard a lady with a deep, gravely voice say.

Langley cringed. *Helga!*

So it was true. His past was now at his doorstep.

Or rather on Lady Standon's. "Yes, please, in here!" she called out. "I am being accosted."

He glanced over at her, more amused than annoyed. "Truly? Accosted? That is the best you can come up with?"

The latch at the door rattled, but it remained closed.

"Oh, dear!" Lady Standon said. "It's locked." Then

she had the audacity to glance up at him. "Would you mind?"

"Mind what?" He knew exactly what she was asking, but he wasn't about to make this easy on her. If she had kept her word and not screeched like a fishwife, he wouldn't be in this mess. Nor would she.

"Opening the door," she said, waving the pistol at the door. "I fear it is locked."

"Locked?" Langley glanced at it and then back at her, smiling. "How inconvenient." Her forethought earlier to bolt her door was now gaining him some time, even as outside her room a crowd swelled—he could hear a smattering of questions in German and Italian, as well as Helga's gruff responses.

"Get out of my way," he heard a rich sultry voice call out, then the door rattled with a determined round of knocking. "Darling! Is that you? I shall break down this door immediately!"

Langley cringed again. Tasha! Leave it to his Russian paramour to come to his rescue. Then again, how many times had she been on the other side of the door while her irate husband had pounded away at the portal, threatening one of her many lovers?

"Then you are him? Lord Langley?" the lady beside him asked without the least bit of the enthusiasm that could be heard rising in the hallway. She actually sounded rather affronted.

He bowed slightly. "At your service, my lady."

"I didn't ask for your service," she shot back.

Yes, definitely not one of the welcoming party. "Well, I didn't ask you to invite in that circus of harpies into my daughter's house."

"*My house,*" she corrected. "Which you weren't invited into either."

"Wasn't I?" He patted his jacket as if searching for something. "I do believe I have my invitation here somewhere."

His charm was lost on the lady, for her reply was the arch of her dark brows over her narrowed eyes.

For a moment he found himself wistfully wondering what color they were. Blue? Nut brown? Green?

The ruckus in the hall drew both their attention back to the door as it rattled loudly, the hinges—unlike the drainpipe outside—holding their own.

"I must say you are a most indulgent hostess," he said as he rose from the bed, "for you seem to draw guests like a moth."

"If only you were all as easily squashed," she replied as she too got up and faced him.

"Poor, darling, Langley, you needn't stay in there with *her*," Tasha purred. "Come out here with me. I have missed you so." The slow scratch of fingernails ran down the door.

"My Langley with her? Are you mad?" This came from Lucia, ever the fiery Italian duchessa. Of course, she would dismiss anyone else as being in competition with her, for she had lived her entire life as the petted and coveted jewel of Naples. "She is nothing, she is but a mouse. As if he would fancy such as *that*."

"A mouse!" Lady Standon straightened. "Whatever does she mean by that?"

"That she thinks you are unworthy of my affections," he said, glancing at the door and then back at the window. He was a good two stories above the ground, which would mean he would most likely break at least one limb if he made a jump for it.

"I knew she was hiding him!" Brigid declared to the others.

This spun Lady Standon around on her heel. "I am not!" she told them through the door.

"Bah! The English and all their high and mighty morals!" Helga sounded in fine form. "Would someone get a pike, an axe, a halberd? I shall break this door down myself!"

"A halberd?" Lady Standon exclaimed. "Oh, yes, I have several of those in the morning room." She glanced over at him. "What sort of lady does she think I am?"

Langley grinned. "I believe the margravine has an entire room devoted to such things."

There was an indelicate snort from the mistress of the house, but whether it was to the fact that Helga had a collection of sharpened weapons at the ready or that he merely knew such women, he didn't know.

Nor did he ask.

Meanwhile, on the other side of the door, the enemy was clearly growing impatient, for Tasha began calling for one of her footmen—most likely not trusting the margravine with an axe. And if his rusty Russian was correct, the princess was calling the situation "a matter of great moral imperative." Nor did he suspect she was creating this fuss in order to save Lady Standon's imperiled reputation.

"This is ruinous!" his unwitting hostess declared, nudging him with her pistol. "Get out of my room!"

"Madame, if I open that door, *I'll* be ruined."

"Then go back the way you came," she said, pointing at the window.

"Believe me, I've considered it." For now there

was a very resounding thud of boots on the steps. Apparently Tasha still favored keeping a few handsome Cossacks about.

"Well—" Lady Standon's foot tapped, and the pistol remained stubbornly pointed at him.

"The drainpipe broke on my way up. The only way out is to jump."

She stepped aside. "Do I appear to be stopping you?"

"I'd break my neck at this height," he said, hands fisting at his sides. Not that the lady looked all that dismayed over the prospect of him ending his illustrious life in a heap of broken bones in her garden.

Truly he could see why the servants muttered about her and Thomas-William got that nervous twitch in his eye every time her name was mentioned.

Nor was she done with him. "So you've not only damaged my house, but now you are going to damage my standing? I am a respectable widow."

He grinned at her. "I've known many a respectable widow in my day."

"I am not that sort of lady!"

"Apparently not," he replied, glancing once again at the window.

"I demand that you leave at once!" she insisted.

Good God! She was every inch the bossy bit of muslin that Thomas-William claimed. And utterly English in her superiority.

Much to his chagrin, Langley had to admit to being a bit charmed.

She continued on in quite an abominable fashion. "Lord Langley, I'll have you know I deplore scandal! Nor will I be party to your . . . your . . . your common, ruffian ways!"

"Ruffian?" He ignored the "common" part of her snub. "The ladies outside this door would probably argue with such a description of my character."

She snorted in reply. Apparently she held them in just as much contempt as she did his "ruffian" inclinations. "Then I'll open the door and straighten them out on the subject."

"Oh, no you won't," he told her, cutting off her path.

"I'll shoot," she warned.

"Please do," he offered. "Better you, my lovely firing squad, than being torn limb from limb from limb by those silken clad wolves." He tossed a knowing glance toward the door.

She appeared to be considering his words, as if they might be a good suggestion. But finally she stepped away from the door, shooting him a baleful glance. "Do not consider this a concession," she said, "for I am not all that unconvinced that you'd be the only one to be ripped apart in the melee."

Smart minx.

"Then, my dear Lady Standon, if it comes to that, stay away from the window. I do believe an open sash was how Tasha got rid of her first husband."

Her eyes widened even as there was another rattle of the hinges. This time the door groaned in protest and looked all but ready to give way. Tasha's footman had most likely arrived. "If you were a respectable gentleman, those . . . those . . ." She waved the pistol at the door as she searched for the words to describe the pack of females beyond.

"Houseguests?" he offered, rocking on his heels, grinning at her. Whyever was he enjoying this? He was about to meet his maker, or at the very least the last four women he ever wanted to encounter again, and all he could do was tease this one.

An irate, entirely proper and upstanding English marchioness.

God, he'd missed Britain.

"You jest? This is hardly funny," she told him as her door shuddered anew. "And now my door is to be ruined as well."

"You could open it yourself," he said, stepping aside. "And feed me to the wolves, as I suggested before."

"Don't think I wouldn't like to, but the moment that door opens I'm ruined." She looked amusingly fierce—standing in the middle of the room in her plain white night rail, her hair falling in a thick braid over one shoulder, pistol in her hand. Unfortunately it was too dark to make out the color of her eyes, the hue of her hair, the true line of her curves beneath that ugly, voluminous night rail.

Egads, was it flannel? Whatever had happened to England since he'd left that they were swathing their women in flannel?

This had to be one of the more devastating results of overturning the French.

And English modesty aside, he made another point. "Lady Standon, you place too much value in respectability. Believe me, it rarely leaves one with an epitaph worth remembering."

"I can well imagine yours!"

He grinned and leaned closer. "Can you now?"

"Oh!" she sputtered and stepped away from him.

"None of this would be happening if you were a respectable man. True to your title."

Langley closed his eyes and shuddered. "And let me guess what you would suggest: that I take a wife and remove myself to the country for the remainder of my days. Would that dull prospect make me respectable?"

"If that is what it takes to get you and your . . ."

"Former nannies?" he offered.

"Companions," she corrected, "and yes, if that is what it takes to get all of you out of my house, then please take a wife. I'd say my house is overflowing with likely and overly willing candidates."

Langley paused, a shiver running down his spine, her suggestion jumbling about with Thomas-William's grumbled complaints.

Hiding . . . Out in the open . . . Take a wife . . .

The door shuddered again, and he realized he had barely enough time to hatch his plan. But leap into it he would, starting with shrugging off his jacket.

Lady Standon gaped at him. "Whatever are you doing?"

"Taking your advice." Flinging his jacket in one direction, he plucked off his cravat with one hand while the other flipped open the buttons on his waistcoat.

She eyed him with open horror. "You're mad! I never told you to disrobe!" Then realizing that her voice was rising, she gasped and lowered her register.

Having added his cravat and waistcoat to the pile, he opened up his shirt a bit and stalked across the room, catching her in his arms. "No, you didn't."

Caught unawares, the pistol fell from her grasp.

Then Lady Standon began to struggle, her fists pounding at his chest. "I certainly didn't tell you to accost me either!"

"No, madame, you didn't."

A loud crash left the hinges groaning their last. One more good hit and—

"Then whatever are you doing?" she gasped, having stilled for a second.

"Exactly what you told me to do. Taking a wife."

And as the door crashed open, he sealed his proposal with a kiss.

Chapter 3

A man will only propose when thoroughly cornered.
Advice to Felicity Langley from her Nanny Lucia

Minerva had no idea what it was Langley was about to do until his lips captured hers and his arms wound tight around her.

There was no escape from his trap—for quite frankly, she was trying like the very devil. Her hands on his shoulders balled into fists and pummeled at him, all to no avail, for the wretched scoundrel had her exactly where he wanted.

A collective gasp rose up as the door swung open to reveal his neatly staged tableaux. A perfect scene of uninhibited seduction, his lips covering hers, his hands cradling her in his steely grasp, the rakish lines of his body entwined with hers.

As if they cared not that the entire household was witness to their passions.

When Minerva tried to twist free, he added to his

deception by dipping her back, so her body arched into his and it appeared to all that he was devouring her, for in truth he was—his hands roaming over her back, along her spine, teasing her, touching her, as if he could not get enough of her . . . which made her struggles appear more like . . .

Oh, heavens, she didn't want to think about how she appeared, not when she was more worried about how it actually felt.

For as shocking as it was, the words "delicious torment" seemed to have found a new place in her vocabulary.

"Langley! Whatever are you doing to her?" Nanny Lucia said in a high-pitched voice that verged on a horrified shriek.

That was the question Minerva wanted to ask— that is, if she could have managed—but right at that moment her lips were occupied, and unfortunately she was having trouble breathing.

Having trouble thinking.

For traitorously, seductively, and eloquently, this wretched, practiced rake was plying his trade over her like a maestro might roam a bow over a violin.

And yes, her strings were trembling. Vibrating with a music that begged one to listen, to move, to respond.

How could she not? What with her breasts pressed to his chest, his hand cupping her . . . her . . . good heavens, her backside, and his lips, oh, those lips, plying hers, nibbling at hers, teasing her to open up to him.

Give in to his seduction.

Give in? She hadn't been dubbed the icy Lady Standon for nothing. She had dodged, avoided, and quelled the aspirations of every ne'er-do-well who had veered in her direction over the last eleven years, since the death of Philip Sterling had freed her from the bonds of marriage. Years of maintaining her spotless reputation were gone in an instant as this one man breeched her defenses without so much as a hint of flirtation.

So even as she considered raising one final note of protest—a knee to his infamous manhood—something unexpected happened.

Unexpected in that Minerva would never have thought such things could happen. At least not to her.

As hastily as he'd caught her up, as tightly as he held her, his lips touched hers with a tenderness, a reverence, that belied his reputation. He wasn't so much devouring her, but teasing her. Tempting her. Tasting her. Slowly, deliberately. His strong lips covered hers, murmured over hers, but what they were saying was like a whisper in a foreign language. She hadn't the vaguest idea what was being said, but all of a sudden she longed for the translation.

Desired it with all her heart.

And as that awareness, the spark of need flared to life inside her, at the very moment when she could feel the traitorous acquiescence in her body, he pulled back, just enough to look into her eyes.

And what she saw there inflamed her. That brazen light of mischief sparkling at her. As if he knew the battle going on inside her . . . and worse yet, that he'd begun to win it.

"My apologies, dearest," he whispered loudly. "There will be time enough for us later."

Later. The word purred over her with a heady promise of passions yet to come.

Like hell, she would have told him, if he hadn't just then set her back up on her feet and she found herself wavering, her knees knocking about beneath her as if her house had suddenly been launched to sea.

In the middle of a storm. With nothing to lash herself to.

Save this solid, muscled man beside her.

I'd rather drown, she fumed silently, staggering a few steps back and catching hold of her dressing table.

"Awch! *Schatzi!*" Nanny Helga cried out, elbowing her way past Brigid and Lucia. "What has become of you, my Langley, that you would stoop to . . . to . . ." Her hands fluttered at Minerva while her nose wrinkled in dismay.

Not to be outdone, Nanny Lucia came bustling forward as well. The elegant lady wore a robe and night rail in a sapphire blue silk that clung to her curves and was so gossamer that next to nothing of the Italian woman's bountiful charms were "hidden" beneath. If the color wasn't enough to catch the eye, she also wore a matching necklace, ear bobs, and bracelets, as if she were about to attend the opera. "*Dolce cuore*," she purred. "Obviously you have lost your way." She tossed a derisive snort at Minerva and at the margravine. "Now, I am here to help."

"You?" Brigid laughed and set down Knuddles. "Look, darling, it is Langley."

Knuddles, true to his affenpinscher nature, set out directly for Langley and promptly clamped his teeth down into the heel of the man's boot, staking his mistress's claim. Even the baron's determined shaking of his foot would not dislodge the little monkey-faced dog.

"Brigid, call off this beast," he muttered, shaking his foot and teetering about with the stubborn little dog attached to his heel.

Which gave the lady the invitation that no one else had received, and she queened her way past the rest of them, pausing before Langley and casting him a seductive glance before she bent over, slowly, purposefully, so that her low-cut night rail billowed out and gave anyone willing to look an eyeful.

Utterly shameless! Minerva stood there stunned by the lady's brazen antics, and her furious glance—why she was furious, she wasn't certain, but then again it wasn't every night she had such a circus parading about in her bedroom—rose to meet Langley's, for he was the catalyst of all this.

As far as she was concerned, they all could have him. While she wasn't particularly fond of the idea of them setting up a brawl in her bedroom, if it would expedite them on their travels, then she would risk a bit of damage and scandal.

Yet to her surprise he wasn't looking down at what the woman was offering, but instead his gaze was on her, and when their eyes met, he had the nerve to wink.

"Ah, thank you," he said as his boot came loose. Immediately he stepped away from the lady and closer to Minerva. "There now, that is better."

Better for who? From Minerva's vantage point it only put her in harm's way, for there was still the Russian princess and her Cossack forces in the background awaiting an opening to make their charge.

And charge they would eventually, she had to imagine, given the narrow glint to the lady's darkly kohled eyes.

Heavens! They were all made up like that—rouged, primped, and gowned as if they had been lounging about waiting for this man to arrive. Next to them she was like a solitary daisy in a hothouse of orchids and orange blossoms. A vestal innocent in a decadent harem.

Her house a harem? Not if she had anything to say about it.

"Out!" She pointed at her door, which now hung by one hinge. "All of you!"

Nanny Brigid put her dog down and her hands went to her hips. It managed not only to show the woman's determination to do just the opposite, but also managed to give her another opportunity to push her breasts up and nearly out of her evening wear.

Really, didn't they make sensible flannel night rails on the Continent?

"Dearest, that isn't necessary," Langley said, sidling up to Minerva and wrapping his arm about her waist, cinching her up against him like one might an unruly mount. "They've come to wish us well."

A suspicious silence fell over the ladies. Including Minerva.

Us? Had he just said "Us?" As in her and him?

Even Knuddles stopped his snuffling and sniffing about to glance at the man.

"Whatever do you mean?" Nanny Tasha demanded. "Langley, you can't be saying—"

"That is exactly what I am saying. I've come home. To marry the woman I love." He gave Minerva another hug, drawing her even closer. "Adore," he confessed. "Allow me the pleasure of introducing the future Lady Langley."

The future Lady Langley? He didn't really mean . . .

Minerva gaped at him just as the others were—good heavens, what had he said just before he'd kissed her?

Exactly what you told me to do. Taking a wife.

Her hands went to her lips as she realized that he'd meant her.

The margravine sputtered something in her own language before she got command of herself and managed to get out in English the one word they were all thinking. "Ridiculous!"

Yes, even she had to agree with the lady. *Ridiculous.* And outrageous. And utterly impossible.

Marry him? She'd rather walk naked through Almack's. She twisted out of his grasp and turned to glare at him, to add her own imperious gaze to the four others that were blazing into this obviously ramshackled rake.

"Married? To such as this?" Nanny Lucia tossed her head, her dark brown locks tumbling around her shoulders in an elegantly tousled state of *dishabille*.

Minerva glanced over at the lady and felt a pang of envy mixed in with her growing annoyance at this pushy bit of Neapolitan temptation. Truly, there was an art and gift to looking like that, one Minerva didn't possess.

Nor do I want to, she told herself, if it had one prancing about in the middle of the night all trussed and trimmed like a holiday pudding.

"Truly, *schatzi*," the margravine said, sending her own scathing glance at Minerva's flannel covering, one brow arching to say in so many words that she wouldn't be caught dead in such material—not even for her shroud. "You tease us, certainly." She sidled once again in front of the duchessa, much to Lucia's annoyance. "Marry this one? Why it is impossible! She has no . . . no . . ."

"Passion," Nanny Tasha finished for her rival. The princess made her move then, taking center stage. "No essence, no fire. Nor has she wit enough to keep you entertained. No offense meant, Lady Standon."

Minerva would like to have possessed enough manners to manage a "None taken," but she found herself boiling mad and filled with an insensible . . . an enflamed . . . well, passion, that suggested the princess had it all wrong. They all did.

"How could she be offended when it is so very obvious," Nanny Lucia sniffed. The others nodded in agreement, as if Minerva wasn't even in the room.

She drew a deep breath, even as her fingers balled up into an uncharacteristic fist. Echoes of her grandmother's taunts that her father would never get away with marrying her to the Marquess of Standon. That he would be doing naught but making a silk purse out of a sow's ear, to all their ruin.

"Oh, but looks are deceiving, ladies," Langley was saying. "And I assure you, Lady Standon possesses all those qualities and more. She has made me the happiest man in England by agreeing to be my bride."

Minerva's head swiveled toward him. His bride? Was the man mad? First he came tumbling into her bedchamber and now he thought them engaged? No, not just mad. Utterly insane.

She should have pushed him out the window when she'd had her chance. And it was on the tip of her lips to call him out, to denounce this lie of his and then happily feed him to these imported wolves, but once again he caught her unawares.

For while she stood there fuming and plotting, he moved closer and slipped his hand around hers. The second their fingers twined, something very odd sparked, a flicker that ran from her fingertips through her limbs as if tapped from a Leyden jar. She couldn't help herself, she looked at him.

And discovered that it only took a spark to ignite a blaze.

His blue eyes danced with a naughty, wicked light that would make a less sensible woman believe they gleamed like that only for her.

Minerva considered herself far too sensible to be swayed by a pair of mesmerizing eyes, by handsome Roman features, by stone chiseled lips and an air of confidence that could inflate a balloon and send it aloft to the farthest corners of the earth.

No, this is naught but more of his rakish parlor tricks, she told herself even as he drew up her hand and then tipped his head down to place a kiss on the tips of her bare fingers.

When his lips touched her, that rare fire burned anew, as if his very breath reignited the smoldering embers. Her knees knocked and trembled in a most insensible fashion.

How could they not when his lips whispered once again over her, a warm, heated kiss that sent shivers trembling out in hurried waves up her arm and down through the rest of her limbs?

His other hand curled around her waist, catching hold of her, drawing her in closer so that she was encircled by him, protected, desired by him.

"Darling, dearest girl," he mused. "I fear our secret is no longer that . . . *our secret*."

If she hadn't been doing her best to keep upright, she swore she could have mustered a snort of derision that would have met with even the approval of Knuddles. But good gracious heavens, how this man could utter two words, "our secret," and make them run down her spine with the same sensual tease as his fingers had earlier.

"You want us to believe you are engaged to her?" Nanny Helga did manage to make an indelicate snort that said everything Minerva wished she could manage, and would muster once she got out of Langley's enticing grasp.

Away from the spell he'd cast over her.

"She is right, *cara*," Nanny Lucia agreed. "It is impossible to believe."

The Russian moved again, in that deliberate, cat-like way of hers. "Yes, none of us are fools, darling. We know all your *tricks*."

Minerva suspected the lady didn't mean just his legendary diplomatic prowess.

Knuddles growled from his post in Nanny Brigid's arms. The lady ran her fingers over the mane of black hair that surrounded the little dog's monkey-like face. "If you think we will leave because you claim to love her, you are quite mistaken."

"Then stay for our wedding and see for yourself," he told them. "I insist."

In one of the small, private parlors of White's, Lord Chudley had been spending a quiet evening reading his paper. Far more enjoyable than escorting

Bedelia and her niece to some soiree or musical or whatever it was she'd been nattering on about over their tea this afternoon.

Bless her heart, he did love his wife, but Bedelia was a busybody by nature, the sort who could cannonade a fleet of American privateers with her forthrightness.

So he'd learned quickly that occasionally he was "utterly needed at his club."

And good wife that she was, she understood and took no offense.

Even so, his respite was interrupted when two fellows came into the room, sharing a whispered exchange that spoke of deceit, and so Chudley watched them through softly shuttered lashes feigning a nap. His high-backed chair was turned slightly toward the fireplace, so the pair didn't see him immediately, that is until they came deep enough into the room.

"Sir Basil—" one of them said, nodding toward where Chudley lounged, looking for all intents like a slumbering old gallant.

"Never mind him," Sir Basil declared. "I daresay even if he were awake, at his age he's as deaf as a post."

Now if Chudley had been a more arrogant sort he would have taken this young pup to task for such cheek.

Deaf as a post, indeed! He wasn't that old, and considering he'd just married his fourth wife, and had no trouble keeping her blissfully happy, he'd like to announce that he was as spry as a goat—they could only wish for such good fortune at his age.

But Chudley hadn't spent his early years working for the Foreign Office not to know that arrogance and a lofty regard for one's manhood had no place in this world.

That, and he still kept abreast of things in the old office, and he'd never once heard a good word said about this upstart Sir Basil. And from the shady looks of the company he was keeping, Chudley had no doubts the pair of them were into something they weren't willing to discuss at Whitehall.

And if that was the case, his curiosity outweighed a slight about his hearing and age.

But demmit, who was that other fellow? He looked vaguely familiar.

"We have a problem," Sir Basil was saying.

"What is it now, Brownie?" the man replied, glancing down at his fingernails. "You always have a problem. And they never amount to the drama that you insist on adding to them."

"You'll think differently when I tell you."

"Then get on with it," the other man said. "Tibballs is downstairs, utterly foxed and in the mood for a few hands of loo. And in a few hands I'll have emptied his pockets."

"You won't have pockets to fill when you find out who is back in Town."

The shake to Sir Basil's voice almost prodded Chudley to open his eyes and give the man a level examination.

"Good God, man, get this over with," the other fellow said, sounding all-too-bored and having taken no note of the fearful tremor to Sir Basil's voice.

"Langley," Sir Basil said in a deadly still whisper.

Chudley's breath froze in his throat and he wondered if perhaps his hearing wasn't up to snuff, for he would have sworn he heard the man say—

"Langley?" The man laughed. "Demmit, Basil, when did you start believing in ghosts? Langley is dead. Now if you'll excuse me—"

There was the thud of boots as the man went to leave, but his departure came to a halt as Sir Basil continued, "Langley is not dead, you fool. He's alive and in London. And you need to get out of Town. Now."

Langley, alive? Impossible. Chudley had seen a copy of the report detailing Langley's last day in Paris. No, the man couldn't be alive.

A skepticism shared by his cohort. "Are you sure you didn't have too much of the Prime Minister's infamous claret? Because you're talking nonsense. Langley is dead."

"Not as dead as you would like," Sir Basil said, reverting to that lofty sort of mushroom tone of his.

Upstarts! Lord Chudley would have snorted. Thought they had to act and sound superior to make up for being utterly common.

Yet, how could Langley live? As distasteful as it was to agree with the likes of this shady fellow, and having had more than his fair share of the Prime Minister's claret a time or three, he was inclined to agree that Sir Basil was as foxed as the poor unwitting Tibballs downstairs.

"Bah, you've gone 'round the bend. He's aloft, I tell you. Now if you will excuse me—"

"He's alive, you fool," Sir Basil insisted.

The strident note to his declaration had Chudley unshuttering his lashes enough not to give himself away, but enough to see the Foreign Office's junior minister take hold of the other man's lapels and drag him up close. "Langley got in my carriage tonight and demanded an accounting of how he was betrayed."

Betrayed? Chudley didn't like the sound of that. Any more than he liked the idea of Langley back in Town.

Devil of a fellow, Langley. Not always on the up and up. Just before he'd been killed in Paris there had been rumors, nasty ones, that he'd been working for the French. Rumors of thefts. And that eventually his French contacts had finished the man off once they were done with him.

Messy business, dealing with frogs.

"He is demanding a full hearing. Wants to see the reports. Wants his name cleared."

Good luck with that, Chudley would have added. *Once a traitor . . .*

"You're serious," the other fellow whispered.

"Haven't you been listening to a word I've said?"

"No, this can't be. I saw him—"

Chudley stilled. *Saw him what, my mysterious friend?*

"If Langley is back in Town—"

Sir Basil shuddered, letting out a breathy sigh.

"Yes, now you see how that could complicate matters."

"Complicate matters? He could—"

Chudley strained to hear more.

"Yes, that's it, exactly." Sir Basil cleared his throat.

"If he delves into—"

"He cannot!" Sir Basil declared, and then realizing he'd raised his voice, glanced over at Chudley.

Both men stood there for a time, an eternity to

Chudley, but he stayed stock-still, if only to sort out everything he'd just learned . . . and hadn't.

Langley was alive? He was still of the opinion that Sir Basil needed to lay off the claret bottle, that is until the other man spoke again.

"Demmit, how did this happen?"

"That is what I would like to know. You told me he was dead, and now here he is popping up like some bloody marionette. The man has more lives than my wife's Persian cat."

The other man made a choking sort of sound. "He'll ruin me, or worse."

"He'll ruin us both," Sir Basil corrected. "You need to get out of Town. Stay hidden. You'll be the next person he comes looking for."

"You've got to stop him," the other fellow hissed out.

"I thought I had," Sir Basil. "Not that he'll escape this time if it is done right and orderly."

Chudley's blood ran to ice. What they were talking about was treason. And for the life of him, he wasn't about to see them murder an agent of England.

Not when he had every intention of being the one to put a bullet through that demmed rogue's heart.

"You insist?" Lady Standon threw her hands up in the air and paced in front of Langley. "You insist with my house!"

"It seemed the practical solution at the time." He leaned forward and lowered his voice. "They weren't exactly falling for the notion that we are wildly in love."

Minerva's brows arched upward and she leaned forward to match him tone for tone. "That is because we are not!"

He waved her off. "A moot point, that."

"A moot point?" she sputtered. "To whom? You? For it is certainly not moot to me." She paced again, stomping back and forth, utterly furious with him.

Her houseguests had been sent toddling off to their beds, not without a few protests, and even more whispered offers that left Langley politely demurring and Lady Standon blushing with annoyance.

So now they were finally alone and Langley was doing his best to find his way through this mess. Like most of his escapades, he was making this up as he went along, but usually when there was a woman involved, she was far more willing than this one.

This stubborn, unyielding Boudicca in flannel.

"Lady Standon, please," he said, looking around her bedchamber and settling for pointing toward the only chair in the room, the one at her dressing table. "Have a seat and calm yourself. Perhaps you would like something to drink to ease your nerves."

"No, I shall not sit down. Nor will I be mollified or plied with drink. I would point out that my nerves wouldn't be in this state if you hadn't come tumbling into my bedchamber like a thief."

"An oversight on my part." One that might work to his advantage. What had Thomas-William warned?

You don't want to be caught in the open.

And while most of Langley's kind preferred to work in the shadows, such tactics had never set well with him.

And now he saw all too clearly how he could draw out his enemy.

By standing in the middle of Society.

And it wouldn't hurt to be surrounded, as it were, by a bevy of deadly beauties.

Present company excluded.

"An oversight?" The lady threw up her hands. "Whatever were you doing on my drainpipe to begin with?"

"I would think that the answer to that is rather obvious—but it hardly matters now. Though in my defense, I will point out that I wouldn't have been forced to climb the drainpipe if you hadn't invited my former . . . former . . ."

"Doxies?"

"Acquaintances," he corrected. "You can hardly call a Russian princess a doxy. It's bad form. Diplomatically speaking and all."

The lady's hands went to her hips and those dark brows of hers arched.

So she didn't like being taken to task. Then again this was why most English diplomats left their wives at home.

English women just didn't understand Continental manners. Were all too judgmental about the mores. And looked askance at most of the customs that made each kingdom and principality unique.

And the lady proved his point by saying, "When one such as your princess arrives—uninvited and unwanted—and takes over one's house as if by divine right, all in pursuit of . . ."

He grinned at her, for the possibilities for completing her sentence were endless.

In pursuit of passion . . . ecstasy . . . pleasure.

But before he could enlighten her, she finished her own tumbled sentence.

" . . . in pursuit of low company, I will call her exactly what she is—a common doxy."

Low? Common? The lady knew how to get to the crux of the matter.

Langley put his hand over his heart. "Madame, you wound me."

The brows arched again, and this time she glanced at him and made a slight withering shake of her head. "I doubt it," she said with every bit of cold rigidity that Thomas-William declared ran through her veins and Mrs. Hutchinson had seconded. But Lady Standon had not been without defenders in the ranks, for Tia believed that Minerva had once been greatly disappointed in love and that was why she was this way.

Leave it to an overly imaginative chit barely out of the schoolroom to see right through the lady's bluff. Because Langley knew something the others didn't about the mistress of the house.

Minerva Sterling, the last remaining dowager Marchioness of Standon, held a spark of fire inside her heart.

He knew that for certain. For he'd felt the heat of her passionate nature when he'd held her.

When he'd stolen that kiss from her lips. With his common, low lips.

Speaking of which . . . "Truly? You thought my kiss low? Common?"

Just as he suspected, her gaze flew up and met his.

Because this was the difference between Lady Standon and her houseguests—for when confronted with the truth about a moment of passion, she gaped at him wide-eyed with guilt and blushed like a May day lass.

"Come now, Lady Standon," he said, closing the

space between them. "Would it be as bad as all that to be engaged to me?"

"Be engaged to you?" Minerva sputtered. "Do I really need to answer that?"

"Apparently not," he mused. "Though I found our kiss quite delightful."

"I did not," she lied. And worse yet, one glance at the insufferable man told her quite clearly that he didn't believe her.

Not in the least.

Did he really have to grin like that? It reminded her of the moment he'd hauled her up in his arms, just before he'd put his lips to hers and—

Minerva scooted around the chair and put it between them. Small comfort it was, because she knew this flimsy piece of furniture would hardly stop such a rogue.

"It seems, my lady," he said, flicking a glance at her choice of protection and giving it scant regard, "we have reached an impasse. For I need a betrothed and you refuse me, even though we've been discovered *in flagrante delicto.*"

"We were no such thing!" Minerva shot back. "You caught me unawares. I had no opportunity to protest."

He grinned again. "No opportunity? Are you certain about that?"

Minerva paused and was about to make a quick retort, but instead found herself replaying those moments over in her head. Slowly. Step by step.

And wished she hadn't. For in every second, from the time he'd taken her in his arms, in the slow descent of his lips onto hers, she could have stopped him.

And she hadn't.

"You took me by surprise," she brazened.

"I suppose I did," he drawled slowly, pushing aside the chair and moving toward her.

She shook her finger at him. "Oh, no, you don't!"

"Don't what?"

"Come near me again!" she told him, dodging past him and opening up her door.

"So we are back to our impasse."

"There is no impasse," she told him. "You and your paramours can leave my house. Leave me out of this madness!"

"If you insist," he said, crossing the room and making as if he was going to leave, but he stopped halfway to the stairs.

"Unless, that is," he began, "you can think of a reason why you might want me to stay." His gaze fell to her mouth, to her lips to be exact.

Minerva pressed them together. Tightly.

"I could be of service to you, Lady Standon, whether you realize it or not." He eased closer to her, his boot conveniently planted at the base of the door so she couldn't shut it.

Not that it would matter much now that the hinges were in ruins.

"Don't you dare!" she managed.

He stared at her for a moment and then nodded. "If you insist."

"I do."

He pulled his foot free and went toward the stairs again. "Until the morning, my lady." And after making a short, elegant bow, he began to ascend the stairs.

Up? What the devil? Minerva blinked and stepped

out in the hallway. "Where do you think you are going?"

He glanced at her, then up the dark stairwell, and then back at her. "To my room," he said as he continued to slowly climb.

"Your wha-a-a-t?" she managed as she followed after him, stopping at the landing.

"My room," he repeated, having stopped a few steps shy of the next landing. "The one you've been graciously providing me for . . . oh, let me see . . . a sennight, is it? Yes, I do believe I've been here a little over a week."

"A week?" she sputtered. "You've been living here, in my house, for a week?"

He pressed a finger to his lips. "Ssh, my lady. Unless you want all of Mayfair to know our secret."

There it was again. The way he said that. *Our secret.* As if that was enough to convince her that they possessed one. Shared something illicit. She ignored the shiver that ran down her spine. The teasing whisper of desire that followed in its wake.

They did have something in common. His kiss had proved that.

"You cannot have been living here for a week," Minerva insisted.

"While I try never to contradict a lady, I fear I must in this case. I have very much been living here. In your house." He needn't take so much delight in pointing out his deception and her unwitting involvement. Oh, but he wasn't finished yet. Leaning down the stairs he whispered, "As it turns out, I am such an excellent houseguest, you hardly knew I was here."

"That is the point, sir. I did not know!"

"Good luck convincing the rest of the *ton*."

Minerva groaned and ground her teeth together. "You are utterly mad!"

The man shrugged. "No, not in the least. And if we are being fair about this, the real madness of my plan requires that I convince Society that *I* am willing to marry *you*, madam. But I am up to the challenge and daresay might find it a tolerable one, indeed."

Minerva sucked in a deep breath, if only to avoid the retort that rose quickly from every indignant nerve in her body.

Why you insufferable bast—

"Good night, my lady." With that, he continued on up the stairs, and when he turned at the landing, he had the nerve to wink at her as if daring her to follow him and make good her earlier threat to turn him out.

Oh, bother! What could she do? Follow him up into the darkness? Kick up a bigger ruckus? Hardly. And that devil of a man knew it. He had her in his crosshairs and there was nothing she could do.

At least not now.

Minerva closed her door and leaned against it—for it was the only way to get it to shut.

Come morning, she vowed, *I'll see the lot of you rousted and moved out.*

And then unwittingly she thought of Lord Langley's kiss and added one more thing to her resolution.

Before there is worse damage than my broken door and ruined drainpipe.

Chapter 4

The creak of the sole remaining hinge on the door into Minerva's bedchamber brought her awake abruptly. Sitting straight up, she spent a heart-stopping moment trying to make right of the world around her—the sunshine pouring through the thin curtains, and the sounds of a London day in full movement—and the equally vibrant dream she'd been wrenched out of.

Of him. Lord Langley. Kissing her. Yet again. And this time she hadn't been protesting.

Not that you protested all that much the first time around.

Minerva ignored that wry observation, for it sounded too much like something Aunt Bedelia might say.

"So sorry, my lady," her maid rushed to say. "I

just thought . . . it's just that you're usually . . . with it being nearly noon, I feared something might be amiss, even though he said he'd left you happily contented."

He said? Minerva glanced up and found Agnes's wide blue eyes scanning her and the bed as if she half expected her mistress to look as ravished as the door. Then the rest of her maid's explanation stopped ringing about her sleep-tousled thoughts.

. . . he said he'd left you happily contented.

How dare he imply that she . . . that they . . . that they'd . . .

Oh, that lying, good for nothing—

Minerva threw back the covers and jammed her feet into her slippers. "Goodness, Agnes! Whyever did you let me sleep this late?"

The girl settled the tray she carried on the dressing table and said, "His lordship said you needed the rest."

Minerva, who'd reached for her dressing robe and nearly had it on, stilled. "He did, did he?"

"Oh, aye. So concerned about you. What a fine, thoughtful fellow he is, my lady, iffin you don't mind me saying. He took great pains to see that Mrs. Hutchinson put your tray together just so." Never still for a moment, Agnes had gotten right to work setting the bed to rights. She glanced up from fluffing the pillows. "He said you might be a bit peckish . . ." The girl paused and blushed, then finished quickly by adding, "After last night and all."

After last night . . . As if there had been a "last night." Which there hadn't.

But there could have been.

Minerva closed her eyes and counted to ten, rein-

ing in her unlikely fancies. She blamed Lucy and
Elinor for all this. She wouldn't have thought once
about such things, save for all their talk of late of
taking a lover and getting married.

And now . . .

Though it was hard to blame Lucy and Elinor
when she knew who the real instigator of these unwanted flights of desire was, and he was downstairs
right this moment wreaking havoc on the rest of
her life.

"You can take that tray back downstairs," she instructed her maid. "I am not hungry."

"Well, he didn't say that exactly," Agnes amended.
"He said . . . oh, it was rather fancy. Just let me recall
it . . ." The girl tapped her fingers to her chin until
suddenly her eyes brightened. "Yes, yes, I remember
what he said. He told me and Mrs. Hutchinson that
you would most likely be famished this morning.
Especially after needing to sleep in so late."

Famished. He hadn't! Oh, yes, he had put that pink
hue of a blush on Agnes's cheeks.

Why, that blasted rogue had deliberately chosen
that word precisely because it wasn't too far from
"ravished"—which is exactly how the story would
be retold by the time his little *on dit* got nosed
around.

Good heavens! The man was mad. Confiding such
nonsense with the servants. Didn't he realize that
such admissions would go from the attics to the
cellar like a flash of Franklin's electricity? Then it
would be over the garden fence and in every house
on Brook Street before . . . Minerva closed her eyes
and groaned as she stopped herself from saying
"noon."

For it was nearly noon by Agnes's own account.

Nearly noon?

Oh, yes, he'd known exactly what he was doing. And let her sleep while his madness took root.

Like small pox. Or the Black Plague.

Not for long, she vowed, ignoring the tray of scones, bacon, and coffee that Agnes had brought up. For damn the man, it did look heavenly, especially with the thoughtful touch of a single red rose on one side. And as loath as she was to admit it, she was hungry.

Famished, really. But she would commit herself to Bedlam before she'd ever admit such a thing. For hidden beneath his words was that unerring knowledge that her appetite and needs could not be sated with just a scone.

Minerva tamped down a groan and hastily donned her gown. "Where is he?" she asked, twisting her hair up and stabbing the pins in place herself, rather than wait for Agnes to help.

"Pardon, my lady?"

"Precisely where is Lord Langley?"

"In the morning room, my lady. Having his breakfast. He bid me to tell you that when you were able, to please join him, for he is ever so fond of your company." Agnes smiled, her bright blue eyes sparkling with happiness for her mistress.

Minerva gaped at her obviously smitten maid. Who would have guessed that plain-spoken, hardworking Agnes harbored a romantic side?

Smitten, indeed! Well, she would see about that. "Agnes, do me a favor and go down and find Thomas-William. Ask him to go over to the duke's stables and direct Mr. Ceely to send around a wagon. Oh, and a carriage as well," she added. Minerva wagered her houseguests would be extraordinarily put out to be asked to walk around the corner to their new home, the duke's residence.

"Are we leaving?" Agnes asked.

"No. But our guests are. All of them."

The maid's brow furrowed. "All of them, my lady?" As in, even Lord Langley?

Especially him, Minerva wanted to say. Truly, what was it about the man that had solid and sensible Agnes broaching mutiny, for it was there on the girl's stricken face. "Yes, everyone."

Goodness, how could the girl be so infatuated when she'd just met the man?

She had just met him, hadn't she? Minerva glanced over her shoulder and couldn't bring herself to ask her own maid if she'd been complicit in hiding Lord Langley in her house.

Meanwhile, Agnes bobbed her head and went to finish her work in the room, folding Minerva's plain night rail and putting it away, muttering as she went, "I don't see how you are going to get them out."

Well, as Minerva saw it, there were two obstacles to this entire plan: the ladies themselves, and Staines, the Duke of Hollindrake's butler, who had turned them away to begin with. Setting her jaw, Minerva was done with good manners. Besides, she still had Thomas-William's pistol. If there were any objections, she would have the leverage to force the issue.

Given what she now knew about her visitors, she suspected it wasn't the first time one of those Continental hussies had been sent packing at the wrong end of a firearm.

As for Staines, she had to imagine that the man would be more than willing to open the door when he found that she'd come armed like a regular rusher. Ignoring the fact that when apprehended, most rushers were hung, Minerva reassured herself that desperate measures were all too necessary.

Besides, she wasn't there to steal anything, just unload what was wrongly delivered to Brook Street.

Meanwhile, the front doorbell rattled awake and startled her out of her reverie. Glancing at the clock, Minerva couldn't for the life of her think of who could be calling so early. "Agnes, was I expecting anyone this morning?"

"No, my lady," Agnes said. "But one of them nannies did send out for some sausages. Mayhap the butcher is delivering them."

The bell rattled again, and this time it sent a tremor of foreboding down Minerva's spine. The butcher with sausages? It didn't make sense.

"Whyever would the fellow bring them to the front door?" she said aloud, more to herself than to Agnes. "No, I do believe someone has come to call."

Which meant Minerva needed to get downstairs and intercede before someone admitted this unknown and unwelcome guest. No, whoever it was needed to be barred from entering, no matter how rude she had to appear. But what else could she do? It would be a disaster if anyone discovered that Langley had been staying with her.

Just then Agnes sucked in a deep breath. "Oh, the devil take me, my lady. I forgot. Your aunt, Lady Chudley, sent a note over earlier. Said she was going to come 'round."

Aunt Bedelia? Minerva tried to move, but her limbs suddenly froze in terror. If Aunt Bedelia made it inside, the first place she'd look for her was . . .

The cacophony of screams that erupted from downstairs confirmed two things.

Aunt Bedelia had been shown into the morning room.

And discovered Langley.

"How is it, Minerva, that you are engaged to *this man* without my knowledge?"

Even Langley had to cringe at the hard cold note in Lady Chudley's question. He almost felt sorry for Minerva, who had come racing down the stairs in response to her aunt's screams.

Well, the lady shouldn't have asked "Who the devil are you?" if she didn't want to hear the answer. And obviously, given the high-pitched screech that followed, she hadn't appreciated his reply.

"Lord Langley, madam," he'd said. "Lady Standon's betrothed."

Then Lady Chudley had begun shrieking like her skirts were on fire. And he suspected it wasn't the sudden betrothal that had the old girl's stockings in a knot, but the fact that Minerva was engaged to *him*. The infamous Lord Langley.

There were times when his reputation came in quite handy. Though given the way his ears were ringing, now was probably not one of them.

"Minerva, answer me!" Lady Chudley demanded. "Is this man your betrothed? And if he isn't, what is he doing at your breakfast table in such a state?"

His state, as it were, was that he'd neglected to wear much more than his breeches and shirt. He'd tossed on his waistcoat, but hadn't put on a cravat. In good English society, he knew this meant he was "undressed," but it was demmed more comfortable to have one's breakfast like this than trussed up like one was going to court.

Enjoying his scandalous state, Langley stretched his legs out and lounged in his chair, meeting Minerva's outraged countenance with a wink and a grin. "I'm so sorry, darling. If I had known we were entertaining so early, I would have put my jacket on. Not that I could find it this morning." He paused for only a moment. "Is it still in your bedchamber?" Then he winked at Aunt Bedelia. "Taken off in haste, so easily forgotten . . ."

"Oh, you wretched man. I am not your darling," Minerva ground out before she turned to her aunt and finished by saying, "and he is not my betrothed."

"*Tsk tsk*," he said, reaching for a scone on the tray. He broke it into three pieces and began to butter one. "I am sure your aunt can keep our secret—that is, if you insist we keep it so." Langley turned his smile toward Lady Chudley and shrugged. "I don't know why she thinks we should hide our happiness."

"*Uggggh*," Minerva ground out. "You are the worst sort of bounder. You interloper. You liar!"

"We'll need to work on your endearments," he told her. "You're a touch out of practice. Why not use the one you called me last night before I left you to your contented slumber?"

There was a moment of shocked silence in the morning room, then Lady Chudley sank into a chair, looking like she needed smelling salts. He poured her a cup of tea, for Mrs. Hutchinson liked to brew her pots like an Irishwoman, as dark as coffee and twice as strong. Picking up the sugar tongs, he asked, "One lump or two?"

"Oh, give me that," Minerva said, coming around the table and snatching the tongs out of his hand. She deftly caught one lump, then another, dropping them into her aunt's tea with the practiced ease of a lady. "Aunt, are you well?" Her voice was low and full of concern. "You mustn't pay Lord Langley any heed. I do believe he is completely mad."

"Mad about you, certainly," he replied, reaching out and curling his arm around her waist. She shoved his hand aside and stormed off to the other side of the table. Langley leaned back and admired Minerva's nerve and mettle as she stood at the head of the table looking quite capable of serving him up as the second course.

Meanwhile, Lady Chudley had picked up a teaspoon and begun to stir her tea at a furious rate.

"I know this must come as a bit of shock to you, my lady," Langley said to the older woman. When she slanted a hot glance at him, he smiled and saw a bit of twinkle in her eye. So she wasn't as outraged as she appeared. Well, it never hurt to have an ally. "I beg of you to believe that I have your niece's best intentions at heart."

They both ignored the indelicate snort that rose from his "betrothed."

Minerva rushed in to get the upper hand. "Aunt Bedelia, if you must know the truth, this rogue turned up last night—"

"Last week," he corrected.

"Last night!" Minerva insisted.

"Last week?" Lady Chudley clucked her tongue. "Minerva! That will never do! A widow is allowed some liberties, discreet ones, but this . . . this . . ."

"None of what he says is true," Minerva insisted,

crossing her arms over her chest. "Who are you going to believe, me or him?"

Lady Chudley glanced from one to the other and then went back to stirring her tea. "This is most distressing, niece."

"I suppose it must be," Langley said, "discovering so unexpectedly that your niece has fallen under my spell. But truly it is I who has fallen." He watched Minerva's brow furrow into an angry line.

"Fallen? I should have pushed you out the window when I had the chance."

"Really, Minerva, such outrageous talk!" Aunt Bedelia said, adding a *tsk tsk*.

"Yes, indeed," Langley agreed. "Let's stick to the facts: I have been living with your generous and very hospitable niece since Tuesday last."

Now it was Lady Chudley's turn to make an indelicate snort. But whether it was over his living arrangements or the notion of her niece being generous and hospitable, he couldn't tell.

"Is it true that he's been living here for a sennight?" This question was posed by Lady Chudley to her niece.

"Most decidedly not!" Minerva told her.

Langley leaned forward and smiled at her. "My dearest girl, we have nothing to be ashamed of, though I am certain some would find our affection for each other scandalous—"

"Ruinous, to be more precise," Lady Chudley added.

"Precisely," he said, nodding in agreement, "but how can we do otherwise when our passion for each other cannot be denied?" He turned to Lady Chudley. "To answer your question, yes, I have been living here. Contentedly. For a sennight."

"Oh, good gracious heavens!" the old girl exclaimed. "This is a scandal!"

"What it is, is utter nonsense," Minerva shot back, before she wagged her finger at him. "You set the matter straight. Immediately."

He bowed his head slightly. "If you insist."

"I do."

Langley glanced up and smiled. "Last night after a delightful tumble into your niece's bed, I proposed to her and she accepted with a most gratifying kiss." He grinned triumphantly at Minerva, for there was nothing untruthful about anything he'd just said.

"Oh you bounder!" she said, getting to her feet. "Get out of my house!"

"After last night?" He shook his head and leaned back in his chair. "Never. Besides, I need my jacket back."

"Minerva Sterling! I should have thought better of you!" Lady Chudley declared. "And this . . . well, this is beyond the pale. I won't have a niece of mine become one of *those* widows—dreadful, licentious creatures that everyone gossips about and who are not received. I don't see how you can do anything other than marry, especially if this man has been living with you for a sennight!" She shuddered and reached for another lump of sugar.

Minerva rounded on Langley. "There is no proof that you've been here as you say. It is only *your* word."

Her implication was clear. Who would believe him—a known rake and a gentleman considered by most to be guilty of treason?

Then again, she barely knew him, for if she did,

she would have known he wasn't beaten yet. For the first rule George Ellyson had taught him all those years ago was to use the truth to one's advantage.

And Langley had the truth firmly on his side. "Minerva, my darling girl, I do have proof. A most reliable witness. One who I am sure will be more than happy to corroborate my story. All over town."

"Who? Mrs. Hutchinson?" Minerva pressed. "Was she sober when you arrived?" She sputtered out a breath. "You expect Society to believe her word over mine?"

"Really, Minerva, we need to work on your diplomacy." Langley spared a glance at Lady Chudley and shook his head. To his delight, the old girl nodded in agreement.

"She's always been overly blunt," Lady Chudley confided.

He grinned back. "Fortunately, I find that one of her more endearing characteristics."

"You're the first," Aunt Bedelia muttered as she tasted her tea, and then dug the tongs into the sugar bowl and selected another large lump to add to it.

"Oh, how dare you!" Minerva sputtered. "How can you find anything about me endearing when you don't know me?"

"You would be amazed what a man can learn about a woman when he kisses her."

Minerva's mouth opened to say something but nothing came out.

Lady Chudley had no such so impediment. "Good heavens, Minerva! You've become quite indecent. Kissing strangers!"

"Betrotheds," Langley corrected, glancing up from his scone. "Hardly strangers."

"Well, I should hope so," Lady Chudley declared. "For it is bad enough that you've gone and gotten yourself engaged without confiding in your only relative." She paused for a moment and then her eyes widened. "I blame Lucy Sterling. Cheeky minx, that one. Living with her about probably put all sorts of notions in your head."

"I'm indecent?" Minerva stammered at her aunt. "Have you not once considered that he is lying?"

"Whyever would I lie about kissing you?" Langley posed, reaching for the plate of scones and offering them to Lady Chudley, who took one and followed Langley's lead by breaking it into pieces as well. "Actually it was quite enlightening."

"Ooooh! Ooooh, you——" she stammered.

"You're a handful as well, aren't you?" Lady Chudley said to him, but there was none of the condemnation that Lucy Sterling had warranted a few moments earlier. In fact the old girl grinned at him.

"This has gone too far," Minerva declared, now pacing at the end of the table. "So who is this witness you purport to have who can corroborate your story."

"Why a lady, of course."

"Not me," Minerva said.

Langley winked at Lady Chudley and then grinned at his unwitting betrothed. "My dear, I wouldn't think to call you that."

Minerva's mouth opened again, this time in a wide O. With her shoulders taut with indignation, she looked ready to club him with the salver. "You wouldn't call me a lady?"

"Well, I must confess we aren't *that* well acquainted so I can make the distinction. Rather, what

I was trying to say is that I wouldn't call you as a witness for my defense."

"How about one for your funeral?" she shot back.

Lady Chudley began to chortle at the sallies flying back and forth across the table. But when Minerva shot her a hot glance, her aunt had the good sense to make it appear as if she was coughing.

"Then who is this witness?" Minerva demanded.

Really, she needed to learn the second lesson of spying. Right after learning how to stay alive, you never asked a question if you didn't want to hear the answer.

And truly, Minerva did not want to hear this answer. But he told her anyway. "Miss Knolles."

"Tia." The name came out like a curse. Minerva had enough sense to realize she'd been outflanked and cornered. She sank into a chair, much as her aunt had earlier.

"So the little imp didn't say a word?" Lady Chudley asked her niece.

She shook her head. "Not one."

Langley snorted this time. "Of course she didn't. She was too busy emptying my pockets every night playing *vingt-et-un*. If I had known what those Bath schools teach young girls, I would never have sent my Felicity and Thalia to one. I shudder to discover how they've turned out."

"So does most of Society," he thought he heard Lady Chudley muttering. "Lovely girls," she amended when she found all eyes on her.

"Aunt Bedelia," Minerva began, her hand resting on her forehead as if it were pounding with a megrim. "Whatever are you doing here this morning? Doesn't your cook make breakfast?"

"I broke my fast hours ago. The early bird, my dear. The early bird." She leaned over and confided to Langley, "Dr. Franklin had a bit of a *tendre* for me and I so adore his sayings."

"From what I have heard of you, my lady," Langley teased, "Franklin wasn't the only one. You've always been the lady to court. I daresay, looking at you, you prescribe to his notion of air bathing?"

Lady Chudley blushed at the implication. "You wicked man!"

Across the table, Minerva groaned, her gaze rolling upward. "Truly, Auntie, whyever are you here?"

"Tut tut," the lady said, waving her napkin at her niece. "Don't you remember, I promised that gaggle of nannies a shopping expedition today."

Minerva's gaze swiveled down to her aunt. "You were serious?"

"You of all people should know I never jest about shopping."

And as if on cue, the ladies began trooping in, Brigid in a sapphire blue gown with Knuddles at her hemline, Lucia following close behind in a pink gown that only accented her dark hair and lithe figure, while Helga had gone with red—garnet red with touches of black here and there—and finally came Tasha, all in black. Tasha always wore black for it set off her fair hair and pale skin, making her seem almost fragile inside it.

A mistake many a man had made thinking she needed to be rescued, protected, cared for.

Langley cringed. He wouldn't make that mistake again.

About any of them.

It would be like thinking one could pluck a jewel

from the case at Rundell & Bridges and not be caught.

Or punished.

"Langley, darling!" Tasha purred as she slid around the others with her catlike grace. "Did you sleep well?"

"The better question is how did you sleep, Lady Standon?" Lucia posed, her smile perfectly set but her eyes focused sharply on her opponent.

Langley had always suspected that the duchessa had more Borgia blood in her than she let on.

Tasha ignored the duchessa's remark and replied with one of her own. "We mustn't pry, ladies. What a betrothed couple does late at night in a lady's bed-chamber isn't that hard to imagine." She swung an assessing glance at Minerva. "Well, most of the time."

"Good heavens, it is true!" Lady Chudley exclaimed. "You were in her bedchamber?"

"Guilty," he replied with a grin.

"You see, I told you," Lucia said. "This betrothal is madness. Not even the aunt knows of it."

"Exactly!" Minerva agreed. "There is no betrothal."

Lady Chudley got to her feet and faced her niece. "If there wasn't an engagement before, there is one now."

Aunt Bedelia was true to her word. And true to her character, she would brook no arguments over the situation.

If Minerva and Langley had been caught in a state of *dishabille*, or as Nanny Lucia so aptly put it, *in flagrante delicto*, then they were betrothed, and the sooner the wedding took place, the better.

So with a stamp of her foot the indomitable Lady Chudley herded the other ladies out the door on the pretense that she wanted their input on an appropriate trousseau for her niece, thus leaving Minerva alone with Langley.

Minerva took a deep breath and told herself she should never have opened the door last night and allowed the nannies in. Further, she should never have allowed Aunt Bedelia in her house.

And certainly she should have called the rat catcher and had the house exterminated from attics to cellars.

The largest rat sat back in his seat, hands folded behind his head as he lounged, looking more like the cat who had swallowed the canary than the vermin she knew him to be.

Well, not quite vermin, for he was far too devilishly handsome to be so crowned.

Truly, how did a man of his age remain so well put together, so charming, so utterly desirable? Then despite herself, she couldn't help wonder exactly how old he was—what with two grown daughters and all.

There's a copy of Debrett's *upstairs. Look him up . . .*

No! She wasn't going to start prying into the particulars of Lord Langley, and she certainly wasn't going to be forced into another marriage. Not by anyone. But in her long years of widowhood, if there was one thing she'd learned, it was patience and timing.

So she sat in her seat, composing herself as Aunt Bedelia shooed the ladies out the front door. Well, all but one of them, for apparently Nanny Helga had other ideas and refused to go out so early, ordering her maid to discover what had become of the sausages she'd ordered and then stomping back upstairs muttering something in her own language that Minerva had to guess was a lengthy condemnation of English hospitality.

Glancing out the door of the morning room, Minerva smiled, for all-too-soon she was going to give the Margravine of Ansbach and the rest of her companions a lesson in English hospitality that would put even those ladies to blush. But the first one to be dispatched was Langley, the root of all her problems.

Once the front door slammed shut and the margravine had done much the same to her door upstairs, Minerva counted to twenty.

Then she got up, walked across the room and stopped in front of him.

Lord Langley grinned up at her, unrepentant scoundrel that he was. "Come to give your betrothed a proper morning kiss?"

Leaning forward, Minerva gently placed both of her palms on his chest, smiling ever-so-sweetly.

Just before she shoved him over backward.

The man landed with a satisfying thud. Brushing her hands together and then over her skirts, the first of the dirty business done, she stalked back across the room.

Meanwhile, there was a scramble of boots and the scrape of the chair as the baron tried to right himself. "Christ sakes, woman! Are you trying to kill me?"

Minerva's gaze once again wandered over toward the silver candlestick on the sideboard and considered the suggestion for a moment. Then she sighed and resigned herself that at least for now killing him outright probably wasn't the best course of action. She had to assume, and rightly so, that the Duchess of Hollindrake would be more put out with her than she already was if added to her crimes against the Sterling family was that of killing Her Grace's rapscallion father.

Meanwhile, Langley had managed to get to his feet. "That was hardly necessary," he told her, straightening up the chair and tugging his waistcoat back into place.

"But very satisfying, my lord," she said, smiling at him.

"Hardly the way to greet one's betrothed," he said, settling back in his seat and reaching for the teapot. "May I?" he asked, nodding at her cup.

"No, thank you," she replied. And much to her chagrin, he poured himself another cup and then began to help himself to the platter of bacon and kippers, as well as another scone. "I wouldn't get too comfortable, if I were you. You are not staying here."

"And where else would I go?"

"We cannot live in this house together." Her stomach rumbled in complaint, for the smell of food was just too much and she was hungry. Against her better judgment, she filled her plate as well. "I will brook no argument on the subject, for you cannot stay here."

"Whyever not?" he said. "We have a house full of chaperones, who are more than willing, I would note, to keep you out of my bed. And further, I am quite capable of restraining myself. That is, if you insist."

"Oh, I do insist. Besides, I never asked for your attentions to begin with."

"No, I suppose you didn't," he conceded. "But from what I can see, they may be exactly what you need."

Minerva had chosen that moment to take a sip of her tea and ended up sputtering it all over. "I beg your pardon?"

He grinned at her, and she couldn't decide if it made him more handsome or more annoying. Both, she decided, ignoring the strong line of his jaw, the crinkle of a dimple on one side, and the sparkle of his blue eyes.

"What I mean to say is that an engagement would be of tremendous benefit to you," he said, as if he had suggested she try the marmalade instead of the strawberry preserves.

"However would an engagement to *you* be of benefit to *me*?" she asked, setting down her knife and fork. Having already given the candlestick another glance, she decided it was probably better not to have anything deadly in her grasp.

He sat back as well. "I would think that would be obvious."

"Enlighten me."

"Gladly," he agreed. "It is well known that your aunt would like to see you married and settled and is not opposed to using whatever means possible to corner you into some sort of union, whether you like it or not."

Minerva flinched. She could well imagine how he'd discovered that much—for while a single meeting with Aunt Bedelia was more than enough to discover this, she suspected Tia's hand in this as well.

The little minx loved to gossip, and Minerva could also imagine what little—and large—*on dits* the girl had shared while playing cards with Lord Langley.

"If you were engaged to me, she would hardly continue to truss you up like Maid Marion and send you off to masquerades only to fill your dance card with aging roués and widowers with seven children." His smile as he finished was like a well-executed touché.

Oh, yes, Tia had done her worst.

"And," he continued, turning his attention back to his breakfast as he spoke. "If you could assume a more loving demeanor, you might even convince your houseguests to give up their stakes and leave. If they have no reason to remain in London, they will be out with the morning tide."

"Oh, no," she said, shaking her head. "They will be out this afternoon."

He didn't so much as laugh, but smiled indulgently at her, as if he found her naiveté quite endearing.

"They will be," she insisted. "I have ordered the carriages, and if it comes to it, I will use Thomas-William's pistol and evict them by force."

"You are going to run a Cossack footman out of your house with only a pistol?" He shook his head. "I hope you are prepared to shoot it, for that is the only way he will leave without his mistress's approval."

Minerva pursed her lips together, but then suddenly brightened. "If I shot you, then there would be no reason for any of them to stay and I would be rid of the lot of you."

"Have no fears, given my reputation and the life I've lived, you may get your wish sooner than necessary," he said in his usual light manner. But Minerva wasn't fooled, for there was something else to his words that filled in around the merry edges.

A sober note of concession.

She eyed him suspiciously, but Langley wasn't a renowned diplomat for nothing. He smiled blandly at her and continued eating his breakfast.

"Whyever would you want such an arrangement?" Deliberately she hadn't said, "engagement."

"Again, isn't it obvious?" He took a swift sip of tea. "I have no desire to marry, but I fear I've had a difficult—if not impossible—time convincing anyone else of that fact. If I were engaged to you, then effectively I would be out of the market and free to live my life without the fear of an unwanted entanglement." He paused for a moment. "That, and an engagement to you, my lovely and staid Lady Standon, would do much toward rehabilitating my standing in Society. I can hardly be as bad as all that if I was able to convince you to enter into marriage again."

There was more to this than just that, she wagered. For if it was only a matter of avoiding marriage, hadn't he proven he was quite adept at it? But there was something so enticing about what he offered . . .

Aunt Bedelia off her back. Her houseguests gone. The freedom to live her life as she saw fit—much as he desired.

Oh, it was tempting to accept what he was offering, but then the chains of matrimony rattled her back to the present. And there was one other factor—Aunt Bedelia. The old girl would only be put off so long before she'd have Lord Langley hauled down to the Archbishop's office and a Special License procured.

The man before her might be the most elusive spy England had ever claimed, but Minerva held a greater fear of Aunt Bedelia's prowess at getting a man married. Lord Langley might have trumped Napoleon, but he'd never outwit the infamous Lady Chudley.

"No," she said, shaking her head. "I will not enter into any sort of agreement. There will be no betrothal. No engagement. I'd rather weather the scandal that will come of refusing you than find myself mired up to my neck in something neither of us could escape or want."

He shook his head and looked ready to start doing what he reputably did so well—cajoling—and certainly not the other thing he was reputed to do so well—when Mrs. Hutchinson came in and stopped him in his tracks.

"There you are," the housekeeper said, thrusting a note out to Minerva. "This came for you. The fellow said he'd wait for an answer."

Minerva took the slip of paper and drew a deep breath, for she could never quite get used to Mrs. Hutchinson's less than stellar manners. She'd be fired from any other employment for her cheek and lack of regard for boundaries, but then again, no one made scones like the lady.

And that had to be worth something, Minerva told herself even as she glanced down at the dirty folded bit in her hands.

Lady Standon.

Minerva nearly dropped it as she stared at the hasty scrawl of writing across the front. *Good God, no! It couldn't be.*

She glanced again at the lettering, even as her heart stilled to a dull pounding thud. She'd know that handwriting anywhere. After glancing at Langley, who was charming Mrs. Hutchinson with lofty praise for her baking, she slid her trembling finger under the plain seal.

Inside it was worse than she'd first feared.

The money is late. Explain yourself. Now.

She folded it back up and stuffed it inside her sleeve, hidden away, though hardly forgotten. Taking another deep breath to still her shaking limbs, she managed a prim smile. "Did the man say he would wait?"

"Oh, aye. Out back. Cheeky devil. Should I send Lucy's man after him?"

"No, no," Minerva told her, rising abruptly. "That won't be necessary."

"Is there something amiss?" Langley asked as he too got to his feet, wiping his mouth with his napkin and setting it down beside his plate. "Can I be of assistance?"

"No," she said quickly, shaking her head. "Just some questions from the painter about what colors I wanted this room done in." She paused, her hand coming to rest on her other sleeve cuff, where the note sat tucked away. "Best I see to it quickly so the work isn't delayed. Please, Lord Langley, finish your breakfast."

"We are not done, my lady," he told her as she rushed out the door, having paid his words no heed. Langley glanced over at Mrs. Hutchinson. "Did you find her ladyship's behavior a bit odd?"

The housekeeper shrugged. "Everything about you toffs is a bit queer in the nob, if you ask me."

"Sorry I did," Langley said, glancing out the door where Minerva had fled.

Chapter 5

. . . though not for long.
Further advice from Nanny Tasha

*M*inerva paused at the back door, her hand trembling as she reached for the latch.

"You can do this," she whispered to herself. "You can face him."

All those years ago. How long had it been? Twelve years since she'd discovered the truth about love. About him. It seemed like a lifetime ago.

At the very least it had been another life. One she didn't want to revisit. Yet here she was, about to face a past she had tried to keep buried all these years. Her fingers wrapped around the latch and pushed the back door open.

Glancing over her shoulder to make sure no one was watching, she slipped into the garden and walked down the uneven path toward the gate, steeling herself for the sight of him.

But when she stepped into the alleyway, she found it empty. She glanced right then left, and for a moment felt a fleeting bit of relief.

She'd been wrong. It wasn't him.

Oh, but it was. For just then, out of the doorway that led to the garden across the way, stepped a tall muscular figure.

"Maggie, me girl, look at you."

Minerva stilled. *Maggie.* She hadn't been called that since the day her father had hauled her down the aisle to marry Philip Sterling.

And instead of finding comfort in hearing some- one use that old, long lost name, it sent a shock of terror through her.

"Don't call me that," she said, drawing herself up. *You are the Marchioness of Standon. You are. He can't do anything to that.*

Oh, but he could.

"What, Maggie me girl, are you too lofty now for old friends? Not so lofty that you didn't come run- ning when I came to call. Just like old times, eh?"

"What choice do I have?" She crossed her arms over her chest and took another furtive glance up and down the empty alleyway. "Now state your business and be gone before someone sees me with you."

Sees me and questions what I was doing out here . . .

"Gotten all hoity-toity, haven't we? But I know dif- ferent, don't I? I knew you when you weren't so fine and you were still my Maggie." Much to her cha- grin, he crossed the alley with the same determined stride that had once caught her eye. And unfortu- nately he was still darkly handsome.

But not as handsome as Langley, she found herself

thinking. For where the baron was charming and lighthearted, this man brooded a dark mystery.

He stopped before her and smiled down at her. One that would have sent her heart pattering a dozen or so years before. But that was the advantage of time and reaching an age where youthful eyes gave way to sight that let one see past the veneer of dark countenances and heavy-lidded glances.

For there was no longer any mystery to Gerald Adlington. Not to her. Everything that seemed so exciting and enigmatic about him had been easy to discover: He possessed no heart, no loyalty.

And he had never loved her.

Still, that didn't mean he couldn't toy with her. Couldn't play cat to her mouse. Something he knew only too well.

"So, Margaret Owens, you can dress yourself up and call yourself by whatever fancy title you like, but deep down we both know you will always be naught but old Gilston's by-blow. My hot-blooded Maggie. My dearest wife."

Langley watched from the morning room window as Lady Standon stole across the garden like a thief. Whatever was she doing meeting her "painter" in the mews? Too many years spent unraveling the secrets of others made it impossible for him not to start wondering what she was hiding.

"So you have your secrets, do you, Lady Standon?" he mused quietly to himself.

From behind him, he heard the telltale creak of the floor in the hallway, and then it was the lady's voice that stopped his speculations.

"*Schatzi*, how could anything hold your attention in this dreary place?"

Helga. He should have known her protestations against going out so early were for naught. He had to imagine that if there ever was an early bird, it was this woman. Sharp-eyed and ready to snatch up whatever came into her sights.

She entered the room without an invitation. "All alone? Goodness, your dear betrothed is a trusting soul. But she doesn't know you like I do."

Langley turned around, for it never was good to keep one's back to Wilhelmenia, the Margravine of Ansbach, for too long. He nodded politely to her. No, she wasn't a woman to be trifled with.

Nor given the least bit of encouragement.

"Where is she?" Helga asked, glancing about the empty place at the table, a slow smile on her lips.

"If you mean my betrothed, she is meeting with a tradesman."

Helga glanced up, her head tipped as if she hadn't heard him quite right. "Meeting with a tradesman? How very common." She paused and ran her finger over the back of the chair. "And how convenient." Then she moved like an eel around the table toward him.

"Margravine," he said as formally as he could.

"Helga," she corrected. "Remember when you called me that?"

"Yes, I do," he told her, stepping away from her and nudging a chair into her path. "I believe your husband found it rather offensive." He paused and glanced over his shoulder at her. "By the way, how is the margrave?"

"Deceased," she said with no sign of remorse, no grief.

"My condolences," he offered, more for himself. He'd been half counting on the old fellow showing up in all his regalia and hauling his errant wife back to Ansbach where she belonged.

"No condolences are necessary," she said, glancing down at her nails. "He was a pig."

True enough. But one who had been able to outmaneuver his manipulative margravine from time to time.

During this exchange, the woman had managed to come closer. "What has happened to you, *schatzi*?"

"Nothing. As you can see I am well."

She shook her head. "You've changed; you're not the same man."

"Time has a way of doing that to all of us," he told her. "Look at me. I am engaged—"

"Bah!" she said, dismissing Lady Standon's place at his side with an airy wave.

"And I intend to retire to the country—"

Now she began to laugh. Loudly.

Langley cringed, for unfortunately it wasn't one of her finest qualities.

"Oh, *schatzi*, no! Stop! You cannot mean such a thing!" She reached for the back of a chair and steadied herself. "You? In the country? Such a waste. Such nonsense."

"Not to me," he said with a conviction that not even he knew he possessed. For standing here, with the margravine, looking back at what had been amusing and energizing for so many years, suddenly paled in the face of coming home to England.

The quiet green meadows. The farmhouses. The stone walls lining the lanes. He had ridden from Dover like a man waking from a dream. "Perhaps I have changed."

"Hmm," she mused. "Most decidedly. Whatever happened to you in Paris?"

He turned to her. "I drank too much wine," he said, making light of the night that had changed his life. Nearly been the death of him. One he barely remembered. No matter how hard he tried. That night was like a candle snuffed out; once the light was gone, it was impossible to remember the world otherwise. "What do you know of Paris?"

"Nothing more than the rest of us. You were there, and then you weren't. The rumors, darling, were terrible. Three years of whispers I have endured. You were dead. You'd helped Bonaparte." She spat the man's name out like an olive pit. "But I never believed any of it. I knew—"

As quickly as her words had come tumbling out, they stopped and her gaze fixed on the side of his head. She reached out her hand and touched the scar that ran from his hairline around his ear and nearly to the back of his head.

Where his head had been bashed in and he'd been left for dead.

"That wasn't there." She shivered as she parted his hair and saw how far back it went.

He brushed her hand away and ducked out of her reach. "Perhaps you didn't notice it before. I fell as a child, you know. While learning to ride."

She laughed again and retreated toward the window, letting the morning sun frame her blond hair. "You've never fallen off a horse in your life.

More like you fell into a cudgel. Or it fell into you. Which was it?"

Since he didn't know, he couldn't say, but this entire round of questions was growing uncomfortable. Nor did he trust her. "You know, madame, one of the reasons I adore Minerva is that she doesn't badger me about my past."

Helga shook her head and glanced out the window as she considered her answer. And when she turned to face him, it was obvious she'd found the perfect answer. "Perhaps it is because she doesn't want you to pry too deeply into hers." She nodded down into the garden.

Against his better judgment, he crossed the room and took a glance out the window.

And what he saw answered several of his earlier questions, and left him with a raftload more as yet to be answered.

"Let go of me, Gerald!" Minerva had tried to flee back into the garden, but he was too quick and caught her in his arms. But not for long. She managed to get her hands on his chest and push him away and close the garden door so they were once again alone in the alley and shielded from prying eyes.

"Hardly the way to greet your husband."

"I am not your wife." Never was.

Though once she'd thought she would be. Had been so madly in love with him. Ready to marry him.

Until her father had come home from London with the alarming news that she was to marry Philip Sterling, the Marquis of Standon, the future Duke of Hollindrake.

"Now, now," he said. "I've got a marriage license that says I'm married to one Margaret Owens and we both know who you are." He eased closer to her again, but this time she slipped away, turning to face him. "Shall we borrow a carriage and ride north to Gilston House? See if any of the old servants remember exactly which of the earl's daughters you might be? Handy for you it is too far north to venture easily or often."

"What are you doing here?" Minerva set her jaw. "Does *she* know you are here?" Her sister. The real Lady Minerva Hartley.

He had the good grace to look a bit repentant. But only for a moment. This was Gerald, after all.

"No, she doesn't. But how could she? She's gone, if you must know."

Minerva's gaze narrowed. "She left you?" That would explain his sudden arrival at her doorstep.

He laughed as if such a thing were unthinkable. Which of course it was. Minnie had been just as head over heels in love with Gerald as her half-sister. But as the earl's legitimate daughter, the likes of Gerald Adlington was far beneath her. And it had been the first time Minerva had ever been able to aspire to something her lofty, selfish sister couldn't have.

"Where is my sister?" she pressed.

"She's dead."

This simple statement brought Minerva's gaze wrenching back to his. Her sister? Dead? No, it couldn't be true. She searched his mocking gaze for some glimmer of deceit.

And when she looked at him, really studied him, she realized something telling. He wasn't wearing mourning. A cold shudder ran down her spine. "How long, Gerald? How long has Minnie been gone?"

Gerald shuffled his feet under her scrutiny and looked away. "Five . . . maybe six—"

"Months?"

He scoffed at her question. "No, not months. Years. About six years now."

Minerva staggered back. "But you never told me—"

"And what were you going to do, Maggie? Wear a black armband for her? Confess the truth? That you married that fancy toff in her stead? That you are naught but your father's bastard?"

Minerva's insides trembled. Not with grief, for she knew her sister never spared a thought for her, save for the money Minerva sent. No, Minnie would never have shed a tear if it had been Minerva's fate, except perhaps because it would have stopped the payments coming.

The payments. If Minnie had been dead all these years . . .

Her gaze narrowed. "How dare you!" she whispered, afraid that if she gave over to the rage, and yes, the grief starting to edge its way into her heart, she would once again be Margaret Owens and give him what he deserved. "My sister was dead and still you took the money?"

"Why shouldn't I have? It's because of me you're top-of-the-trees and worth a plum."

"Because of you?" she sputtered. "You courted me, then eloped with my sister behind my back. Behind our father's back."

"Which is why you've got your fancy name—a

good one, I might add. I deserve a little something for raising you out of the back halls and below-stairs where your father kept you."

A little something? " 'Tis blackmail."

Gerald shrugged, a negligent tip of his shoulders. "Rather an ugly way of phrasing it, Maggie, but I suppose there are some who might see it that way. Not me, though." He had the audacity to wink at her.

"Get out of here," she said, pointing down the alleyway.

He shoved her hand down. "Not without my money. That's why I'm here in the first place. When I went to Brighton this week to get the quarterly, that rum-cake solicitor said your account was closed. Emptied. Cavey business, that, Maggie. To leave your own kin high and dry."

Now she saw all too clearly why he was here. Her accounts! She'd completely forgotten the part of her accounts that she quietly funneled to a solicitor in Brighton, who in turn saw the money turned over to her sister.

Since her banishment to this house on Brook Street, all her accounts had been closed, as had Elinor's and Lucy's. There hadn't been any money to send on. Not anymore. She glanced up at him and smiled.

"I fear I've run afoul of the new duke and his wife. They cut me off. There is no more money to be had."

He cocked his head and eyed her. "Oh, aye, what's this nonsense? I won't be bobbed by the likes of you."

"I am not conning you, Mr. Adlington, if that is what you are saying. Not in the least," she told him coolly. "I have this house to live in and naught much else."

He glanced up at the house. "Any silver in there?"

Minerva ran out of patience with him. "Good heavens, I'm in the suds enough with His Grace without adding to my crimes. And have you taken a good look at this house? I can tell you quite honestly there is nothing of value in it." She put her hands on her hips. "You'll have to live within your means. Isn't your army pay—"

Then she realized something else that had been bothering her about him—his arrival in her midst not withholding: He was out of uniform.

"You sold out!" Her words came out like an accusation. For of course he'd sold out. And then squandered every coin.

How had she ever loved him? Fancied him her hero? Again, for whatever reason, her thoughts turned to Lord Langley and how different he was. Oh, Langley was a rake and a seducer, but he wasn't a complete cad, a man who would live on a woman's coattails.

"What if I did? Not that it's anything to you. You still owe me my quarterly, and that's all that matters." His jaw worked back and forth. "Got any jewels?"

She sighed in exasperation with him. "No. All the Sterling jewelry belongs to the duchess."

Including the Sterling diamonds, which Minerva had neglected to turn over. Luckily for her, the Duchess of Hollindrake seemed to be ignorant of her rightful claim to them. And if she hadn't relinquished them to their true owner, she certainly wasn't about to give them to the likes of Gerald Adlington.

Not even to keep her secret. She'd rather hand

them over to the duchess. Which came in a close second.

"Come now, Maggie," he coaxed. "You're still a bit of a looker. There's no one about you could hook? Another one of those old culls, the sort with a heart ailment and one foot in the grave like the last one you had? I'd say one of those sorts would come in right handy about now."

What would come in handy right now was Thomas-Williams's pistol.

Minerva cursed herself for not thinking of it sooner. Especially now that he was pressing her to get married. Why in heavens was everyone in London seemingly bent on seeing her wed?

Good heavens, this snake was as bad as Aunt Bedelia. Worse, perhaps.

"I fear, Mr. Adlington, that our arrangement is over." She went to step past him, but he caught her by the elbow and held her fast, and to her shock, his other hand rose as if to strike a furious blow.

"You listen here, Lady Toplofty," he whispered into her ear, his words blustering over her hot and wet. "You'll get me my money and I'll hear no more of your tomfoolery, or I'll march myself over to that duke's house and tell him who you really are. Then I'll show him my wedding license—the one that says I'm married to one Margaret Owens—and I'll demand he hands you over to me." He shook her for good measure, just to make certain she heard him loud and clear.

Oh, she had. "You wouldn't dare, Gerald."

"I would, don't think that I wouldn't. Then what, Maggie? Whatever will the Sterlings do when they discover they nearly had themselves a bastard for a duchess? What will they say about the little switch your father made all those years ago? Do you think they'll let you back in their house?" He shook his head. "You'll be tossed out with only the clothes on your back, if they leave you those."

She reeled a bit, her knees wavering, the nightmare she'd feared all these years beginning to come true.

"So if you can't find anything of value in that house to give me what I'm owed," Gerald told her, "then you had best find yourself a new husband, and right quick."

Minerva tried to shake him off, but his grip was like a blacksmith's vise. "There might . . . perhaps . . . there is someone."

"Now yer talking sense," he said, easing his grip a bit. "But this isn't some flummery of yours? Just to gammon me?"

"There is someone," she insisted. "Actually, I recently became engaged, though it isn't widely known." He eyed her as if gauging the veracity of her claim, and so she brazened him out. "A baron. With means." She had no idea if Langley had a farthing to call his own, but she doubted Adlington would know either.

"To whom?"

"Lord Langley."

Like she suspected, Adlington shook his head. "Never heard of him."

"Why would you have?" she shot back, finally shaking him off. "He's an honorable man." That was probably a stretch, but then again, this was Gerald.

For a moment Minerva feared she might have spoken too quickly. She had gotten used to being a marchioness, a lady, one a gentleman wouldn't strike or contradict. But to this man, she was simply Margaret Owens, the Earl of Gilston's by-blow.

But to her surprise and relief, he grinned at her and lowered his hand, instead chucking her under the chin like he had when he'd courted her. "Still got that bit of fire in your belly and the mouth to match. Maggie, you just proved what me mum always said, 'You can take a girl out of the cellars, but you never take the cellars out of the girl.'"

Something inside her snapped. In all these years of being treated with the deference due a marchioness, the daughter of an earl, she'd forgotten what it meant to be merely the bastard in the kitchen. But it came back in a heady flash.

She caught hold of his sleeve, met his gaze and said with every bit of fire she still possessed in her belly, "And you would do well to remember my mother's favorite saying, 'When an old rooster crows too loud, it's time to cut his throat.'"

Beneath her fingers, for only a moment, she thought she felt him tremble. *Good.* Let him know she hadn't completely forgotten her backstairs origins. Her father might have been the lord and master, the earl of his realm, but her mother . . . now, she'd been feared for different reasons.

Gerald eyed her and then let out an uneasy laugh as he tugged his sleeve out of her grasp. "Get yourself married to this baron of yours, Maggie. And use that sweet mouth of yours for something other than threats. Talk him into giving you a generous allowance—I've grown used to your way of life."

He bowed slightly to her and then turned to leave. "Oh, and don't think I won't be watching you,

Maggie, me girl. Try to make a dash for it without me, it will be your ruin."

Minerva spent a few moments composing herself as Adlington strode out of sight.

Not that she believed for a moment he was going very far. No, if there was one thing she did know about Gerald Adlington, it was that when it came to money, there was nothing he liked more.

"Wretched, horrid bastard," she muttered as she came through the garden door and up the path.

"Problems with your painter?"

Her gaze wrenched up, and to her horror she found Langley leaning against the doorjamb, looking quite innocent.

Too innocent.

"Nothing I can't remedy," she said, drawing herself up and standing ramrod straight.

"Anything I can do to help?"

She stumbled then, and didn't dare look at him, for once again he'd posed the question in that nonchalant air of his. And if there was anything she had learned about this man in her short acquaintance with him, it was that there was nothing innocent or nonchalant about him.

He always had a plan. Or was forming a new one.

"No, nothing," she demurred. Well, lied. "If you will excuse me, I have my accounts to review. I don't like them to go unattended. Details go missing if you don't stay on top of every expenditure."

"Thorough and practical," he mused. "Are you sure I cannot help? I might not be all that good with accounts, but I have other talents you could avail yourself of."

She had to imagine he did. For truly, as she stole a glance at him and managed a wan smile, she wondered if he knew anyone who could arrange for an accident. But then dismissed that thought. If she asked him—or for that matter, Thomas-William or Lucy—then she would have to explain to them why it was she wanted Gerald Adlington to end up at the bottom of the Thames.

And what would she say?

He was my betrothed until he secretly eloped with my sister and I was brought to London in her place.

For it would be exactly as Adlington had said: The Sterlings would cast her out without a second thought. And what of Aunt Bedelia? What would happen to her if it was discovered that her beloved niece wasn't really her legitimate niece at all?

No, there was nothing she could do but stall the man, and one way to do that was to . . .

"Actually, Lord Langley," she said, pausing on the step beside him. "There is something you can do for me."

He inclined his head. "Anything, my lady."

"I have given some thought to your proposal—"

"You have?" He slanted a glance at her.

"Yes," she said, hurrying the conversation along because she didn't want to get into the particulars of her change of heart. And she'd also learned in her short acquaintance with Lord Langley that he was the sort with a hawkish eye for details. Very much like his daughter, Felicity. "And as such, I accept your proposal—" He looked about to say something to her, but she staved him off by raising her hand. "However, I do have three conditions."

"Only three?" he teased.

Ignoring him, she continued, "I will not share your bed."

"My bed in the attic is rather narrow. I had hoped we would share yours. From the little time I did get to enjoy it, I found it quite delightful." She cocked a brow at him, and he shook his head. "If you insist. No sharing beds."

"And there will be no more kissing."

"No more kissing? However do you expect us to convince anyone—especially my old boon companions—if we are not seen as wildly and passionately in love?"

"It will go a long way toward reforming your reputation. As you said, you are a changed man," she told him tartly.

"More changed than I like," he muttered, then again waved her off. "Agreed, no kissing. What is your third condition?"

"That I will not be embarrassed by any untoward behavior on your part."

He paused for a moment and then his eyes sparkled with amusement. "Whatever do you mean, Lady Standon?"

Pursing her lips, she considered giving him another shove. Demmed man knew exactly what she meant, but he was going to force her to say it.

Well then, she would. "I will not have my betrothed carrying on with other ladies while he is engaged to me. I have my reputation to think of, as well as that of my family."

"And after we are married, am I free to roam then?"

"Lord Langley, this engagement is a temporary situation."

"Well, thank goodness, for you have cut me off at the knees for the time being."

"Surely you can restrain yourself for a few weeks?"

"If I must . . ." He edged closer, grinning and looking about to seal their bargain with a kiss.

"You must," she told him, pushing him back.

He shrugged and seemed hardly put out, for he said, "I also have terms of my own."

Minerva had been about to brush past him and go into the house, but she paused, immediately suspicious. "And what would those be?"

"That you agree to the very same terms you have rendered down upon me. You agree not to share my bed, there will be no begging for my kiss, and most importantly, you will not carry on with other men." He glanced over at the garden door that led to the alley and let one elegant brow arch upward.

Minerva froze. Good heavens above! What had he seen?

Or even worse—what had he overheard?

She stared at him for a moment, waiting for him to ask, to reveal what he knew, but he only stood there, charmingly handsome and appearing as innocent as a lamb.

In other words, he wasn't about to show his hand.

"Agreed," she told him through clenched teeth. "You need have no concerns on my side of this bargain."

"I should hope not," she heard him say as she hurried past.

Langley watched Lady Standon flee into the house. She could run all she wanted to, but he had every intention of discovering why she had just lied to him and why it was she had suddenly agreed to their faux betrothal.

He suspected it had nothing to do with Lady Chudley's constant machinations and more to do with her "painter" in the alley. A fellow he needed to get a better look at.

Crossing down the garden path, he pushed open the door and hurried down the alley in the direction he spied the man leave.

For as much as he had hurried downstairs and crept out into the garden to overhear what was being said, all he'd managed to discern was the last thing the man had said to Lady Standon.

" . . . it will only be your ruin."

Whatever could this fellow be holding over her head that could be ruinous? She didn't seem the type.

Then he thought of the kiss they'd shared last night . . .

Who would have thought there was that much passion inside such a tightly wound lady?

Langley shook his head. No more kissing! What nonsense. The lady burned to be kissed. Even if she didn't know it.

Which was the other point. She certainly wasn't some Merry Widow seeking her affairs here and there and living the freedom that her dowager status afforded her. Quite the opposite.

Everything he'd heard over the last sennight from her staff, and his impression from meeting her, said quite clearly Lady Standon lived her life completely above reproach.

The perfectly respectable lady.

But he wasn't so convinced. Not now. Not since

he'd kissed her. And in his experience, such tautly held respectability was usually naught but a veneer to protect oneself.

But from what?

He had reached the corner and was so lost in thought he nearly ran into a large fellow coming in the other direction. He glanced up to find Thomas-William planted in front of him.

"Just the person I need," he said, thinking to recruit the man into discovering who Lady Standon's painter might be.

However, the very investigation Langley had thought to launch into his new betrothed melted away the moment Thomas-William said, "My lord, I think I have found someone to help us."

Langley glanced down the busy streets of London where her "painter" had disappeared, the man having slipped away.

No, it appeared for now that Lady Standon and her secrets would have to wait.

Chapter 6

Lord Langley is every bit a scoundrel as we have long suspected. I was all aswoon when I met him at Lady Standon's this afternoon. He is truly the wickedest man alive.

However will such a dull lady like Minerva Sterling ever keep him entertained now that they are engaged? Yes, my dear Lady Finch, they are betrothed. Can you imagine what the Duchess of Hollindrake will say when she discovers . . .

An excerpt from a letter by
Lady Ratcliffe to Lady Finch

So you decided not to flee," Langley said as he and Thomas-William made their way across London to meet with a possible contact from inside the Foreign Office.

The man shrugged, for he didn't like to speak much. Silences were Thomas-William's strength.

"Let me guess," Langley said, sitting back in the

seat of the hackney. "You realized that if you went back to Lucy and told her you weren't going to stay with Lady Standon, you'd have to admit that you were frightened off by a mere houseful of women."

The man blew out a disgruntled breath and crossed his arms over his chest, staring out the window. "Seems you aren't."

Langley grinned at him. "My stock and trade."

The man's level gaze met his. "And marriage? To that one?"

Lady Standon. "Oh, so you heard about that."

He nodded curtly.

"Never fear. The lady and I have an agreement. Will come to naught."

Thomas-William's brows rose. "Does that aunt of hers share in your agreement?"

"Who? Lady Chudley?"

The man shuddered. "Aye, that one. Throw off her niece and she'll have your head."

"I don't intend to cry off in some havey-cavey manner." He paused for a moment, thinking of Lady Standon as she'd come in from the garden— shaken and frightened. No, the last thing he wanted to do was add to whatever was troubling the lady. "Besides, I can handle the likes of Lady Chudley. It isn't like one wouldn't see, or rather hear, her coming."

At this, Thomas-William laughed a bit, but his humor didn't last long. "Yes, but that won't save you from Miss Lucy. If you break Lady Standon's heart, Miss Lucy will see you finished." He paused for a moment. "And you won't see her coming."

No, he wouldn't. Langley had the good sense not to take Thomas-William's warning lightly, for it was no laughing matter. As good as he was, there wasn't a man in the Foreign Office who hadn't been trained at the Ellyson house who didn't hold a silent terror of the man's daughter in his heart.

"Have no fear for Lady Standon," he told his friend. "She is far too sensible to fall for my charms."

The carriage pulled to a stop and Thomas-William nodded toward the door.

By habit, Langley took a quick, assessing glance out the window, to gauge the surroundings of where he was about to alight. And what he saw did little to raise his spirits. "Here?"

Thomas-William smiled. And since he was about the only man in London who Langley trusted, he shoved open the door and stepped out, realizing at once that they were in one of the more infamous spots in the city. For behind him had once stood a great tower and clock to mark where seven streets came together, but was now no more than a warren for thieves. Even in broad daylight the place had a murky, dark sort of air about it.

And more notably, it was the perfect place for a fellow to be murdered and no trace left of him. And conveniently, no witnesses.

"Seven Dials?" he asked, less as a question and more as a wry remark to his companion.

"My contact thought it best."

Apparently their driver didn't, for the hackney—who had insisted Thomas-William pay him up front for such an address—now drove off at a mad pace.

"Your contact?" Langley said, glancing around at the milling crowd, trying to spot who this might be.

And then came darting out of the shadows a bunch of street urchins, circling like Gypsies and picking at his coat, turning him about, calling out to each other and jeering at him.

"Hey, there!" Langley protested. "That is my watch . . . and my wallet. And I do say, that was my hat." He tried to snatch back his beaver—he'd had that made in Paris—but the little dodger was too fast, toothlessly grinning as he danced out of reach. "A little help, Thomas-William?"

The other man just stood on the curb and laughed.

By the time the little rutters stopped, he'd been picked clean and stood wavering in the muck, dizzy and dazed. When his eyes finally focused, he found Thomas-William had gained a companion, a fellow with rough breeches, a plain shirt and jacket, and a pair of solid boots.

Who was this? Their keeper come to finish the task?

And so it was, in a sense. For the man—make that a young man, Langley realized when the fellow tipped back the wide brim of his hat—shoved out his hand. "I am Lord Andrew Stowe, in His Majesty's service. My fellow agents and I are honored to be of assistance to you."

By the time Minerva reached the sanctuary of her room, her accounts were all but forgotten.

"Men!" she muttered as she stormed inside and shoved her door shut behind her—at least as far as it would close with the damaged hinges. "Blast them all."

Her father . . . Gerald Adlington . . . the Duke of Hollindrake . . . Thomas-William . . . and . . . and . . .

Her list came to a fumbling halt as she spied a black wool jacket folded neatly on the corner of her bed.

And most of all, Lord Langley, she finished, stomping across the room and sweeping the man's forgotten jacket off the bed and onto the floor.

She was of half a mind to toss it out the window, which is what she should have done to the owner, when she glanced down at the offensive bit of clothing that had contributed to her current ill luck.

But instead of plucking it up and sending it aloft out the window, she paused, for Langley's jacket had fallen open when she'd pushed it to the floor, and there inside the coat peeked an odd slit in the lining.

As if for a pocket or a place to conceal something one didn't want easily discovered.

No, you shan't, she advised herself. Prying into other's secrets was more Lucy's domain, not hers, she reasoned.

Then again . . .

Glancing around—not that she needed to, for she was utterly alone, but still, she wasn't inclined to snooping—she eased off the bed and sat down beside the jacket, sliding her hand inside the opening and pulling out a slim packet wrapped in a handkerchief with the initial *T,* and adorned with tiny flowers done in simple embroidery in one corner.

T. Who might this be, my lord? Minerva mused. *A former lover? A mistress? An admirer? Someone so important that you carried this for some time, if the worn little bit of linen is any indication.* Carefully, she unfolded the small handkerchief and found inside a bundle of letters, tied in a pale blue ribbon.

Yet another mystery, she realized, for the frayed ribbon barely held the letters together, having obviously been tied and untied too many times to count. The careworn corners and edges of the yellowed stationery also spoke of having been read and reread over and over again.

Whatever these letters contained, they were precious beyond gems and gold to Lord Langley, for she knew without a doubt they had traveled with him for years and he kept them as it were, in the pocket over his chest, over his heart.

Minerva bit her bottom lip and considered the letters she held, and what could be inside them.

And while her thoughts ran along the lines of Langley's rakish reputation, when she turned the packet over, she found she could easily discern the contents of the bottom letter and the mysterious T who held such a special place in Langley's affections.

Dear Papa,

Felicity says I mustn't write to you on this matter, but I beg you to come back to England and take us out of Miss Emery's school. She says you cannot come home until you have cleared your name, but it is ever so horrid here without you . . .

Minerva's chest tightened with a sharp pang. For here she'd considered the worst about the man, instead of suspecting where his true regard lay. How hard it was to consider that Langley—*the* Lord Langley of mistresses and infamous affairs, of infamy too scandalous to share—held such a tender regard that he carried these letters in secret.

Not mementos from some tryst, or a painted Incognita with an odd foreign title and kohled eyes, but lovingly written pleas from his "T." As in Thalia Langley. His daughter. Felicity Langley's twin.

She needn't read any further, but sat for some time holding the packet in her hands, Thalia's words echoing in her thoughts.

. . . until you have cleared your name . . .

The very notion sent a shiver through her, for Minerva realized that Lord Langley hadn't come back to merely set Society on its ear, but to finish something very dangerous—for certainly he hadn't wanted his daughters involved in whatever havey-cavey business had drawn him away from England. Away from them.

No, he'd left them at Miss Emery's to clear not only his name, but theirs as well, and he most decidedly hadn't wanted them mixed up in it.

Still, that didn't calm her nerves or change her opinion of the man, for Minerva knew without a doubt that now she was in middle of his troubles.

Whether she liked it or not.

Sometime later Agnes came in clucking "that she wasn't ready."

Minerva glanced up from where she still sat on the floor. *Ready for what?*

Then she realized it was Tuesday and her afternoon in.

Which meant for the next few hours she had to sit through the idle chatter and inane compliments of fortune hunters and rakes, who, having heard that the Earl of Clifton had married Lucy and the Duke of Parkerton had carried away Elinor after a whirlwind courtship, were now dropping by to see what all the fuss over the Standon widows might be about.

And stacked up like well-aged firewood besides these ne'er-do-wells would be the usual assortment of widowers looking for a second or—horrors upon horrors—a third or fourth wife. These codgers came with the compliments of Aunt Bedelia, who had assured them that her dearest niece was the choicest pick of the three dowagers.

But even from the second landing she knew today was different. For it was still a good half an hour before she was known to be "at home," and already there was a cacophony of voices coming from the downstairs parlor.

Female voices. A gaggle of clucking and pecking like a henhouse stuffed to the rafters with chatty birds.

"But darling, she has no *joie de vivre*! No style! He will be bored before the first month is out," Nanny Tasha was saying.

"Yes, yes! Exactly! He is a man of the Continent. Of the world," Nanny Lucia agreed. "He will never marry her, for he will be done with her in . . . in . . . oh, how you English say 'due' . . . 'due' . . ."

"Deux semaines," Tasha supplied in French.

"A fortnight, dear," Aunt Bedelia supplied. "We call it a fortnight."

How kind of you to help, Auntie, Minerva mused from her spot on the stairs.

"Yes! A fortnight," the margravine chimed in. "If that."

"I think my niece will surprise you." Aunt Bedelia sounded supremely confident.

There was a tap on her shoulders and Minerva nearly leapt out of her gown in shock to be caught eavesdropping. "Jamilla!" she exclaimed.

For indeed, here was yet another of Lord Langley's mistresses, Princess Jamilla Kounellas, who had come to London nearly a year earlier, and since then had lived in and out of the house here on Brook Street and set the London *ton* on their collective ears with her outrageous manners and fashions.

But Minerva had always found Nanny Jamilla rather a delight, for the lady always spoke her mind.

"I cannot believe Langley will do this! Not with her!" complained Tasha from inside the parlor.

Jamilla's brows perked at the distinct accent. "That Russian she-wolf has taken over my room!" she complained, nodding toward the parlor and looking quite put out. "Bah! I should have known that once it got nosed about the Continent that Langley was alive *they'd* show up."

Minerva stilled and then glanced over her shoulder at the other woman. "You knew he was alive?"

Her countenance brightened. "Yes, of course. It was why I came to this dreadful London last year. To tell my dear girls that I'd been having an impossible time getting their father out of prison—"

Minerva took a step back. "Lord Langley was in prison?"

Jamilla's hand fluttered at the question. "But of course. Where else would he have been all this time?"

Where indeed? Minerva thought, a bit taken aback. Still . . .

"You knew Lord Langley was alive and you kept it a secret?" she asked, honestly quite amazed, for Jamilla was hardly known for her discretion.

"But of course, though I thought I had been more discreet in my bribes to get him out," she said, "for this is what I feared." Again she glanced down the stairs and shook her head, like one might upon finding a pack of mongrels had wandered in from the streets. "Such awful creatures! And I fear, my dear, impossible to be rid of."

Rather like you, Minerva mused, thinking of all the ways the Duchess of Hollindrake had tried—most unsuccessfully—to send Jamilla packing back to Paris. But now she understood a little more about why the former nanny had stayed.

"You've been waiting for him to come back," Minerva said, not so much a question as a statement.

"Once, perhaps," Jamilla admitted, her gaze still fixed down the stairs, "but no longer. He is in my past, and hardly rich enough to afford my tastes. No, for my darling girls I stayed, to see them reunited with their father, and once Langley has straightened out this mess," again her hand fluttered, but this time toward the parlor, "I can move on."

Mess was exactly the word Minerva would use to describe the collection in her salon.

From down below, a strident declaration echoed upward. "But to marry her? Acch! It is dreadful!" the margravine was saying. "Why, my *schatzi* hardly knows her, and if he truly did know her—" The lady made a rude sort of noise, and Minerva could almost see the dismissive wave of her beringed fingers. "She will not be able to keep him. How can one such as she?"

"Married?" Jamilla met Minerva's gaze. "Langley is to marry? What utter nonsense is that idiot woman going on about?"

"Lord Langley is engaged," Minerva supplied.

Now it was Jamilla's turn to snort. "Langley get married? He isn't the sort. Not unless he was trapped into it by some unscrupulous, ridiculous creature of questionable—"

"He's engaged to me," Minerva snapped. "Langley is betrothed to me."

Jamilla paused, then smiled widely. "La! Lady Standon, who knew you could jest so!"

"But I am not joking," Minerva told her.

"*Est-ce vrai?*" she asked, reverting to her native French, as she did when she became overcome.

"Yes."

Jamilla glanced toward the parlor. "Langley must have his reasons," she said under her breath. Then she brightened and smiled at Minerva. "And the others, they don't like this?"

"Not in the least."

The former nanny lit up. "Oh, darling, how wonderful for you." She glanced over Minerva from the top of her brown hair tucked into a plain chignon, down her sensible day gown, to the plain slippers on her feet. "But of course they are right," she said. "However will you keep him?"

Langley knew immediately he'd found an ally in Lord Andrew Stowe.

Though young, impossibly so, most likely no more than twenty, Lord Andrew was the last agent Ellyson had trained before the man had died five years earlier. And being a Stowe meant Lord Andrew came from a long line of men who'd served their kings and queens loyally. The third son of the Marquess of Drayton, he was not yet at his full height, but he was a commanding sort even in his low attire.

Having given Langley a hearty handshake, Lord Andrew invited him to come have a drink, and off they went into the bowels of Seven Dials, to the rooms where the young man lived, with the line of guttersnipes bringing up their rear.

That is, after Lord Andrew had admonished the little pack of thieves to give Lord Langley back his belongings.

"Unfortunately there were those in the Foreign Office who thought me too young and too much of a liability to send over to the Continent when I finished with Ellyson," the young man said, as he gestured for Langley and Thomas-William to sit at the table in the middle of the large room. He shrugged as he put a decanter and glasses down for them and poured drinks for the men.

"Was your hair," Thomas-William laughed.

Lord Andrew raked a hand through his dark auburn locks. "I suppose I do look rather a bit too English." The young man laughed. "Kept me here. Much to my mother's relief, though not so much to mine. Then after a few years chafing about Whitehall—"

"Making a pest of yourself," Thomas-William noted.

The young man grinned. "Yes, a bit, I suppose. But it did get me this assignment. Or got me demoted, as some might aver." He waved his hand at his large apartment, which looked like a replica of George Ellyson's map room in Hampstead Heath—with the large table in the middle, books overflowing their shelves, and collections of oddities and bits of aristocratic comforts filling the room—a globe, a tusk from something mounted on the wall, a few etchings and paintings. Comfortable furniture filled every corner and a good, thick carpet kept out the chill of the floorboards.

"And that assignment is?" Langley asked, glancing around, eyeing particularly their audience, the seven youngsters all perched about the room.

"Training my crew for the work ahead," Lord Andrew said, sending a wink to one of the lads. "Now that you've all gotten a very good look at Lord Langley, upstairs with you and see to your lessons. I do believe Mr. Crunkshaft is waiting." There were good-hearted groans and muttered complaints, but the lot of them made their way to a narrow set of stairs in the back of the room. "And Goldy, mind you, I won't have you stealing poor Crunkshaft's pocket watch again and resetting it so classes end early." The young imp grinned, a toothless smile glowing back in the shadows. "Oh, and good work this morning, the entire lot of you! I'm quite proud."

They all trooped up the stairs and then were heard tromping across the floor overhead.

Langley glanced back as the last of them disappeared into the attic. "A crew of street children?"

Lord Andrew grinned. "Yes. And an excellent lot they are. You'll see—they are going to be your guardians, your watchdogs, for the next few weeks until we get this all sorted out."

"My what?" he stammered.

Lord Andrew glanced over at Thomas-William. "Didn't you explain this to him?"

"Thought it best coming from you."

"Left me to the dirty work," Lord Andrew teased back.

The other man shrugged.

"Goldy and her companions are going to fan out around Brook Street or wherever you go, and make sure no one is lurking about. No one will give them a second glance. Then, if they notice anything odd or suspicious, they'll be able to give you fair warning."

Langley did a second take at the attic stairs. "That little bit of baggage was a girl?"

"Oh, aye. Actually there are three of them in the lot. Three girls, four boys. But the girls dress like boys—keeps them safer, not that I worry about Goldy much. She's never without a knife, and rumor around the Dials is that her father was the finest miller around."

The baron glanced over at the stairs again, for he knew in the cant of the Dials what a "miller" was: a murderer. That aside, it was a ridiculous notion. To keep him safe by using children.

Children capable of slitting throats . . .

Still, he met Thomas-William's dark gaze with the question in his own. *Are you certain of this?*

The large man just sat back in his chair, arms crossed over his barrel of a chest, looking quite content.

"Now, my lord, how can I help you?" Lord Andrew said, settling into his seat and looking far more assured of himself than a twenty-year-old lad should.

After taking a deep breath, and remembering this was—as Thomas-William had assured him on the ride over—his best chance at clearing his name, he continued, "I need to get into the Foreign Office, specifically into the intelligence files from Paris in the months before I was attacked."

"Get into the Foreign Office files?" Lord Andrew let out a low whistle. "It would be madness to attempt."

Thomas-William added a snort of agreement.

But Langley was undeterred. "But I must, it is the only way."

Lord Andrew shook his head. "Not always. George always said to start at the beginning: So what do you remember of Paris, sir—that is before we decide to get ourselves killed by making a suicide run into Brownie's files."

The baron rubbed the side of his head—the one that had been struck that fateful night. It always ached when he tried to force up the memories. And as always, there was nothing much to remember. Just flashes of things—the ripe stench of the alleyway, the chill of the cobblestones beneath his fingers, and voices, a babble of voices with not a single word that could be discerned.

Closing his eyes, he tried to bear the pain of it and pull something up, anything that would help.

"He doesn't," Thomas-William said. "He can't recall a thing."

Lord Andrew pushed back from the table and sighed. "Would be helpful, but just the same, perhaps we can sort out some other clues."

Langley wished he shared the young man's optimism, for right now his head rang like the bells of St. Paul's, driving out any coherent thought.

"How did you make your reports?" Lord Andrew asked.

"I was known in diplomatic circles as an art collector with very little taste—an easy mark, so to say. I'd buy horrid counterfeits, the sort only the most ignorant rube or mushroom would own and send them back to England via Strout who would forward them to Langley House for storage."

"And with them, your reports," Lord Andrew finished.

"Yes, exactly. Inside sculptures, behind paintings. Pieces of work so worthless no one would bother stealing them—"

"A paum," Lord Andrew said. "Like a shell game."

"Exactly," Lord Langley said. "But I would address the box slightly differently if it needed closer examination, so to say, and my tenant, Mr. Harrow, would forward that collection on to George so he could gain the reports."

"Did this Harrow know about George?" Lord Andrew asked.

Langley shook his head. "No. All Harrow knew was that George Ellyson was a fellow collector."

"What was the last thing you remember sending?" Lord Andrew asked.

Langley shook his head. "That's just it. I don't recall what last I sent."

"Then perhaps that is the best place to start—discovering what last you sent," the young agent said.

By God, he was right. Langley had all but forgotten about his shipments. Could it be that he had sent one just before he'd been attacked?

"Then once we find that, we can go about confronting old Brownie," Lord Andrew was saying.

Harrumph, Thomas-William snorted.

"What's this?" Lord Andrew said, sitting up straight.

"I've already met with Brownie—"

Thomas-William shook his head.

"Yes, well, I rather jumped into his carriage last night," Langley corrected. "And shoved a pistol up his nose and demanded answers."

Lord Andrew laughed. "Good God, you don't know how many times I've longed to do just that. Not that I imagine he was all that forthcoming even with your pops in his face. Surprising bit of bottom for such a low fellow."

Langley nodded in agreement. All too true. Brownie had surprised him, for he thought that faced with his own mortality, the man would have given over everything he knew.

Which only meant the man was in deep. And like Lord Andrew said, had enough courage to protect himself.

"I thought I might startle him into giving me what I want, at the very least rattle his cage a bit." Langley thought of Brownie's shock when he'd plucked off his scarf and the other man realized the baron wasn't dead.

"A little pressure to put him off his game," Lord Andrew said. "I can see you don't like it, Thomas-William."

"Get us all killed, going out in the open," the man said. "Not the way it should be done."

"Well, Sir Basil will be more dangerous now that he's been forewarned," Lord Andrew agreed, "but he will also be more likely to make a mistake in his haste to finish you off."

"Exactly," Langley said. "I intend to keep him on his toes. Watch him. Shake him up a bit."

"Get yourself killed," Thomas-William grumbled.

"That is where my crew can help," Lord Andrew said.

"What I need is to get into his files," Langley told the younger man, getting straight to the point.

The young agent shook his head and let out a low whistle. "Nosing about those files is what got me sent here to the Dials. You're right to suspect Brownie. Odd bits of business going on around the office, and he's at the center of all of it."

Cupping his glass in his hand, Langley stared down at the amber liquid inside. "What exactly?"

Lord Andrew lowered his voice. "Rumors that you and Ellyson were in league with the French to damage English relations. Sealed reports and shipments with your name and Ellyson's name attached—all of which went directly to Brownie or through Nottage and then were hushed up and buried who-knows-where—"

"Nottage?" Langley said, glancing up. "As in Neville Nottage? My secretary?"

"Yes, the two of them were as thick as thieves after you were reported missing, and then—" Lord Andrew began.

"What you mean after I went missing?" Langley said, straightening in his chair, a rare shiver running down his spine. "Nottage died in Paris. He was killed in the same alleyway where I was attacked."

Thomas-William and the younger man exchanged puzzled glances.

"Nottage isn't dead," Lord Andrew told him.

Langley shook his head. "He's dead, I had it from the prison guard."

Again Lord Andrew glanced at Thomas-William and then back at Langley. "Then you have been misled. Nottage is the one who came back to England with the reports of your demise."

Langley tried to take it all in. "Are you telling me that Neville Nottage is alive?"

"Yes," Lord Andrew said with a bit of a huff. "Where there should have been a formal investigation into what happened to you, there wasn't, just a lot of rumors floating around about your loyalties, the secret reports and shipments, like I said, and then all of a sudden Brownie is elevated to a knighthood, and Nottage inherits a small fortune from some distant uncle, and both of them are living in the clover."

"Nottage." Langley muttered the man's name like a curse. Here he had trusted the man for over a decade, mourned his death, and now the baron feared his all-too-capable secretary had taken all those years of experience in his shadow and put them to some devilish use.

This put an entirely new light on his troubles.

Lord Andrew glanced over at him and then continued, "I must say, Brownie's sudden elevation was odd enough, but when *Sir Basil* moved into that fancy house of his, his wife started looking like one of my father's mistresses, all covered in rubies and such, well it was just too much to ignore. So I began to ask myself, how the devil could he afford it all? It stank of something buried much deeper."

Yes, indeed, Langley pondered silently, as he let the young man continue.

"And then there were the implications that George Ellyson hadn't been entirely loyal." Lord Andrew's brow furrowed. "The man was dead, and I wasn't going to see his name sullied. He was more of a father to me than my own. At the very least he spoke to me, which to this day mine can barely manage. Doesn't approve and all."

Glancing over at the young man, Langley nodded. "Yes, I know how that goes."

"Well, I wasn't about to let George Ellyson's name be tarred with a traitor's brush, so I began poking about. Asking too many questions," Lord Andrew grinned, "which old Brownie didn't like. He had me sent here. Probably assumed I'd get myself killed inside a sennight, living in the Dials and all. Be out of his hair, with the minimum of paperwork."

Thomas-William snorted.

"Exactly," Lord Andrew agreed. "Which is why I propose that we eliminate you, Lord Langley."

Langley blinked and then cocked a brow at the impertinent young man. "Excuse me?"

"I think we could lure Brownie out into the open, my lord, if you were to stick your spoon in the wall."

"You want me dead?" Langley asked, glancing over at Thomas-William.

And demmit if the man wasn't grinning at the idea.

"Exactly," Lord Andrew said enthusiastically. A little too enthusiastically. "And I know just how to do it."

Minerva, having ignored Jamilla's assessment of her wardrobe choice for her afternoon in, had gone downstairs and taken her seat.

And while the nannies gathered there—Lucia, Tasha, and Helga—all smiled at her and greeted her kindly, it was akin to watching an entire nest of vipers coiling around her, just looking for a chance to strike.

Aunt Bedelia, on the other hand, appeared in rare spirits, the news of her niece's engagement like a magic tonic. The lady bloomed as if the malice and venom around her was naught but posies and sunshine. "Minerva, my dear girl, there you are! And on this very important afternoon. I feared you were going to hide upstairs."

"Whyever would I do that?" she asked, having settled herself into her chair.

"Well, because you know it will be quite the crush this afternoon." Having said that, Aunt Bedelia busied herself with the tea tray, rearranging the cups and saucers and looking anywhere but at her niece.

Knowing her aunt as she did, Minerva was immediately suspicious. "What have you done?"

"I might have mentioned to a few close friends—"

"Mentioned what?" she blurted out. For Aunt Bedelia could meander around a point endlessly if she wanted to avoid a subject.

The lady took a deep breath and sighed. "Why, your engagement to Lord Langley, of course!"

Minerva groaned. It was her worst fear being realized. "You didn't have to say it was him."

"Well, goodness heavens! How could I not mention Lord Langley when I spoke of your being engaged?"

Sinking into her spot on the settee, Minerva closed her eyes, her fingers pressed to her temple. Usually she had the makings of a megrim at the conclusion of her afternoon in, not before the first guest had arrived.

"You look distressed, Lady Standon," Nanny Lucia commented, looking anything but a nanny in her bright yellow-orange gown that was cut enticingly low. "I would think that the very mention of your marriage to Lord Langley would have you glowing."

"That is if you are going to marry him," Nanny Tasha purred. She stood in the corner, like a regal black cat.

"Oh, she will marry him," Jamilla said from the doorway, having waited a few moments to time her entrance.

"You!" hissed the margravine.

"Oh, yes, Helga, dear," Jamilla said. "I am here. And Tasha, darling, you had the impudence to take over my room. But I am not insulted. You have always coveted what is mine. Not to worry, I have made the necessary changes by moving you to the back bedroom. Oh, it is overly drafty and terribly cold, I daresay very much like your beloved St. Petersburg. You will feel quite at home." She spared a glance at the duchessa. "Lucia," she said with a slight nod.

The duchessa nodded back. "Jamilla."

Not to let such a cold greeting stand as a warning, Jamilla continued, "Darling, that color does not suit you. Whatever were you thinking?"

"It doesn't?" Lucia said, looking down at her striped gown.

"Not here in England. Or maybe it is this dreadful room." She glanced around at the faded walls and peeling paper. "It makes you quite yellow. Why, I had thought you were your mother for a moment."

The margravine began to laugh, which then was quickly turned into a polite cough.

Still, it was enough to propel Lucia to her feet. With her nose in the air, she left with a deliberate, regal ease. But when she hit the stairs they could all hear the hurried patter of her slippers as she dashed up the steps.

Jamilla brushed her hands on her skirt and then sat down in the chair Lucia had occupied.

"You know each other?" Minerva managed to sputter.

"But of course," Helga said. "How else were we to find Langley if we didn't join forces?"

And as Minerva glanced about the room, she could see the similarities in these women, though not in looks—for they were all as different as a bouquet of blossoms, but they all possessed the same confidence, what the Russian princess had been saying before, that *joie de vivre* that made them stand out.

While I . . . Minerva wavered and glanced toward the door thinking she still had time to flee, but then the bell over the door rattled and to her horror Lady Wallerthwaite—one of Aunt Bedelia's favorite cronies and one of the *ton's* biggest gossips—arrived.

"Bedelia!" she called out to her friend. "How did I just know you would be here?"

"Where else would I be on such an afternoon, Aurelia?" Aunt Bedelia replied unabashedly.

Good God! If Aunt Bedelia had told Lady Wallerthwaite . . .

The bell rang again, and again after that, and

within half an hour the sitting room overflowed with guests.

Specifically, ladies. The news that Lord Langley was back in town had brought out the curious, the flirtatious, widows of questionable virtue, and a few more who had never shown the least propensity for impropriety, but apparently even the hint of perhaps seeing the scandalous rake in person was enough to get them to abandon their embroidery hoops and order their carriages to take them to Brook Street.

"Good heavens, I don't know what is coming to Mayfair," Lady Finnemore complained when she arrived, having all but wedged Lady Ratcliffe out of her seat. "The street outside your house has the worst case of urchins—one of them had the temerity to ask me the time. As if a guttersnipe had an appointment to keep!" She glanced around the room, weighing the company and doing what everyone else had done, search the room for a sight of him. But she was far less discreet than her companions. "Why where is he, Lady Standon?"

"Who, Lady Finnemore?" Minerva replied, following her aunt's lead from earlier and rearranging the cups and saucers.

The baroness continued, "Lord Langley, of course. I hardly came here to see you!"

"Lord Langley? Here?" Minerva feigned horror. Well, it wasn't entirely feigned. The entire situation was a nightmare. "I don't know why you would think I would have a gentleman in my house."

"But my dear child, it is all over Town," Lady Ratcliffe chimed in. "That he has been living under your roof."

Oh, yes, and how had that happened? She only

need make one guess. Minerva's gaze swung to her aunt, who was conveniently and intently glancing up at the cracks in the plaster overhead.

But Minerva hadn't been a marchioness for all these years without a few withering glances that could quell even the likes of Lady Ratcliffe. "I fear you have been misinformed," she replied with haughty grace. "And I am surprised a lady of your distinction would lower herself to listen to such gossip."

There was a tense moment in the room, until Tasha chimed in, "There is no reason for hiding, Lady Standon." Then she turned to the gossipy hens perched about the room and announced, "Of course Langley has been here. He is in love. He will not be parted from Lady Standon. Not when he is in a passion."

The other nannies nodded in agreement, as if such a thing were natural.

Not in England, Minerva wanted to shout at them even as the matrons in the room began to cluck among themselves. *English ladies do not engage in passions.*

"I have always found men who are madly in love are like wolves, hungry and insatiable," Tasha continued. "Why once, I had a Cossack lover who insisted that every morning we make love atop his—"

"More tea, Lady Finnemore?" Minerva said, shoving the pot toward the lady's cup.

Lady Finnemore glared at her, and Minerva had no idea if it was from the outrageous turn of the conversation or that she'd stopped the flow.

"Cossacks! I am surprised you still let them in your bed," the margravine said, waving her hand at such a notion. "Now you may not think it to look at them, but I've had not one, but two lovers from Cologne, and they were naughty fellows. So very satisfying." She made this mewing sort of sigh, one that stopped every conversation in the room. Not that there had been that many left. With her audience's full attention, she went on. "There was a night, oh what was his name, the burgher who traveled with the French advisor . . ." Helga glanced over at Lucia. "Do you recall?"

"The fat one or the narrow man with beady eyes?" Lucia asked. She had returned to the room wearing a blue gown and taken an immediate interest in the subject at hand.

"You had a fat lover?" Lady Ratcliffe blurted out, and almost immediately covered her mouth, as if she couldn't believe what she'd just asked.

"Oh, no, dear lady," the margravine said. "The Frenchman was fat. My lover had a magnificent body. Who would have thought a burgher could have such a big . . . big . . . Oh, how is it said in English?" She looked over at Aunt Bedelia.

Of all the days for her tottering house not to fall down, this had to be the one, Minerva thought as her aunt supplied the word Helga was seeking.

"Manhood, my good margravine," Bedelia said, passing a tray of scones around. "I do believe the word you are looking for is 'manhood.'"

Several of the matrons nodded in agreement.

Helga beamed. "I think it might be more accurate to say his manhood matched his enormous investments."

Lady Finnemore tittered like a schoolgirl. "Lady Standon, does Lord Langley have a large—"

And if that wasn't enough, the front door opened and into the room strolled the man himself. Larger than life, as it were.

The ladies in the room all cast searching glances, and Minerva wanted to clout the lot of them. Really, did they have to examine the man so thoroughly just to determine his . . . his . . . assets?

Then again, when she glanced over her shoulder at him, she found herself entranced as well.

From his light brown hair tied back in such an unfashionable queue, to his Roman features—the hard-cut jaw and the deep cleft in his chin, the strong shoulders. Tall and handsome, there was no sloth to the man, but a physique that spoke of athleticism and masculine power . . . or rather, assets. But what stopped Minerva most was that mischievous light that always seem to burn in his eyes.

Like he had a secret he longed to share.

Well, I can just imagine what that is, she thought with a huff as he smiled at all the ladies in the room, some of them sighing without any thought of propriety. He could have charmed a cat away from a dish of cream with those eyes.

And she didn't know why she was put out by his appearance—perhaps it wasn't so much his arrival, but the other ladies' reactions. Oh, such an unfamiliar bit of ill-ease ran down her spine. Like jealousy.

Which she wasn't. Not in the least.

Especially since he saved his most dazzling smile for her.

"Minerva, my dearest," he said as if on cue, his eyes lighting upon her as he crossed the room with long, solid strides. "How like you not to remind me that it is your afternoon in. I would have forgone my club and been here." He leaned over and placed a kiss on her forehead and then turned and bowed to the ladies in the room with an elegant Continental grace that wasn't often seen.

"*Oooh,*" came another collective sigh.

While they were busy commenting on his arrival, Minerva was doing her best to compose herself. Oh, he had promised! No kissing.

Yet here he was doing just that. His lips, warm and smooth on her forehead, left her feeling utterly ruffled, quite undone. For it was naught but a prelude of what had happened last night when he'd gathered her in his arms and kissed her thoroughly, leaving her limbs languid with desire, her insides trembling, and worst of all, passions she'd thought long lost awakened and clamoring with hunger.

Worst of all it had taken naught but the brush of his lips on her forehead and she was awake—like the bright clear note of a clarion call had roused her—his touch awakening her body, her desires. Her thighs tightened, her insides melted, her nipples hardened.

Minerva groaned as he took his place at her side as if that was exactly where he belonged, his hand resting possessively on her shoulder. With all eyes on her—or rather on him—she couldn't very well brush his fingers away or shrug him off.

Besides, there was a delicious bit of warmth that curled from his fingers into her shoulder and magically through her limbs with an intoxicating heat, unfolding inside her, once again trumpeting her desires to the forefront. Rallying them to come forth from where she'd held them prisoner all these years.

Honestly, she wasn't sure she would have pushed

his touch away even if they hadn't had an audience. But pretenses had to be maintained and so she left his hand where it rested, and lied to herself that he had no power over her.

None whatsoever.

"Lord Langley, such rumors we've heard about you!" Lady Finnemore exclaimed. "That you were dead of all things, and now here you are. How is it that you've come back to London?" The baroness was never one to let an opportunity to pry pass her by.

"I would think the answer is obvious," he replied, glancing down at Minerva and smiling at her.

"However did the two of you meet?" Lady Ratcliffe rushed to ask.

Minerva pressed her lips together. For as much as she would like to have said, *Why, he fell into my bedroom while attempting to break into my house,* such a reply would seal her fate for the rest of her days.

Married to Langley. Under his thumb, even as she was now . . . with that promise in his eyes teasing her every morning over the breakfast table as he'd done earlier . . . with the warmth of his hand covering hers . . . stealing her sensibilities away . . .

Lost in her own wayward thoughts, she barely heard Langley's smooth reply.

"We met last month. In the country. At the Duke of Hollindrake's estate. I was there recuperating from my journey home, and it was then that I met my dear, darling Minerva. You could say she was the very tonic for my soul."

Her startled glance rose to meet his. "You could say that," she muttered. "But you needn't."

"Whatever did the duchess say about your obvious *tendre* for each other?" Lady Finnemore asked, obviously fishing for yet another *on dit* to pass along.

As if the nannies hadn't given her enough . . .

But the lady made an excellent point. One Minerva had overlooked until this moment. However had she forgotten the baron's daughter?

Dear God, what would the Duchess of Hollindrake say when she heard that her father was engaged to one of the Standon widows?

Minerva shuddered, and wondered if there was still time to catch the afternoon mail coach to Scotland. The Sterling family hunting box was looking more and more like welcoming refuge than a remote place for banishment.

She could even hope for a late spring snow to keep the duchess at bay until at least June—when her temper might have waned.

A bit.

"Felicity? She is delighted," Langley said, filling in for Minerva's stunned silence. "My daughter is utterly happy for me to have found love once more."

Tasha and Lucia both coughed, for they were of the same private opinion that Minerva was drawing to—the duchess was going to be a holy terror when she discovered her father's sudden arrival in London and just as hasty betrothal.

"The little duchess will be so happy for you, darling Langley," Tasha purred, smiling at the pair of them as if imagining Felicity dragging Minerva before a firing squad. "How could she not when you have found such a lady. I am surprised you haven't carried Lady Standon off already, if only to secure her."

Minerva shot a scandalized glance at the man beside her. "I don't think—"

"Lady Standon is ever so modest about their passion," the margravine told the scandalized matron sitting beside her. "Why last night, when we left them together in her—"

"Lady Finnemore, have you tried the scones," Minerva said, shoving the tray toward the lady, cutting off Helga's ruinous prattle.

"Last night?" the lady whispered anyway, undeterred by the offer of scones.

Helga nodded and smiled with a coy glance over at Langley. "He is ever so wicked, don't you agree?"

All around the room heads nodded.

Minerva began silently composing a letter to Bow Street. *Dear sirs, I request your help in removing several dangerous vagrants from my home . . .*

"And do you have plans while in Town, Lord Langley?" one of the ladies asked. For the life of her, Minerva couldn't recall the woman's name, but then again, she wasn't all that well-acquainted with most of her callers today. The matron with her heavily lidded eyes and puffy lips made a ridiculous moue and fluttered her fan. "Other than taking a wife."

The others added their own titters and smiles.

Minerva added another line to her letter. *You will not miss my house, it is the one on Brook Street that resembles a Vauxhall circus.*

"Nothing of note," he said, brushing away the lady's query as one might lint on a sleeve. "Though I've managed to procure a box for us tonight. They are doing *The Merchant of Bruges* at the Drury-Lane Theatre tonight."

"Excellent!" Aunt Bedelia declared. "Chudley and I will be there."

"I have other plans," Minerva said. She didn't,

other than devising another way to get all of them out of her house.

"You cannot, my dear," Langley insisted. "I would be bereft to attend without you at my side."

Minerva glanced up at him. *Really, bereft? Now what was he about?*

"Oh, Lady Standon, you must go with Lord Langley! It will be all the talk if you don't," Lady Finnemore insisted.

And more talk when I do attend, Minerva wagered.

Langley wasn't done making his case. "Besides, it is one of your favorite plays, you told me so yourself. And Kean is to do the merchant." He grinned at her, and that sparkling light in his blue eyes and the mischievous turn of his lips left Minerva gaping.

"How thoughtful," Lady Finnemore remarked in an aside to Lady Ratcliffe. "I doubt Lord Finnemore knows my favorite color let alone my favorite play."

Minerva wanted to groan, for his pretty speech almost had her believing *The Merchant of Bruges* was her favorite—well, she did like it immensely, but so did half the *ton*—and now he had this room of gossips believing that he actually knew those sort of things about her.

And after such a short acquaintance. She could almost hear Jamilla chiming in, *But darling, when you are in love, you just know these sort of things about one another.*

And when Minerva didn't answer—for truly how could one to such a speech?—Langley turned to his audience. "Just as I suspected. She is speechless." He laughed and winked at the ladies in the room. "I hope to keep her thusly for the rest of our lives."

To prove his point, he kissed her again, his lips

warm and seductive against her brow, lingering a moment longer than proper, and when he slowly, regretfully pulled away, he bowed once more to the ladies. Then, as if he couldn't help himself, couldn't resist her charms, he caught up her hand and brought her fingers to his handsome, smooth lips, murmuring over them, "I leave you to your guests, my goddess, my Minerva, and I look forward to our evening." His glance smoldered over her as if he spoke not of their engagement for the theatre but of something later, an encounter far more intimate.

The room stilled, as if no one wanted to breathe, no one wanted to break the spell, as if they were all sitting in her place and this man was enchanting them, and only them.

And heaven help her, Minerva shivered, for no man had ever looked at her that way. Kissed her so possessively. And as much as she knew he was doing this to convince every one in the room theirs was a love match, and that a recitation of his performance would be repeated from one side of London to another before the curtain rose tonight, God help her, she found herself wishing he wasn't acting.

For what would it be like to have a man as handsome and seductive as Lord Langley truly desire you?

Chapter 7

*When a man makes a promise to a lady, do realize he
has no intention of keeping it.*

Advice from Nanny Lucia to Felicity

𝒯he house on Brook Street bustled with activity
as all the ladies in residence got ready for an evening at the theatre. In her room, Minerva and her
maid Agnes ignored the endless trod of servants
running up and down the stairs and the shouted
complaints—mostly from the margravine—about
the lack of hot water and other "essentials."

Standing in her room with Agnes fussing around
her, Minerva would have liked to remind her houseguests that they had chosen to stay with her, and if
they didn't like the condition of their surroundings,
they could take the next boat down the Thames.
She'd be happy to check the sailing times.

To Botany Bay . . . or the southern tip of Africa . . .
or even Java.

But she had another problem that far outpaced her desire to get rid of the nannies.

Whatever was she going to wear to the theatre? As complaints and orders flew about the halls of the house, Minerva realized she was about to be outdone utterly and completely. And while she'd never thought much of it before, suddenly . . .

Oh, that wretched man and his kisses and twinkling eyes. He had her at sixes and sevens. And there was no reason for it. None at all.

"What about the plum one, my lady?" Agnes said, her head cocked to one side as she surveyed the gowns laid out on the bed.

Minerva shook her head. "No, I don't think that will do." Not that there was much to choose from. She had never been overly extravagant with her wardrobe—much to Aunt Bedelia's chagrin.

"But it is what you always wear to the theatre," Agnes said, clearly perplexed by her employer's sudden pique over her choices.

And that was the problem. She always wore the plum gown to the theatre. The blue gown to soirees and musicales. The mauve gown to balls.

"Oh, heavens none of these will do," she avowed, pushing them all to one side of the bed and flouncing down on the space she'd just cleared away. For one wild moment she thought of dashing off a mad note to Elinor and begging her to send over the crimson gown, the daring one her friend had worn to catch the Duke of Parkerton's eye.

But there wasn't time, she realized as she glanced over at the mantel clock. Oh, why hadn't she thought of it earlier?

A knock at the door startled her out of her reverie and she glanced up to find Jamilla and Nanny Brigid entering her room. And of course Knuddles, who came trotting in and glanced up at the gowns on the bed before he jumped up and settled down in the middle of them, sniffing in disdain as he went, as if such poor silks and brocades were barely suitable for his respite, but what was a dog to do?

Soon he was snuffling and snoring away.

Jamilla swept in and gave Minerva's choices much the same dismissal that Knuddles had. Already dressed for the evening in her usual flamboyant style, she entered with regal ease and a cloud of exotic perfume. "It is as I told you, Brigid," she said over her shoulder to the woman behind her. "I think we have come just in time."

To Minerva's surprise, the contessa stepped forward, also elegantly dressed for the evening, but also carrying a gown, her arms buried in silk. "Consider this my wedding gift to you, Lady Standon." She held out her offering and smiled at Minerva.

"Oh, Contessa, I couldn't," Minerva said, shaking her head as Nanny Brigid shook out an emerald silk.

"Bless my soul!" Agnes gasped as the contessa held up the most daring and eye-catching gown either of them had ever seen.

"But how can you not accept, my dearest Lady Standon?" Brigid waved her own maid into the room, and the girl went to work settling the gown over Minerva's head. "And from now on, you must call me Brigid," she said as she surveyed her maid's handiwork.

"Tell Lady Standon all about the man you met today," Jamilla said, casting a wink at Minerva as she pushed Knuddles over and sat down on the bed.

"Oh, yes," Brigid giggled. "Your aunt introduced me to the most elegant of gentleman. A marquess, which is good, no?"

"Very good," Minerva said, a little disoriented as Brigid's maid bullied her over to the dressing table, pushed her into the chair and began to dress her hair with a series of brusque, exacting movements. Quickly, the grim-faced servant had Minerva's hair artfully, if not painfully, tugged into a series of cascading curls.

Meanwhile, Brigid continued extolling her new conquest, Langley obviously forgotten. "According to the little duchess's book," she was saying, "he is very rich."

The little duchess's book? The woman had gotten her hands on Felicity Langley's *Bachelor Chronicles*?

Minerva tried to twist around, but the maid barked at her in German and gave her hair a sharp tug. All Minerva dared after that was a hot glance at Jamilla. "You didn't!"

"But it was in the room, on the mantel," the princess demurred. "I merely helped her with the translation."

Oh, how could she have forgotten the duchess's infamous matchmaking journal was still in the house? Leaving it around this lot of grasping, title-chasing women was like offering each of them their own personal keys to the Tower treasury.

"I think he is perfect," Brigid said, admiring herself in the tall glass propped up in the corner.

Brigid's maid, enlisting some help from Agnes, got the gown pinned and tucked with a few quick stitches until it fit to Jamilla's and Brigid's satisfaction. Next came out a small case of pots, and the two supervised as Brigid's maid powdered Minerva's face, added a bit of paint on her lips, kohl on her eyes, and ended by waving for a pair of high heeled shoes. Last, but not least, Agnes carried over the Sterling diamonds and sighed with delight as they were settled around her ladyship's neck.

Minerva felt dizzy from all the attention. That, and the bantering, frank comparisons by Jamilla and Brigid of past lovers and potential ones gleaned from the *Bachelor Chronicles*, though it seemed the contessa was genuinely taken by this mysterious marquess of hers.

"And tonight," Brigid said, turning Minerva toward the full length mirror in the corner, "every man at the theatre will envy Langley."

Hardly, she scoffed silently, that is until she looked at her reflection in the mirror and didn't recognize herself. How had they done this to her? However could this be her?

For looking back at her from the mirror was Nanny Minerva—a veritable goddess having risen from the plain and sensible ashes of what had once been Lady Standon.

Langley stood at the bottom of the stairs and listened to the tromp of feet overhead and cringed with each shout at a maid or slam of a door.

He'd spent a good part of his life romancing women, learning their nuances, knowing how to charm them and when to leave, but in all his experiences, he'd never understood what took so demmed long for them to get ready.

Especially since he knew how quickly they could get undressed.

Glancing at the clock, he sighed, for there wasn't much time left to get to Drury-Lane, but what could he do? Not for a dukedom would he venture up those stairs and prod a single one of those ladies along.

What about her? Would you dare for her?

Langley shook his head as images of Lady Standon filled his thoughts. In that dreadful night-rail, no less. Yet when he'd held her, oh, what unbelievable curves his hands had discovered. And the kiss he'd stolen, her lush, full lips, her fury, and then that moment when she surrendered and caught him unaware with the fire smoldering inside her. He tried to tell himself his reaction, the jolt of desire, the need she'd awakened inside him, had merely been that of any man who'd been alone as long as he had.

But that wasn't quite the truth.

That certainly didn't explain this afternoon—when he'd come into the parlor and greeted her with a kiss, in front of a roomful of gossips. Kissed her not once, but twice.

His only excuse was that when he entered the room she was the only one he'd seen. For a second he thought her all alone, for that was where his gaze had landed.

And where it stayed.

Fixed on Lady Standon. When he finally noticed the others, then her regal stance, her uplifted chin, the tight line of her brow had made sense. No longer the marchioness, she was in his eyes Minerva, the goddess of wisdom . . . of war.

For there in the keen intelligence sparking in her eyes—he could tell she blamed him utterly for her predicament, and well she should. But also he

thought he spied a fire, a hint of the passion he'd
barely tasted last night, and suddenly found himself
parched to drink from those lips once again, despite
his vow to keep their arrangement chaste.

None of which he should even be thinking about
since what he needed to be doing was sticking to his
search for Nottage—which had come up empty this
afternoon. The man's rooms were hastily packed up
and vacated, and his landlady hadn't seen him go.

Which had her in a state, for Nottage owed her for
his rent.

Which indicated, more than likely, his former secretary wasn't planning on coming back.

Which only made the search for Nottage, and his
quest to get the evidence Langley needed to clear
his name from suspicion, more urgent.

And put him at greater risk.

As well as those around him.

Including her . . . He glanced upward again, his
brow furrowed into deep rows. He shoved that
thought aside, since for the first time in months, nay
years, he was so close to clearing his name, regain-
ing his life . . .

But those niggling fears didn't stay tucked away
for long.

"Going out?" Thomas-William asked, having
come silently up the backstairs.

"Yes," Langley told him, tearing his gaze away
from the steps leading up.

"Have you a care about what could happen to
her?"

He knew exactly whom Thomas-William meant.

Lady Standon.

"This isn't Paris," he said aloud, more for himself than to answer his friend's query.

"No, but it is just as dangerous. Going out in the open isn't—"

"Yes, I know," Langley said, cutting him off. "It wasn't what George liked to do. But Lord Andrew's plan is sound." What it could be better described as was quick and cunning.

Thomas-William snorted and shook his head. Then again, he never liked haste, but certainly he had to appreciate the cunning part.

"And if you are worried about the lady, don't forget, she's got that bloody pistol of yours, threatened me with it last night," Langley argued. "I think you should be more worried about my hide than hers. The lady can take care of herself."

Before Thomas-William could add another Ellyson-inspired lecture on carefully thought out strategies, they were interrupted by a loud explosion of breaking glass upstairs, followed by the margravine letting loose a harangue in no less than three languages.

When the lady finished, Thomas-William made one more appeal. "How will your honor be restored if Lady Standon is harmed in the effort? There is no excuse for sacrificing her for something so fleeting." Then he bowed his head slightly and left, his parting shot taking a bit of Langley's confidence with it.

Damn Thomas-William and his philosopher's sensibilities!

Not that he had time to consider them or even compose a retort—not that there was one—for just then the doorbell jangled, and when no one came in to answer it (most likely every servant in the house had been harried to the point of deafness), the baron opened it himself.

"Swilly!" he exclaimed, shoving out his hand at his old school friend. "What the devil are you doing here?"

"Me? I should say! Is that you, Langley?"

"It is. In the flesh." They shook hands enthusiastically and Langley all but drug him into the foyer. "Swilly, how is it that you are here?"

"Swilly no more, my good man," the fellow said. "Throssell now. Inherited about five years ago. That demmed uncle of mine seemed all but determined to live on like a veritable Methuselah, but I finally got the chance to put him to bed with a shovel, and I did so with great vigor."

Langley laughed. "Got your hands on the title and that old pile of stones to boot."

"And a fine pile of money," Throssell added, his chest puffing out. "I will say this for the old goat: He lived well past his time, but turns out he was a regular Midas. Kept all his gold neatly piled up. So there it was just waiting for me. Put it right to good use, I did, fixing up the kennels. He left them in a shameful state of disrepair. Shocking, don't you think?"

The baron slapped his old friend on the back, for Swilly, as he'd been known at school, always had pockets to let and high expectations of his uncle dying "at a moment's notice." That and he'd always been hound-mad—no wonder the kennels at Throssell Castle had been the first to see his attentions. "I'm happy for you, but that still doesn't explain what you are doing here, of all places."

"I'm in Town for the Season," the marquess explained. "Never really thought about taking a wife, but it seems that a marquess must have one. At least that's what my mother natters on about." He glanced at his reflection in the mirror and gave his wild brown hair an absentminded pat. "So when I ran into Lady Chudley this morning—demmed fine woman that Lady Chudley—and she introduced me to one of those foreign chits she had in tow with her, a countess with the oddest bit of terrier I've ever seen—got the lines of a devilish little ratter to him, I will say, but demmed if the little chap doesn't look like a monkey. Caught my eye, she did."

Langley shook his head. "Brigid?"

"No, no, I think the dog had another name, Noodles, or something like that. Hard to understand what that gel was saying, but she claimed the dog had come from a long line of sires owned by none other than—than—" He snapped his fingers as he tried to come up with the name.

Langley closed his eyes. "Marie Antoinette."

"Yes, yes. Of course you'd know. All that time on the Continent and such." Throssell shuffled his feet a bit and took a glance up the stairs. "Liked her lines, good stance, and so I asked her to the theatre with me tonight."

Langley was almost afraid to ask if his friend meant Knuddles or Brigid. But then he got his answer when the lady in question came down the stairs.

"My Lord Throssell, is that you? Why I nearly didn't recognize you—looking so very resplendent," Brigid cooed like a lovesick teenager, and to Langley's shock, Swilly—no, make that Throssell—blushed like a lad.

The poor man tried to come up with a response as Brigid, her red hair falling like a waterfall of curls over one bare shoulder, her gown fitted to her curves as if her maid had painted it on, glided down the stairs. And while Langley knew the lady preferred horseback and hounds over Town life, when it came to making a sensation, Brigid could stop a man in his tracks when she dressed for seduction.

"I hope I haven't kept you waiting," she said as she stopped in front of Throssell.

Langley knew why she had paused thusly, and nudged his old friend in the back and whispered, "Take her hand, Swilly."

"Oh, what? Yes, suppose so," he stammered, before he caught hold of Brigid's gloved fingers and brought them to his lips. "My lady, you look divine," he managed in a voice that sounded far more sophisticated than Langley would have ever thought Swilly could muster, but there it was. "Shall we?" he said, leading her toward the door.

"Do you mind if we bring my friends?" she asked. "For Langley's carriage is far too small for all of them and I would be loath to have them travel about so cramped."

Langley's gaze followed Swilly's as it went up the stairs. Perched on the various steps were his daughter's former nannies, Jamilla, Lucia, Tasha, and Helga. It was a dazzling sight to behold, the colorful gowns, the glitter of jewels and the scandalous décolletages.

All that Swilly could manage in response was a stammering "We-ell, I—I—I—"

That was enough for Brigid. "Come along, ladies. Lord Throssell is delighted to have our company."

The ladies trooped down the stairs, filing after Brigid and her conquest.

"If you prefer, *schatzi*," Helga said, "I could stay behind and keep you company."

"No, I think this is Throssell's night," Langley said. "I'll be along in a few minutes."

She continued on, a bit of frown on her features.

Tasha and Lucia said nothing as they passed him by. But then again, neither of them needed to say a single word to convey what they were thinking. Or offering. Tasha with her swaying hips and Lucia with her come-hither glances would probably put Swilly into apoplexy.

Then again, the Marquess of Throssell was about to become the most envied man in London.

As Jamilla came by, she winked. "Enjoy your ride with Lady Standon."

"Yes, darling," Brigid called from the window of the elegant Throssell carriage. "Enjoy your ride to the theatre."

Then he understood what had just happened. Brigid and Jamilla had conspired and outmaneuvered the others so that he and Minerva had the duke's carriage all to themselves.

All to themselves?

Perhaps that wasn't the best idea. She still had Thomas-William's pistol tucked away somewhere.

Especially since he'd kissed her this afternoon. Twice. In front of witnesses. When he had promised quite faithfully not to . . .

Oh, she might have had a spark of passion in her gaze, but he hadn't forgotten that furrowed brow of hers hinted at a goddess's wraith.

Still, she was merely a London dowager, he re-

minded himself. Hardly the dangerous sort like
Brigid and her poisons, Tasha and her Cossacks,
and Helga and her threats of a sharp pike to the
mid-section . . . or lower.

Whatever did he have to fear from Lady Standon?

Behind him there was a slight rustle of silk, and he
turned around, only to discover that a secluded carriage wasn't Brigid and Jamilla's only bit of mischief.

For they'd gone and worked their matchmaking
magic on Lady Standon, and for the life of him,
Ellis, Baron Langley, the rake who'd romanced and
charmed every beauty the Continent had to offer,
found himself as dry-mouthed and stammering as
Swilly.

Oh, they knew him too well, he realized, all his
smug masculine superiority taking flight as the lady
descended the stairs, slowly, deliberately, one step
after another.

High-heeled slippers peeked out from beneath
her hem, giving a flash of the slender, silk clad legs
hidden beneath. The gown, an emerald green, shim-
mered with the same haunting depth that an actual
jewel might, but as his gaze rose higher, he found
himself gaping.

Her figure, hidden before by sensible gowns, was
no longer concealed, but swathed in silk, leaving no
man who gazed upon her in doubt of the curves,
the delights she possessed. Hips that a man could
claim, a waist to wind your arm around, and a pair
of breasts, full and round, that would make even
Aphrodite weep with envy . . . and every man who
couldn't possess her. Claim her. Take her to his bed.

The lady on the stairs was no longer merely a dowager. No London matron. She was, in every sense of the word, a goddess come to life.

Her hair, nut brown in daylight, seemed more mahogany now, having been brushed and tugged into a tempting array of curls spilling down from the jeweled coronet sitting atop her head. Painted and adorned, she could have been stepping down from a high altar, Olympus itself, instead of the rickety steps of this house where she ruled.

Oh, Jamilla and Brigid had done what they knew best. They'd contrived to make Minerva a temptation he couldn't resist. A woman he'd have to have.

Would surrender his heart, his honor, his very life to possess.

But resist he would. He swore he would. He was no Swilly. No country cub. He was Lord Langley, the breaker of hearts, and his would not be swayed by tricks that were naught but a courtesan's slight of hand.

At least that was what he vowed until he took Minerva's hand, brought her fingers to his lips and found himself utterly undone.

For her part, Minerva would have liked to remind Langley that he'd promised not to kiss her. But right now seemed hardly the right moment to ring a peel over his head.

Besides, she was having a devil of a time standing on these high-heeled shoes of Brigid's. However did the woman manage to slink about so seductively in these towering things?

And all done up as she was, she wasn't all that sure that at any moment now Langley wasn't going to burst out laughing at her, dolled up like a high-priced Incognita.

She certainly felt like one with Langley's kiss lingering over her fingers, for her insides fluttered about and urged her to be as passionate as the lady she'd seen staring back at her in the mirror.

The one she barely recognized as herself.

Truly, whoever was she going to fool? For certainly everyone would see past this transformation and realize that it was only Minerva, Lady Standon, behind the paint and silks.

Certainly not a practiced rake like Lord Langley!

Not that she wanted his attentions—which she didn't—but just once it would be something to be looked upon and regarded so intimately . . .

Oh, what was she thinking? She could hardly be as desirable as Brigid and her startling red hair and divine angles, or Tasha and her petite, fair looks, or Lucia and her come-hither glances.

No, this was all so foolhardy! She should turn on one heel—carefully so—and flee upstairs, wash her face and put on her sensible plum gown.

That is exactly what she should have done, just as she should never have answered the door the previous night.

But then she made the mistake of looking into Langley's startling blue eyes, and saw something she could never have imagined staring back at her.

The heat that swept through Langley's body as his lips touched Lady Standon's fingers left him staggered.

It was only a kiss, a greeting, but suddenly it wasn't. Her faint perfume of roses, the tremble in her fingers, the way she wavered on her high-heeled slippers. All of it threw him completely over, as if he'd been tossed under the wheels of a mail coach.

Oh, God, he wanted her. Forget the theatre, forget their plans. He wanted to catch her up in his arms, carry her up the stairs, and spend the rest of the night undressing her, discovering every nuance, every curve, where he could make this enchantress sing with pleasure.

His chest tightened, and his body . . . well, he was embarrassed to say what state he was in. He was as bad as Swilly.

However could this be? He'd kissed how many ladies in the past two decades since Franny died, and not one of them had stirred such a response in him.

And when he looked up into Lady Standon's eyes, lined as they were with kohl, making them both exotic and enticing, he gazed deeper and swore he could see the fire, the passion buried inside her very soul.

Like a distant flickering candle meant to guide him home, these flames of hers teased him to come closer, to listen carefully, dared him to try and tame them.

At that moment Thomas-William's ominous words echoed in his thoughts.

There is no excuse for sacrificing her for something so fleeting.

For while Jamilla or Brigid, Tasha or Lucia, and especially Helga, all knew the risks and rules of this game, he doubted Lady Standon did.

Wrenching his gaze away and ignoring the tightening in his chest, he said, "Lady Standon, shall we go?"

Best to get out of the house, before he did give in to his rakish inclinations and reputation.

But that didn't mean he let go of her hand.

"Yes, that sounds lovely," she said, her formal, proper tones just the right note to remind him that theirs wasn't a true match. Merely a ruse.

But it didn't have to be . . .

Oh, demmit, he was in over his head when he started thinking like that. False engagement or not, he needed to keep his wits about him.

Perhaps it is because you have never had a betrothed before.

For he hadn't, he realized as they made their way silently to the carriage. With Franny it had been a whirlwind courtship, just as he got his first assignment, a posting to Constantinople. He'd always suspected her father, Lord Hawstone, had used his influence in seeing him, a young baron with not much more than his name, sent so far away. Yet when Langley suggested—half in love, half in jest—that she, Miss Frances Hawstone, come along with him, she'd readily agreed.

They'd eloped that night, and the ship's captain had married them—despite the lack of banns and that both of them were underage. Better to marry them straightaway, he'd told his first mate, than to have a worse scandal in the months to come when they docked at some far off foreign port and the miss was far gone with child.

So it had been done with no fuss, no foolishness. And no proper betrothal. Just two overly romantic teenagers madly in love, with no thought about what they were actually doing.

So why was it, twenty some years later, he was bumbling along like Swilly, while Lady Standon maintained her perfect composure in the seat across from him?

He took a deep breath and tapped on the roof for the driver to move on. "You look lovely."

She shook her head, a dismissive sort of flutter.

"But you do," he insisted.

"'Tis the gown and the diamonds—none of which are mine."

"I disagree," he said. "The gown reveals your figure to perfection." He leaned forward. "Much better than that night-rail of yours."

"Langley!" she exclaimed. "You promised!"

Langley. She'd called him "Langley." Not "my lord," not "sir," nor several other unflattering sobriquets that could have been flung in his direction.

And like holding her hand, kissing her fingertips, he rather liked hearing her use his title in such a familiar way.

"Do you hear me?" she said. "You promised. No scandals. And that includes references to situations that may not be understood by others."

"So let me get this straight," he said. "No kissing and no innuendoes."

"Exactly," she told him, hands folded in front of her. "I'll excuse this afternoon, but no more."

If she was willing to excuse those lapses . . .

"If you insist," he demurred.

"I do."

"But you are looking lovely this evening."

Her brow furrowed as if she didn't quite believe him. "Not overdone? I fear I look like a . . . a . . ."

"A what?"

Now she leaned forward. "A courtesan. Or an Incognita. Some gentleman's vestal."

He sat back and grinned. "Lady Standon, now I am scandalized. Wherever did you hear such words? Learn about such company?"

"I opened the door to my house the other night and found it filled with such company," she said tartly.

She had him there.

"Perhaps the diamonds are overmuch," he said. "But they are stunning, and are only brightened by the light of the lady wearing them."

She snorted at his gallantries. "I've never heard such nonsense."

Langley was a bit taken aback by her skepticism. He didn't know if he'd ever met a woman who didn't adore being fed compliments as if they were squares of Turkish delight. "Then you haven't been properly courted—though those diamonds would say otherwise. Who loaned them to you? Tasha? Or Lucia?"

Her fingers went to the throat, where they fluttered nervously over the stones. "Neither. I probably shouldn't even be wearing them."

Never had he heard anything that sounded more like a confession. Still, he joked, "I doubt you stole them." And laughed at the notion until she blushed and glanced out the window.

Langley's amusement came to a halt. "Lady Standon, what mischief have you been about? Have I discovered your darkest secret?"

Her gaze flitted back to his, wide with alarm.

So you do have your secrets, he mused, thinking of her mysterious "painter."

"If you must know—"

"I must," he replied.

"These are the Sterling diamonds," she explained.

"Ah, family heirlooms. I'm surprised—given what I know of the Sterlings—you were allowed to keep them after your husband died. I would have thought they'd been—" He was about to say *gathered up with the rest of the heirlooms,* but her eyes widened even further, telling him he needn't say the words aloud. "Good God, Minerva! You are a cheeky bit of muslin. You kept them when old Sterling stuck his spoon in the wall!"

This brought her up straight in her seat. "I did no such thing. I handed them over to the next Lady Standon. Elinor wore them at her wedding to Edward."

He folded his arms over his chest and sat back, cocking one brow at her. "So how is it you have them now?"

"Oh, gracious heavens," she said, her brow furrowed to be caught so. "The diamonds are for the wife of the heir, who will eventually become the Duchess of Hollindrake. But it was decided when Lucy Ellyson married Archie—"

Oh, he saw it only too well. "The diamonds went into hiding rather than be handed over to the daughter of a thief and a dolly mop."

She pressed her lips together and nodded.

But there was more to this than just one unlikely bride. "But Lucy didn't become the duchess," he mused aloud. "Archie died and then Felicity—" Langley stopped. Egads, those diamonds were supposed to be around his daughter's neck! And then his supposition went one step further. "Am I to suppose that Felicity is unaware of the Sterling diamonds?"

Minerva glanced down at her gloves and tugged at them. "It might be that no one has told her. I believe she has been rather occupied since she married the duke."

"And you haven't had an opportunity to convey them to her?"

"No," she shot back. "And why should I? She's the one who banished me—me and Elinor and Lucy—to that shambles of a house, who had us cut off, who's been the ruin of everything!" She settled deeply into her seat, arms crossed over her chest, though one hand slid back onto the stones, cradling them possessively. "So no, I haven't given them to her."

Langley pressed his lips together to keep from laughing. He knew he should be offended—at least for Felicity's sake—but he wasn't. Oh, he had no illusions about his daughter. She'd been a high-handed, opinionated, matchmaking terror since childhood. She'd once laid out a chart for the Queen of Naples as to the likely European and English princes and princesses for her children to marry, much to the queen's amusement and the horror of the English ambassador.

"There is no need to ring a peel over my head," he told her. "Felicity won't hear about them from me. And all I will say to you, Madame Jewel Thief, is that I do believe your coloring lends itself better to diamonds than that of my fair daughter." He winked at her, pleased this time that she blushed at his compliment.

"Thank you. For I do love them."

He laughed. "Then you should wear them often."

She bit her lip and glanced out the window, and he realized something else. "You do—you wear them quite often, don't you?"

"You are the very devil, Langley," she scolded. Then she paused and added, "And yes, if I am feeling a bit out of sorts, there have been a few times when I've worn them . . . just for myself."

Something about the way she said this left Langley with the lascivious image of her wearing just the Sterling diamonds and not much else. But he also suspected that if he suggested such a thing, the proper Lady Standon would box his ears.

Still, such a proposition might be worth the risk—for suddenly he found himself lost in the memory of how it had felt to tease a kiss from her lips, hold her hand, the heat of her fingers in his sending shocks of desire through him.

The Sterling diamonds were but the outward fire of the lady before him. For like the cool stones, when the light hit her just right she burned from the inside with the same dazzling brilliance.

"What are they playing tonight?" she said, breaking the awkward silence that had filled the carriage as he sat there contemplating the impossible—of seeing her naked save for those diamonds.

He barely heard her.

"Lord Langley?" she prodded. "The play? What are they doing tonight?"

"Uh, *The Merchant of Bruges*," he said, answering quickly to change the direction of his thoughts.

His very wayward thoughts.

"Oh, yes, you said that earlier. How odd of me to forget." She glanced out the window, her reticule strings twisted around her fingers.

"Kean is playing the merchant," he added, if only to keep himself from contemplating the lady across from him . . . naked. Beneath him. Calling out his name.

Langley, oh, Langley! Yes, Langley, oh, yes!

"My lord? Are you well?"

"Uh, yes, of course," he managed.

"As I was saying, I saw him play it a few weeks ago," she replied, sounding relieved as well to have something, anything, to discuss. "It is an excellent portrayal. I hope you will enjoy it."

He nodded in agreement. "I should. I've heard much of Kean, so it is with some guilty pleasure that I finally get to see him perform. I love the theatre, you know."

Her gaze wrenched away from the window to meet his. "You do?"

She needn't sound so amazed. "Yes, Lady Standon, I do."

"I just didn't think that *you*—" She stopped there, but he could well imagine what she had been about to say. The blush on her cheeks and her nervous glance back out the window were enough evidence.

"Believe it or not, I have interests beyond seducing widows and carrying on infamous affairs."

"I didn't think that," she shot back. Far too hastily. For she also sat up straight and glowered a bit from behind her kohl-lined eyes, as if daring him to contradict her.

If only she knew how much more desirous and tempting she looked when she got into a pique.

Dangerously so.

"Well, perhaps," she admitted. "But in my defense,

one hears things about gentlemen . . . and their . . ."

She listened to gossip about him? Oh, this could be interesting. He raised a single brow, and it was enough of a prod to have her confessing.

"Well, one hears about their . . . prowess, and it is difficult to believe that such persons have time for other pursuits."

"Are you saying, Lady Standon, that I have spent most of my adult life perfecting my, as you say, 'prowess,' to such an extent that I wouldn't have any other time for such frivolities as the theatre?"

This time she furrowed her brows. "I might."

He sat back in his seat, arms folded over his chest now. "I do hope the king hasn't heard these rumors," he muttered, more to himself than to her.

This startled her out of her prudish stance. "The king? Whatever has he got to do with all this?"

"My good lady, contrary to popular prattle, I have spent more than twenty years in His Majesty's service. If he were to think that all I'd done in that time is merely sport about the Continent and collect his gold for nothing more than my prowess—"

"Well, when you put it that way—"

"I didn't. You did."

She pressed her lips together. "Oh, I suppose I did, didn't I?"

"You did."

"Then it isn't true?" she asked. "What they say about you?"

"You'd have to tell me what 'they' say."

To his delight, she blushed. He rather liked it when she blushed. One wouldn't catch Helga blushing. Or Tasha, for that matter.

"My lord, I don't repeat such gossip." Her primly folded hands went from her lap to crossed over her chest in a defiant stance.

"But apparently you aren't adverse to listening to it."

"Oh, you are incorrigible!"

"The same could be said about you, Lady Standon," he pointed out. "Did you ever protest the recitation of these reports? Refuse to listen? Leave?"

"It is hardly polite to up and leave when someone is relating a story," she told him, her hands going back to their respectable place in her lap. "Besides, I didn't even know you then."

"Oh, no, far more polite to allow an innocent man's reputation to be sullied by secondhand reports—"

"You are hardly innocent, sir. I have a house full of guests that speaks to the contrary."

He casually glanced out the window as he said, "Still, I suspect you rather liked hearing about my affairs."

"I never!"

He turned to meet her indignant gaze. "Never?"

"Not in the least," she said, even as her fingers wound and rewound her reticule strings around her fingers. "Surely not." Then she sat silently for a few moments as she straightened her skirt.

"Madam, you are a liar," he said, crossing the carriage and taking her hand in his again—if only to provoke her, certainly not because he'd been dying to touch her again.

No, it wasn't for that reason. Not at all.

"You liked listening to the tales of my prowess because your life was dull and passionless," he said, even as she tried to pull her hand from his. But he held on, and to emphasize his point, he wound his other arm around her waist and hauled her right up against him. "You've longed to burn, to have a lover, to be kissed senseless, to be carried away to far-flung places and never look back."

She opened her mouth to protest, but all her lips could do was flutter a bit. "How did you . . ."

"I'm a mind reader," he teased, studying the way her cheeks were rising in color again.

"Oh, of all the utter nonsense," she managed to bluster.

"Not entirely," he said, leaning closer, taking a deep inhale near her neck, letting the soft rose-scented perfume fill his senses. "It was my job to know, my lady. Not seducing wives and collecting mistresses—though that often helped mask what it was I was about—but what I really did was know my opponents. Know their wishes, their desires. Discover their *secrets*."

As he let that word whisper over her, she shivered. "And you think you've discovered mine? You think me a romantic, longing to run away with some ne'er-do-well?"

"Yes."

Her eyes widened a bit. "Ridiculous."

Langley leaned closer. "Come now, Lady Standon. Is it all that ridiculous? Truly? We both know the truth."

She shivered slightly, trembling really. "How could you know?" she confessed. He could tell that had cost her. "You hardly know me."

If she were any other woman, he would have flirtatiously told her that there was much a man could tell from a lady's kiss, but that wasn't entirely the truth. And he knew that Lady Standon, this living, breathing embodiment of the goddess of wisdom, wouldn't want to be dallied with.

And more to the point, there was far more he didn't know about her, but he wasn't about to tell her that. So he told her what he did know.

"You have two books out from the lending library. *The Capitals of Europe* and *The Mysterious Harem of Constantinople*. A travelogue and a rather risqué novel of French origins. The first book suggests you would like to leave London well behind you, and I won't comment on the second one, only that it says much about your unfulfilled desires."

"My unfulfilled—" She shook her head, as if trying to break the spell winding its magical way around them. "I have no such—"

He put a finger to her lips. "Oh, but you do. I know your secret."

This time her gaze narrowed, challenging him, yet that didn't mean he couldn't feel the tremble moving inside her. "And whatever do you think that is?"

"That as much as you protest otherwise, you long for me to kiss you. You want nothing more than to throw your vow away."

Chapter 8

. . . then again, what lady wants a man to keep his word?
Advice to Felicity Langley from her Nanny Lucia

*M*inerva's heart leapt in her chest. The warmth of his finger teased her lips, a promise of the fire that could be ignited, if only she said the word. *Yes.*

Please, sir. Kiss me, she wanted to plead. *Yes, please.*

And demmit if he didn't see the desire in her eyes. This charming, wretched devil. It was as if he could truly read her mind, for his other hand was at the small of her back, caressing her, soothing her, moving her closer, until she was up against his chest.

Her breasts, barely concealed as they were in Brigid's scandalous gown, rode up even higher, her nipples tight as they were pressed against the super-fine of his jacket.

Langley glanced down at her bodice, and she knew without a doubt that wolfish twinkling gleam in his eyes as his gaze rose and met hers wasn't for the diamonds around her throat.

And in that moment she knew. Like a woman does, that a man desires her. Wants her. Wants to see her naked and sprawled across his bed, so that he can explore her every curve, her every desire.

His hand, which had left her lips—when, she couldn't recall—was now cupping one of her breasts, his thumb rolling over her nipple. His gaze never left hers, as if daring her to stop him. And when she didn't, he leaned forward, and she thought—no, she wished—he would kiss her, but instead his head tipped and the whisper of his breath, warm and enticing, washed over her as he nuzzled her neck, her earlobe, her hair.

Minerva opened her mouth . . . to complain . . . to protest . . . perhaps only to try and breathe . . . and all that came out was something she'd never heard.

"O-o-o-oh," she gasped. "Oh, Langley."

Good heavens! What was that?

And when his hand slipped one of her breasts free of her gown and his fingers curled around it, explored it, drew her nipple into a taut knot of desires, she did it again.

"O-o-o-oh." She couldn't help herself, couldn't stop herself, for this man was lighting every desire she'd held in check for far too long.

Well, quite honestly? Forever . . .

Why was it now that her ardor was finally finding the light of day? Or rather the pleasures of night as she and Langley rocked together in the carriage as it ambled through the dark streets.

He murmured something to her, but what, she didn't know, for his hands were roving over her, igniting a trail of desire wherever they went, her back, her breasts. Then they were moving her, pulling her beneath him.

She lay on her back on the seat and he was atop her, his body hard.

Truly hard, and instead of being shocked as she should be—for she'd never had a man like this—her body thrummed to life with the same unwitting abandon as the moans he'd elicited with his heated touch.

A whisper of cool night air rushed over her legs, and she glanced down to find he'd moved her gown up so that her stocking clad legs were bared to his explorations.

While the night was chilly, his touch was fire as his fingers ran up her thigh, over her garters, and then paused slightly before they brushed over the curls at her apex.

She moaned again. How was it that one touch could leave such a delirious ache in its lingering path?

His lips were murmuring at her throat again, over her breasts, as his fingers continued to explore her, slowly, tentatively at first, as if testing the waters and then . . .

Minerva's hips arched of their own volition as he touched her where no man had ever touched her thusly, at least not for *her* pleasure.

And an unholy pleasure it was . . .

Torturous waves of passion ripped through her as his fingers found what they'd been searching for and began to tease, circle, and stroke her.

This time when her lips opened to moan, nothing came out, for she couldn't breathe. She couldn't think. All she could do was feel, her body throbbing with need. Raging, aching need for this man to never stop.

He was licking her nipples, suckling them, even as her hips began rising and falling to the movements of his hand.

Her hips arched higher, bucking against him, seeking out more, wanting more, her body clamoring with need. And then her hips rose for the crescendo, for that final release.

"Langley," she gasped. "Langley!" And then she was undone, unraveling, the waves crashing around her, leaving her gasping for air, shamelessly clinging to him. "Oh, Langley."

She lay there for a time, realizing that *this* was what all the fuss was about. Oh, yes, indeed she understood now.

His mischievous eyes twinkled in the dim light of the carriage. "Do you still?" he asked.

Did she what? Minerva gazed up at him, dazed and languid from his seduction.

"Do you?" he whispered in her ear, his warm breath leaving her shivering—and she couldn't tell if it was from aftershocks of her passionate explosion or anticipation that he would do it all again.

Oh, yes, again, her ripe and long-unused body pleaded. *Again and again.*

And then she remembered what he'd said just before he started this deviltry.

That as much as you protest otherwise, you long for me to kiss you. You want nothing more than to throw your vow away.

Good heavens! What had she vowed? It was nearly impossible to keep a straight thought, not here in his arms, with his lips nibbling at her earlobe.

Not to kiss him and not to share his bed.

And here she was, thoroughly tumbled. Well, nearly so.

"Well?" he whispered. "Do you?"

Oh, she knew what he was asking. Would she break her vow and kiss him?

Minerva sat up, which was difficult because he had her pinned down, still held her as if he would, with but a word from her, tease her back to that delicious state of wonder and this time leave nothing undone . . .

She guessed that the infamous Lord Langley could probably get her out of her gown faster than the finest lady's maid, the confines of a moving carriage hardly a hindrance to such a rake.

And oh, as loathe as she was to admit it, if only to herself, she wanted to be naked. Beneath him. And to have him kissing her. Devouring her with his lips. Filling her . . .

For her collection of French novels had given her a rather intimate knowledge of what should happen between lovers, though she had to admit, the practical application left her pages in shame.

Now that she'd had a glimpse of what it could be, what a man's touch, his lips, his body, could do to a woman—as her husband never had, never been able to manage—she wanted nothing more than, well, more.

She wanted it all.

But to do that she would have to break her vow, and when she gazed up at that seductive, self-assured light in his eyes, that arrogant glimmer that said he had her exactly where he wanted her, something inside her snapped.

And not in a good way.

"I do not. I will not," she told him, pulling herself out from beneath him. Not that he let her get very far. His arm snaked out and he pulled her back up against him, as if he didn't want her to forget for a moment what had just transpired between them.

As if she could.

"I do not want to kiss you and I do not want to share your bed," she lied.

The rakish, intelligent devil, this diplomat of seduction, grinned. "And so you haven't. For this carriage is no bed." Her mouth opened in a wide moue to protest, but he continued on. "Nor have I kissed you."

No, he hadn't, she realized. And in that moment she knew he'd only cracked Pandora's box open, that there was so much more to discover, so much more this man could give her, show her, tempt her with.

"All it will take is one word, my lady," he whispered into her ear, while his hands worked their seductive magic over her.

Yes, she wanted to shout and give in. And she very nearly did, for there was his head tipping down, his lips about to claim hers, and her body was thrumming back to life under his skilled touch. Already she was starving for more, delirious with a passionate hunger.

He'd quickly teased her back into this state and she should be furious, but instead was only in desperate need for more.

Yet just before his lips claimed hers, Langley pulled back. "How unfortunate for both of us that I cannot."

She very nearly said, *Why the devil not?* Nearly. For

she remembered just before the indelicate and utterly unladylike phrase slipped from her lips that she was the Marchioness of Standon, and as such, she didn't say those things.

"I promised," he was saying. "As did you. I couldn't be the instrument of you breaking your word . . . Of seeing you beg for my kiss . . ."

Of her breaking her word? Begging? She ground her teeth together. What of his vow?

Of all the smug, presumptuous . . .

"You, sir . . . you, sir . . ." she stammered as she tried to push him away. Tried. For he wouldn't let her go. Held her as if he still hadn't quite made up his mind. As if he might still try to . . .

Minerva's body thrummed in protest. *Good heavens! Don't be a fool. Kiss him!*

The great oaf grinned at that very moment, as if he, like he had claimed earlier, could read her mind. That he knew exactly how much she desired him.

Oh, the very devil! His name was Langley! This time she used every bit of strength she possessed to wrench herself out of his grasp and cross the carriage to take up the place where he'd been sitting.

It only made her indignation worse when she realized he was still grinning at her. Well, if he could resist, she certainly could. She set to work straightening her gown, tucking her hair back into place, trying everything she could to make her insides as respectable as her outward appearance.

"You are hardly going to maintain the illusion that we are happily engaged if you choose to sit over there glowering at me."

"I am not glowering," she shot back. She was well past glowering. More like furious. Outraged.

Frustrated.

Worst above all, she was furious and outraged more at herself than at him.

And not for every stone in the Sterling diamonds would she admit she was most angry for not having taken the chance and discovered truly what his legendary prowess was all about.

She flitted a glance over at him and nearly sighed. Did he have to be so handsome? Brown hair all tousled—had she done that?—cravat tied with a rakish flourish, blue eyes alight, as always, full of mischief and deviltry.

An intoxicating, enticing deviltry that was like no other lure, for his eyes promised pleasures untold for any lady who caught his wandering eye.

Untold pleasures . . .

Minerva felt her usual iron resolve waver. Now that she'd had a taste, however, would she be able to stop until she'd drowned in his arms?

But whatever her capricious convictions might have been, they came to an abrupt halt as the carriage pulled to a stop before the theatre, and mere moments later the door swung open.

Langley got out ahead of her and then turned to hand her down. He smiled up at her, his brows waggling as if to encourage her to do the same. "Remember, we are madly, passionately in love," he whispered in her ear.

Oh, he would have to put it *that* way!

"Indeed," she said, pasting a pained smile on her face, taking his hand and getting out of the carriage only to find a good part of the *ton* gaping at them.

"And despite our mutual desires," he said under

his breath, "I trust you can keep your word as to our agreement."

She could keep her word? Oh, the arrogance of the man.

"I can keep mine as long as you keep yours," she said, smiling at Lady Finnemore, who must have been waiting on the steps for their arrival, and was even now pushing her way forward to greet them.

"Trust me, I can," he said, nodding to a man who'd offered a short, curt bow.

"Oh, but I don't trust you," she said back as she was jostled from one side, teetering on her heels.

"I would do well to remember that the next time you throw yourself in my arms," he whispered softly so only she could hear him. Yet before she could correct him or even give him the set down he so richly deserved, the wretched fellow had turned to a distinguished looking gentleman. "Sir Basil, how good to see you again, and so soon! I must assume this lovely vision is your daughter. No? Your wife? I never . . . Have you met my betrothed, Lady Standon . . ."

As Langley greeted Brownie, he made a surreptitious scan of the crowd around them. The thick crush unnerved him, for it had been such a gathering in which he'd been attacked in Paris.

Paris. He couldn't stop the shiver that ran down his spine, the sense of foreboding that it was happening all over again.

This is London, he told himself, smiling at Lady Standon and doing his best to quiet the fears and alarm that usually arrived with these wrenching fragments of memories. *You have nothing to fear.*

Yet just then someone bumped into Minerva

and she stumbled, swaying on her high heels. He caught her easily, steadying her elbow, his other hand winding around her waist and pulling her up against him.

Merely to keep her from falling, he told himself, surprised by the sense of possessiveness tightening his chest, especially now that he saw the number of heads turning at the sight of her.

Just as his had earlier.

Oh, yes, now you notice her, you fools, he wanted to chide, but instead put a self-satisfied grin on his face, the sort of statement of male arrogance that said, *However did you miss such a rare jewel? Well, she's mine now.*

Not that she was, but the rest of London didn't know that. But she nearly had been in the carriage.

Good God, how was it that this stubborn, practical, delectable widow had him at sixes and sevens? Especially when, as Thomas-William liked to remind him, he had more important matters to attend to.

Like figuring out who had tried to kill him in Paris.

And most likely still wanted him dead. He glanced over his shoulder and found Sir Basil's gaze boring into his back.

No wonder he still felt the chill of Paris in his bones.

"Posies, my lord?" a child called out just before they made it to the door. She tugged at his sleeve. "Posies for her ladyship?"

He was about to brush the urchin aside, but a flash of red gold hair and a smile with a missing tooth caught his eye.

Goldy!

He paused for a moment, letting Minerva step ahead with Jamilla and Brigid, who had been waiting for them to arrive, then leaned over and handed a coin to the little urchin.

And while he made the pretense of selecting just the right spray of orange blossoms from her grasp, she whispered to him, "That bloke, the one who's hurrying off to get inside—"

Langley slanted a glance in that direction and spied a tall figure in a dark great coat.

"—he slipped yer lady a note," she finished.

Langley glanced first at Goldy, shocked by what the child had spotted, and then at Minerva, who was at that moment furtively tucking a slip of paper into her reticule.

What was this mischief? Then he glanced up again and toward the door, where the fellow was just dodging inside. A man about the same size and build as her "painter."

Perhaps he should have spent a little more time considering her sudden reversal earlier.

After all, what the devil did Lady Standon have to gain from this betrothal farce? Why had she agreed to her role in all of this?

And who was the "painter" she'd met in the alley, and why had that encounter propelled her to change her mind so quickly? Certainly, he had no doubts this stranger was the catalyst for her acceptance of his proposal.

But why?

"Ah, here is the perfect one," he told the girl as he made his selection. Flowers in hand, he set after his betrothed, all the while Goldy's bright voice called out to the latecomers behind them, "Posies! A lady isn't a lady without her posies!"

"Or her secrets," he muttered under his breath.

Not even the magic Kean worked on the stage could hold the audience's attention—not while a whirlwind of gossip and speculation swirled through the audience like a rewritten script. Lord Langley's box—full of his former paramours and his new betrothed, one of the now infamous trio of Standon widows—was a delicious scandal, rife with possibilities and endless points of conjecture.

In other words, the night was a grand success.

That is for everyone but Minerva. She spent the first act fidgeting in her seat, trying to determine how she was going to give Lord Langley the slip at intermission and meet Adlington, as his note had demanded.

When she shifted yet another time, Lord Langley leaned over. "Bored?"

"Not at all," she whispered back. "Enchanted."

"Then you might want to stop twisting your reticule strings into knots—you'll break them, and then where will you tuck away whatever it is you ladies keep inside those things?" His hand slid over and came to rest atop hers, as well as her reticule, and all she could do was stiffen and stare straight ahead.

She didn't dare glance at him to gauge why he would say such a thing. Not when in the carriage she'd sworn he could see right through her, knew all her secrets.

All her desires . . . Well, he'd certainly done an excellent job of uncovering, or rather unraveling those.

A hot blush rose on her face as she recalled how

wanton she'd been. Nearly naked beneath him. His fingers plying from her the most delicious notes of passion, and how she'd fallen so easily under his seductive spell. Her insides warmed and she shifted in her seat, trying to find a comfortable position.

Langley leaned over again. "Warm? You look flushed." He grinned at her and then winked.

Oh, the arrogant man! He thought she was woolgathering about him—never mind that she was—but of all the impertinence.

"Would you watch the play," she told him, pointing at the stage.

"I prefer the one being conducted up here."

She glanced over at him. What was he up to now? Studying her as if he knew of the note in her reticule. Minerva pried her gaze from his and fixed it back on Kean. And the play. Anything other than the man beside her.

Oh fiddle! She was being ridiculous. Of course he didn't know what was in her reticule. He couldn't have seen Adlington pressing his horrible note into her hand or her hiding it.

Nor did he know all her secrets.

Not that he wasn't apt at ferreting them out or making a few very good, albeit educated guesses. Still, that didn't mean she should underestimate him; she suspected he was a dangerous foe—just look at how he'd gotten her babbling on about the Sterling diamonds.

Better the necklace than other subjects, she mused, curling her fingers into the knit stitches of her reticule.

His fingers were still atop hers and appeared to have no intention of leaving. The warmth of his touch curled into her hand, up her arm, and as much as she knew she should slip free of his intoxicating touch, she just couldn't.

She wanted him to hold her hand, touch her.

And if she was willing to admit it—which she wasn't—she wanted him to do so much more.

Minerva shifted in her seat and tugged her hand free of Lord Langley's grasp.

"Whatever is the matter?" he whispered to her, picking up the spray of orange blossoms he'd purchased for her and taking an appreciative sniff. "I thought you loved the theatre?"

"I do," she replied, retrieving her blossoms. "But I find it distracting to have everyone staring at us and not the stage."

"They are staring at us?" he asked, his voice full of innocent surprise, as if he hadn't noticed the none-so-discreet pointing and whispers aimed at them.

"Why wouldn't they?" Minerva shook her head. "This box is akin to Astley's circus."

He glanced over his shoulder. "What? Has the margravine taken to riding naked again while I was watching Kean?" He winked at her, settled deeply into his seat and fixed his gaze on the actors as if it was the only amusement to be had.

Minerva pressed her lips together to keep from laughing. Oh, bother the man! He truly was incorrigible.

Nor was he done.

"It isn't just your houseguests who have everyone staring in our direction," he mused quietly.

"*Your* guests," she corrected.

He reached over and took her hand again. And

this time he held it so there would be no slipping free. Not without making a scene. *"Our guests."*

Our guests! Minerva wanted to box his ears. There was no "our." Just a facade of a betrothal. This mire of scandal into which she'd tumbled.

Rather, he'd done the tumbling and she'd been the innocent victim in all of this. At least, she'd been the innocent one until the carriage ride over.

Though given the wry looks Jamilla and Brigid had cast at her when they'd joined her on the steps, she had to imagine they'd guessed the truth.

She only hoped no one else had.

They hadn't, had they? She sat up in her seat and surveyed the faces staring up at her.

"Whatever is the matter now?" He leaned over closer. "Mr. Frisk has just made Miss Kelly an honorable proposal of marriage. The squire shall not win her hand."

Minerva shook her head. "Whoever is Mr. Frisk?"

He smiled indulgently. "Are you not paying attention to the play?"

The play? She glanced at the stage as the actress was taking the young actor's hand and declaring her love. Oh, that Mr. Frisk. "How can I?" she said in her defense. "With everyone staring at this box."

"They are not staring at this box," he demurred.

"They aren't?"

"No," he said with a slight shake of his head. "They are staring at you."

"Me?" She let out a sigh. "You're mad."

"For you," he said, grinning like the wicked baron he was.

This time she didn't care if she made a scene. She pulled her hand free. "Will you please stop that."

"Whyever for?" He stubbornly reached over and took her hand again. And demmit if her heart didn't patter a little to be once again in his grasp. "We have a performance to give. Remember?"

"They can watch the play," she told him tartly.

He squeezed her fingers slightly, but it was enough to send her heart racing again.

"It appears all of London is in the mood for a romance," he said, his glance smoldering with a look that said, *As am I.*

Devilish fellow. He knows exactly how handsome and charming and worldly he is . . . Minerva pressed her lips together. *But he is only acting, putting on a performance for the entire* ton *to witness.*

He didn't desire her. A dowdy London widow? No, he couldn't.

Oh, but if only he did . . .

She tamped down the most uncharacteristic sigh that nearly slipped from her lips and reminded herself of one simple fact: This was Lord Langley. And if that wasn't enough to stomp out these ridiculous foolish fancies, then she obviously needed to remind herself that this man was the Duchess of Hollindrake's father! When Felicity heard of her father's impromptu betrothal, there would be hell to pay.

She took a deep breath, ignored his fingers still wound around hers, and instead glanced around, scanning the crowd, and immediately wished she hadn't.

For there was Gerald watching her. Not her precisely. His avaricious gaze was fixed a little lower. On the Sterling diamonds to be exact. And most likely mentally weighing the stones and adding up their worth.

And here she'd told him she didn't have anything of value. Oh, foolish, foolish, foolish. Why had she worn them?

If only she didn't know the answer to that. The same reason she liked to put them on late at night when she was all alone, when she wanted to imagine herself as beautiful and desired and loved.

Because she wanted to burn with the same fire that they did when touched by the right light, just as Langley had said earlier.

Still, she couldn't have imagined the blaze he would ignite in the carriage ride over. Now all she could wonder was how she would ever put such a fire out.

For like her decision to wear these jewels tonight, now there were repercussions, just as the vile note folded away in her reticule promised.

There were always consequences to everything. *Always.*

And this the bastard daughter of an earl, masquerading as a marchioness, knew better than anyone. Probably even better than Langley himself.

Chapter 9

Never put anything in your reticule you wouldn't want your dear maman or even your best confidante to discover. And your bodice is never a good second choice. Your lover will most decidedly discover it there.
Advice to Felicity Langley from her Nanny Brigid

*W*hen the curtain fell for intermission, Lady Standon plucked her hand from Langley's grasp and leapt to her feet, saying in a heady rush, "Yes, well, there it is. I'll be right back."

Langley caught her by the elbow. "You needn't go without me, my dear." He watched the emotions—frustration, concern, and pique—play out behind her kohl-lined eyes. No, she certainly didn't want his company. "I can go fetch whatever you desire."

"I don't desire anything," she told him, trying to pull her arm free and not succeeding.

He should just let her go, let her play out her intrigues, for Lord knows he had his own pile of troubles to contend with, but something inside him tugged possessively at his heart.

You need to help her, it urged. *You must help her.*

Those words echoed through his thoughts, like the hiss of a stage manager off to one side prompting a forgetful actor to remember his lines.

But he didn't want to be prompted to do what was right, what was honorable.

Just let her go and concentrate on keeping Sir Basil off balance, he told himself, recounting the plans he had made with Thomas-William and Lord Andrew.

Including the one that would start tonight.

But intervention came in the form of Tasha, stepping between him and Minerva with all the ease of a sleek cat. "Darling, sometimes a lady doesn't need a man's company," she told him, her brows arched as if to say, *In certain circumstances.* She extracted Minerva from his side and pulled her to the aisle. "Come, Lady Standon. Men, even one such as Langley, can be so obtuse about a lady's needs."

The two women departed, and Langley watched them go, his lips pursed in frustration. He shouldn't be frustrated, he should be relieved, so he could get on with what he needed to get done, but at the door, Minerva took one furtive glance over her shoulder at him—a guiltier look he had never seen—which only served to drive his curiosity wild.

What the devil was Lady Standon up to?

Then as his gaze swept around, he spied the one thing that would answer his question.

Her reticule.

Dropped and forgotten when she'd bounded to her feet.

He reached down and plucked it up, making a

good show of returning it to its rightful place in her seat, even while his fingers slipped inside and plucked out the note she'd concealed.

Surreptitiously, he flipped it open and read it.

Time's up. Meet me at intermission. Or else.

Langley sniffed. Good God. *Or else?* What sort of mushroom writes such melodramatic nonsense?

Any number of reasons for such a demand ran through his head—gambling debts, an insult or slight, a love affair gone sour. That last one he dismissed as quickly as he thought of it. Ridiculous notion, that.

Proud and proper Lady Standon in some sort of sordid love affair? He snorted and tossed the thought aside.

Besides, the image of another man with her left him with a pit in his stomach. For what reason he couldn't fathom, but he didn't like the idea of it. Not in the least.

Crumpling the paper and then shoving it in his pocket, he made his way through the press of people, determined to put this distraction to an end; that is, until a large gentleman stepped into his path.

"Langley! It is you! Heard you were in Town."

"Lord Chudley! Why it's been years. Good to see you, sir," Langley replied, holding out his hand.

"Take your hand away, you cad. I will not shake it," Chudley declared. "You are a dead man to me."

"So that's him," Adlington sneered as he glanced over Minerva's shoulder.

She looked across the foyer, where Langley was coming out of the doorway of their box.

"Leave me. Leave me now!" she said, moving to dodge away. "Before he sees us."

Gerald stopped her flight almost immediately, catching hold of her elbow and towing her back into place. "What if he does? Doesn't look like much," he said. "Besides, I hear tell he's a traitor."

Minerva drew in a sharp breath. For while she didn't know Langley very well—oh, good gracious heavens, she barely knew the man at all—she couldn't, wouldn't, believe that of him.

But before she could refute such a lie, Adlington continued, "Is that the game, Maggie? Marry him and then watch him dance at the end of the rope?"

She recoiled in horror at such a suggestion, yanking her arm free.

Adlington clucked his tongue at her. "Bad idea, my girl. They take everything from traitors. There's no profit in marrying one."

No profit . . . Never had she wished more for Thomas-William's pistol in her grasp. She wouldn't even be in this predicament if profit wasn't Gerald's middle name.

"I'll leave London if you don't stop this," she threatened.

"No you won't," he said. "Not until you give me my money." He glanced at her décolletage and shook his head. " 'Nothing of worth,' she says. You little liar. Those diamonds would keep a king in style."

"The money was never yours, it was for Minnie," Minerva corrected as she watched—with some relief—Lord Chudley step into Langley's path and bring him to a halt. For the time being. "And neither are these diamonds—they belong to the Sterling family. They are the duchess's, if you must know."

"A duchess probably won't miss a few baubles."

Baubles? Only an idiot like Gerald would call such stones "baubles."

"Then you are a fool. The Duchess of Hollindrake would hunt you down herself," she told him. *After she finished me off for losing a family heirloom.*

Adlington leaned closer. "We could both go, Maggie. Take that necklace and leave."

She scoffed at him and tried to escape, but he had her pinned in place, with her back to the wall and his hand planted just over her shoulder.

"We could go to America," he continued. "You fancied that notion once; you could again."

She made her answer with an inelegant snort. "I'd rather spend the rest of my days in Newgate."

He pointedly ignored her sarcasm as if it weren't meant for him. "Boston would be a far sight better. Or New York. Mayhap down South—there's land a plenty there, so I hear, and those diamonds would buy us a kingdom and all the help we'd ever need."

"Slaves? You'd buy slaves?" She couldn't fathom such a thing. But apparently Adlington wasn't averse to the notion.

"You've forgotten what living is like without a household of maids and cooks and fancy fellows at your beck and call. You'd change your mind right quick if you were tossed back into the kitchens." He snorted as if that thought was a great jest, then leaned closer and said softly, "And over there, none of that rabble will care if you are naught but an earl's by-blow. Might even give you some standing amongst the blighters."

"Hardly," she scoffed, "if I arrived with the likes of you."

He leaned closer still. "You've turned out uppity, Maggie. That title of yours has gone to your head. But when they throw you out, what then? You'll be in the gutter, just where you would have been if I hadn't seen the way clear for you to marry that old goat." He leered at her, and Minerva knew immediately who had replaced her former husband as London's most ghastly old goat. "Come with me now, Maggie," he cooed. "Just say the word."

She recoiled as best she could. "How about this one: 'No!' Or to be more precise: 'Never!'" Truly, did he think her so daft? "Why, you'd run through whatever coins came your way for this necklace before you got to Plymouth." She paused as his brow furrowed tellingly. "That's it, isn't it? You're in deep, aren't you? And to someone who isn't as forgiving as my sister was?"

"That is none of your business," he whispered, his teeth grinding together like a wolf, his face turning an angry shade of red.

But as much as he taunted her about her lowly origins, he seemed in the same measure to have forgotten where she'd come from as well. Minerva wasn't merely the earl's natural child. "As my mother always said, 'I may be only a woman, but a man has to eat and he's got to sleep.'" She straightened up on her high heels so she almost looked him in the eye. "Have a care, Mr. Adlington, what you take for supper tomorrow night and where you decide to slumber."

He paled, but before he could rally, counter her threats, a loud voice stopped them. Stopped all the conversations in the foyer.

"I'll have satisfaction, Langley! I demand it!" Lord Chudley bellowed.

Everyone turned toward this pronouncement, even Adlington.

Minerva used the distraction to slip out of Gerald's trap.

"Chudley, there is no reason to—" Langley was saying.

"Demmit, man! Are you going to back away from a challenge like a coward?"

There was a collective inhale of breath.

Minerva was stopped from stepping into the fray by Nanny Brigid, who stood on the inner circle of witnesses, Throssell hovering protectively at her side.

"Seconds, sir. Name them!" Chudley bellowed.

Seconds? Had Aunt Bedelia's husband gone mad? But then the madness spread as Langley nodded in agreement and the foyer buzzed with the news.

A duel!

Good heavens! Blackmail and now this . . . Minerva found her once staid life being thrust into a maelstrom of scandal.

She was starting to think that, perhaps, a quiet cell in Newgate might be a welcome respite.

Gerald Adlington was about to go after his quarry when a lady tapped him on the sleeve with her fan.

"Excuse me, were you just speaking to that lady?"

"What business is it of yours?" he said, not really looking at the woman, but trying his damnedest to keep Maggie in his sights. Bitch! She wouldn't slight him so if she knew it had been his idea to have the earl send her in her sister's place to marry Philip Sterling.

Bloody stroke of genius that, if he did say so himself. Maggie's placement so close to the Sterling coffers had given him and his suddenly useless bride an endless supply of illicit cash.

Especially after the old earl had made it clear he wouldn't give his errant legitimate daughter and her new husband a shilling, not even when he turned up his toes.

Useless. That was what Minnie had become. Then again, weren't most women useless? Save for when a man wanted . . . He watched Maggie's hips sway, the curve of her backside as she departed, and he groaned a little bit. She'd always found a way to stir him. And London whores were expensive. Perhaps he should just find a way to nab her, her bloody diamonds and make off to America.

But that notion would have to wait, for the overdone bird at his side became overly insistent. "I would have a word with you—in private," she was saying, this time taking his arm and tugging him back into an alcove.

Gerald gave her a hard stare, and found his gaze was met with an equally merciless one. Instantly he knew who she was, one of those fancy foreign pieces who was rumored to have been one of Langley's warming pans.

"Stop gaping like a fish and close your mouth," she told him, giving him another nudge with her elbow. "You will listen to what I have to say, if you know what is good for you."

Gerald's temper flared to be spoken to thusly. Obviously Langley liked them bossy. Fool. Personally, he liked his birds a bit more submissive.

"What do you want?" he asked, puffing out his chest and facing her down.

She was, after all, just a woman.

She took a slow glance over at Minerva and said, "I think we have mutual desires that need to be addressed. Much to be gained if we worked together."

He liked the sound of that. "What do you have in mind?"

And so she told him.

"I thought you said you would handle this?" Neville Nottage said, sidling up behind Sir Basil and watching the growing fracas between Lord Langley and that old fool, Viscount Chudley.

"What the devil are you doing here? I told you when we parted at White's to hide! Better still, leave London," Sir Basil said, pulling him into an alcove. Not that anyone was looking, for they were too busy watching the escalating scandal.

"I think not," Nottage said. "Every day Langley is alive puts us in danger." Still, he pulled the collar of his coat up higher and the brim of his hat down lower.

"Very soon he will be under attainder for treason, and it won't matter what he knows," Sir Basil replied, glancing down at his program as if scanning it for something interesting in the next act.

"When?" Nottage demanded.

"When what?" Sir Basil said, taking a peek over at Chudley's buffoonery.

"When will he be arrested? I detest this loathsome cowering."

"By the end of the week," Sir Basil told him.

Nottage shook his head furiously. "No! He needs to be eliminated now."

"We wouldn't be discussing this at all if you had finished the task in Paris. After all, you said he was dead. That Paris was the end of our concerns."

"I would have sworn—" Nottage muttered, glancing furtively over his shoulder, but keeping his back to the crowd.

Yes, well your swearing didn't do it, now did it? Sir Basil mused silently, vexed at living in the baron's crosshairs, for here was the seemingly unstoppable Lord Langley still alive.

Though perhaps not for long.

"This may be better," he said aloud. "Lord Chudley is a demmed good shot, even at his age. He'll finish this business for us. Besides, Langley hasn't got any evidence against us. Remember he came to me begging for help." Sir Basil snorted and went back to looking over his program.

"I know Langley," Nottage grumbled. "He's playing with you. And even if he doesn't have anything, what if he discovers something before Chudley manages to send him aloft?"

"He won't find anything. I've covered my tracks well. I wish I could say the same about you."

Nottage colored. Dangerously so, but Sir Basil was confident in his own position.

There was nothing left that could point the finger at him save a few suspicions and the jealousies that came with rising in the ranks as he had.

"There is that one missing shipment," Nottage pressed.

"Yes, which was lost. And if we couldn't find it, why do you think Langley will be able to make it materialize out of thin air?"

"Because he's Langley," Nottage said, watching

his former mentor with a narrowed gaze. "Listen well, Brownie, I'll not be hanged for any of this. Not I. There is nothing to be done save stop the man. Without delay."

Nottage turned to leave, but Sir Basil stepped into his path. "Stop bleating like a lamb. I have this well in hand. If this isn't done with care and caution, we will both fall."

"I beg to differ. I don't think you do have this in order," his co-conspirator replied. "Nor do you have the stomach for what needs to be done. Easy to order his murder when the man is across the Channel, but you haven't the nerve to kill a fellow when he's standing right in front of you, now do you, Brownie?"

"These things need to be done wisely. There is too much at stake."

"This is no time, my good man, for care or reason," Nottage told him, "Langley must die. Now."

Sir Basil shuddered, and clenched his teeth together. Whatever did the man want him to do? Pull out a pistol and shoot the baron in front of the entire *ton*? Ridiculous notion. These things took careful planning, deliberation, timing . . .

"So I thought," Nottage sneered. He leaned closer and whispered, "Time for you to step aside and I'll show you how it is done in the field."

"Like you did in Paris?" Sir Basil said, managing a brazen bit of courage.

But it was too late, for Nottage had already slipped into the crowd, moving like an eel through the excited throng that was even now rushing back to its seats for the next act, if not for the play, but to make sure they had the finer points of the scene they had just seen enacted in the foyer.

No one noticed Nottage, but then again the man was like that—familiar but utterly forgettable.

Alone, Sir Basil fumed, watching Nottage stride boldly out the door and into the night, where most likely the man was planning a murderous final act of his own.

"A duel?" Minerva said to the baron as they exited Drury-Lane Theatre. "Really? That is how you avoid a scandal, Langley?"

"I can hardly be held accountable for Chudley's sense of honor," he replied. "Nor is it the time to have this discussion." Langley glanced up and nodded at the gaping crowd that parted to let them through. Then he took her hand, placed it on his sleeve and began a slow, staged descent down the steps.

Minerva glanced up and immediately her fingers curled tighter around her spray of orange blossoms.

Oh, good heavens! It seemed everyone in the theatre—whether they'd witnessed the exchange or not—had lined up on the steps to watch them leave, just in case there happened to be an encore performance.

"What do they think is going to happen?" she asked under her breath as they walked along, her hand firmly pinned to his sleeve by his other hand.

He needn't hold her so, she would have told him. She wasn't about to let go.

"Perhaps they are waiting for another aggrieved husband to step forward and challenge me as well."

"How many more are there out there?" she asked, pausing at the curb as he waved for their carriage to come forward. The driver pulled into place and

Langley stepped out into the street and opened the door for her.

"More than you would like, I'm willing to wager," he joked.

Oh, you would jest, she mused as she picked her way to the carriage. It had rained while they'd been inside, and the puddles were everywhere. It wouldn't do to ruin Nanny Brigid's elegant shoes, for with her accounts cut so drastically, Minerva knew this finely crafted pair wouldn't be easily replaced, nor would the gown if the hem got soiled.

Happily she made it to Langley's side unstained and was just about to step into the dry confines of the Hollindrake carriage when she spied the flower girl from earlier—her bright copper curls so hard to miss—dashing up the street from where the carriage had come, darting around the crowds and horses, her face twisted in terror.

Something was terribly wrong, but what, Minerva had no idea. Just this jolt of warning racing along her spine that said her entire world was about to be turned upside down.

Then it seemed everything around her stilled, as if the seconds that usually ticked easily by were slowed by the hands of Fate. The little girl shouted something, but what it was, Minerva couldn't discern, not over the hullabaloo around them. But the child, realizing she had Minerva's attention, pointed up.

She twisted around to see what had the little urchin so frightened and her heart stopped.

The driver had risen up in his post—only it wasn't the usual fellow who drove the Duke of Hollindrake's spare carriage, but a stranger, wearing a mask, with a low-slung hat and his collar pulled up high. But there was no mistaking his intent—from inside his coat he was drawing out a pistol and aiming it.

Right at Lord Langley, who with his back to the man had no idea what was about to happen.

Minerva twisted again, this time so she faced Langley, terror robbing her of her wits, her ability to speak. And here was the baron smiling at her, probably coming up with another flirtatious quip about his unsavory reputation, and she knew in that split second she didn't even have time to warn him.

Only to save him.

Catching hold of his lapels, she shoved them both into the crowd, even as the driver's pistol fired.

They hit the street hard, Minerva atop him, splashing in the mud and muck. Ladies screamed and men shouted in terror as the horses bolted forward, then took off in a mad dash down the street to escape the chaos.

Langley's arms had wound tight around her. He held her close, not only in shock, but in a possessive sort of way that she could feel all the way down to her bones. His eyes, robbed of their usual mirth, held a different sort of light altogether—amazement, shock, fear, and then an unholy fury.

"Are you hit?" he asked, his question clipped and short.

She shook her head. Amazingly, she wasn't. "Are you?"

"No," he said, righting them both with amazing

speed. He strode out into the street and watched with narrowed eyes as the carriage sped around the corner, then he turned to look at her. "Did you see him? Who was it?"

"I don't know. He wasn't the usual fellow. Not the one who drove us here."

Langley glanced back down the road, then returned to her side, catching her in his arms. "You could have been killed!" he scolded. "Whatever were you thinking? You foolish, madcap woman!"

Well, good heavens! Minerva ruffled at his description. She'd just kept him from being shot and he was of a mind to ring a peal over her head? "I did what I thought was best. 'Twas the little girl, the flower girl, who warned me—"

She couldn't finish her sentence for suddenly her eyes welled up with tears and she looked around for the child, but she'd disappeared from sight.

Langley smoothed back the long curls that had fallen from her once perfect and enticing coiffure. "Minerva, you have more bottom than any woman I have ever met, and now I owe you my life."

She swallowed back a gulp that she feared would turn into a sob.

It wasn't exactly the most perfectly worded bit of praise she'd ever heard—truly, bottom?—but it pierced her heart just like the sight of her lovely little spray of orange blossoms, which lay trampled and lost in the mire of the muddy street.

That could have been Langley, she realized. Or her. Lost in the mud, lost forever. Oh, dear, how had her life gotten so tangled?

For the first time since her wedding night, she

began to cry. And worse, in public. Welling up like a regular watering pot.

Oh, the devil take her! She was crying over a spray of orange blossoms. Wasn't she?

Langley caught hold of her and pulled her close. "Are you sure you weren't hit? That you're un-harmed?"

She nestled closer. Discovering the steely warmth of being held thusly.

"Whatever were you thinking?" he whispered into her ear.

"Saving you for Lord Chudley, I imagine," she replied, wiping at her eyes.

"I'm hardly worth the effort," he told her.

"Yes, I can see that now," she lied. "It won't happen again."

But she had to imagine that with a man like Langley at her side, it would.

Chapter 10

Men and their honor! Such a noble idea, and to
what lengths they will go to protect it. Too bad they
are not as concerned about a lady's honor—for they
will go to ruinous lengths to gain her attendance in
their bed.

Advice to Felicity Langley from her Nanny Lucia

Minerva came downstairs the next morning,
her thoughts awhirl from the events last night. However had her life come this?

Chudley had challenged Lord Langley to a duel.
And then Langley had been shot at, and she, of all
people, had saved his life.

And while she had shrugged off the event to the
others as naught but a botched hold-up—her own
fault for wearing the Sterling diamonds so pub-
licly—she held every suspicion that there was far
more to the attempt on Lord Langley's life than just
a robbery.

Nor had the nannies seemed to find it plausible. They had all glanced out the carriage and looked at everyone but her, as if they pitied her for being such a fool.

For they knew, as Minerva did now, that the man was a dangerous enigma.

Flirtatious and rakish. By all accounts a favored hound by every living woman who'd ever met him.

And yet he'd been living in her house in secret. Added to that, what about all the rumors about his death, hints of treason? He had only been a diplomat, nothing more.

Hadn't he? Certainly the stint in a French prison suggested otherwise.

She paused, her teeth catching her lower lip as she continued to puzzle it all out, but kept coming back to Chudley's challenge.

Why, the entire thing was ridiculous to fathom. Here she'd thought Aunt Bedelia's fifth husband quite the stodgy, dependable sort—which up until last night she'd thought an odd choice for Aunt Bedelia— but apparently her aunt had seen the lion's heart beating beneath the viscount's tweedy exterior when no one else had.

But a duel? Lord Chudley was going on seventy, if he was a day. And whatever sort of mischief had Lord Langley wrought that Lord Chudley had held a grudge this long, and obviously so deeply?

Pausing on the landing, she came to the only correct conclusion. Of course this was over a woman. Good heavens, given Chudley's age, Langley must have been in short pants when the slight occurred.

Not that it wasn't an impossible notion. No one who knew Langley would put it past the baron to have been charming women even back then. Rakish devil.

Good thing he'd never had sons, only daughters.

His daughters . . . Minerva's heart pattered slightly as she thought of the letters in his jacket, faded and worn, and obviously so very dear to him.

Dear Papa . . .

Whatever he was in life, there was no denying his daughters were devoted to him and he loved them with all his heart.

Thank goodness he'd never had sons.

Then for the life of her she couldn't help but see a pair of lads—tawny like their father and just as charming. Tall and strong, with blue eyes alight with mischief and delight as they came running across a wide meadow dotted with snowdrops in bloom, each racing the other to see who would reach her first.

For the first time in her life, Minerva's heart burned with a longing for a family. To kneel down and hold a child close, ruffle his hair and inhale deeply, taking in the salty air of a fresh-faced lad—all sweet meadows and trout and horses and the things a mother probably didn't want to know about.

Minerva, who had never desired children, never even been comfortable around them, suddenly ached for nothing more than the safe haven of a home and family. A pair of boys, and the man who stood beside her in her vision . . . a man she could see so clearly with his golden brown hair and blue eyes, desired so deeply . . .

She caught hold of the railing to keep from sinking down atop the step.

She didn't want this . . . a home . . . children . . . a

true husband. No, she knew better. She *couldn't* want this.

The shuffle of boots in the foyer below stopped her wayward thoughts. Thank goodness something had, she mused, until she heard the bits of conversation rising up the stairwell.

"Yes, gentlemen. I do think everything is in order."

Langley! Oh, she had a few things to say to him this morning. After Chudley's challenge, the entire evening had been chaos, and then after his near murder, he'd hustled her and the others into Lord Throssell's carriage, ordered them home and slipped away into the night.

Whenever had he come back? She'd waited up for him, until all hours . . . that is, she 'd tried to wait up for him, but despite her best efforts, she must have eventually drifted off into an exhausted sleep atop her bed, for she'd awakened not that long ago still in her muddied gown.

"Then we are agreed, my lord?" came a deep voice she didn't recognize.

"Yes, two days from now, Primrose Hill at dawn," Langley was saying.

Primrose Hill at dawn? She shivered and then leaned farther over the railing, trying to catch sight of him. This could only mean he meant to go through with this scandal. Wasn't being shot at once already this week enough for the man?

A duel indeed! Over her dead body . . .

Or his, she thought grimly.

"Swilly will stand with me, along with Thomas-William," Langley continued. The boots shuffled again, and then some murmured discussion drifted upward even as the creak of the front door revealed it was being opened.

That was it? Just a few civil words over what was nothing more than politely organized murder?

Well, certainly not in her house.

But by the time Minerva whirled around the landing and hurried down the last flight, the foyer was empty and all she could spy of Langley was his coattails disappearing into the dining room.

"Who were those men?" she demanded when she caught up with him.

Langley had settled back into his chair and was already tucking into a half-eaten breakfast that must have been interrupted by his guests. He didn't get up at her arrival.

Apparently one interruption to his breakfast was enough.

"Chudley's seconds," he said as if merely commenting on the lackluster state of his now cold eggs.

Seconds! Oh, this was madness. Though apparently not to Lord Chudley or her faux betrothed, who sat there calmly, coolly dispatching his morning repast.

"Langley, you cannot do this," she told him, coming around the opposite side of the table and facing him. It made her feel more solid to have the breadth of the table between them. Even if it was as narrow as this one.

"Of course I must. I was challenged."

"Challenged? 'Tis foolery! Nothing more."

"Not to Chudley," he pointed out. "It is a matter of honor."

"You'd do this . . . this murder . . . to appease an old man's honor?"

He looked up at her, his gaze level and straight-forward. "Yes. Actually I would. I would have you know, Lady Standon, that sometimes your honor is all you have in this world."

And he wasn't speaking of Chudley—this she knew right down to the heels of her slippers. And something about the solemn light in his eyes, the calm manner with which he spoke, made her pause, left her unable to breathe.

Honor. She'd lived without that notion her entire life, and yet here was a man who would hold onto it with both hands, valued it above all else, wore it as proudly as others wore a perfectly cut coat.

But still, the end results of holding onto something as ethereal as honor . . . She closed her eyes for a moment trying to blot out the vision of either man—or both—lying atop Primrose Hill in a pool of their own blood.

"Please, Langley—"

"I like that," he said softly.

Minerva paused. "Like what?" She could hardly see what there was to like about a discussion of him being shot at.

"I like it when you call me Langley," he confessed, smiling at her. "It is quite endearing."

"I would never be so informal," she said, realizing that indeed she was being so utterly intimate with him. She'd been calling him that ever since . . .

Last night in the carriage. Her gaze flew up and she found him smiling wickedly at her as if he too was thinking the very same thing. Recalling their inter-lude with some delight, if that wretched grin of his was any indication.

"I won't make that mistake again," she informed

him, not sure if she was speaking of her use of his name or their encounter in the carriage.

"We are betrothed," he reminded her. "And you are a widow. Both are perfectly acceptable."

"We are not," she corrected. "Betrothed," she added hastily. They had gone right past acceptable and respectable last night.

"But no else knows that." Then he reached for another piece of toast from the rack and began to butter it. After he was finished, he glanced up at her, obviously not willing to continue until she agreed.

"Lord Langley—"

"Tut tut," he said, shaking a piece of toast at her.

"Langley, then," she ground out. "Please . . . please, don't do this. You promised me you wouldn't compromise my reputation if we went forward with our agreement—"

"And thus far I have kept my part." Then he paused, tipped his head and studied her. "Have you kept yours, my lady?"

That piercing gaze of his went straight to her heart.

"No other men?" he prodded.

"No!" she sputtered. "When would I have—"

And her words abruptly came to a halt as she recalled her meeting with Adlington. How could she have forgotten it?

While she might, not so Langley. He must have seen her with Gerald and . . .

Minerva straightened. Not that there had been anything to see. Besides, Langley couldn't have noticed her situation with Adlington; he'd been too busy with Chudley.

Which meant he was bluffing.

"There is no other man in my life," she asserted.

"That is good news," he said, letting up his scrutiny. "I'll have you know I am the jealous sort."

"Truly? Will it matter much when you are dead?"

He grinned at this. "Worried for my safety?"

"Not in the least," she said, pacing a bit. She stopped and whirled around, shaking a finger at him. "But if you die up there, I'll be the one left to live with the scandal."

"I can hardly be held accountable for Chudley's challenge, or that he had to make it in the middle of Drury-Lane Theatre."

She pressed her lips together. He did have her there. Still . . . "And why was such a challenge necessary?"

He waved her off and dug back into his breakfast.

"Langley!" Minerva reached across the table and pulled his plate away.

He tossed down his napkin. "If you must know—"

"I must."

"Good God, woman, it was fifteen years ago, is this truly necessary?" He reached for the teapot, and in a quick motion she pushed it out of his reach.

Taking a deep breath, he sat back in his chair, arms folded over his chest. "I was posted in Naples at the time, and Chudley and his wife—not your aunt, his second wife—were there. She was a foolish young thing and she flirted shamelessly with any and every man at court."

"Including you?"

"Yes, including me," he said, shaking his head. "Then one night Chudley spied his errant wife with a man out in the gardens, but he couldn't see who it was. So when he demanded she name her paramour, rather than reveal her lover's name, she said it was me."

"Whyever would she do that?" Minerva asked.

"Because, if you must know—"

"I must—"

"I had rebuffed her on more than one occasion and she was a petty bit of muslin." He raked his hand through his hair and then shook his head as if trying to discard the memory. "I wasn't interested in her. Besides, any man would have been a demmed fool to dally with her, given Chudley's reputation with pistols."

"Was there a reason you rebuffed her?"

He blew out an exasperated breath. "Contrary to the common gossip you seem to ascribe so much value to, I have not bedded every woman I've met. Besides, she wasn't my sort. A more foolish and vain chit never lived." He paused, then leaned over and fetched his plate back. "Vain I don't mind, but I've never suffered a foolish woman." He dug back into his breakfast defiantly, as if challenging her to refute his version of the events.

Minerva took a step back and considered what he'd said. And then she glanced upward and considered his former paramours, all still soundly asleep upstairs. Oh, they were all vain creatures, but as he said, not one of them was a fool. Calculating, yes. Devious, definitely. But foolish? Not in the least.

And neither was she. For like his honor, she knew he was telling the truth. She didn't know how or why, but she would have staked her honor on it.

What little she possessed.

"To avoid a huge scandal," he said, continuing the

story, "I was hastily reposted to Paris—not to mention, peace had broken out and the Foreign Office wanted to take advantage of the moment to gather every bit of intelligence on Napoleon that they could muster. Thus, Chudley's insult and challenge have lay lingering all this time—though I have to admit, I'd all but forgotten about it, at least until yesterday."

Minerva sighed, completely exasperated over the entire situation. A fifteen-year-old peccadillo? Oh, she'd never understand men.

She pulled out her chair and sank down into it, unwilling to even think of the consequences of such a rash act.

"You don't believe me," he said, having mistaken her dismay. And if she didn't know better, sounding quite affronted.

She glanced up at him, took in his furrowed brow, the indignation. "Actually, I do, that is what has me in a mare's nest."

This took him aback, his eyes widening as if he was seeing her for the first time. "You believe me?"

Minerva nodded, then reached for the teapot and poured him a cup, as well as one for herself. It wasn't steaming as it ought and it had brewed too long, but then again that seemed to be par for the course at the moment.

"Why?" he asked quietly as he cradled his cup in his hands.

"I don't know," she confessed, unwilling at first to look at him. But then she willed her gaze to meet his. "But I do."

And inside her heart, those words took on an entirely different meaning.

* * *

Langley didn't know what was more disconcerting—having Lady Standon's conviction in his favor or the way his heart beat faster as she gazed steadily at him. Not just faster, but actually thudded and pounded as if applauding.

For it couldn't be something else. Certainly not *that*.

He knew he should say something, but what you said to a lady when your heart went on some errant course of its own, he knew not.

For whatever he was going to say to her, he knew he had to damn well mean it.

"Minerva, I—"

His confession came to an abrupt halt as the front doorbell jangled. Not just the usual rattle, the poor thing sounded as if it was being yanked off the hanger.

They shared a glance that said the same thing. *Aunt Bedelia.*

Most likely having spent the night unsuccessfully bullying her husband to give up his folly, she had now come to Brook Street to continue her tirade.

As the bell tolled again, Langley bolted to his feet. Given what he knew of Lady Chudley, he assumed he wouldn't get a third warning. "That is my signal to leave."

"Leave?" Minerva protested, getting to her feet as well. "You can't just abandon me to her."

And just as he predicted, the front door banged open. *"Where is he?"*

They both glanced at the door. "'Tis your relation, my lady, not mine," he said in the way of an apology.

Minerva stepped into his path. "What does it say

about your precious honor that you flee in the face of my aunt?"

"That my honor isn't always what it should be," he teased, before he leaned forward and, staring at her lips, half considered putting a kiss on them. But he stopped just short and said, "Alas, I promised."

His near kiss was enough to distract Minerva, and he dodged around her and escaped down the hall toward the kitchen even as Lady Chudley rounded the corner.

He continued apace down the back stairs to the kitchen and had planned to cut through Mrs. Hutchinson's domain, then depart using the servant steps that led up to Brook Street, but what he spied in the kitchen halted his escape.

For there sat Mrs. Hutchinson, Thomas-William, and one of Lord Andrew's urchins, all on stools beside the lift that carried plates to the dining room.

"What the devil—" he began.

"Sssh!" Mrs. Hutchinson said, finger on her lips. "The next round is about to start."

As he drew closer, he could clearly hear Lady Chudley saying, "This is ruinous, Minerva! You must put an end to this nonsense!"

Egads, the shaft between the walls conducted conversations perfectly down to the kitchen for all to hear.

Why this was the worst sort of eavesdropping!

But before there was anything more from above, the incorrigible housekeeper leaned over to Thomas-William and nudged him in the ribs. "Owe me two bob, you do. Told you himself would be down here in a thrice when that caterwauling mort arrived."

For his part, Thomas-William shot Langley a scathing glance, not that much different from the one Lady Standon had sent him when he'd gotten to his feet to flee.

"My lord," the boy began, "Lord Andrew sent me with the carriage—"

"Sssh," both he and Mrs. Hutchinson directed at the lad.

"But I am supposed to—" the boy persisted, but stopped when he realized no one was listening to him. Huffing a sigh, he sat back on his stool and shook his head.

Not that Langley really noticed, for down from above came Lady Standon's strained voice, "I hardly see what I can do—"

"What you can do?" Lady Chudley clamored. "I'll tell you what you can do—"

"A slight delay in our plans," Langley whispered to the lad. And having not a single bit of honor when it came to such practices, and every measure of his wits, Langley pulled up a stool and settled in like the veriest tabby.

"I will have him arrested," Aunt Bedelia declared, still standing at the head of the table like she was presiding over the House of Lords.

"Who? Lord Chudley?" Minerva asked as she gave up and sat down, pushing Langley's deserted plate aside.

"No, of course not!" the woman sputtered. "That wretched betrothed of yours—he is the cause of all this. Whatever was I thinking giving you my blessing for such a union? The man is a scandal!"

"A scandal? He wasn't the one who issued some

foolhardy challenge in the middle of Drury-Lane Theatre!" Minerva shot back, wondering at her own vehemence.

Good gracious heavens, she was defending Langley.

"And why shouldn't Chudley have issued his challenge? Granted, he is a bit of a hothead when provoked—though usually he roars in that manner in more private moments." Aunt Bedelia sat down and pulled out her handkerchief, fanning herself a bit.

Minerva's gaze shot up to her aunt. Had she just heard the lady correctly? Oh, if the blush on the older woman's face was any indication, she had.

And wished she hadn't.

"Please, Aunt Bedelia, let us not fight over the hows and whys of this mess." *And please no more intimate details about your marriage to Chudley. It is going to take a month of Sundays to get the image of Chudley roaring through your bedchamber scrubbed from my mind.* "Let us work together to discover a solution to all this."

"Find a solution to what, darling?" Tasha said as she sauntered into the dining room, glancing at the sideboard and taking naught but a piece of toast.

"The duel," Lucia chimed in, coming in behind the Russian princess. She fluttered her hand at Minerva. "You English are so odd—always ready to argue—but also so ready to condemn a sensible solution." She sighed and took a plate as well.

"A duel is a wonderful moment for a man," Helga said, having come in behind Lucia. "The honesty, the bravery, the courage. Never fear, my *schatzi* will put a bullet through that old goat and be done with him." She snapped her fingers and sat down at the table, glancing around for a servant to fetch her a plate.

"I'll have you know, my good margravine," Aunt Bedelia began, bristling with indignation, "that my Chudley is an excellent marksman and will most likely put your scandalous Langley in an early grave!"

"He can try, darling. He can try," Tasha said, reaching over and patting her hand, as if already offering her condolences. "But as the margravine says, Langley is a devilish rogue. I fear your Chudley has challenged the wrong man."

At this, Brigid came in, Knuddles at the hem of her gown. "But of course Chudley has challenged the wrong man. Whatever did Langley do? Flirt with his wife?" She made an inelegant sort of snort, as if such a thing were trifling and hardly worth the bother. "But I grieve for you, Lady Chudley. I do. For I doubt with your coloring you look all that well in black."

Minerva glanced over at her aunt, who looked ready to give every single one of them a severe wigging, so she stepped into the fray and announced, "There isn't going to be any killing. No need for widow's weeds."

The nannies shared a collective glance and sighed in unison, a sort of unanimous, *Oh, these English.*

Tapping the heel of her slipper down hard, Minerva folded her arms over her chest. "I mean it. There will be no duel. Langley will never go through with this. He promised me he wouldn't drag my name through scandal and he won't."

Tasha shook her head. "If you were worried about scandal, Lady Standon, whyever did you become engaged to the baron?"

"Yes, why did you, Lady Standon?" the margravine echoed.

Minerva found herself as the focal point of the room, with all eyes on her. Even, she suspected, Knuddles. "Well . . . because . . . I would say . . ."

Lucia waved her off. "Say no more. You love him. Of course you do. All women love Langley, rogue that he is."

There were nods all around, save Aunt Bedelia, whose opinion of Minerva's betrothed no longer glistened.

And while she would have liked to correct their assumption—that she was in love with Langley—she just offered a wan little smile. "I don't want to see either man harmed. And neither does my aunt."

"Of course no one wants to see a good man die," Brigid began, "but however do you stop them when they get their blood up?"

Lucia shrugged in agreement at this, ever the Italian.

"Well, if you must stop him—" the margravine began.

"I must," Minerva insisted.

"You could always poison him." Having given up on any hope of a servant, the lady got up and helped herself to a plate full of eggs and sausages. "Ask Brigid for help—she's the expert."

"Poison?" Minerva gasped.

"Not so much to kill him, Lady Standon," Brigid advised, handing down a piece of bacon to her monkey-faced little dog, cooing at him as he snapped it up. "Just enough to keep him down for a day or two."

"If his horse were to go lame, he would not make it in time," Tasha added.

"Hide his pistols," Lucia offered.

"Tie him up," the margravine suggested. When the others glanced at her, she scoffed at them. "As if any of you haven't done as much."

There were shrugs and nods all around, including Aunt Bedelia, and Minerva couldn't believe what she was listening to.

"I still say having the rogue arrested is the best choice. Lock him up in Newgate and throw away the key," Aunt Bedelia avowed.

"On what charges, my lady?" Tasha asked. "You English so adore your charges. Is it against the law to find a lady interesting? When Langley finds a lady charming, nothing can divert him."

"Yes, yes, that is it," Lucia agreed. "Lady Standon, Lady Chudley, you have naught to do but to keep your gentlemen diverted until the appointed time has passed." She smiled wickedly.

Minerva thought her aunt would be outraged, but to her shock her aunt's eyes widened with relief. "Yes, yes, that is the perfect idea. I shall keep my husband delightfully entertained and so exhausted that he will not be able to rise in the morning."

"I hope he can still rise, darling, for your sake," Tasha teased. "And if you do the same, Lady Standon, Langley will be well occupied as well."

Once again Minerva found herself the center of attention. "I cannot do that!"

"Whyever not?" came the chorus of protest.

"We are not yet married." She looked around the room waiting for the respectable support she would expect. Except she was prattling on to the wrong crowd. "We can hardly—"

Oh, it was no use, they all looked at her as if she had grown a second head.

"Minerva, you have always led a proper and respectable life——" Aunt Bedelia began.

Well, thank goodness there was one voice of reason in the room. Seducing Langley indeed! As scandalous as dueling. For hadn't last night in the carriage nearly been her undoing?

But Minerva was in for a shock.

"My good niece, this is no time for propriety. We have a grievous situation. One that warrants extraordinary mettle," Aunt Bedelia said, her voice ringing with conviction. "You must do everything in your power to lure that man into your bed and keep him there!"

Down in the kitchen, Lady Chudley's demand was met with a stunned silence.

Then Thomas-William leaned over and nudged Mrs. Hutchinson. "Now *you* owe *me* two bob."

Chapter 11

A man manacled to your bed is nothing to be ashamed of.
Advice to Felicity Langley from her Nanny Tasha

This is no time to play the pious widow!" Aunt Bedelia told her niece in no uncertain terms. "You must take that man to your bed."

Actually, Minerva thought it a perfect time to play the pious widow and run for the nearest nunnery.

"And why wouldn't you want to have Langley close?" Nanny Helga asked in that coy manner of hers. "You are, after all, madly in love with him, are you not?"

With all eyes on her, waiting for her to either declare her love or her engagement a hoax, as most of them suspected it to be, Minerva instead bolted to her feet, filled with a sudden urge to flee.

And as it was, Providence concurred with her sudden spate of cowardice, offering her the perfect excuse to do just that. For there, out the window, she spied the retreating figure of Lord Langley, along with Thomas-William and a young lad, ambling down the garden path toward the mews, where, much to her chagrin, a carriage awaited them.

Oh, damn that man! she silently cursed. He truly thought he could slip away and leave her to all this scandal? Not to mention, they hadn't finished their conversation about the duel or that "robbery" last night.

Robbery, indeed. She'd wager the Sterling diamonds that it hadn't been a mere robbery. But she'd get no answers to any of it if she let him slip away.

"Excuse me, Auntie," she said. "I just remembered I promised Lord Langley I would accompany him on an errand." She nodded politely to the others. "Ladies, if you will excuse me." Pleasantries aside, she dashed from the room, ignoring the round of questions and complaints that followed her.

Up the stairs she went to catch up her bonnet, pelisse, and gloves, and then raced down the back stairs to avoid a second chorus of queries from the dining room. At the back door, she nearly collided with Mrs. Hutchinson, who was coming up from the kitchen lugging a basket.

"Oh, my lady! Are you going as well?" the housekeeper huffed. "For I would have packed more if I'd known you were off to the country with himself."

Off to the country? Damn that Langley! Jaunting off and leaving her behind to deal with . . . well, everything.

"It is no matter, Mrs. Hutchinson," Minerva said, catching up the handle and going out the door. "I'm quite sure Lord Langley won't mind sharing with me. Not in the least."

The lady answered as honestly as she always did. She snorted loudly and then chuckled her way back down to her kitchen lair as if she knew Lord Langley wouldn't like Minerva's arrival into his plans.

Not in the least.

Minerva smiled to herself, but didn't waste another moment, hurrying out the back door and down the garden path. Langley was just settling into the seat of a plain curricle when she caught hold of the railing and pulled herself up and in beside him. "What a pleasant surprise, my lord. Mrs. Hutchinson says we are off for a ride in the country." She smiled at him and settled her hand on his sleeve. "How odd I didn't get the news until it was nearly too late to join you. But here I am. Happily, we are in this adventure together. Isn't that so?"

Langley glanced up at Thomas-William, who sat in the driver's seat. The older man offered no help, just a shrug that tossed this problem back into Langley's lap.

"Lady Standon, get out of the carriage," he ordered.

Thomas-William winced.

"No," the lady said, in a tone that suggested she wasn't about to brook any objections.

In the tiger's seat, Grady, one of Andrew's lads, cheeky little fellow that he was, let out a low whistle, like a warning.

Beside him, Langley found Lady Standon not only settled in but, having tied her bonnet on, was even now inspecting the basket she'd brought, no doubt packed by Mrs. Hutchinson. When she plucked out a scone, she turned to Grady. "Have you had anything to eat this morning, child?"

"No, milady," the boy whispered, awed to be so addressed.

She handed over the tasty morsel and smiled at the lad, conquering his stomach and heart in one fell swoop. "Scone, my lord?" she offered him.

"I will not be bribed with scones. Not even Mrs. Hutchinson's. Now get out."

"No, thank you." She settled deeper into the seat. "Where are we off to this morning? Mrs. Hutchinson said something about the country."

Before he could reply—which he wasn't going to—Grady piped up from the back, "To Langley House, ma'am."

This time, Thomas-William let out a loud guffaw, for the man knew, as did Langley, that now there would be no stopping Lady Standon from coming along. For if they did toss her out, she'd just follow.

Langley shot a black glare over his shoulder at Grady, but the boy was too happily eating his treat to notice. Instead, he made a note to himself to speak to Lord Andrew about feeding his brats more so they weren't susceptible to bribes with scones . . . or a pretty face.

"Lovely day to show me my new home," Minerva was saying. "You do delight in surprising me, Lord Langley, don't you?"

"Your new wha-a-a-t?" He tried to make sense of what was happening, but even as he stammered out his dismay, she waved her hand toward Thomas-William, a sort of by-your-leave gesture. One the other man wasn't going to argue about, for much to Langley's dismay, the man picked up the reins and had the horses off and down the mews, driving with a steady, capable hand.

Oh, it wasn't as simple as that, Langley vowed. Reaching forward, he caught the reins and pulled the horses to a stop. "You are not going, Lady Standon."

"Langley, like it or not, I can be of use to you. You determined that when you proposed this engagement of ours. You wouldn't have offered it if it didn't help whatever cause it is you have embroiled yourself in."

"Lady Standon, this is hardly the time or the place—"

She wasn't done yet. "I can be of use to you. I proved that last night. If I hadn't seen that child's warning, you would be lying in the parlor with candles around your body and that circus of doxies you've got installed in my house wailing in mourning."

"I don't think they'd be wailing—" he began to point out. He doubted the margravine could even work up a plausible case of tears.

"Last night aside, if you think you can leave me home in that house—having to face callers and listen to the advice of those nannies—I will shoot you myself and save Chudley the trouble." She folded her arms over her chest and stared at him, as if daring him to contradict her. "I still have Thomas-William's pistol."

"Aye, she does," Thomas-William concurred. Well, he needn't grin when he did.

"Please, Langley, let me be of some use," she pleaded. "Even if I am naught but an outward distraction as to the true purpose of this outing."

Langley set his teeth together. She was right on all counts. And he could see now why she had never remarried—she was probably sharper and more astute than half the bachelors in London put together.

Still, he shook his head, but before he could explain his reasons, or more to the point, think of some reasonable ones, she continued blithely on. "If anything, my presence gives this jaunt a far more respectable air than the three of you sneaking off on whatever nefarious business you have up your sleeves. So if anything, I would say my addition to your party is fortuitous. Especially if you plan on being shot at again. I daresay I will make every attempt to save your life again, but please, my lord, don't expect me to make it a habit. I quite ruined my gown last night."

There was another whistle from the tiger's seat, and this time Langley turned and glared at Grady. "Listen well, you little kinchin cove," he said, "I can put you out as well."

The boy gave him the same sort of look Minerva had. The one that said, *You can try.*

For she had him dead to rights. Having her in the carriage iced their journey with a sweet coating of innocence.

That, and he wouldn't put it past her to go fetch the pistol, if only to further her point.

"Oh, demmit," Langley muttered, letting go of the reins and throwing himself back in his seat. "I am getting too old for all this," he muttered, but said nothing further, realizing that setting them both out would cause more gossip than leaving them in. As it was, it was exactly as Minerva had said, that it would appear to anyone watching him—and he was positive someone was—he was out for an early morning carriage ride with his betrothed.

Taking this as a sign of defeat, Thomas-William clicked his tongue at the horses and they once again began to trot down the empty street.

"You are getting too old for all this," Minerva agreed as they came up to Grosvenor Square and she said to Thomas-William, "You will want to turn on Oxford Street." So she even knew the way. Why was he surprised? "Now Langley, at your age—"

"At my age?" He straightened up. "How old do you think I am?"

Lady Standon shook her head and glanced down at the buttons on her gloves. "I know how old you are."

"Been checking up on me?"

To this she sent him a scathing glance. "Wouldn't you?"

"Perhaps I should do the same with you, Lady Standon."

"Whatever do you mean?"

"Do some checking up on you," he said. "And the company you keep."

She flinched a bit before she bluffed and said, "Be my guest."

Oh, he would, once he got done with his own troubles, but he wasn't going to tell her that. Instead, he wrapped his coat up around his neck and leaned against the wall, closing his eyes.

"Langley, what are you doing?" she asked, nudging him.

He opened one eye and looked at her. "Trying to get some rest." With that said, he closed it and nestled deeper into the corner.

"Has Thomas-William been to your house before?"

"No." He didn't bother to open an eye this time.

"Does he know the way?"

He could hear the rising annoyance in her voice and didn't feel like abating it. "No."

"Then how are we supposed to get there?"

This time he opened both eyes. "You seem to be quite informed as to my business—you direct him, my lady."

Instead of an argument, she nodded and leaned forward to give the man directions. "Take the Blackfriars Bridge, then make your way to the Kent Road—"

"Westminster is closer," he offered without thinking.

"I thought you were sleeping," she said, arms crossing over her chest. "Certainly, Blackfriars is a more direct—"

"Westminster, Lady Standon, or you can get out."

"Well, then," she huffed, "Westminster it is, Thomas-William. But if Lord Langley gets us lost, he's the one getting out to ask for directions."

"Lord Langley," came a soft voice, nudging him out of a deep sleep. After a night spent searching for Nottage, he was exhausted and still too tired to be roused quickly—not that he could avoid it. Lady Standon finished her task with a heavier jab to his ribs and a stern order, "Wake up. We've come to a village, and I don't think you want me to call a lot of attention to our arrival by announcing ourselves at the local inn."

Langley opened his eyes and straightened, glancing around to get his bearings. For indeed they were in the village near his ancestral home, at the crossroads that would lead one on to Croydon or across the green hills to Langley House.

And she certainly had the right of it. He didn't want to call attention to his arrival. The prodigal son as it were.

"Lady Standon, are you always so astute?"

"I've learned to be," she replied.

Once again there was that mysterious, wistful note to her words, the one that said there was more behind her confession, but just as he wasn't quite willing to reveal his true intentions, he didn't think he had the right to press her.

He stretched again, this time coming fully awake, and found the carriage sitting atop the hill that looked down on the pretty little green valley where his family had lived for generations. In the middle sat a familiar, good-sized manor house, done in brick with three great chimneys rising from a steep gabled roof.

"Is that Langley House?" she asked.

"Aye," he said, feeling a bit of awe and trepidation. Home. He'd traveled halfway round the world and back only to stand here and feel as awed as he had in the Sultan's palace. No glittering gold, no towering minarets, just the green grass and tall oaks that called to his very roots.

"It's a lovely place," she mused.

"It is," he said, shaking his head for a moment, as if he didn't quite recognize it. Behind them, Grady slept, curled up in the tiger's seat, Minerva having at some point put the lap robe over him.

At least he assumed it was Minerva.

She turned in her seat and smiled. "How long has it been since you were here?" she said in a soft voice, so as not to wake the boy.

Langley sighed. "Since I joined the Foreign Office."

Minerva's mouth fell open. "So long?"

"Yes, so long," he said, nodding to Thomas-William, who turned the carriage down the drive. "My father and I quarreled and . . . well . . ."

"I take it he didn't approve of your choice of professions," she said, her gaze scanning the well-manicured lawns and the line of pretty trees coming into view.

"My father rarely approved of anything I did," he told her. Farther along, the pond sparkled with dappled sunlight, and there were children by its edge, fishing poles in hand and their laughter a sweet greeting.

The pond! Good God, he had all but forgotten about the pond. It had been one of his favorite places as a child. One of many, he now recalled. How ever could he have forgotten it?

"My father loved this place, and all I could ever see was the horizon beyond it."

"That isn't all that unusual," she said, her gaze sweeping over the meadows and the graceful trees.

"He said someday I would come home and regret ever leaving."

She murmured something, perhaps her own remembrance of a place lost. "Do you?" she said after some time.

"Yes . . . I mean to say, no," he corrected. "Oh, bother, I don't know."

"Don't fret over it. You can't get back the time you've lived, and all you have is what is before you," she said sagely.

"Egads, I find myself betrothed to a bluestocking," he teased. "Who was that, Aristotle?"

She laughed. "No, Aunt Bedelia."

Then they both laughed, as did Thomas-William.

Now they had dropped down from the hill and were coming up the main drive where it curved through the lawn. Minerva was leaning over the edge and smiling.

When the lady did, her entire face lit up from its usually staid expression. There was something almost magical about seeing her so.

"What is making you grin?"

"The snowdrops—such pretty little things." She waved at the white blossoms blooming in happy clumps throughout the lawn. "It is so odd, because just this morning I was thinking of just these flowers."

"And now you find them," he said, glancing over them, but not feeling the same joy, rather a sort of melancholy.

"Have they always been here?"

"Yes. At least as long as I can remember. My mother loved them. She paid the local children to dig them and divide them and then let them plant them wherever their fancy took them." He tapped Thomas-William on the shoulder and the man stopped the carriage. Langley climbed down and held out his hand to Minerva.

She hesitated for a moment, but then slipped her fingers into his and came with him. He waved at Thomas-William to drive on, and they set off along an ambling path that cut across the lawn. He reached down and plucked a handful of the flowers for her, and like the orange blossoms last night, she accepted them with a bit of a blush on her cheeks.

"She liked to scatter hope," Minerva said, taking his offering.

"Pardon?"

"Snowdrops. They represent hope. The first flowers in the spring. Hope for a new beginning." She took a sniff of the delicate blossoms and then shyly glanced over at him. "Perhaps you were meant to be here today. To find your hope."

He arched one brow. "Lady Standon, you harbor an Eastern philosopher beneath that very English exterior of yours."

Minerva laughed. "Don't let Aunt Bedelia hear you say that. She'll accuse you of corrupting me utterly."

It was almost on the tip of his tongue to ask who was the worse corrupter, he with his high praise, or her aunt urging her to take him to his bed.

But then he'd have to confess to eavesdropping, which he suspected she certainly wouldn't approve of.

"Langley, why are we really here?" she mused, having taken a deep sniff of her flowers.

"My dear Lady Standon, we are here to visit with my tenants, the Harrows, nothing more." He glanced ahead at the house as it came fully into view.

"Minerva," she said, also looking straight ahead at the house, still blushing from his offering or at her own boldness.

"Pardon?"

"Minerva. I would rather you call me Minerva. Lady Standon sounds so terribly formal."

"If that is what you wish," he said, bowing his head in acquiescence.

After a rather too long moment of silence, she glanced over at him.

"Yes? Is there something more?" he asked.

"Aren't you going to offer me the same courtesy?"

"What courtesy?"

"To call you by your given name, Ellis."

"Absolutely not," he avowed, shaking his head. He'd never liked his name, the moniker of some great uncle who'd been a renowned scholar and theologian.

"Whyever not?" she persisted.

He pulled to a stop, for not far ahead came a man carrying a handful of fishing poles.

"Langley! Whyever won't you let me call you by your given name?"

He turned and faced her, his hand coming to cup her chin. "Because my dear, lovely Minvera, I prefer it when you call me Langley, as you just did. It sounds as if you can't decide whether you want to box my ears or kiss me." He leaned closer, right up to her ear, so close that his breath whispered over her, "And because I like seeing you puzzle out which desire will win."

Then he had the audacity to give her a cheeky wink, and before she could utter another exasperated "Langley," he turned to the man approaching them.

"Hello, there. It has been a long time, Mr. Harrow!" He extended his hand and shook Harrow's with vigor. "And most excellent to see you in such good health. I hope you don't mind my intrusion, but I was in the neighborhood—"

"Mind? But of course not! This is your home," Mr. Harrow said, nodding toward the house. "And you look in good health as well, my lord. All those rumors about your demise. Me and Mrs. Harrow never believed a word of them!"

Langley glanced over at him as they crossed the yard and headed toward the stairs. "You didn't?"

The man waved a hand at the notion. "No! Why would I when your boxes kept coming just as regular as ever?"

It was only after an hour or more of pleasantries, a round of visits and happy greetings from the servants—for word of Lord Langley's return ran through the house and out into the gardens like wild fire. Then there was tea and refreshments served by Mrs. Harrow, dozens of questions posed by the younger Harrows—who had heard of the legendary Baron Langley and his travels from grand tales told by the servants—and a full report by Mr. Harrow as to the well-being of the tenants and the estate, before Langley finally got to the point of his visit.

For ever since Harrow said that Langley's boxes had never stopped arriving, he'd been in an impatient state of nerves.

They'd kept coming? How could that have been when he'd been in Abbaye Prison all that time?

"As you mentioned, I've had regular shipments of crates sent here—" Langley began.

"Yes, of course," Harrow said eagerly. "And as you instructed, we've stored them in the attic. Save the boxes you asked I send on to your friend in Hampstead."

"Aye, about those—" Langley began.

"Poor Mr. Ellyson," Mrs. Harrow said, passing a plate of biscuits to Minerva. "I am sure you heard of his passing."

Langley paused. "Yes, I did. And I had hoped—"

Mr. Harrow nodded. "I was just about to send off some of your collections to him when Mrs. Harrow noticed a line in the paper about his passing."

"My sister sends me the papers from Town," she explained to Minerva.

"So we kept it safe for you—"

"It's here?" Langley blurted out, losing his characteristic debonair manner of cool disdain.

Even Minerva gaped at him.

But how could she know what this might mean? His last box to George? All his hopes.

Langley tried to tamp down his rising cheer. This was better than he could have imagined. Still, he reined in his passions and said with a more detached air, "Would you mind if I were to look through it . . . and the others as well?" He paused for a second. "There is a particular piece I would like to retrieve as a wedding present for my bride. And then we will bother you no further and be on our way."

At this point he reached over and caught Minerva's hand, and to his amazement, she played her part of surprised and grateful fiancée with amazing believability, by smiling graciously at him.

Mr. Harrow glanced over at his wife and then back at the baron. "You aren't here to inspect the house?"

"Well, if you would like me to—"

"You aren't here to show Lady Standon the residence?" Mrs. Harrow asked.

"You haven't come to put us out?" one of the younger lads ventured.

Langley glanced at Mrs. Harrow's strained face and realized that for all their happy manners, beneath their hospitality was a greater worry.

That they were, as the younger Harrow had said, about to be put out of the house.

It was, to his amazement, Minerva who put the lady at ease.

"Mrs. Harrow, you haven't anything to worry about on that account. Langley and I wouldn't think of asking you and your happy family to leave Langley Hall. You have a good lease, and from every indication, you are excellent tenants of the estate." She leaned toward the woman and whispered loudly. "Men! They just bluster in and don't understand our fears, do they?"

Both the older Harrows sighed and then Mrs. Harrow smiled warmly. "Oh, but I must warn, my lord," she said. "Your boxes are not all that organized. It is rather a tumble up there."

"Does he mean to go up and look at those shameful paintings and sinful pieces of pottery?" one of the lads piped up.

"Joshua!" Mrs. Harrow scolded, blushing a deep pink.

"But Maman, that is what you called them," he protested. "Before you forbid us from looking at them." The irrepressible boy wasn't done yet. "Lord Langley, did you really steal all those things from ol' Boney?"

Langley wanted to laugh at the curious light in the boy's eyes, for he well remembered when an uncle of his—his mother's brother who'd gone to sea—would come to visit with tales of exploring with Cook. Well-embellished and lacking all the realities of a long sea voyage—the dreadful food, the boredom, the wretched conditions—he'd lived to hear about the odd native customs, the exotic creatures and the strange markings, the sort of tales he could regale his friends with for weeks to come.

"Aye, lad. And if you can find me a bar to open up the boxes with, I'll tell you about the night I snuck into Versailles and snatched them right off ol' Boney's walls."

"Gar!" the boy whispered, wide-eyed and thunderstruck with awe. "Will you also tell me about when you were captured by the sultan and locked in his palace?"

"Oh, aye," he agreed, his arm over the boy's shoulder as they walked out of the room, Minerva and Mrs. Harrow in their wake. "But he didn't lock me in just his palace, but in his harem."

"Langley!" Minerva protested.

And when he turned around to gauge her expression, he found her eyes alight and her lips pressed tightly together—to keep from laughing aloud.

Oh, yes, she'd come to her decision on which she desired more.

And it had nothing to do with boxing his ears.

Minerva looked around the attic space at the line of paintings stacked against the wall, alongside vases and statues lined up all in a row. They were as Mrs. Harrow had told her son, a shameful lot.

Truly, here she had always heard Lord Langley described as a connoisseur, but there was only one word to describe his art collection.

Dreadful.

Langley stood studying his collection, a metal bar in his hand. They were all alone, for though he'd promised to regal the Harrow children with tales, Mrs. Harrow had announced that despite Lord Langley's generous offer—or because of it, Minerva suspected—the children needed to rejoin their nanny in the nursery.

"You won't need that," she told Langley, nodding at the pry bar in his hand. "Apparently young Joshua has made it a habit to enjoy your collection." She nodded at the open boxes and the scattered pieces sitting atop the crates and chests that made up the attic storage.

"Oh, I need it," he said, walking up to a statue of a shepherdess. The painting beneath the glaze was shoddy, leaving the poor miss cross-eyed as she searched for her lost lambs.

But she wasn't so for long.

Suddenly, Langley raised his arm and swung the bar atop the girl's head, shattering the pottery.

"Langley? Are you mad?" Minerva gasped.

Ignoring her, he picked through the shards as if searching for something, and when he found nothing, turned to the nymph beside her and smashed her to smithereens.

Minerva caught his arm. "What are you doing?"

"If you must know," he said as he picked though the pieces, "occasionally, I would send home sensitive information inside pieces of art."

"So you weren't just a diplomat," she said, nudging him for information.

"No, not always," he confessed, already eyeing another statue.

Minerva took another glance around the attic, with a new understanding of what she was looking at. They hadn't been chosen for their beauty or their rarity, and certainly not for their value, rather quite the opposite. "Oh, thank God."

"For what?" he asked as he broke apart a pair of lovers.

"I thought I was marrying a mushroom," she said with a giggle.

"Had visions of the morning room decorated with that lot?" he asked, waving his hand at a line of cross-eyed milkmaids.

"Yes, or worse." She shuddered, picking up one of the paintings. "Dear heavens, this is as bad as the painting hanging in my room."

"Next time I am in your bedchamber, Minerva, I shall have to be the judge of that. I took great pains in choosing pieces no one would covet."

He handed her the bar. "Go ahead. I know you want nothing more than to consign that sea nymph to an untimely end."

"Gads, is every one of these pieces cross-eyed?"

"I fear the man I bought these from used his daughter as his model."

"She wasn't one of your conquests, was she?" Minerva teased, just before she took up the bar and smashed the little piece into bits. She glanced over at the wreckage. "Oh, you are perfectly correct! That is most satisfying. But what am I to look for?"

"In the potteries, it would be a slim piece of paper

that was inserted through the potter's slit in the bottom."

"A piece of curled paper, I imagine," she said as she picked up one of the pieces and peered inside the hole. "For it would unwind along the sides and remain unseen."

Langley paused. "Minerva, you continue to surprise me! I avow you would make a most excellent agent. I would not want to cross paths with you."

"Then keep that in mind when you are tempted to vex me," she teased back. Then she turned serious. "Langley?"

"Um, yes?"

"What do you hope to find?"

"Answers," he replied.

"Nothing more you'd like to share?" she prodded. "It might help me to know what I am searching for."

"Your reputation," he told her with a grin.

"My reputation? Sir, if this collection was to see the light of day, what little standing I have left in society would be in tatters."

"Better that than engaged to a traitor," he said.

"As important as that?" she whispered.

"Aye."

Turning to the rest of the collection, Minerva's determination to help only grew more resolute. "And the paintings? I don't believe smashing them is in order—though probably most satisfying."

"No, we cannot damage them—no more than necessary," he said, reaching into the bag he'd brought up. "We'll need to cut the canvas out of the frames. Some of them have an extra canvas beneath, and others might have a note or writings on the interior of the frames. We'll have to take extra care with those."

"Too bad," she mused as she held up a poorly composed pair of lovers. "Good heavens, is that a third arm on that poor woman?"

He glanced at the painting. "If that fellow is lucky."

Langley's optimism evaporated over the next few hours, as they discovered their search was in vain.

While he found the box that had been intended for George Ellyson, it also appeared that someone had beaten him to the contents, for there wasn't a note to be had, not a single clue inside.

Only more questions.

And the boxes, the ones that arrived after he'd been confined in Abbaye Prison, held nothing but more conundrums.

"It appears that this crate had a rather rough voyage," Minerva speculated as they gazed in at the ruined contents. She pulled one of the paintings out, a small landscape of a ruined castle. When she turned it over, her brow wrinkled and she handed it to him.

The frame had been oddly hollowed out, a narrow trough inside the sturdy wood.

"What is that?" Minerva reached inside and pulled out a bit of black velvet. She studied the frame closer. "It looks like there was velvet all along that groove. There are bits of it stuck in the wood."

He shook his head and put it back down in the crate. None of it made sense, and worse, it appeared he wasn't going to find any answers here.

So they made their way downstairs, thanked the Harrows for their hospitality, and returned to the carriage.

"Langley, what does this mean?" Minerva asked

after they climbed in, having finally gained some distance from the Harrows.

Thomas-William glanced over his shoulder, most likely about to ask the same thing.

Langley shook his head at his old friend and then turned to Minerva. "It means I have to go back to the beginning."

Thomas-William muttered a curse and started the horses toward London.

"Is it as bad as all that?" she asked.

He tried to smile for her sake. "It means you are most likely engaged to a traitor."

To his surprise, she scoffed at such a thing. "Really, Langley. It hardly concerned me before, what makes you think I would change my mind now?"

Chapter 12

*Sometimes there is naught you can do for a man, save
stand silently beside him and believe.*

Advice to Felicity Langley from her Nanny Rana

They returned to Brook Street well after dark,
and Langley let her out and escorted her to the
door.

But he hadn't come in with her. He silently sent
her inside and then disappeared into the night.

Minerva spent much of the next day pacing about
the house and peering out the windows, watching
the crowds on Brook Street and the comings and
goings of the servants in the mews behind the house
in hopes of catching a glance of him.

Demmed man! Oh, she knew marchionesses were
not supposed to use such words, or even know of
them, but right now being Lady Standon was far too
confining.

If she were mere Maggie Owens, perhaps then Langley wouldn't be so reluctant to let her help.

And in her worried state, she even thought she'd spied the little flower girl from the theatre, milling about the lamppost across the way. Madly, she'd rushed outside to catch the child, for as impossible as it seemed, she suspected the urchin was somehow connected to the mystery behind Lord Langley's return to London.

But when she flung the front door open, the girl caught up her basket of flowers and took off like a rabbit through the pedestrians, disappearing before Minerva could even cry out.

And when Minerva realized that everyone on the street was gaping at her, she'd beat an equally hasty retreat back inside her house.

Not that the inside offered much in the way of sanctuary. Her address was suddenly the most sought after one in London.

She'd never realized how many gossipy tabbies lived in Town, for suddenly there was a cream-lined trail leading straight to her door. No matter that it wasn't her afternoon in, the curious and the gossips called anyway, delivering their cards to a vexed Mrs. Hutchinson in hopes that "Lady Standon might like some sympathetic company."

Sympathetic, indeed! She'd instructed her housekeeper to send them all packing. There were some consolations in having a housekeeper who had been raised in Seven Dials. No one could get rid of unwanted guests better than Mrs. Hutchinson—save of course the foreign sorts who just moved in.

According to Aunt Bedelia, who had called in the

afternoon, even those who weren't at the Drury-Lane Theatre the night before had their own rendition of Chudley's dramatic challenge and Lord Langley's scandalous acceptance.

"Why I hardly knew London had such a collection of tattle tongues," she avowed. "They are savaging my poor Chudley and ruining my standing! Such behavior! Such rash displays of ill-manners! What is society coming to when demure respectability is no longer the order of the day?"

Thus speaks the woman who not a day earlier ordered me to seduce my betrothed, Minerva had mused silently. Nor was she moved by her aunt's plight, for Lady Chudley had been Society's leading gossip for more than thirty years. But it was obviously a bitter broth for Bedelia to swallow, especially now that she was on the other side of the spoon, so to say.

But the day had passed, and now it was well after midnight, and Minerva had more pressing concerns than the maelstrom of gossip and scandal swirling around her. Glancing out the window of her bedroom, she willed the darkness to reveal the one thing she wanted to know above all else.

Where the devil was Langley? And Thomas-William as well?

Whatever were those two up to?

Not that she cared, she tried telling herself. She didn't. Not in the least.

Oh, but she did. And she could help, if only he'd let her.

Then perhaps he'd help you . . .

Pushing away from the window, she snuffed out her candle and flounced down on her bed, a thin shaft of moonlight streaming through the gap in the parted curtains.

No, she couldn't ask Langley for help. The man had enough worries not be saddled with her poor problems.

Treason . . . She shook her head at the evil implications that word held, but she also suspected the answers could be found with the clues at hand . . . *the grooves in the frame . . . the bits of black velvet . . . the nannies arrival . . . Langley's hidden intelligence shipments.*

Minerva sat up as the parts came together.

It was obvious that someone had learned of his means of sending intelligence home to England and then used the same devious channel for their gains, leaving Langley's reputation to be sullied. And when he returned, they had tried to kill him.

Minerva shook her head. Oh, it was all too far-fetched. Wasn't it? Aunt Bedelia would say she'd been reading too many novels of late, but still . . .

Oh, if only Langley would come home and tell her he had finished the wretched business once and for all. Then they could . . .

They could what?

She rolled over and punched her pillow. However had this happened? This . . . this anxious, devilish concern.

No, concern wasn't the right word. Concern was what you felt when a friend fell ill. Concern was something you wallowed in when your quarterly accounts ran over.

This ache in her chest, this trembling in her limbs, was something altogether different.

Yet how had it happened? And even as she searched her memories of the past few days, it was that wretched vision from the other morning that continued to haunt her.

The pair of boys, with Langley at her side, a life that could be hers if only she would . . . if she dared . . .

Risk her heart.

Minerva shook her head. Oh, no, that would never do. Trust her heart? Look where it had gotten her the last time. She'd trusted Gerald Adlington and he'd betrayed her by marrying her sister in hopes of gaining an heiress's fortune.

"It isn't just that," she whispered, thinking of that meadow, the white drifts of snowdrops blooming in haphazard clumps. It wasn't just the pair of mischievous lads.

But something else.

For Langley's confession that sometimes all a man had was his honor had prodded her about her very dishonorable existence.

Honor.

For that had to be why Langley was lurking about London in some secretive attempt to clear his name.

To regain his honor.

There is nothing to regain, she would have told him. No, he had more honor than any other man she'd ever met.

And that called to her. So very deeply. How she longed to live free of her own deceptions. The lie that had imprisoned her as Minerva Sterling. Kept her living in the strictest confines for fear someone would see the truth: She was no lady.

Mayhap if she could help Langley, restore his name, then that would redeem hers . . . for there would be no stopping Adlington, not until he was placated or finished off.

For a moment she lay atop her bed in silence, the entire house asleep around her, nothing stirring, not even a crackle from the coals in the hearth.

The vastness and the emptiness of the night weighed heavily upon her, and once again she glanced toward her window and sent up a silent wish.

Please. Let him come home. Yet, she didn't have the courage to add the very secret prayer she had tucked in her heart.

Let him come home to me.

She paused for a moment, hoping to hear the telltale creak of the gate or the kitchen door being picked open, or however it was Langley and his Foreign Office cohorts got barred doors to yield to them.

But there was nothing but silence to greet her, so she closed her eyes and tugged her pillow close to her breast.

Close to her heart, where for so many years she hadn't dared to let any man come near.

Until now.

The house was dark and still when Langley slipped through the gate and made his way up the garden path in the back, his steps laden with discouragement.

After finding nothing at Langley House, save more questions, he and Thomas-William had shadowed Sir Basil, not letting up their surveillance of the man in hopes he'd slip up or that Nottage would show himself. But to his dismay, the mushroom continued to lead his smug and orderly life as if he had everything well in hand.

Nor had there been any sign of Nottage.

No, Langley realized, the only way to discover the truth was to search Sir Basil's office at White-hall, despite Lord Andrew's protests that it would be foolhardy.

There he would find the proof he sought. He had to find something and quickly. For Langley felt his time running out, the danger to Minerva cutting him to the core. She was in far too deep, and if the incident at the theatre hadn't shaken him, it was her earnest desire to help him that had.

Even Thomas-William had reluctantly agreed to his mad plan and come along, though most likely only to ensure that he didn't get himself killed in such a foolhardy endeavor.

But gain the man's office they had, though it was as dull as Sir Basil himself, with nothing out of the ordinary to be found—and they had nearly taken the place apart searching it.

No, it was as Lord Andrew had said, whatever evidence there was left, it would not be easily found, if it even existed.

All they had discovered was the signed paper-work that indicted one Ellis, Baron Langley, for high treason.

Then the situation went from futile to downright dangerous as they slipped back into the corridor, the one that had been empty not twenty minutes earlier, and found half a dozen guards blocking their path.

Luckily for them, Whitehall never changed, and since Langley had spent his first two years with the Foreign Office running errands all over the labyrinth of halls and offices, they were able to put up a merry chase, at least so it appeared until they found themselves cut off with only two choices: surrender or fight their way out.

It hadn't really been a choice. Not with Thomas-William there. Nor had it been easy, but they'd managed to outpummel the younger guards—Thomas-William handily knocking three of them cold in quick succession.

But that didn't mean the last three had given up as easily, and Langley and Thomas-William had suffered for it—though in the end they escaped, dashing down a long unused stairwell that led to a door concealed by a large bush. From there they slipped into the darkness of St. James Park and then doubled back to the river.

While Langley knew his identity was safe, Thomas-William was too familiar a face with the agents in the office. When his description was passed around, it wouldn't be long before a warrant would be issued.

So with some regret, Langley had sent his friend upriver to the Earl of Clifton's estate. He knew Clifton and his wife, Lucy Ellyson, would conceal and safeguard her father's loyal servant with their very lives.

But as he watched Thomas-William rowing away, moving quickly along with the tide as it pushed him upstream, Langley shivered. It wasn't from the cold, but that he was alone.

Out of chances, out of ideas.

Save his meeting tomorrow morning with Lord Chudley on Primrose Hill. Perhaps he would be better off just letting the old viscount put a bullet through his heart and be done with the matter.

For twenty some years he'd lived what some might call a charmed existence: mistresses, adventure, travel, and perhaps it had been just that. Magic.

Then it all had changed when he'd brought the girls to England to go to school. Without them it had been as if the light had gone out of his heart, and without their brightness in his days, he'd been blind to the darkness that had eventually enveloped him.

Treason. Oh, good God, there would be no stopping Brownie now that he had the order signed. While it was all but his end, the last thing he wanted was for that stain to touch Tally and Felicity's lives. If he was hung for treason, it would ruin them, their futures.

And it would ruin Minerva as well.

Cold, bleeding, and shivering, he'd warily crossed Piccadilly and St. James, through the byways and alleys of Mayfair, until he came to the mews behind Brook Street.

Minerva, his heart chimed at the sight of her window. *I am so sorry.*

For very soon their betrothal would mire her down in scandal, something he knew she'd abhor, come to despise him for.

Much to his chagrin, the kitchen door was locked. Mayhap this was her way of telling him to bugger off.

Not just yet, he thought grimly, reaching into the concealed sleeve inside his boot where he kept his picks.

He quickly got the door open and staggered inside, pausing for a moment on the stairs down to the kitchen, if only to catch his breath.

"My good man, you are getting too demmed old for this nonsense," he muttered to himself, a wry smile coming to his lips. Never would he have thought all those years ago, when his old school chum Robert Jenkinson had talked him into joining the Foreign Office, that at two and forty he would still be getting into roustabouts and lurking about like a thief in the night.

And what did he have for all of his troubles? Half his memory, his reputation in tatters, and ruination looming over everyone he loved. Langley considered one other choice.

What if he were to slip into the night, leave London? Tally and Felicity already thought him lost, had probably gotten used to the notion; they were better off without him.

Then, unbidden, came the image of Minerva standing before Langley House with a handful of snowdrops in her hands.

Hope, she beckoned. *Remember to hold onto your hope.*

Oh, aye, he had hope. Hope that Chudley was still a good shot.

As it was, when he got to the bottom of the stairs in the kitchen, he swayed a bit, then staggered over to a chair and sank into it.

Well, hopefully he'd given as well as he'd gotten, rubbing his aching jaw. Slowly, he sorted out his various aches and pains and realized he was worse off than he first thought.

"Demmit," he muttered.

There was naught but the glow of coals in the kitchen range, and no sign of Mrs. Hutchinson. The lady was probably off with her "dear Mudgett." Which was good. And the glowing coals meant the water in the tank on the side of range was hot and there was no one about to witness his battered state.

Though tomorrow there would no hiding his bruised jaw and nose, which was still flowing like tapped claret.

Groaning as quietly as he could, he dragged a tub out from under one of the workbenches and began filling it from the range.

While the rest of the house was a tumbledown pile of neglect, the kitchen was of the first order. Mrs. Hutchinson said Felicity had insisted on re-doing it for her, if only to keep the unlikely cook and housekeeper happily baking scones. Hence the dumbwaiter and the fancy cooking range. With each panful of hot water he emptied into the tub, he raised a toast of thanks to his scone-mad daughter.

Now all he had to do was bathe, bind the worst of his wounds, and get himself upstairs to bed. Then this night would be over.

Or so he thought as he stripped off his torn jacket, bloodied shirt, and mud-splattered breeches, be-cause when he reached to remove his smallclothes, there was a creak on the stairs behind him.

Already wound too tight from the night's events, Langley grabbed up his pistol and whirled around, only to find himself ready to shoot his white-faced betrothed.

"Good heavens, what happened to you?" Minerva gasped, not even looking at the pistol in Langley's hand, her gaze fixed on his bloodied nose and the dark purple coloring on one side of his jaw. She crossed the space between them, her hand coming up to cup his face but stopping short when he winced. "Who did this to you?"

He set down the pistol. "Haven't you a concern for the other fellow?"

"No. None." She took another measure of his injuries and brushed past him. Good heavens, how far had he come, staggering about like this? Whatever had happened? A thousand questions she knew he wouldn't answer filled her thoughts as she pulled up on the handle of the pump, and then went to work filling a bucket.

They'd need far more hot water than he had.

Then it struck her. *They.*

The bucket sloshed over and she stopped pumping. Stopped herself from considering such a notion. Carrying it to the reservoir in the range, she filled it back up. Then lighting a taper, she went to the cupboard in the back of the kitchen, raiding the cabinet of towels, cloths, and soap.

It wasn't her mother's kitchen back home, with its pots of unguents, needles for stitching, and binding strips, but this meager selection would have to do.

When she turned around, she found Langley slumped in the chair, his feet in the steaming tub of water. His eyes were closed and he looked utterly lost.

He hadn't found the evidence he needed. Oh, if only he would let her help him. Damn the man for being so bloody proud, for coming from such a long line of heroic sorts, for yes, she had done her checking on him.

If only . . .

Minerva ignored the pang in her heart, ignored the impropriety of the situation, and did her level best to remember the times she'd watched her mother put some other poor, battered soul to rights.

Still, having watched a deed wasn't the same as the actual doing. She wasn't even sure where to start.

Get him clean, she could almost hear her mother say. *Clean and dry.*

Wash him? She'd never washed a man before, never seen such a man all but naked. Yes, she'd been married, but to Phillip Sterling, who, by the time she'd wed him, was well past his prime—and she'd never seen him naked, mercifully—for he always came to her late, after a night of debauchery, to make a few drunken fumbled attempts in the dark, and then left.

Thankfully . . .

But Lord Langley was different. In excellent shape, his muscled shoulders, taut back, and lean frame left her breathless, slightly intoxicated. Even battered and broken as he was, the sheer masculine power beneath the bruises and dirt left her wavering.

As it had the other night in the carriage . . .

Heavens! It was just as Lucy and Elinor had said. *That the right man . . .*

Now Minerva wavered.

No, Lord Langley was not the right man for her. He couldn't be.

Still, the notion terrified her. What if he was? Then the last thing she could do was fail at this. He needed her.

Certainly he wasn't asking her, but her heart was.

Sighing to herself, she dipped the pan into the tub and glanced at him. *Where do I begin?*

Then it was if her long-lost mother gave her a nudge filled with courage. *At the beginning.*

Minerva whispered softly to him, "Lean over."

He did, and she gently poured the water over his head, letting it run through his matted hair and down his shoulders. Then without another word she lathered up her hands and went to work. Silently she cleaned his hair and began to carefully wash his face.

His gaze met hers as she wiped away the blood around his nose, the silence between them putting her on edge. "You were gone all day," she said quietly.

There, it wasn't a question. Just a statement.

Filled with questions.

Langley winced as she ran the cloth around his jawline. "Did you miss me?"

"I was worried," she said honestly. Nor could she help adding, "And you reek of the Thames."

"It wasn't by choice," he offered. But that was all he offered.

So she rinsed the cloth and went back to work on his shoulders, the breadth of his back. Beneath her fingers she felt long, thick welts, and she shivered. Reaching for the candle, she held it up to reveal a series of deep scars running from the top of his shoulders all the way down.

"Is there something wrong?" Langley asked.

Minerva shook her head and set down the candle. Rinsing out the cloth, she continued, shocked by what she'd seen.

Yes, she knew he'd been imprisoned, Jamilla had said as much, but this was far worse than just being locked up. He'd been whipped at some point in his rapscallion life. Beaten savagely. She shuddered to think of how such a thing happened, and when she ran the cloth down the length of his arm, she found more scars around his wrists, the sort that comes from bindings.

Arrested? Kidnapped? Set upon? She didn't know, didn't dare pry. But one thing was for certain, he'd been taken and beaten. But then again the scar along his hairline that ran all the way back behind his ear said that much. But that hadn't been the only time. The masculine body beneath her fingers was not that of a spoiled toff, nor of a man accustomed only to the comforts of regal palaces and seducing women as his reputation suggested.

Lord Langley had lived a very different life than the one she'd so blithely assumed.

Minerva didn't realize it, but she'd paused, and the stillness of the house and the room around them suddenly loomed like the darkness of night.

"You needn't do this," he said to her, reaching for the cloth. "You shouldn't be involved."

She pulled the cloth back from him and continued working, trying to ignore the lines and planes of his muscles, of the hardened power beneath the bruised veneer. "I became involved the moment you tumbled into my bedchamber, when you moved into my house without asking. No, I am involved whether I like it or not."

"I won't ask which."

"That's sensible of you," she told him tartly, glancing at his nose. She handed him a cloth and then pressed his hand to it to staunch the bleeding. "Is it broken?"

"No," he said, shaking his head slightly.

She went to the stove and dipped the pan into the

tank. The water was no longer cold, but it wasn't scaldingly hot either.

But it was cleaner than the growing bilge in the tub.

"I didn't think so from the look of it," she said, "but you would know best."

"You have a talent for this," he said softly.

Minerva glanced away. "My mother had the talent. I only watched."

"And helped. I can't imagine a bossy chit like you just watching."

She smiled. "I helped when she was busy with other matters."

He watched her tear a set of cloths and pick through the pots of unguents. "Not the usual talent one finds in a lady. Especially a countess, or a future duchess."

"My mother was an unusual woman." And not the countess. Just the daughter of the local witch, as most liked to say.

"As is her daughter," he murmured as he stretched and tested his shoulders.

Yes, quite unusual, she mused silently. The bastard daughter foisted off as the legitimate one. Certainly not your average marchioness.

Then again, she thought, slanting a glance at him over her shoulder, he might not be so surprised. He might not even care that she wasn't . . . who she was supposed to be.

What would Lord Langley think of plain Maggie Owens?

"Here, I would have thought the lofty Lady Standon would call Mrs. Hutchinson to help," he was saying. "This seems more her territory."

Minerva shook her head. "Never. She gossips too much. Something I don't think you want or need."

He didn't answer.

"At least she'd offer me a strong drink," he teased. "A good measure after being tossed around a bit. Steady my wits."

Minerva snorted. "You don't need a strong drink. As for your wits, I think they've been addled enough for one night. What you need is to get clean and dry and the bleeding stopped."

"Minerva Sterling, you are the most sensible woman I have ever met."

And here she'd spent all these years hiding behind a veneer of propriety and sensibility, but being branded so by his lips rankled her. She didn't want to be sensible in his eyes. She wanted to be . . . oh, like the others . . . wild . . . irresistible . . . worldly . . . desirable . . .

"You are too old to be taking such risks," she heard herself saying. Oh, heavens, she was too sensible for words!

He raised his weary head and managed to wink at her. "I'm not so ancient that I can't take care of myself. I'll have you know, there were six of them."

She poured the less than warm water over him and set the pan down so she could settle her fisted hands on her hips. "And that is supposed to make me feel better?"

Six of them? He'd been set upon by six men? Why it took her breath away. And she told herself it wasn't because he'd managed to best them—at least enough to escape with his life. No, not in the least.

For she'd been terrified since she'd found him down here in the kitchen.

Then something else occurred to her and she cursed herself for not asking sooner. "Is Thomas-William . . . is he . . ."

She didn't dare finish the rest of the question.

But Langley did. "Alive? Yes." He glanced down at his bloodied and battered hands, which she was carefully wiping clean.

She nodded. She'd grown overly fond of Lucy's taciturn servant. Still, "alive" didn't tell the whole story. "Is he injured?"

"He's a bit worse for wear, but he'll heal."

Minerva drew a deep breath and then sighed. "Is he safe?"

"Yes."

She saw no need ask any more. But then again she'd been puzzling over the events at Langley House ever since they'd returned—and now, added to the evidence she'd seen on his back . . .

"Langley?"

"Hmm."

"How was it that boxes continued to arrive at Langley House when everyone thought you dead . . . and I suspect you were . . ."

He glanced up at her, his expression unreadable for once.

"Detained?" she offered.

"Minerva—" He shook his head at her.

She was prying when he didn't want her help, but she persisted. "Please, I want to be of assistance to you. Who could have sent them?"

He sat silently for a while, then sighed. "I don't know."

"Someone you worked with? An aide? A secretary? Another . . . diplomat?" She thought better of saying what she meant.

Another agent. One capable of betrayal.

He shook his head. "Good God, Minerva, is that all you've been doing since I left you? Coming up with theories?"

"Well, yes," she told him. "What else was I to do?"

"Oh, demmit, if you must know—"

"I must—"

"Yes, I suppose you do. And most likely won't let up until I do answer your questions." He fixed a weighted glance on her, but Minerva held her ground.

"No, I won't, and since you are in no condition to run off, I believe I have you at my mercy."

He blew out a breathy snort. "I had a secretary, Neville Nottage." Langley glanced away and took another deep breath before he continued. "He was a third or fourth son, I don't recall, but he had no prospects, and he hardly made a splash in the diplomatic corps, but he did a remarkably good job at managing my business, though I never would have thought him capable of . . ."

Revenge. Betrayal. Even possibly murder. Minerva's imagination ran wild. Good heavens, could that dangerous man in the carriage have been this ordinary secretary?

"And then?"

"When I went missing in Paris, I was told he was dead . . ." Langley blew out a breath.

"But he isn't," she said with conviction.

"No. It appears that he and Sir Basil in the For-

eign Office have been working together for years."
He rubbed his head. "I must have been hit hard, for
I shouldn't be telling you any of this."

But she was ever so glad he was. "They did this to
ruin you?"

"No, I think I was merely their means to something
else. They needed a scapegoat, someone to point to if
they were caught. This is treason we are talking about,
Minerva. Something that cannot be taken lightly."

When he glanced over at her, she could see the
pain in his eyes. Nottage's betrayal. The dangerous
straits he was in.

"I'm ever so sorry," she whispered.

He nodded and glanced away.

Oh, bother. And here she'd thought perhaps she
could help, when all she'd done was stir up more
painful memories. Glancing at him again, she took
his hand in hers and gently pulled it away from his
nose. To her relief the bleeding had stopped.

Now if only everything else—whatever madness was circling around him—could be as easily
staunched.

Getting another pan of clean, warm water, she knelt
down in front of him to wash his legs. Thick, muscled
lengths covered in crisp hair. Filling the cloth with
soap, she continued to wash him, running the cloth
up and down his legs, marveling at the heat of his
skin, the way it felt to caress him so . . . wishing she
could take him in her arms and do more than just
this . . .

And when she ran the cloth up his calf to his
thigh, he stopped her, his hand covering hers.
"My lady," he said in voice thick with need.

She glanced up and saw something there in his eyes that tore at her heart even more.

Desire. Painful, aching desire.

This wasn't seduction, this wasn't a man trying to charm her, tease her as he had the previous night, but a man who desired to be lost in her arms. Lost from a world closing in around him.

Minerva felt herself unravel. She didn't know what to do, but like the choice of helping him, cleaning him up, she knew if she failed him, she would never forgive herself.

That and she desired him. Longed for him. She looked into his eyes and once again swore he could see all the way to her soul.

Yet she also saw a dark pain shadowed in his gaze. Could it be that his secrets were so much like hers?

Yet he took her hesitation altogether wrong, and lifted her to her feet. "Go, Minerva. Please. I won't involve you any further."

She gazed into his eyes, where the conflict was easy to see.

And he must have known it, for he turned away, catching up the towel and wrapping it around him.

"It is for the best," he said quietly. "Besides, in a few hours I need to be . . . Well, I need to go . . ."

"The duel with Chudley?" Minerva gaped at him. "Don't tell me I've gone to all this trouble just to see you shot."

"Minerva, I must. Can't you see that?"

"No, I cannot." Vexed and furious—mostly at her own indecision—she picked up the wet clothes and dirty rags and put them in the wash basket.

Silently, she cleaned up, while he wound another

towel around his waist. Concealing himself, just as he concealed so much more.

"My lord," she said, her words coming out in a tumbled rush, "do you wish for someone to confide in? Someone to help you?"

He glanced over his shoulder at her, as if surprised to find her still there. "I would ask the same of you, my lady."

Minerva took a step back. "Whatever do you mean?"

"Do you have anything you wish to tell me? Something that you need assistance with?"

Right now? Hours before his ridiculous duel with Chudley and suddenly he wanted to help her? As if she would even ask, and add to his already obvious problems. Wasn't that why he'd come to Town without telling his own daughters, if only to avoid involving them? She glanced up at him, biting her lip, then shook her head and went back to tidying the kitchen, if only to avoid going up to her bed.

If only to keep from being alone.

He wouldn't confide in her, anymore than she would him, because, she mused, they didn't trust each other enough.

Was that it, or was it as he said, too dangerous to involve her?

Minerva shook her head. She was involved, whether he liked it or not, and she was about to turn around and tell him so, but when she looked up, she found he'd slipped from the kitchen and disappeared up the stairs as silently as a cat.

Leaving her utterly alone.

* * *

Langley got up to his room in the attics and cursed himself the minute he closed the door.

What the hell was he thinking? She had been willing and desirable, and he refused her. Rubbing his skull, he realized he'd been hit in the head harder than he thought.

No, it wasn't that. It was because when he was with Minerva, everything was different.

The lady was so infuriatingly sensible. And capable. And smart. Not some bluestocking—but intelligent—sharp-eyed and capable of thinking quickly.

And she doesn't trust you, a wry voice teased. Another point in her favor.

That needled him more than he cared to admit.

Minerva didn't trust him. She wouldn't confide in him. Wouldn't ask for his help.

Damn her! If she had any idea of the scrapes and dangers he'd faced, endured . . .

Well, she does now, he realized.

Her fingers had traced the lines on his back. The ones he'd gotten in Abbaye, the prison in Paris where he'd been detained until Napoleon's defeat.

Why, she'd shivered as she washed them, as if they were still raw and open. But she hadn't recoiled. Hadn't stopped and backed away.

She'd finished what had needed to be done and asked no questions. Well, no more than she could resist. Nor had she been prodded to pry when she'd seen the scars on his wrists—the ones he took great pains to keep hidden.

And after years of living a life of lies and deception, he knew exactly why she hadn't asked.

Because she had a dark secret of her own that kept her from prying into the hearts of others.

No, Minerva Sterling's secret wasn't an overdrawn account or an expensive obsession for endless shoes and gowns. And it pained him more than he cared to admit that he was powerless to help her—at least until she trusted him enough.

She trusted you enough to offer herself to you . . .

He made an inelegant snort. Because her aunt had exhorted her to do so to keep him from making his meeting with Chudley. Digging around under his bed, he found the bottle of brandy he'd stolen from Mrs. Hutchinson a few days earlier and took a long pull.

Yes, that was why she'd looked at him that way, as if he were the first man she'd ever desired.

And if he was being honest, the reason he refused her, left her, was because when she'd looked at him with those wide, honest eyes, he knew—knew like he'd never known with any other woman—that they were . . . that she was . . .

Unlike any woman he'd ever met.

Oh, he'd loved Frances all those years ago, but with the wild careless passion of youth. And it had been lost long before it had ever been tested when she'd died in childbirth, leaving him with their infant twin daughters and a brief line of memories.

In all the years since, he'd done naught but imitate that heedless, reckless love, poor imitations all, but it was also all he knew how to do.

All he'd thought himself capable of doing.

He glanced down at himself and realized he'd put on a clean shirt and breeches.

Because he had no intention of going to bed.

Go to her. Tell her. Before tomorrow. Before your entire life unravels.

He left the attic and began the slow descent to her room. The steps creaked beneath his steps, as if echoing his thoughts.

So she will confide in you.

So she'll trust you.

So you can find your heart.

That thought stayed his progress.

Find his heart? Ridiculous! He simply needed to thank her for her assistance. He continued until he reached her door.

Yes, thank her.

And beg her to reconsider her offer.

The door was cracked open and he went to push it open.

I am not here to seduce the lady. As I told her, I can't involve her.

But you have . . .

He was about to call to her when he spied her standing before her mirror.

Her brown hair, so staid and ordinary in its tight chignon, now fell in tumbled curls down past her shoulders. She wore only her chemise, which revealed what her sensible gowns hid—a lush and curved figure—round breasts, full hips, the body of a woman who could enflame a man into insensibility.

Then she turned and he spied something that had his lips turning up in amusement.

The Sterling diamonds.

What had she said last night in the carriage?

Oh, yes, now he remembered.

. . . if I am feeling a bit out of sorts, there have been a few times when I've worn them . . . just for myself.

And just as he'd suspected, she liked to wear them when she was half dressed. Dangerous minx.

Though nearly naked as she was, she outshone the cold stones like the most precious jewel he'd ever seen.

He slipped into the room and quietly closed the door behind him.

"Minerva?"

She gasped and whirled around, hairbrush in hand, ready to defend herself.

But when she saw it was him, the brush fell from her fingers, landing in a dull thud on the carpet.

"I . . . I . . . I . . ." she stammered.

They stood there for a moment, both unwilling to speak. The desire in her eyes, that aching need, was so clear. He should say something, he had to tell her . . .

"I came to thank you," he whispered. "Properly."

She shook her head. "A proper thank you?" Slowly, she crossed the room and reached up to cup his battered face. "Langley, surely you've come here for more than that."

Chapter 13

*Do you think Lord Langley is as legendary—
in certain matters—as they say?*

A confidence overheard at
Lady Ratcliffe's afternoon tea

*M*inerva could not believe her bold desire. Instead of ordering him out, as she should have, she was now standing half dressed in front of Langley, and practically begging him to take her to her bed.

Langley, surely you've come here for more than that?

However had she come up with such a brazen line?

His stubbled jaw teased her hand, still cupped around his poor, battered face. A handsome man in his finery, there was something all too enticing about Langley once he was stripped of his polished veneer and all that was left was the virile man beneath.

"I've come . . . that is to say, I came down here

to . . ." he stammered, sounding like a befuddled bridegroom rather than an accomplished rake.

His reluctance, his disquiet, only emblazoned her desires. He wanted her, she knew that, but something was very different about this night. This moment.

For both of them.

His open shirt revealed a smooth, hard chest, and to her bemusement, his feet were bare.

Why that was amusing, she didn't know, but then again, it wasn't every night she had a handsome, barefoot man come padding into her bedchamber . . . She smiled up at him. He had come to her. Just as she'd wished when she put on the Sterling diamonds.

"I don't know what I am doing here," he confessed.

"It couldn't wait until the morning?" she asked coyly. Lady Standon no more, Minerva cast away everything that had held her life in bindings.

"No, it couldn't," he murmured.

"I should throw you out," she whispered back. "But I won't let you go without one thing." She slid closer to him, one hand pulling his face down a bit while the other curled around his waist so she could hitch herself even closer to him.

Langley, the man with the easy quip, the man used to inviting a lady for a tumble with merely a flick of his mischievous, devil-may-care glances, opened his mouth to say something, to ask that one obvious question, but nothing came out.

Like a siren of old, she smiled at him, inviting him to do that thing she'd vowed she would never allow him.

To kiss her.

Parting her lips, she rose up on her tiptoes and said, "Are you going to make me beg?"

"No," he said, pulling her closer still. "That will come later."

And then he kissed her.

His kiss the other night, while tantalizing, had been hastily given and abruptly ended, so it made this one all the more mesmerizing. Slowly, his lips covered hers, claimed hers. Somewhere, he'd found Mrs. Hutchinson's stash of brandy, and the hints and rumors of that rich brew whispered over her senses. As his tongue tangled with hers, her body swirled with passions, as if his kiss filled her with its own intoxicant.

Oh, and it was a heady brew. His hands roaming over her back, her bottom, drawing her ever closer to him, up against him, while his lips, his tongue, teased her to drink even deeper. To fall headlong with abandon into his seduction.

Though wasn't she the one doing the seducing?

It was ever so hard to determine who was seducing whom. Having tackled her fears earlier with naught but bravado, now Minerva found her heart, her own power.

The command every woman yields when she finds her heart's desire. Her soul. Langley's kiss, instead of leaving her wavering and shocked, now awakened a potency she'd never known she possessed.

It filled her heart with a vitality, a knowledge, that she'd never dared claim, for fear that someone might realize she was no proper lady. But it seemed Langley didn't need a proper lady.

He wanted her. And only her.

Her hands ran up and under the front of his shirt, starting at the top of his breeches, where a hint of crisp hair ran down to where his manhood even now strained against his plain breeches.

He stilled, as if waiting to see which she would choose—north or south—and for the life of her, she paused, spellbound by the heat of his body, the notion that her touch drove him to this drawn-out pause, awaiting her next step with the same trembling desire that was racing through her fingers, up her arms.

And then he did the impossible. He covered her hands and brought them up, inviting them to explore his chest, to give in to the slow, tantalizing explorations he was enjoying.

No. No. No. That wasn't what she wanted.

She wanted to erupt, ignite, burn. She wanted to touch him, hold him. Now. And if she did, she knew they would tumble headlong onto the floor and give in utterly. Completely.

"Oh God, Minerva," he whispered as he freed one of her breasts from her chemise and took the nipple in his mouth, teasing the tip with his lips, his tongue, his teeth, while his hand slowly moved between her legs and found her hot, wet core, where he began to touch her, slide over her taut nub, leaving her panting, breathless.

It was the carriage ride all over, but this time . . .

There was no theatre at the end of the block, only the two of them and her bed, waiting for them to fall into it. To give in to this desire he'd awakened with a stolen kiss and left to smolder between them ever since.

Her hips began to move, rising in crescendo, her knees buckling as she began to lose control.

And all she wanted was to touch him. Hold him.

"Langley," she gasped. She gazed into his eyes, pleading where words failed her.

She saw herself beneath him, as in the carriage. She could nearly feel what it would mean to have him inside her, filling her, stroking this growing need of hers.

Of theirs.

Oooh, what would it be like to have him inside her?

Even now Langley was intoxicating her, like aged brandy, deceptive with its dusty bottle, potent when it unfurled inside you and all that tempering ignited in a burst of passionate fire.

What had he said? That he was going to make her beg.

Having merely tasted the elixir he was offering, she would do anything to have him continue. Breathless, she pulled back from him for a second and looked into those startling blue eyes. There was no grin on his lips, no flights of teasing, just the same dark, dangerous urgency that now claimed her heart.

"Please," she managed.

"Are you begging?" he asked, his lips nuzzling over her earlobe, down the nape of her neck.

Really? Did he have to do that? It sent shivers down her spine, and if she couldn't stand before, now she clung to him.

Begging.

"Yes, ever so much." There, she'd said it.

And in reply he caught her up in his arms. He shouldn't have the strength, the wherewithal, considering all he'd been through this night, but here he was, catching her up.

Now all he had to do was cross the room and . . .

and . . . Yet, to her utter vexation—really, who knew that such a thing was possible when one was in the throes of passion—he stood there in the middle of the room, holding her in his arms and not moving.

Wasn't this the part where he tossed her on the bed and tumbled her? Dishonored her? Thoroughly, completely, utterly?

At least that was how it always worked in French novels.

Yet here he was, as immobile as the Colossus of Rhodes.

She nodded toward her bed, worried that perhaps he'd been hit harder in the head earlier than she'd suspected. Could a man forget how to—

"I fear, Minerva . . ." he began, nuzzling her again.

Did he have to do that? It really made it impossible to think.

" . . . there is one other matter to contend with," he finished.

Oh, there were several matters to contend with, she would argue, but instead asked, "What now, Langley? I've begged. I'll beg again, if that is what you want."

He glanced over at her bed. "I promised I wouldn't share your bed without your invitation."

"Oh, good God, man, I thought that was implied when I didn't toss you out earlier."

Langley didn't know what he found more fascinating about Minerva—her prickly nature or the deep passions that rose with the same mercurial fire.

And right now she was burning with both.

"Are you taking me to my bed or not, sir?"

Cheeky minx. What he should be doing was dropping her on her backside and running for the Dials, where she would never find him.

Though even if he did run, he wouldn't put it past her to follow and demand her due.

So he tossed her atop her bed and grinned down at her.

Minerva's mouth opened in a wide moue, but he knew it wasn't one of outraged protest. No, quite the contrary, for then she beckoned him to join her.

And he did, yanking off his shirt and following her with equal abandon.

"Thought you'd never get here," she whispered as she caught hold of his face and drew it close to kiss.

His heart did that odd tumble again. The same *thud* it did whenever she touched him.

Long ago, on a trip between Paris and St. Petersburg, there had been an old Gypsy woman who had stopped him and caught his hand, peering into the lines there.

She'd smiled at him and said very cryptically, as her type were wont to do, that he could love as many women as he dared, but one day a woman's touch would lay claim to his heart and he would be hers forever.

He'd thought then that her words were nonsense—the promise of eternal love—if only to gain a few more coins. Yet, from time to time, when a woman would come to his bed, lay her hand atop his sleeve at a ball, or he'd clasp her fingers to bring them to his lips, he couldn't help but think of the old crone's words.

She'll hold you like no other.

And now, as Minerva cradled his face with her

hands, stroked his stubbled chin, curled the curves of her body into the angles of his, he found himself lost.

Falling.

Claimed.

And instead of sending him hying off to another posting, another engagement, stealing into the night never to return, he wanted nothing more than to spend the rest of his life in her bed.

Listening to her beg for his kiss, his touch.

But if he was honest here, he was the beggar.

Minerva offered him something that he'd never thought possible.

His heart.

Her arms wound around him and drew him close. Her soft breasts pressed against his chest, her long legs winding around his.

He resisted grinning, thinking of the Minerva in the ugly flannel gown he'd met the other night.

Who would have ever suspected a supple, gorgeous women resided beneath that wretched flannel tent? But even her lacy chemise was too much for his desires, and skillfully he plied it from her body, leaving her adorned only in the Sterling diamonds, the stones glittering against her pale silken skin.

He began to kiss her anew, exploring her body, kissing her, running his tongue over her erect nipples, suckling her. His fingers slipped inside her, and Minerva was hot and wet, her hips moving seductively, setting the rhythm as he slid over her nub.

She was panting again, writhing and moving beneath him. Her bare foot wound around his leg, running up and down it, stroking him, and he imagined her hands doing the same thing to his manhood. Stroking him, pulling him closer, drawing him toward his completion . . .

So when her hands went once again to his waistband, this time he didn't stop her, he let her open his breeches, let her slide her hand inside and free him. Where before he'd wanted to wait, he didn't think he could last much longer.

Nor did it seem could she.

"Oh God, Minerva," he gasped as her fingers curled around him, running down his length until they wrapped around his balls and gave them a tentative, gentle squeeze.

"Does it feel good?" she asked.

"Better than good," he rasped out. So she stroked him again, exploring him from the base to the head, her thumb rolling over the wet bead that rose up and using its slickness to add to her teasing.

Langley sucked in a deep breath, thankful he wasn't some callow youth, for he'd have spilled his seed for certain when her fingers wound all the way around him and held him tight as she ran her hand up and down.

"This will never do," she complained as she continued to stroke him, her lips nibbling at his shoulder and then up along his jawline, her tongue raking over the stubble there.

Oh, God, it was bewitching the way she was exploring his body, giving over to her to desires. "No, this will never do," she was muttering.

Langley didn't think he'd heard her correctly. "Excuse me?" he managed. He'd never heard any complaints before.

"Your breeches," she said, her fingers tugging at the waistband. "I won't be tupped like some dairy maid."

"Tupped?" Langley laughed. "I certainly hope I do better than that."

"Oh, I have no doubts," she told him, her hand winding around his length, "but the breeches must go."

Who was he to argue with the lady?

Minerva could have clamped her hand over her mouth. Ever since Langley had come into her life, it was as if he was giving her long stilled tongue and unconventional upbringing license to be set free.

Tupped, indeed! Whatever had she been thinking to say such a thing?

And whatever was she doing? She was holding him, stroking him like a courtesan might. But he was so long and thick and solid. *Hard*. Never had she been with a man like this, with one so virile and capable.

Her aunt had been right a few nights ago. Sterling had never been able to consummate their marriage and his fumbling attempts had been a horror.

So here she was, a widow and a virgin. She should be as innocent as a bride, but Minerva had always been so very curious. And she hadn't been raised in the closeted world of a debutante like her sister, but spent her early years in her mother's cottage and then in the kitchens of her father's house, where she'd seen enough coupling to know that it offered its own piece of heaven.

And with Langley, she felt a freedom to be as licentious as she'd ever dreamt of being. As brazen as the books of French prints Jamilla had casually left in the parlor one evening. Minerva Sterling certainly wouldn't have looked at such a book, but Maggie Owens?

And it was hardly brazen to ask him to take off his breeches. For she'd wanted him naked. Completely so.

Then again, he didn't seem to mind, for a wicked grin pulled at his lips, and he helped her slide his breeches off.

"Oh, yes," she sighed happily now that he didn't have a stitch on. "This is more how I imagined it."

Langley stilled, one brow rising sardonically in an arch. "You thought of me doing this?" he teased. And before she could answer, he kissed her neck, her earlobe, while he nudged her knees apart and set his manhood so it was nestled almost inside her cleft.

The most delicious ache of anticipation ran down her spine even as her hips rose up to meet him. She couldn't breathe. She couldn't even beg.

But oh, thank heavens Langley was a disreputable rake, for he knew exactly what she wanted, and without a word he slid inside her, his manhood opening her, easing into her, and then even though she still couldn't breathe, she moaned, softly, then louder still.

"Oooh," she breathed out. "Langley—"

He kissed her, moving slowly, in and out, easing deeper and deeper into her. With each stroke she moaned, her fingers running over his back in a desperate search to find something, anything, to hang onto, for her world was suddenly opening up beneath her.

He'd rocked his way into her, his movements starting to come quicker and harder, and then with a sudden thrust he buried himself inside her, sweeping past her barrier with unwitting speed.

Minerva gasped, both at the moment of pain and

then the utter joy of having him there, filling her. It was hard and tight and delicious all at once.

But for Langley it was another matter. He stilled, for apparently—as suddenly as he broke through her veil—he realized what he'd done. "Good God!"

Her lashes flew open, and he was looking down at her with an expression of utter shock. Never had a man looked more confounded.

"You've never—" he began, about to pull out of her.

But she caught hold of his buttocks and held him fast. "Please, Langley, don't stop. Not now."

"But I can't—"

She rocked her hips so her body slid over him. "I think you already have," she told him, with a bit of a smile on her lips. She rocked against him, feeling the slick friction that rode over her nub all the way through her. "Please, Langley, don't make me wait any longer." Before he could say another word, she rose up and covered his lips with hers, kissing him, her hands now running up and down his back with the same slow steady movements with which he'd entered her.

"Please, Langley," she whispered.

"Oh God, woman, how can I say no to you?" he groaned, pinning her to the mattress, his body moving with long, slow strokes, filling her completely with each one.

Minerva, one hand wound into the sheets, the other wound around Langley, hung on for dear life as her body began to move and ache, to tremble and take on a life of its own.

The world began to spin around her, and she couldn't see much beyond the look of pure desire in Langley's eyes. He groaned deeply as his movements became more hurried, more frantic. He was going faster and faster, and she met each thrust with her own clamoring passion.

And then the world gave way, and she reached her crisis, her body dancing amongst the heights, freed from every constraint, a celebration of desires finding their place in the very heavens.

She knew in that moment there was nothing else but this night, this man, this very dangerous passion.

For here was Langley, having found the same dizzying bliss—wildly thrusting into her, over and over again, as if he never wanted to stop chasing the passion between them, and with each movement filling her with his seed, claiming her as his own.

His only. For this night and forever.

"Where are you, Langley?" Minerva whispered sometime later.

After they'd both found their completion, they'd fallen into each other's arms, exhausted and languid.

"Lost," he told her.

"Found, I would hope."

"Aye, that too."

"But it frightens you," she guessed all-too-wisely. Minerva rose up on one elbow and looked over at him.

He paused, for this was venturing into an honesty that he'd never crossed into. Had avoided with a rake's practiced expertise. "It should."

"Should it?"

He laughed. "That is the odd part. It doesn't. You

leave me breathless. Taken unawares. And odd as it sounds, I feel as if I have come home."

"Home? Here?" She laughed. "Your standards are sadly lacking, sir, if you find this ramshackle house comforting." Minerva waved her hand at the painting hanging over the bed. "With its fine artwork and tumbledown drainpipes."

He tipped his head back and glanced up. "Certainly such a painting wouldn't have been found in Versailles, not with that folly. I daresay, is it lopsided?"

She nudged him with her elbow. "You are looking at it upside down." Minerva glanced up at it as well. "And yes, it is crooked."

He laughed and rolled atop her, then looked back up at it again. "Decidedly crooked. Perhaps we knocked it loose from its nail when we were—"

"Langley!"

"I know how we could straighten it out," he teased, and began to kiss her anew, his hands seeking out the spots he was coming to love—her lush breasts, the curve of her hips. Immediately, his body came to life, and happily so did hers, rising up to meet his, and her lips eagerly seeking his own.

"If you think this will help," she said in that arched way of hers. "I've never liked a lopsided folly."

"Most decidedly this will straighten out everything," he promised as he filled her again and they rocked together, her every touch a reminder of what he'd found . . . and what he was risking.

Chapter 14

Choose a ~~lover~~ husband carefully. Do not dally with any man who cannot love you senseless.
  Advice to Felicity Langley from her Nanny Tasha

*M*inerva awoke to the clamor of the bell over the front door and the strident cries of a lady ringing her own peel through the house.

Good heavens, whatever was the matter now?

She blinked her eyes and gazed at the hint of dawn peeking through the windows.

Then in a flash, the events of the last few days sparked through her thoughts.

The kiss in the carriage . . . The report of the pistol as it fired . . . The kitchen shrouded in the light of a single candle . . . Langley naked and over her . . . the hint of dawn peeking through the curtains . . .

Langley! The duel!

She bolted upright, even as Aunt Bedelia burst into her bedchamber. "Where is he?" she thundered.

Minerva looked with some shock at the empty spot beside her, and instinctively her hand went to the curve in the mattress.

The sheets were cold. He'd been gone for some time.

"He was here . . ."

"Dear God, gel! You had him in your bed and couldn't manage to keep him there?"

Minerva shook her head, running her fingers through her thoroughly tousled hair. "I had no idea he'd left."

"Harrumph!" Aunt Bedelia sputtered. "But I must admit, Chudley did the same thing to me." She crossed the room to the corner closet and flung the door open. Almost immediately she began tossing clothing over her shoulder at Minerva—a chemise, stockings, a gown. "Don't just sit there gaping, gel, get dressed! And don't forget to take off those diamonds." The old girl paused for a moment and then asked, "Whatever were you doing with them on in the first place?" Then she shook her head. "No, don't tell me!"

Minerva did as ordered and scrambled out of bed, pulling on her clothes as quickly as she could. Then she removed the Sterling diamonds and settled them in their case, and as her fingers ran over the velvet lined box, she trembled. "Oh, Aunt Bedelia, I tried to divert him, it was just that . . ." The night had been everything and more than she could have imagined, but still he'd left.

And now . . . and now . . . Her vision clouded with tears as all she could see was a green meadow with Langley lying atop the thick grass in a pool of his own blood.

Like the worst sort of simpleton, a regular watering pot, she burst into tears.

This gave Aunt Bedelia pause. The lady who never stopped for anything, the veritable whirlwind of activity, actually stilled and stared at her niece.

"I think I love him," Minerva confessed between gulping sobs. "However did this happen?"

And then Aunt Bedelia did the unthinkable. The old girl wrapped Minerva in her arms and held her like a mother might.

"There there, child. I should have known that rogue would love you until you were insensible. He has that look about him." She smiled at her niece and brushed her rumpled hair out of her face. "Just like my Chudley."

"I am not worthy of Lord Langley. I am not even—"

Aunt Bedelia pushed her out to arm's length. "Sssh," she chided. "You are the woman you were meant to be, and that is all that matters to a man. How you got to be Lady Standon is of no consequence."

Now it was Minerva's turn to still. "What do you mean by that?"

"I mean," Aunt Bedelia whispered, "that you are as much or more of a marchioness as that feather-brained sister of yours ever would have been."

Chills ran down Minerva's spine, and they had nothing to do with the drafts running in from the cracks in the window frames. "You know?"

The lady huffed with impatience. "Of course I know who you are, Maggie. Known since the day that bosky fool of a brother of mine married you off in Minerva's stead. Oh, you two gels always bore a startling resemblance to each other, so I can see why he thought it would work, but I knew. How could I not?" She nodded toward the bed where Minerva's stockings still lay, while she returned to the closet, bending over to hunt around for a pair boots. "Tell Agnes to have more care with the state of this closet. Why, it's a disgrace."

Minerva sat down on the bed, albeit to put on her stockings, but quite honestly she didn't think she could stand. Aunt Bedelia knew the truth? "You knew and you never said a word?"

Truly, given that this was Aunt Bedelia, it was rather hard to believe.

But she was underestimating Bedelia's loyalties.

The lady glanced over her shoulder. "And what was to be said?" She went back to hunting around for shoes and plucked free one boot, then another. "Good heavens, the scandal would have ruined us all. And heaven knows, the Sterlings would not have taken the deception lightly. The weight of their wrath would have fallen not only on your shoulders—but your father's and mine as well—if they'd ever learned the truth."

"But you've said nothing! Not once in all these years."

"Oh, I had my say when I realized what your father had done. Confronted him right after the ceremony— told him exactly what I thought of the entire debacle! Utterly unfair to you. Not that he saw it that way— thought you were landing in the clover. Married to an aging sot twice your years! Rotten clover that, not that he would listen to me."

"No more than he'd listened to me," Minerva said softly.

Bedelia laughed. "Yes, he mentioned you weren't

all that cooperative. And what he threatened you with if you didn't follow through."

"My mother," she whispered.

Her aunt shook her head. "Threatening to put her out. He'd never have done it. But how were you to know that?"

"Not that it would have mattered," Minerva said. "She was gone before I could ever—"

"There there," the older lady said, setting the boots at Minerva's feet and sitting down beside her. "You carry her nerve and wits with you, and thankfully not the Hartley nose!" She tapped her own hawkish beak and smiled. "But you definitely have her way of seeing things, of being able to make sense of the oddest connections."

"You knew my mother?"

Aunt Bedelia laughed. "But of course I knew her. She and I grew up together. She was like a sister to me. Oh, how I loved your grandmother's cottage, though I wasn't supposed to go there or even know the trade she practiced or that some called her a witch." The lady paused for a moment, smiling at the memories. "So I've kept your secret, not so much for your father's sake, but for hers. I failed her when I didn't stop the wedding, but I've done my best for you since, as well as I could." Her eyes glistened with tears and she wrapped Minerva in another hug. But the rare show of affection didn't last long, for Aunt Bedelia was soon on her feet, pulling her composure together. "Now now, this isn't doing either of us any favors nor stopping that foolish pair of devils we love from shooting each other."

Minerva nodded and wiped the tears from her

cheeks. "Aunt Bedelia, what if . . . what if we don't make it in time?"

"Chudley doesn't dare die. I told him quite roundly I would use my widow's portion to buy a brand new wardrobe—no widow's weeds for him—and have a new husband before the month was out. Some spendthrift pup who would run through Chudley's fortune in a fortnight and leave me with naught but my garters."

And knowing Aunt Bedelia, Minerva mused as they hurried out to her waiting carriage, she would do just that.

Primrose Hill, where once Henry Tudor hunted and his daughter Elizabeth rode with abandon, was a popular spot for the aggrieved of London. Cuckold husbands, cheated gamesters, and insulted rivals came to settle their differences with honor across the grassy knoll rising at the far end of Regent's Park.

Aunt Bedelia's driver had been ordered, threatened, and harangued not to let anything get in his way— so the good man gave the horses their heads and the usually staid beasts raced through the empty streets, the carriage rocking and tossing the occupants back and forth in their seats. Minerva clung to the strap on the wall and prayed they would make it in time.

How could a few hours change one so? she wondered. For now she understood what it meant to love another, and this wretched duel could end it all in a single shot.

"Oh, I do wish he would hurry," Bedelia complained as the carriage rattled and screeched around another corner and began to climb the hill. "We will be too late and they shall both be dead."

Minerva glanced over at her aunt. "I daresay we may be joining Chudley and Langley in the afterworld if your driver hurries much more."

As it was, a few minutes later the careening carriage came to a plunging stop and both ladies tumbled out on wavering legs. The hillside swirled in an early morning mist, and it took Minerva a few moments to get her bearings.

Not so for her aunt. "Oooh!" Bedelia gasped, pointing the way.

Minerva turned to find the two men about fifty yards away. As the wisps of fog began to curl away on a hint of a morning breeze, it revealed Chudley and Langley, having marked off their paces, turning to aim and fire. On either side of the field stood the witnesses—their seconds and a black-clad surgeon, none of whom paid the newly arrived ladies any heed.

Besides, it was too late.

Even before Minerva could protest, both pistols barked to life, the sharp retorts and the puffs of smoke tearing through her heart as if she'd been struck. She sank to her knees.

Langley's bullet neatly trimmed a small branch over Chudley's head, dropping the leaves like a May Day crown atop the viscount's dignified beaver hat.

She would have smiled at such a roguish feat if it hadn't been for the sight that caught her eye as the last of the mist cleared from atop the hill.

There, just beyond the opponents, sat a man atop his horse, his hand outstretched with a smoking pistol aimed directly at Langley.

For Langley and Chudley's shots hadn't been the only ones fired at that moment. And while Langley purposely fired honorably up into the tree above his opponent, this man had fired with deadly intent.

Minerva tried to shout, tried to warn the seconds, anyone, but the only thing she saw was Langley wavering, his hand on his chest.

Oh, heavens! He's been shot! She hauled herself up and ran headlong toward him, stumbling twice, yet before she reached his side, he dropped like a stone to the ground. Throwing herself beside him, she heaved him over, and to her horror a great stain of blood spilled across his chest.

Bedelia, who had hurried after her, arrived just then and screamed, a piercing, keening wail that might well have been heard across the distant Thames.

Minerva glanced up at the rider in the distance, even as the surgeon and Lord Chudley came striding over. Bedelia's cacophony seemed enough confirmation for the assassin, for he saluted Minerva with his pistol and rode off.

Chudley arrived at his wife's side and gave her a companionable pat on the arm. "There there, my dear, no need for hysterics."

Bedelia pointed at Langley's bloodied chest. "Oh, Chudley, what have you done?"

"I only meant to nick him," he said, taking another bored glance down at the baron.

"It wasn't you, my lord," Minerva said, looking up. "There was another man, over there." She pointed at the now distant figure riding off at a furious pace. "He fired as well. It wasn't the viscount's bullet that struck Langley, but that man's." The seconds and surgeon gaped at her, and she continued, "I will testify to it. This isn't Chudley's doing."

"Fine way to ruin my reputation, you madcap

girl," Lord Chudley scolded, nudging his toe into Langley's side. "Of course it was my bullet that hit this good-for-nothing devil. I've as good as killed him."

Minerva staggered to her feet. "My lord, this is nothing to take credit for! There is a killer who is getting away!" She looked from the seconds to the surgeon and then back to Lord Chudley. "Aren't any of you going to stop him?"

"Good God, Minerva!" Langley muttered from his spot on the ground. "Do you have to be so demmed observant?"

Langley warily opened his eyes and gazed up at her. He refrained from laughing as her face went from shock to relief and then a sort of white fury that had him wondering if he wasn't going to be truly dead in a few moments, instead of only feigning dead.

"You . . . you . . . you . . ." she stammered.

The light in her eyes said she'd settled on relief, but this was Minerva, his Minerva, and he knew she could be a prickly, mercurial sort.

'Twas why he loved her. Furious one moment, just as passionate the next. Steady and calm in a crisis, ready to do battle when necessary.

Langley grinned. *Yes, he loved her.* It was a staggering notion.

Even as he started to get up, if only to gather her into his arms and kiss away her now murderous gaze—for truly, he still wasn't completely sure she wasn't going to take up one of the second's pistols and finish him off—Chudley planted his booted foot atop his chest, pinning him down. "Not so fast, Langley. He's not quite out of sight yet. You need to remain mortally wounded a few moments more."

"Needn't sound so pleased with the notion, my good man," Langley said, winking at Minerva.

"Was a rather galling notion to have to miss you when I shot, but duty first, I've always said," Lord Chudley replied.

"Andrew, will they be able to keep track of him?" Langley asked, nodding toward the road that led down the backside of the hill.

Lord Andrew, dressed as a somber London surgeon, pulled his wide-brimmed hat from his head. "They'll keep him in their sights. He won't get away. Not this time."

"Excellent plan, if I do say so," Chudley said.

"Thank you, Uncle Chudley," the young man said, grinning. "I knew you would be perfect for the task."

Minerva glanced over her shoulder at the viscount and then back down at Langley. "This was all a ruse? You wretched beasts! You could have told us."

Aunt Bedelia added her dismay by hitting her husband squarely in the shoulder with her reticule. "Chudley! You had me believing I was about to spend the remainder of my days hiding on the Continent surrounded by naught but low, horrid company. How could you?"

The viscount rubbed his shoulder. "Completely necessary, my dear. Why, you and Lady Standon added just the necessary drama to our little scenario. I daresay, your excellent shrieking will have all of London thinking that Lord Langley is dead, or at the very least, mortally wounded."

"And you, Lord Andrew!" Aunt Bedelia added,

rounding on her husband's nephew. "I shall have some sharp words for your mother about your part in all this!"

Lord Andrew groaned, and Langley felt a moment of pity for the young man.

"Is he gone?" Langley asked, changing the subject.

Lord Andrew glanced around. "Yes. You can sit up."

Langley did so, plucking a silver salver out of the front of his shirt.

"My salver!" Minerva gasped as she retrieved it. "Whatever were you doing with my salver . . ." He didn't want to tell her, but of course the lady put the pieces together quickly. "You came here knowing you might be shot at." She shook the dented thick metal at him as if she meant to finish the fate that the salver had saved him from.

"Not 'might be,' for indeed, I *was* shot at," he corrected. Langley shook out his shirt, and the spent lump of lead dropped to the grass. "Though I knew it wasn't going to be Chudley's bullet that I had to be concerned with." He turned to the viscount. "But you might have pulled your shot a little more to the right. I demmed well felt your lead go whistling past my shoulder."

Chudley guffawed a bit. "Had to make it look good."

"But the blood," Lady Chudley said, with a shudder. "Good heavens how could that be?"

Lord Langley held up a small bladder. "Pig's blood. An old Foreign Office trick. When I fell over, I nicked it and . . ." He waved at the mess on his shirt.

Minerva took a step back. "So this was all a farce?"

Langley nodded. "No, not all of it. Lord Chudley's

challenge was real—though twenty some years in the making." He glanced over at Lord Andrew. "Why don't you do the honors?"

The young man shot a wary glance at Bedelia and then took up the story. "I meant no distress to you, Aunt," he began. "It was only done to keep Langley alive."

"Harrumph!" the old girl sputtered, as if she thought that a foolhardy notion in itself.

Langley picked up the story. "Lord Andrew and Chudley thought it would work to our advantage if everyone believed I'd cocked up my toes and died for real. If only to lure our enemies into a sense of complacency."

"That man," Minerva said, pointing to the empty spot on the hill where the rider had been, "was here to ensure that no matter what, you didn't come down from this hill alive." Her brow furrowed, and Langley could only guess at the conjecture going on inside her head. "Was that Nottage?"

"I don't know. I didn't get a good look."

Aunt Bedelia stepped forward. "Whyever would someone want you dead, Lord Langley? Beyond the obvious reasons."

Lord Throssell, who had stood as a second, let out a bark of a laugh.

"Because of what I know," Langley told her. "Or rather, what I knew."

"What you knew? Are you addled, sir? Because I am starting to think you are all 'round the bend," Aunt Bedelia prodded, as only she could.

"There was a time when I would have agreed with you," he told her. "You see, about three years ago I was attacked in Paris—struck from behind. When I woke up, in Abbaye prison, I barely knew who I was, let alone where I was. It was nearly a year before I began to remember anything." He glanced over at Minerva. "Like who I was or why I was in Paris." He shook his head. "But the events beforehand, why someone wanted me killed—try as I might, I can only remember shadowy bits and pieces."

"So your lack of memory isn't enough for your enemies," Minerva pointed out, hands fisted to her hips. "They still want you finished off."

"That's the rub, my lady," Lord Andrew chimed in. "No one but those of us here know that Lord Langley can't recall the necessary evidence needed to bring down Sir Basil, and from the looks of it, Neville Nottage. For this much we suspect: Sir Basil Browning is the mastermind behind a series of crimes that could disgrace England, and worst of all, put the shaky peace on the Continent into chaos. Anger many of our allies."

"Allies we will need in the coming months," Chudley added. "Especially now that there are rumors Napoleon has escaped and is raising his army anew."

"Sir Basil? Do you mean to say you think Brownie is behind some grand scheme?" Aunt Bedelia scoffed, brushing aside the shocking news about that horrid Corsican. "Lord Andrew, it's no wonder your mother won't speak of you. You make it sound as if he'd gone and stole all the crown jewels of Europe!"

All the crown jewels. . .

Those words, spoken in haste, lit something in his memories. And from the way Minerva's eyes widened, it seemed they sparked something in her mind as well.

"Langley, think of it," she said. "The arrival of the nannies. The grooves in the picture frames. Lady Brownett at the theatre." She ticked off the evidence like an excited child. "The velvet we found at Langley House. The case that holds the Sterling diamonds is lined like that as well."

"Yes, by God, you have it!" he said. "Jewels. They were stealing jewels and then shipping them home in my art collections."

Everyone gaped at them.

He grinned at her. "My lady, you are too smart by half."

"I am just pleased I could help," she said, smiling back at him.

Then Lord Throssell piped up. "Jewels, you say? Why the contessa was going on and on last night about her missing pearls and the duchessa's lost rubies." He glanced at the others. "I fear she'd had a bit too much to drink." Then he rubbed his head. "I think I had as well, for I daresay I promised to replace those demmed pearls."

"There you have it," Aunt Bedelia said proudly, beaming at her niece. "Now go arrest the lot of them and we can all go home and put an end to this nonsense."

"Unfortunately, my dear," Chudley said, "we haven't enough evidence, save our suspicions, and Lady Standon's excellent theories."

"Break into the Foreign Office!" Bedelia declared. "Find it."

"It isn't there," Langley told her.

"Ooh! You foolhardy man!" Minerva gasped, shaking a finger at him. "That is where you went last night, isn't it? You broke into the—" She stopped herself and sucked in a deep breath, as if she didn't want to finish the sentence.

"Minerva, we are going to have to work on your discretion," Langley said.

"Yes, I suppose," she demurred. "I should learn not to speak out of turn." Then she grinned and said, "Though not just yet." Turning to Lord Andrew and Lord Chudley, she asked, "What do we do next?"

Not really asked, more like prodded. Demanded. Ordered.

"Lord Andrew's crew is following our assassin—"

"Nottage," Minerva corrected.

"Yes, yes, if you insist. Nottage," Chudley said, his whiskers bristling to be so corrected. "Then once he's reported in to Sir Basil, which I have no doubt he will, we'll nab him and have him held on charges of murder."

She didn't look all that convinced. "How will you hold a man for murder charges when the victim was shot at a duel with another man?"

Lord Chudley huffed again. "I have a friend at Bow Street who owes me a favor. He'll keep that fellow locked up where no one will find him. In the meantime . . ." The viscount took his wife's hand and brought it to his lips. "This is where you come in, my dear. You need to return to Town—"

Aunt Bedelia beamed with delight. "And do what I do best?"

"Yes, precisely," Chudley told her. "Recount this morning's events high and low. Lament to anyone who will listen that I am off to the Continent, and that Lord Langley is . . ."

"Lost. Gone. Dearly departed," Langley instructed. "And do make my stance in the face of your husband's noted marksmanship a brave and valiant one."

"Turn you into a hero?" she scoffed. "As if you deserve such an honor, you rakish devil!"

"Because I have an offer to make," he told her, "a private one."

"Careful there, Lord Langley, or I will shoot you," Chudley said.

Bedelia rapped her husband on his shoulder. "I am no light-skirt, sir. You should have known better than to marry the likes of Susannah Sullivan all those years ago."

"I thought we agreed never to discuss our previous spouses," Chudley said.

Aunt Bedelia's brow furrowed, but so reminded said nothing more. Rather she knelt beside Langley and he whispered his offer into her ear. She paused for a moment, then her mouth spread in a wide smile. As she got up, with Chudley's help, she said to Langley, "There won't be a dry eye in London, my lord. When I get done, they will wonder why you haven't been elevated to a saint."

True to their deception, the seconds carried Lord Langley to the carriage as if he were in mortal danger.

Chudley kissed his wife good-bye and rode off toward the Dover road.

But Minerva lingered for a moment, gathering her thoughts, trying to pull together the details. As she glanced over at the spot where the man had shot from, she tried to reconcile her nagging doubts.

What was it Chudley had said? *A demmed fine shot.*

And was it by a Foreign Office agent? Or perhaps a hired assassin?

Mayhap . . .

For she couldn't help shake another suspicion. That the man who fired that shot had been someone else.

Like a former army officer.

But what would Gerald Adlington have to gain by killing Lord Langley? She bit her lips together and stole a glance back at Langley as one then another possibility raged through her thoughts.

To force her hand, perhaps? For the Sterling diamonds? Definitely. Then he wouldn't have to wait for her supposed nuptials to get his money; rather, he could just make good his threat to take the Sterling diamonds and be gone.

Could it have been Gerald the other night, beneath that greatcoat and low-slung hat? He was certainly the right height and build as Gerald . . .

And he'd been at the theatre . . . threatened her . . . Oh, why hadn't she considered this before now?

And if it was true, that this Lord Andrew was going to capture him, and it was Gerald, then she had no doubt Adlington would sell her out if he thought it would gain him his freedom.

Minerva shivered. She could only hope it had been someone other than her devilish foe.

"Is something wrong?" Langley asked from inside the carriage. "You looked demmed pale out there in the cold."

She shook her head. "No. 'Tis nothing," she said, climbing inside the carriage and sitting down next to him.

At least she hoped it wasn't.

When they arrived at the house at Brook Street, it seemed that news of the duel had preceded them.

A crowd was gathered outside, while inside the house the nannies lined the foyer. Tasha's footman, as well as a couple of servants from across the street, were called to help carry the wounded baron up to Minerva's room.

How he did it, Minerva didn't know, but Langley nearly had her believing he was on his deathbed. In addition to his bloodied shirt, he groaned and moaned with each jostle, hanging onto her hand as if it were his last lifeline to this world.

When the duchessa saw him, in true Italian fashion she dropped to her knees wailing and crying. Tasha patted her shoulder and stood as straight and upright as a solitary pine, tears glistening on her cheeks.

Brigid clung to Knuddles, while beside her, Lord Throssell had his arm around her shoulders.

"Not good," the man muttered. "Not good at all. Won't last the night, I daresay. Shame that. Demmed shame."

Jamilla surveyed the proceedings with a handkerchief stuffed to her lips, her kohled eyes revealing nothing.

Minerva followed the litter up the stairs, and when she came to the landing, she glanced back and found that only the margravine seemed unmoved, as if she wouldn't believe any of it—at least not until she saw Langley breathe his last.

"Do you need anything, dear Lady Standon?" Nanny Helga asked, almost sounding sincere. "We could take turns sitting vigil with you."

Minerva tapped down the shiver running down her spine at the woman's offer and instead shook her head. "I think it best if he has naught but peace and quiet until . . . until . . ."

This implication made the contessa sob even harder, and the lady's wails prodded Aunt Bedelia into the next act of their plan.

"Come now, all of you, the man needs peace and quiet. I think it is best if you all take refuge at Hollindrake House—it's just on the next block over. If only to give Lady Standon these last few hours—"

"Yes, yes," Jamilla readily agreed. "There is nothing more for us here."

Tasha nodded as well and helped Lucia to her feet, while Throssell guided Brigid out the door. Only the margravine lingered, waiting for Tasha's footman to come down.

"How bad is he?" she asked.

"The lead is still inside him. Even if they could get it out, the surgeon will only finish him off in the trying."

The margravine put her handkerchief to her lips and nodded, looking as aggrieved as Lucia.

Or was she smiling? Minerva wondered as she took one last furtive glance over the railing.

"Are they all gone?" Langley asked.

"Yes," Minerva said, glancing back over her shoulder as she pressed the door closed. "Apparently with you on your last breath, that lessens their chances of finding their missing jewels."

"Don't rule out their determination just yet," he told her. "Gemstones have a powerful hold over their owners."

"They do indeed," she agreed, opening the case that held the Sterling diamonds and dangling them in front of her.

"And we are all alone?" Langley asked, a wicked smile on his lips.

"Yes."

He waggled his brows at her and patted the spot next to him on the bed.

Minerva stifled a laugh. "Aren't you afraid the exertion will kill you in your state?"

"Only if you keep me waiting," he teased back.

"I may finish you off myself. You had me worried sick."

"Truly?"

"Yes." She crossed her arms over her chest and glared at him.

"Why?"

"Langley, do I have to answer that?"

"Yes," he said. "But if you would rather, you can show me how worried you were." Again he patted the spot on the bed beside him.

"I am still in a pique. Haven't you the least concern I might finish you off?" she asked, sauntering over to the bed, then falling into his open arms.

"That is what makes it so much more fun," he whispered before his lips claimed hers.

Chapter 15

A former lover is like a dog that bites. Never think that just because they slept in your bed and held a tendre *for you once, they won't take off your hand at the least little provocation.*

Advice to Felicity Langley from her Nanny Brigid

"If you do not stop pacing about, I will shoot you myself," Minerva told Langley, who continued to wear a path in front of the hearth despite her warning. "You are supposed to be on death's door."

They'd taken refuge in her bedroom, with only her trusted staff in the house: Mrs. Hutchinson, the woman's daughter Mary, and of course Agnes. Mr. Mudgett had been sent over to ensure that the nannies were well settled at Hollindrake House, and set Staines to rights if the duke's butler protested.

This left the house uncharacteristically quiet, which was unnerving in itself.

"I will be dead if I don't find a way to uncover the truth about Brownie and his lot." Langley paused and glanced at the painting hanging over his bed, cringing at the lopsided folly.

Or was it just a reminder of his own folly? she wondered.

"Langley, what would you be doing if you hadn't this inconvenience before you?"

"I'd call it more than an inconvenience," he muttered.

"Yes, well, I thought it more diplomatic than to ask you what you would do if you weren't under threat of attainder, or what coat you would like to wear to your trial."

He stopped, and for a moment she thought he was going to explode with anger, but instead the mirth returned to his eyes. "I don't think they'd bother much with a trial."

She smiled and got up, crossing the room and reaching under her bed, then dragging out a great atlas. Hefting it atop the bed, she patted a spot beside her. "Come, let us plot our escape."

"Us?"

"I won't be left behind to answer all the questions. Risk being sent off to who-knows-where all because of this faux engagement. If you are going to make a run for it, I am coming along." She flipped the pages and then stabbed her finger into a spot.

"Bossy baggage," he said, sitting down and glancing at the place her finger marked. "No, that will never do," he went on, shaking his head.

"Abyssinia? Whyever not? Sounds wonderfully exotic."

"Hot and full of the most dreadful bugs, some the size of your thumb."

Minerva's brows drew together and she pulled her finger back hastily. "Then you tell me where we would go."

For the next hour he did just that, trailing his fingers across the pages, regaling her with tales of all the places he had seen—many of which she assumed were wild exaggerations.

"And I wager the sultan would grant me sanctuary, give us a fine house, as well as my own harem."

"A harem!" she protested.

"Yes, it would be expected," he said, grinning as he lay back, his hands behind his head.

Minerva tossed a pillow at him. "I think not. Hasn't the last week in this harem been enough?"

He snorted. "I didn't say I intended to fill it. I daresay you would keep me well-occupied for some time."

"I would, would I?"

"Oh, yes," he said, edging the book aside and pulling her into his arms. She made a slight protest, but only slight, for the moment his lips nuzzled her neck, any hint of pique she'd felt vanished.

"We'd spend our nights making love in the gardens with only the tinkling music of fountains, the air perfumed by an array of flowers that would still seem pale beside your beauty."

"You are naught but a charming rogue, Langley," she said.

"A rogue no more," he promised before kissing her, thoroughly, soundly.

But their interlude wasn't meant to be, for downstairs the bell over the front door jangled loudly.

"Your aunt!" he groaned. "Doesn't that woman have anything else to do?"

Minerva shook her head, rising from the bed. "No, that isn't Aunt Bedelia." She paused for a second, and then glanced at Langley in alarm when she heard the front door creak open.

"Dear heavens, they are just coming in," she whispered, going straight for her night table and reaching inside the drawer for Thomas-William's pistol.

"Give that to me," he told her, holding out his hand.

"No. And do be still. You are supposed to be on death's door. Besides, no one would think that I'd be carrying such a thing."

Minerva went to her door and eased it open.

Of course it creaked, but she could hear a whispered argument down in the foyer. Slowly she eased her way to the railing to glance down, and to her annoyance, Langley followed right on her heels.

"You are supposed to be dying."

"I won't have you going first."

"I know exactly what I am doing."

"That is what I fear."

Cautiously she pointed the pistol over the railing before she tipped her nose over as well.

"Good God, Lady Standon!" came a beleaguered voice. "Do you always have to be pointing that demmed pistol at me!"

"Lord Clifton?" she asked.

"Minerva darling, whatever is going on?" Lucy Sterling, now Lady Clifton, pushed past her husband, unconcerned by the loaded pistol pointed at her. "Do put that away, I fear it gives Clifton hives." She glanced over Minerva's shoulder. "See there, Clifton, I told you and Elinor that Lord Langley could hardly be as ill-used as everyone is saying."

Then she glanced from Langley's dark expression to Minerva's tousled state. "And sir, just so we are clear, if you are merely dallying with my friend, the reports of your demise will not be in vain."

It only took a few minutes to sort out their newly arrived company, with Minerva and Lucy settling into the dining room. Langley gave Clifton a hearty handshake and a nod to join him down in the kitchen. As it was, the earl had news from Lord Andrew.

Meanwhile, Elinor Sterling, now the Duchess of Parkerton, had gone straight to the kitchen, and was even now coming up from Mrs. Hutchinson's lair with a tea tray.

"For you know how long it would take if we dared asked her to do it," she said with a laugh as she settled the tray down and began to pour for her friends.

Minerva had deliberately chosen the dining room, because she didn't want them to be seen in the front parlor where some noisy old tabby might decide that "poor Lady Standon" was taking callers.

"What are you two doing here?" she asked.

"Come to help," Lucy said.

"Most decidedly," Elinor agreed, passing the plate of scones around.

"You shouldn't have come, this isn't like before." When they all lived in the house and Minerva had helped them both gain their true loves.

Then she glanced at her friends. Honestly, if ever there were two women capable of helping her save Langley, it was Elinor and Lucy.

Lucy grinned. "Yes, you are seeing sense now. We can help, and I daresay you have need of us."

"What have you heard?" Minerva asked.

"The situation isn't good," Lucy said, lowering her voice. "The man who shot at Lord Langley escaped."

"No!" Minerva gasped. "But Lord Andrew and Lord Chudley seemed so confident—"

"Aye, they were. But this fellow is far more deadly than they had assumed. He killed the agent who tried to capture him."

Minerva sank back, her teacup rattling in its saucer. Oh, this was terrible news. "How do you know this?"

Lucy shrugged. "Lord Andrew came to call not an hour ago, and I might have been—"

"Eavesdropping?" Elinor made a *tsk tsk* sound. "Lucy Sterling, you are a countess now. Proper countesses do not snoop about." Then she grinned and all three of them laughed, for they all knew Lucy would never be an ordinary or proper countess.

But the mood returned to its somber air all too quickly, for Minerva let out a long sigh. "However will Langley get this Brownie character to confess now?"

"Brownie?" Elinor asked. "Do you mean Sir Basil Brownett?"

"Yes," Minerva said.

"Why he's on the guest list for Parkerton's soiree tonight." She glanced at both of them with upraised brows. "The soiree he is throwing to celebrate our marriage? The one you've both been invited to attend?"

"Oh, dear, Elinor, I forgot!" Minerva confessed. With everything that had happened in the last few days, her social calendar had been the least of her worries.

"Sir Basil is going to be there tonight?" Lucy asked, her dark expression giving both her friends pause.

"Yes," Elinor replied. "Everyone is going to be there. Parkerton rarely throws a party, so no one will miss it—especially the likes of Sir Basil— mushroom that he is, for the Prime Minister will be there as well."

Lucy grinned. "Then I know exactly what we can do."

"We?" Minerva shook her head vehemently. "No, I cannot allow either of you to get mired in this mess."

Elinor shrugged. "Just try and stop us."

"Minerva Sterling, you have no choice in this," Lucy told her, winking at Elinor. "For if you don't let us help, I shall tell Felicity that you've had her diamonds all this time."

Down in the kitchen, Langley sat back on his stool. "He got away?"

Lucy's news had run quickly down the dumb-waiter.

"Demmit, I had hoped to tell you before my wife did," Clifton said. "But yes. Lord Andrew came by just an hour ago. He thought it would be of little notice to have Lucy come calling on Minerva."

"He killed an agent?" The baron's blood ran cold.

Clifton nodded.

"I can't believe this is Nottage," Langley said, pushing his stool back.

"He came back from Paris after you were reported dead a changed man." Clifton glanced up the dumbwaiter. "I think he learned more from you than writing reports."

"I never murdered anyone," Langley shot back.

"No, but you were always considered one of the most devious agents out there."

Langley accepted this as praise, but right now he wished he were also as ruthless as Nottage so he could guess the man's next move.

Before anyone else lost their life.

"I appreciate you coming, Clifton, don't mistake the matter, but I wish Lord Andrew hadn't dragged you into this as well."

Clifton sat up. "Ellyson was Lucy's father. I'll not have his name sullied. Or yours either."

Langley nodded his thanks before he retook his stool. He went to say something, but Clifton put his fingers to his lips, his head bent toward the opening.

"What the devil are they up to?" Langley whispered.

"Concocting some harebrained scheme, if I know my wife."

"Demmed if I will let Minerva get caught up in this any further," Langley said.

But as they listened to Lucy lay out her plan, as meticulous and cunning as anything her father could have devised, Clifton turned to his old friend and grinned. "It just might work."

Langley shook his head. "The hell if I am going to let Minerva walk into some trap. A man died today because of this folly. I won't let her—" He couldn't even say it.

"That is the beauty of it," Clifton replied, sitting back and taking a drink—coughing a bit, for they'd poured healthy measures from Mrs. Hutchinson's private stock, a brew she bought from a Seven Dials distiller.

The sort that could have been used to clean out the Paris sewers.

"We won't let them carry it out," Clifton said. "Minerva can be the lure, but she'll never make it anywhere near Brownie. We'll all be close at hand to make sure their meddling ends there. Then we'll spring our own trap."

But from the corner of the kitchen came an argument that stopped them both.

"Don't you two gentlemen go and underestimate me gels there," Mrs. Hutchinson said, waving a boozy hand at him. "Let them get the job done. Got bottom, they does. Get it done right without your infernal meddling."

But Langley had no intention of letting Minerva meddle in his affairs. Not if it put her life at risk.

Long after Lucy and Clifton and Elinor had left, Minerva brought up the supper tray, her hands trembling. She didn't know if she would be able to pull this scheme off, but Langley's future—and perhaps even hers—depended on it.

Their future.

Of course he'd never said a word about them being together once his name was cleared, and even this afternoon, for all their fanciful talk of travels and far off adventures, he'd never once given any indication that it was naught but a way to pass the time.

But she knew what she had to do. Get him to drink the wine and then slip away. Elinor had already sent around a gown—her scandalous scarlet dress she'd bought in Petticoat Lane—and Agnes was getting it ready downstairs in the morning room.

"Here is supper," she said, pushing open the door to her room.

To her surprise, Langley wasn't at the small table by the fireplace, but in the bed.

"Excellent, I'm famished," he said, his brows waggling suggestively.

"For a man who is supposed to be dying, you are showing a cheeky amount of verve."

"How can I not?" he teased. "You bring me to life every time you walk in the room." To prove his point, he plucked the sheet back to reveal he was completely naked, and as he'd said, happy to see her.

"Langley, now is hardly the time," she said, wishing her body wouldn't warm so when she looked at him. Gracious heavens, the man was sinfully handsome.

"Come to bed, Minerva," he beckoned.

"We should eat first, while it is hot," she argued, though even to her own ears it was hardly forcibly put, for now her insides were growing wet and tight.

Distract him and get him to drink the wine, Lucy had advised.

Well, making love was thirsty work, she mused. And there was a good hour and a half before Elinor's carriage would come around to pick her up.

"Langley—" she protested faintly, even as she crossed the room to the bed, "you are incorrigible."

He caught hold of her and pulled her into bed atop him. "I prefer insatiable, desirable, irresistible."

She laughed and let him pull her gown up, baring her legs, letting his hands roam and explore her, while his lips captured hers and kissed away any further arguments.

Moving past her undergarments, he touched her, stroking her, bringing her right up to where she was panting with a passionate lust. He'd eased her gown over her head and she wore naught but her chemise, though barely, for he'd freed her breasts to lavish them with his tongue, suckling deep until both nipples were taut.

"However do you do this to me?" she gasped, reveling in the heady desires running through her limbs.

"You drive me to it," he told her. "I want you like I've never wanted a woman. You make me rock hard just by walking in the room."

"I'm usually arguing with you," she teased back, reaching down and touching him, stroking him in return.

Langley groaned, and he raised her by her hips and settled her down atop his erect member. "Love me, Minerva. Love me."

She slid down over him, relishing every bit of him as he filled her.

Having forgotten everything she needed to do this dark night, she let herself give over to the bliss of making love with him.

She rode him slowly at first, as much teasing him

as herself, but then slowly their pace grew quicker, more anxious, as they both gave in to their desires.

Minerva felt wanton, brazen as she rode atop him, her body driving back and forth along his hardness, teasing her, leading her toward the bright dawn.

Beneath her, Langley groaned, deeply and with longing, like a wolf calling to its mate. His body thrust upward and she could feel him come alive inside her, savage, deep thrusts that pushed her over the edge with its wild cadence.

"Minerva!" he cried out. "Oh God, Minerva!"

She moaned and continued to ride him, letting the same waves wash over her. Over and over, leaving her spent and content.

She collapsed into his arms, his heart hammering wildly beneath her ear.

He stroked her hair and whispered endearments and promises for later, his arms warm around her, a safe harbor from all that lurked in the night beyond.

Everything that threatened to destroy him.

And for a time she lay there, letting him coax her into believing every night would be like this until he grew quiet and still, having fallen asleep. He hadn't drank the wine, but perhaps this was better for he was sound asleep and she wouldn't have the guilt weighing on her that she'd tricked him.

Then she heard a carriage pull to a stop outside. "And it will be like this always," she whispered as she slipped from the bed, then gently lay the coverlet back over him. Tossing her gown over her head and catching up her boots, she went to the door.

Having taken the precaution earlier of oiling the hinges herself, she closed the door silently, and then sighed as she locked the door and took the key with her, slipping down the stairs out into the night, where Agnes was already waiting in the carriage to help her change.

Langley waited until he heard the carriage begin to drive away and then sprang into action. But when he got to the door, he was more than a little piqued to find she'd locked him in.

Not that he couldn't get such a simple lock open, he mused as he grabbed up his boot and dug into the sleeve concealed inside.

But this was delaying him more than he wanted.

For he needed to catch up with Minerva before she entered the trap with Brownie and Nottage, especially if his former secretary was willing to kill to keep his freedom and his ill-gotten bounty.

Clifton planned to do the same with Lucy and had promised to give the same instructions to Elinor's husband, the Duke of Parkerton.

The last thing Langley wanted was one of the three former Standon widows blundering into a confrontation—no matter how much bottom they had.

With a few twists of his pick, the lock opened. He grinned as he got to his feet.

Only to find a pistol shoved into his nose.

He looked up at the lady holding it. "Good God, woman! I haven't time for this."

"Aye, darling, but you do. And whyever do you look surprised to see me? You had to know I rarely give up what is mine."

* * *

Minerva arrived at Parkerton House not long after. Agnes, having grumbled about the unconventional dressing room, had managed to get her mistress in order, including the Sterling diamonds.

As she climbed out of the carriage, Minerva turned every head, as Elinor and Lucy claimed she would.

" 'Tis naught but the dress and the diamonds," she muttered under her breath as she walked up the steps, head held high despite the gasps and whispers that parted the way before her.

"I wouldn't think she would be out—"

"No, not tonight!"

"Shameless!"

"Whoever would have thought she would—"

Yes, truly, Minerva would have agreed, who would have ever thought she, of all the Standon widows, would fall in love with a notorious baron and risk everything to save his reputation.

Truly, she found all of his noble "for King and country" notions a bit over the top and cared only for seeing his name restored.

Because she loved him. Minerva tipped her nose a little bit higher. She loved Langley. It was a dizzying notion. Rather like having the man make love to her.

He's going to be furious with you.

Yes, she argued with herself. *He will be. But he cannot do this alone.*

Nor can you.

Minerva shivered, her fingers going to the Sterling diamonds around her throat.

But she didn't have to do this alone, for not long after she entered the house, first Lucy and then

Elinor flanked her, the three of them laying out their final plans.

"The toad is over there," Lucy said with a slight tip of her head.

"Aunt Bedelia calls him naught but a dull stick," Minerva said as she glanced in that direction. "Just a moment. I know him. Langley introduced us the other night at the theatre. I remember his wife was quite the preening mushroom."

"Dreadful woman," Elinor added. "Arrived dripping in gems, and had the audacity to point out that they were real, unlike so many other ladies' jewels."

"Yes, and now we know who they really belong to, don't we," Minerva said, more under her breath than as a question, her gaze swiveling toward the woman.

Lucy nodded, while Elinor smiled and said, "Allow me to distract Lady Brownett so you can work your wiles on her husband."

"My wiles, indeed!" Minerva scoffed.

Lucy shook her head. "No, Minerva, I daresay you have found your heart, for you have bloomed in the last week. Langley must be magnificent."

Elinor nodded.

"He is," Minerva whispered as she began her turn through the crowd, her gaze fixed on Sir Basil as Elinor lured Lady Brownett off toward the refreshment table.

Setting to her task, Minerva sauntered past him, like one of the nannies might, carefully and seductively casting a come-hither glance over her shoulder at the man until she caught his eye.

"Lady Standon!" he sputtered, wide-eyed with surprise.

She paused and glanced at him as if she couldn't quite place him, then smiled. "Ah, yes, Sir Basil, just the man I was looking for."

"For me? I would have thought you would be home. With Lord Langley! Dire straits, I hear."

"Dead," she replied, making a nonchalant shrug as she gazed out at the crush in the ballroom.

Sir Basil paled. "Dead, you say! Shocking."

She looked over at him. "Yes, rather shocking indeed." Then she took a step toward him.

"But you are here—" he stammered as he backed up, glancing around and realizing she was cornering him into an alcove.

"Of course, where else would I be? I had to find you."

"Me? Lady Standon, I think your grief has impaired your judgment. Perhaps you might have a relative or a friend close at hand—"

Minerva closed the gap between them. "Sir Basil, I don't need anyone but you."

"Madame! This is becoming scandalous. What you need—"

"What I need is money for the surgeon so he'll keep quiet as to why it wasn't Chudley's bullet that killed Langley, but the second one fired by your associate."

This time Sir Basil looked like a three day old fish, eyes unblinking, his mouth stuck open.

"I have no idea—"

She put a finger on his chest and prodded him. "I think you know exactly what I mean. And since you saw fit to ruin my chances for a good inheritance as Langley's widow—truly, Sir Basil, you couldn't have had him murdered until after I married him?—so I have come for my cut."

"Your wha-a-at?"

"My fair portion," she told him, glancing down at her gloves and then up into his beady, porcine eyes.

"Madame, this is madness!"

"Is it?" she mused. "Before Langley passed on to his reward, he realized he was leaving me in dire straits, and wrote a rather detailed account as to what he was doing in Paris before he was attacked."

This caught Sir Basil's full attention.

"While I am sure the Prime Minister would find it excellent reading, or the *Times* might find it enlightening to print, I daresay it has other values."

The man swallowed—gulped, really. "I have no idea what you mean, madame."

But Minerva knew he was bluffing. So she said, "I wager you do, or I can go ask your wife where exactly she got her necklace. I know an Italian duchessa who might find those rubies quite familiar. And I doubt her Borgia blood would make her all that forgiving over the matter."

He began to shake.

"Yes, you do understand my meaning, and you'll meet me after the next dance upstairs, in the room at the end of the hall."

She started to walk away, but he caught her by the elbow. "I will not be blackmailed, nor will I meet you anywhere."

Shaking her arm free, she met his gaze with her own black, haughty stare. "Oh, you'll meet me. And you will be in a generous mood when you do, for if you find my blackmail—as you call it—

outrageous, I am sure there are others who will reward me handsomely." With a nod toward the doorway where the Prime Minister had just come through, she walked away, hoping her trembling knees did not give her away.

"Helga," Langley said, backing into Minerva's room.

"*Schatzi!* I don't understand why you look surprised to see me." She glanced at the rumpled bed and sniffed. "Such low tastes you've developed. How unfortunate you hadn't such a touch for the common before you stole from me."

"Stole from you?" Langley shook his head. "I have no idea what you are talking about."

Certainly there were things he didn't remember, but stealing from the margravine he would remember. For he couldn't believe he'd ever be that foolish.

"My jewels, you wretched cur. You stole my jewels. The crown jewels." She stalked closer. "Why do you think the others are here? You've stolen from all of us. You were quite productive those years you were 'lost.' But I know what you were doing. Retracing your steps and stealing from every crowned head who once hosted you."

Langley shook his head. Madness! This was utter madness. "I've been in Abbaye prison all this time."

"Bah!" she spat at him. "Who else could have climbed into my bedchamber and known where I kept them? I want my sapphires back!"

He would have liked to point out that there were about half a dozen likely candidates who knew the lady's bedchamber intimately, at least that he knew of, but being a gentleman, and the fact that she was holding a pistol, kept him from stating the obvious.

"I haven't your sapphires," he told her.

"You dare deny it? That you stole the Crown Jewels of Ansbach? And Tasha's necklace, the one that the Tsarina Catherine gave her, or Brigid's pearls—a rope that once belonged to your Queen Elizabeth, and Lucia's rubies—the Borgia rubies?"

"Egads, they've made off with a fortune," he muttered vaguely. An image of dark stones around a woman's throat flooded his thoughts. Lady Brownett! She'd had on rubies at the theatre. "Helga, it wasn't me. This entire plot was made to look like I stole your jewels. It was my secretary, Nottage, who took them."

For a moment the lady's eyes flickered with recognition at the name.

But was it more than that? Was she familiar with more than just the man's name? Had she taken him to her bed as well? He wouldn't put it past the insatiable margravine.

Even with that flicker of doubt, she wasn't about to change course. "Bah!" she scoffed. "I am not so foolish to listen to more of your lies."

She brought the pistol closer, and Langley, instead of being alarmed, realized there was no talking reason with her. Well, that was one disadvantage of being a rake. Eventually your charm ran out.

"These crimes are not mine," he insisted, sticking to the truth of the matter. "I came back to London to prove just that. The man you seek is Sir Basil. I have nearly got him caught, if only you will let me—"

"Harrumph!" She waved her pistol at him. "Where are my sapphires?"

Down below, the front door opened, and for a heartbeat Langley feared it was Minerva having returned. But then the thick trod of boots told him it wasn't.

But what he didn't expect was the sight that greeted him in the doorway. "The painter?"

"The what?" the fellow stammered.

"She told him you were the painter," Helga supplied.

"Ah, apt little liar, my Maggie is. Langley, isn't it? I'm Adlington. The man who is married to your betrothed."

Langley did a double take. "You're what?"

"Never mind who he is," Helga said, stamping her foot impatiently. But then again, the margravine never liked it when the conversation focused on any other woman than her.

"We've come for Lady Standon's diamonds," the man supplied, glancing around the room as if he expected them to be laying about.

"Ahem," the margravine coughed, glaring at the fellow.

"And her sapphires," he added.

"I have neither," Langley told them.

"But you know where she hides them," Helga said, sneering.

"Actually, she left wearing the diamonds," he said. "So unless you plan on storming the Duke of Parkerton's house and taking them in the middle of his soiree, you are out of luck."

Helga didn't take two seconds to consider the notion. "Do it," she said to Adlington.

"Do what?" he stammered, busy glancing around the room as if looking for anything else of value.

"Go to this Parkerton's house and tell Lady Standon that if she doesn't give you the diamonds, her precious Langley is dead."

"She won't give them up," Adlington said.

"Then kill her," Helga told him.

Chapter 16

When you fall in love, it is not with a name or a title or a fortune (though all those points are indispensable) but with the heart that beats inside.

Advice to Felicity Langley from her Nanny Lucia

𝒟own the block on Brook Street, a carriage sat in the shadows between the gas lamps. As the occupants watched Adlington hurry down the steps and set off at a fast clip, the lady's brow furrowed.

"There is something odd going on there," the woman said to the man sitting beside her.

"There is always something odd going on in that house," he advised.

The lady nodded in agreement. "This is more than my father being back in Town, as Lady Finch's letter said." She started to climb down the steps, but her companion stopped her. "I am going to get to the bottom of this," she said over her shoulder.

"Do you think you should go alone? From what you've told me about your Nanny Helga—"

She smiled at her husband. "I would love you to come with me, but you will make a dreadful racket. I can slip in and out without a sound."

There was no arguing that. The lady was as light-footed as a cat. Just like her father. But that didn't mean he wasn't going to stay close just in case.

Because oftentimes where the former Felicity Langley dared tread, not even angels would venture.

"Wish me luck," Minerva whispered as the set came close to ending.

"Luck," Elinor whispered back.

"There is no need," Lucy said, giving her hand a quick squeeze. "We will be right behind you."

And so Minerva crossed the room and made for the stairs as nonchalantly as she could.

"She truly wears that dress well," Lucy remarked.

Elinor tipped her head and studied her. "I daresay she does," she agreed.

"What is this?" Both women jumped at the question that rose up behind them.

"I believe it is our wives, deep in their plots," a second man replied.

Lucy and Elinor exchanged glances as first Parkerton, who took his wife's hand, and then the Earl of Clifton caught Lucy in his grasp.

"What are you doing?" Lucy demanded as she struggled to get free of her husband.

"Asking you to dance," he replied, pulling her out to the floor.

"But I am not in the mood," she told him, glancing over at Elinor, who was in much the same straits.

"Truly, Parkerton, I have a matter to attend to," she was saying.

"Foolishness," he told his duchess. "Our staff is the finest in London. They will see to whatever needs to be done."

"Including seeing Minerva safely out of harm's way," Clifton advised them.

Lucy's gaze flew up to meet her husband's.

"Yes, we know," he said, for he knew her well enough to know she would never confess her machinations, not in a thousand years. "And if you think you are going up there, just the two of you, to spring your trap on Sir Basil, you've both gone mad."

"But Minerva can't do this alone," Elinor protested.

"She isn't going to," Clifton assured them. "By now Parkerton's brother Jack and Lord Langley are in place and ready to put an end to all this."

"Helga, for the last time, I didn't steal your jewels," Langley told her.

From her post in the doorway, she scoffed at him. "Bah, *schatzi*, what makes you think I will believe your lies a second time?"

He groaned and rubbed his forehead, and in that moment he could have sworn he heard someone coming up the stairs.

Someone with the stealth of an agent. Friend or foe, it mattered not, for all he needed was to have Helga distracted for enough time to gain possession of her pistol.

So he gave them what help he could. "Oh, and what about the lies you told me?" he said, getting up.

She ruffled a bit at this. "I never lied to you! I loved you!"

Now it was his turn to scoff. "Loved me? You had me arrested to keep me in your country."

"But *schatzi*, you were going to leave me."

"I was a diplomat. I was ordered to leave. I had no choice."

"Bah! You could have found a way."

"I certainly didn't need you helping me!" he shouted at her.

"Such a small thing," she shot back. "You fuss like a child!"

"You accused me of selling secrets to the French! In my country that is treason."

She waved the pistol at him. "I withdrew the charges."

Yes, he well remembered what he'd had to do to get her to do just that. "I was disgraced at home. You would not believe the reports I had to file to straighten out your lies!" And her vengeful charges had probably given Sir Basil and Nottage the idea of using his former lovers to ensnare him.

Around the corner came a sight he couldn't fathom. At first he thought he was imagining things.

Fanny. Fanny come back from the dead. Just as fair-haired and with the same determined set to her brow.

But then his heart swelled with pride. No, it was his Felicity. All grown and as lovely as her mother had ever been.

And carrying a large candlestick.

Just like he'd taught her.

"*Schatzi*, we could have all that again and more, just like that night in the castle when we drank too much and you insisted we go down into the armory and—"

Clunk.

The margravine fell over in a heap.

Neither Felicity or Langley bothered to catch the lady.

"I have no idea what you did with her, but I preferred not to know," Felicity said, setting down the candlestick and wiping her hands on her skirt. For a second there was a shy, awkward silence between them. Father and daughter, so long parted.

But the time was of no matter when he swept his daughter into his arms. "Felicity, you dear girl."

"Papa," she whispered, looking up at his bruised face with concern. "I thought, Tally and I both feared—"

"No more," he said, smoothing back her fair hair and gazing with awe at her face, so much like her mother's. "I am back."

And then, so much like Felicity, she got right down to business. "I got the most high-handed letter from Lady Finch this morning. What is this nonsense about you being betrothed to Minerva Sterling? It is as ridiculous as the reports that you were dead."

Minerva!

Langley caught up Helga's pistol and stepped over the lady. "Do you have a carriage?"

"Yes, but where are we going?"

"To Parkerton's. Minerva is in danger."

Felicity cocked a brow at him. "Minerva? Not Lady Standon? Not my new nanny, but Minerva? Truly?"

"Yes, truly," he said, setting a quick kiss on her brow.

"Has this anything to do with that common looking fellow I saw leaving a few minutes ago?"

"He is after Minerva and her diamonds."

"Diamonds?" Felicity protested. "Papa, you are mad. Minerva hasn't any diamonds." Then she paused. "Not unless you gave her some."

"Diamonds?" asked a tall fellow at the front door.

"Oh, dear! This is hardly how I imagined this meeting. Papa, this is my husband, the Duke of Hollindrake. Thatcher, darling, this is my father, Lord Langley." She hurried down the steps toward their carriage with the two of them trailing quickly after her. "Diamonds, indeed!"

"Do you mean the Sterling diamonds?" Thatcher asked. "I was wondering just the other day what had gotten to those."

Langley flinched. For if Sir Basil didn't end Minerva's life tonight, he suspected his daughter would be next in line as her unwitting husband described the priceless gemstones that were hers by rights and were at this very moment in danger of being lost forever.

When Minerva got to the end of the hall, she found Sir Basil standing in the middle of the parlor waiting for her.

She bowed her head slightly, acknowledging the man, and entered the room.

But to her dismay, the door closed behind her and

she turned around to find a stranger standing there, barring her escape.

Hardly a stranger, though.

"The theater . . . You were the one." And then she looked him over thoroughly. "And today at the duel. You're Neville Nottage."

"You are far too astute for your own good, Lady Standon," he said, pushing her forward into the middle of the room.

"So I've been told," she muttered. Oh, dear, two of them? Sir Basil was naught but a bureaucrat, but this other fellow . . . She stole a glance at his cold dark gaze. He was deadly.

But any moment, Lucy and Elinor would arrive and they would finish this. Still, she needed to gain them a bit more time.

"Yes, I know everything," she said. "You were Langley's secretary. You and Sir Basil concocted this scheme—to steal from Langley's old mistresses, and make Langley look like the guilty party. How you used his art shipments home to hide your crimes— for if any of this was discovered, it would be on his head, not yours."

Sir Basil paled but said nothing.

"You truly are as intelligent as you are beautiful, Lady Standon," Nottage replied. "And far too knowledgeable to live."

If Lord Langley liked the cut of his daughter's husband, he grew even fonder of his new son-in-law when the man drove like the very devil toward Parkerton's. They were there in a flash, but to his dismay they hadn't caught up with Adlington.

Which meant the man was already here, or he'd yet to arrive.

He hoped the latter, but suspected the former.

"Demmit," he muttered as he entered the crush inside. It would be nigh on impossible to find the man, let alone catch him in this crowd before he found Minerva.

So instead he let his gaze sweep over the plumes and turbans for Clifton's tall, commanding figure. And when he spied him, he dashed across the dance floor, stopping the earl in the middle of a set. "Where is she?"

"Where is she?" Clifton repeated. "What are you doing here?"

"Yes, indeed," the Duke of Parkerton echoed. "You and Jack are supposed to be on the balcony."

"I was detained," he said. "Where has she gone?"

"She just went up naught but a few moments ago—that way," he said, pointing to the stairwell.

The two of them started for the stairs, but were stopped by the imposing figure of Lady Chudley. "You cannot go bursting in after her," she told them.

"Excuse me?"

"I have been watching all that is going on tonight, and when I saw Minerva cornering Sir Basil, I knew she was up to mischief. Then he went upstairs, and then she did. And now that dreadful Gerald Adlington has gone up there."

"Adlington?" Langley gaped at her. "How do you know the man?"

"Dreadful rube. He has been blackmailing me for years. Most likely Minerva as well, now that I think about it." She caught hold of Langley's sleeve. "If anything happens to my dear girl—"

Moving quickly, Langley went for the stairs, but Clifton stopped him. "Her aunt is right. If you go barging in there, Lady Standon could be harmed. We still don't know where Nottage is."

It took every bit of willpower he possessed not to go dashing up the stairs, but Clifton was right. He had to be careful. Hadn't one man died already today over all this folly?

"Jack will have all this in hand," Parkerton told them.

Jack! Langley had forgotten all about Jack. "Which side of the house is that balcony on?"

Parkerton led the way, racing through the corridors past his astonished staff. Once outside in the garden, they moved quietly along the side the house until they were directly under the balcony.

"Tremont," Langley whispered up at the outcropping of stone.

A familiar face leaned over the edge. "Late to the party, as always," Jack Tremont teased. "About demmed time. Looking rather dicey up here."

"Can you stop them?" he asked.

" 'Fraid not. Brownie's no fool. He closed the doors the moment she came in, demmed near spotted me." He turned and glanced back inside. "Hold on a moment, who the devil is that?"

The door to the room barged open, and immediately Nottage, behind Minerva, wound his arm around her neck and dragged her back, using her as a shield.

"Who the hell are the two of you?" Adlington

sputtered as he came into the room, a pistol in his hand.

"I'd ask the same, sir!" Sir Basil demanded, having leapt to his feet.

"Her husband," Adlington declared. "What is this, Maggie? Got more than me on the hook? Or are these blokes after those baubles of mine?"

"Gerald, get out of here," she told him. "And he is not my husband," she said to Sir Basil. "He's a madman, a fool. Gerald, be smart for once and leave."

He shook his head, stubbornly, stupidly. "Not without what I got coming to me."

Sir Basil sat up. "And what might that be?"

"Them baubles, the ones around her neck," Adlington said, nodding at the Sterling diamonds. "Those are mine."

Minerva groaned. This entire trap was turning into a circus. Her gaze swept the room, even as she struggled to come up with some way to get out of this alive.

And as she did, she spied a figure out on the balcony.

If she wasn't mistaken it was the Duke of Parkerton's nefarious brother, Mad Jack Tremont.

What the devil . . .

He nodded to her and drew back into the shadows beyond.

Help was coming. She only needed to stall.

"Gerald, if it is gems you want, you should know that these gentleman have been stealing stones for years. Rubies, pearls, probably diamonds as well. From some of the richest ladies on the Continent."

"Shut up," Nottage said, winding his arm tighter around her neck.

"You blokes haven't seen a set of sapphires, have you?" Gerald asked with a sly smile, his pistol now pointed at Sir Basil. "If you were to give me her and the sapphires, I'd be glad to dispose of Lady Standon for you and forget all about this."

"Whatever is going on?" Felicity whispered, having caught up with her father and the other men.

"Minerva is trapped by Sir Basil, Nottage, and now this Adlington fellow," Langley told her, eyeing the distance up to the balcony.

"The one who is intent on taking my diamonds?" she asked.

"Yes, rather," he remarked.

"Well, what are you waiting for? Climb up there and save them."

"You mean save Lady Standon?" he corrected.

"Yes, that is exactly what I meant," she said, sounding not-so-convincing to anyone. "Oh, bother. I don't care about the diamonds, Papa. Go save the lady," she told him with a wave of her hand toward the drainpipe. "And—"

"Yes, yes, I know, if I can, save the diamonds." Langley glanced at his daughter's husband. "You had to mention the diamonds."

"Sorry, I rather forgot myself," Thatcher apologized.

With speed and agility Langley climbed up the drainpipe until he reached the balcony. As he came over the railing, Jack grinned.

"Good to see you, old friend," he whispered.

"And you," Langley said.

"Now I know where you've been all this time," Jack remarked as he nodded toward the scene being played out in the room beyond.

Langley leaned over and pulled his lock picks out of his boot. "Where is that?"

"The Paris circus," Jack said, keeping an eye on the scene inside.

"Very amusing," Langley told him. "Actually managed to get out of Abbaye in much the same manner. Twice."

"Ellyson would have told you that once should have been enough."

"It should have been, but my hosts were a rather determined lot."

"You are not going to like who you see in there," Jack remarked.

"So it *is* Nottage. Rotten bastard," he muttered. But there wasn't time to consider much more, for inside the room the conversation was now rising to an argument.

"She's turning them against each other," Jack explained.

"As only my minx can."

Jack's gaze swiveled over toward him. "Really engaged to her?"

"Will be once I get her out," Langley told him.

"Can't scamper out of wedlock like a monkey," Jack remarked.

"Not if you marry the right woman."

"True enough," Jack agreed.

Langley quickly got the lock undone and slipped the door open slightly, so the full conversation wafted through the opening.

"They've got a king's ransom in jewels stashed away," Minerva was saying. "These diamonds of mine are nothing compared to what they have."

"Is that true?" Adlington asked the pair, his pistol wavering between Sir George and Nottage.

"Aye, but it wasn't my idea—it was his," Sir Basil said, rising from his chair and taking a step away from Nottage. "It was all his idea. Stealing the jewels, shipping them to London. I merely used my contact in Strout's office to make sure the jewels were removed before the crates were sent on to Langley's house in the country. I did nothing else."

"Nothing else?" Nottage scoffed. "You set Langley up to be arrested, you planted information in the reports that made him out to be a traitor, all so you could get him attained for treason and get his house and title, you *cit* bastard."

"And my brother calls me a disgrace," Jack muttered.

Sir Basil's face grew bright red with rage. "It was all him," he said, pointing at Nottage. "He forced me, he—"

Nottage moved so quickly, it was like a flash of lightning. He shoved Minerva into Adlington's path then reached inside his coat, pulled out a pistol and shot Sir Basil, the man falling back in the chair. Then he turned to flee out the balcony, but what he met with was the full force of his former mentor, who tackled a shocked Nottage to the floor.

Langley had the advantage of surprise, and before the man could raise a hand, the baron planted a solid, well-aimed facer—full of every bit of anger and fury he possessed—knocking his former secretary out cold.

Meanwhile, Clifton and Parkerton broke through from the hall, but not before Minerva twisted in Adlington's grasp and faced her old suitor.

"I have been waiting a long time to do this," she said.

And then she brought her knee up as hard as she could and nailed him squarely in what she considered the area that had guided the wretched man all his adult life.

Gerald's mouth opened in a wide O before he toppled over.

She kicked the gun out of his hand, and would have kicked him one more time for good measure if Langley hadn't pulled her back.

"It is over," he told her, cradling her close. "All over."

But it wasn't.

For having seen the writing on the wall, Gerald made good his threats.

"She's not Lady Standon. She's naught but Maggie Owens, the old earl's bastard. The man married her to Sterling instead of his own daughter. Her mother was the village whore. She's not a lady. She's nothing but an imposter."

But if he thought he was going to be rewarded for sharing the truth, what he got was a gag over his mouth and his arms bound, and was left in a chair while the rest of the mess was sorted out.

Still, the damage was done, and Minerva felt the weight of all the eyes on her and the whispered speculation that now encircled her.

By morning she would be completely ruined.

Lucy came over and wrapped her arm around her friend, and then later, when it was time to move Sir Basil's body, Clifton gathered them both up and took Minerva home, while Langley stayed behind.

The entire carriage ride no one said a word, and the heavy silence inside it weighed on Minerva as much as her broken heart did.

Why would Langley ever return to her now?

They found Mrs. Hutchinson passed out in Minerva's room and the margravine missing.

Minerva took one glance at the empty wineglass and realized that her bosky housekeeper had drunk the wine intended for Langley.

"Serves her right," Lucy said as she directed Clifton to return to Parkerton House with the news of the missing margravine, while she stayed with her friend.

Minerva collapsed onto the bed and cried as Lucy sat beside her and waited for the flood of tears to subside.

And when they did, Minerva asked, "Can you forgive me?"

Lucy blinked. "Whatever for?"

"For not being who I am supposed to be? For being so awful to you for all those years, acting like I was an earl's daughter and you were—"

Staring across at her, Lucy pressed her lips together and then laughed aloud. "Good God, Minerva! Is that what's bothering you?" She laughed again and then pulled her into a bear hug. "You are exactly who you are supposed to be, the most courageous and intelligent woman I have ever met. I am honored to have you as my friend. Best we leave the past behind us, for I had my fair share in our previous disagreements."

Minerva wiped at the tears on her face. "Yes, I suppose you did."

"And I'll always be your friend, unless you start insisting that I not eavesdrop, like Elinor is always prattling on about."

Her heart close to breaking, Minerva hugged her dear friend. "Oh, Lucy! I think we owe a debt of gratitude to the Duchess of Hollindrake for putting us all together."

"Are you just saying that so I'll stand by your side when she rings a peal over you for hiding her diamonds?"

They both laughed, and for a time they sat together, Minerva relating the events that led to her marriage—a story she had never told any other living soul—and Lucy, good friend that she was, listening.

Then Clifton returned to fetch his wife, but to Minerva's pain, he had not come with Langley.

With nothing better to do, she sought her bed and lay there for some time, staring up at the painting of the crooked folly until she drifted off to sleep.

How long she slept, she knew not, but she was awakened when her window sash creaked open.

She sat bolt upright in bed and gaped as Lord Langley came climbing in her window.

"Ho, there, minx. Sorry to wake you up," he said, leaning over and warming his hands at the fireplace grate. "The fellow you hired did an excellent job of repairing the drainpipe."

"Whatever are you doing here?" she asked, feeling suddenly shy. "And whyever did you climb up the drainpipe?"

He grinned. "Because I still can." He let out a big sigh. "You will be pleased to know that Nottage confessed to everything, but of course blamed it all on Sir Basil. Your excellent sleuthing and powers of deduction made it quite easy to lay all the evidence out to the Prime Minister—ah, it is good to have an old friend in high places—that, and the margravine arrived, with Brigid and Lucia in tow, and Lucia identified Lady Brownett's rubies as the Borgia stones. Lady Brownett kicked up quite a fuss to be relieved of her jewels, and if old Brownie hadn't been dead already, I think the old girl would have done him in herself."

He glanced around the room and spotted the tray left over from earlier, picking up a piece of bread and cheese and munching happily. "Oh, I daresay I am famished."

"So is it all over?" she asked.

He nodded. "I am still under attainder for the time being—that demmed Sir Basil had it filed earlier today. But no matter, I will be cleared before long. The Prime Minister has promised to gain me a king's pardon, perhaps even an elevation— though not for a few years. We'll have to wait for the scandal to die down a bit. Still, I have you to thank for all of it."

Minerva couldn't find the words to say anything, for she was still in shock that he was here. With her.

Dear God. Had he just said "we"?

And before she could manage to find the nerve to ask what he meant, he continued, "And you will never believe this, the margravine would only sign her statement if she could take Adlington with her when she left London. She wouldn't go without him, and he thinks he's found his boon." Langley shuddered. "Poor stupid fellow. Well, he'll learn soon enough when he finds himself manacled to her bed." He glanced over at her, "Not that I was ever—"

Minerva waved her hand at him, for clearly she'd heard enough. Besides, this was all great news— save perhaps the part about the margravine and Adlington—and it was only after a deep breath and when he paused long enough for her to find her wherewithal that she was able to ask, "Langley, whatever are you doing here?"

"Where else would I go?" He shrugged off his jacket and sat down on the edge of the bed to tug off his boots.

"But you know the truth now," she persisted. "You know who I am, and yet you are still here."

He paused for a long moment, and then glanced over at her, "I love you, Minerva. You. Not your name. Not who Gerald Adlington thinks you are. I love *you*." With that said, he simply went back to pulling off his boots.

Minerva shivered. Had she truly heard him correctly? He loved her? "But I am not Lady Standon."

"Of course you are. It matters not who you were before you married Philip Sterling. But once you married him, you became his marchioness. For better or worse. Though not for much longer," he told her, his eyes alight with a passionate mischief. "I think you will make a much better baroness." He reached out and pulled her close.

Minerva pushed him back. "Langley! I am not a lady. I am not even a proper Lady Standon."

"And I am still being examined for treason," he teased back. "Simply put, we make an excellent pair. I think we should be married immediately and capitalize on our notoriety."

"Married?" Minerva couldn't believe her ears. Or her heart—for it hammered in her chest with a wild cadence. He truly wanted to marry her.

She gazed into his eyes and found nothing but serious intent mirrored there. No teasing, no mischief, just a burning passion for her and her alone.

"You've loved princesses, and duchesses, and real ladies. Whyever would you want me?"

He huffed a sigh and sat up. "First of all, you are decidedly wrong about all of that. I never loved any of them. I didn't know what it meant to love until I met you."

"But I am not a lady," she told him.

"That is where you are wrong," he said, leaning over and searching in the drawer of the nightstand. He pulled out a velvet pouch and drew out of it a gorgeous emerald necklace.

Silently, he put it around her neck, then sat back and admired his handiwork. "I knew emeralds would suit you much better than diamonds."

Minerva's fingers went to the stones and then she looked up at him. "Where did these come from?"

"Langley House," he told her. "I fetched them while you and Mrs. Harrow were admiring her garden. I knew then that I would need them."

Minerva's brow furrowed. "Then? Why that was before we'd—" She came to a stop and blushed. *Before they'd made love.*

"Not for me," he told her. "I might not have been able to say it, but I knew then I loved you and that our betrothal was not in vain." He paused and looked at her. "Will you have me, my dearest, beloved Minerva Sterling?"

And even before she could say yes, he caught her in his arms and began to make love to her.

And very soon she was saying "Yes!"

Several times over.

Epilogue

London, 1825

"*A*re you going to tell Papa and Minerva about what you found inside that painting?" Thalia, Baroness Larken, asked as she tipped onto her toes to catch a better look at the ship coming into the Southwark dock.

"Whatever do you mean?" Felicity, the Duchess of Hollindrake, asked, nose tucked in the air.

Her twin was hardly fooled. "That wretched painting of the folly. What you found inside?" Tally raised her brows and gave her sister a hard stare.

It had no effect on Felicity. "If I hadn't gone to the trouble of having the house on Brook Street redone for them, that painting would still be on the wall and no one would be the wiser."

"But that painting came from Papa's private collection, and he most likely knows who those sapphires belong to."

Felicity shrugged and went back to watching the ship draw closer. She'd recently had the painting taken down, and when it was, the frame fell apart and with it a velvet pouch containing a sapphire necklace.

"Wasn't there some fuss with Nanny Helga all those years ago and her missing sapphires?" Tally mused. "You don't think those might be—"

"Thalia Langley!" her sister said, all indignation and mock horror. "You have the most rampant imagination, and at your age! Whatever would Papa have been doing with Nanny Helga's sapphires? 'Tis scandalous to even suggest such a thing. It is just a very odd coincidence, nothing more."

Tally thought it no such thing, but said nothing.

"You aren't going to mention them, are you?" Felicity asked as the ship began to turn into the dock.

"No, but I have to imagine you are keeping them a secret because you haven't forgiven Minerva for not telling you about the Sterling diamonds," Tally replied.

"I have so," Felicity shot back. "But it only seems fair that I wait a bit before I inform her and Papa about them. Besides, they have been gone all these years in China, and I hardly want to burden their happy homecoming by dragging up past peccadilloes."

Tally pressed her lips together and tried not to laugh out loud. Her sister was as incorrigible as ever.

"Can you imagine it? Papa is finally home," Felicity said, letting out a contented sigh. "He wrote of looking forward to hearing the sound of laughter filling Langley House." The duchess glanced over at her four children. "I suppose that means he will wish for all of us to visit and visit often."

Tally laughed. "That might be one way of looking at the matter." She rocked on her heels and glanced at the ship.

There on the deck, a trio of unruly children raced underfoot, scampering across the lines and weaving in and out of the sailors as the poor men worked to dock the ship.

"Poor Minerva," Felicity muttered, shaking her head.

"Whatever do you mean?" Tally asked.

Felicity nodded at the ship. "Rounding the Horn with such children on board! Wherever is their nanny? Or their mother, for that matter?" She made a *tsk tsk* sound and shook her head.

Her twin, on the other hand, smiled at the boys' antics. "Handsome children, don't you think?"

"Rambunctious devils, more like it," Felicity remarked. Then the duchess glanced at the children again.

Tawny hair, bright eyes . . .

No! It couldn't be.

"Tally—" Felicity began.

"Hmm, yes?" her sister asked, waving at their father and Minerva, who had arrived at the deck rail. Minerva, smiling and looking elegant in a silk gown, leaned over and kissed one of the lads on the forehead, while her father leaned over and picked up the smallest one, holding him up to see London spread out around them.

"Is there something everyone neglected to tell me?" Felicity demanded.

"That our father and Minerva are bound to cause more scandal?" Tally mused. "Oh, dear, I do believe young Ellis is about to fall over the railing." Quickly, Minerva tugged the boy back to safety.

"No, not that!" Felicity bit out. "That we have two—no, make that three—half brothers?"

"Oh, yes, I daresay we do," Tally agreed.

"And why didn't anyone tell me?"

Tally grinned and waved happily at her father. "I do believe Papa thought it best to wait and tell you when he was back in Town."

Turn the page for a sneak peek
into the world of the Standon Widows,
from author Elizabeth Boyle!

$\mathcal{W}$hile I was writing the last couple of books in the Bachelor Chronicles—*Love Letters from a Duke, Confessions of a Little Black Gown,* and *Memoirs of a Scandalous Red Dress*—I was going over the elaborate family tree that I had developed for these stories and realized that I had an entire branch of widows—all of whom had been married to the onetime heir to the Hollindrake dukedom. Three Lady Standons. Because their husbands died before inheriting, and another heir had stepped into line, each widow hung on the tree like a solitary leaf.

But I became intrigued. Here were three widows, all possessing the same courtesy title: Lady Standon, and a divided widow's portion. Then, like most writers, my imagination ran wild. What if the Ladies Standon didn't get along? What if they were more trouble than they were ever worth? What would you do if you were the Duke of Hollindrake, the one who finally inherited, and you had the care, responsibility, and feeding of these fractious widows?

Then I came to the question that answered it all: What would that matchmaking dynamo, Felicity Langley, do with all these widows? The only possible way to get rid of them, short of a long Continental tour or outright murder, would be to marry them off. And I knew that is what Felicity would do—as quickly and efficiently as she has done everything else in her life.

This was serendipity that I couldn't ignore, stories I had to write, and thus was born the next series in the Bachelor Chronicles: The Standon Widows. I hope you enjoy these peeks into the first two books, *How I Met My Countess* and *Mad About the Duke*.

HOW I MET MY COUNTESS

Object: Marry off Lucy Ellyson Sterling

Unlikely Hero: The Earl of Clifton

Years earlier, Lucy helped her father train Lord Clifton in the arts of being a spy. Needless to say, the noble earl found the unlikely Lucy a handful, and she, well, she thought Clifton completely unqualified for the dangerous work ahead and did her best to discourage him.

"Still, you might consider returning to London for the Season," Lucy continued blithering on like Mariana might, "so as to find a wife."

"A wha-a-a-t?"

She swore his shudder ran all way down to his boots.

So the Earl of Clifton had a fear of matrimony. That might work in her favor.

"A wife," she supplied. "A countess. A lady of good bloodlines to supply you with an heir and a spare."

"Yes, yes," he said. "I know what a wife is for."

"Aren't you worried about leaving your title without an heir?" She paused and lowered her voice. "If you don't come back, that is."

He glanced over at her, a hint of annoyance flashing in his eyes.

Oh, she'd hit the mark with that one.

"I have an uncle who is in line," he said stiffly.

"Excellent. Is he married?"

"Yes."

"A sensible fellow, then?"

There was a long, measured pause from the earl. "Not particularly."

"How unfortunate. But perhaps he has heirs with the necessary qualifications?" she asked.

"Yes. Two sons." The answer came out like a dog snapping at a bone.

Lucy pressed her lips together to keep from grinning. Oh, she had him now. Then she composed her next sally very carefully. If only so it landed like a cannonball at his feet.

"So you'll marry when you return—that is to say if you return."

His brows knit together and his arm stiffened.

Lucy wondered if, perhaps, she might have pushed him too far.

"I'll return." He said this with a finality that should have been enough right there to end the subject—that is if this had been an ordinary polite conversation.

But it wasn't enough to stop Lucy.

"Of course you will, my lord. Most certainly," she said, patting his arm as if consoling him over a lost wager. And a paltry one at that. Then she continued, "What sort of lady will you look for?"

"Excuse me?" He stumbled a bit and Lucy waited for him to get his footing and composure realigned before she once again thrust her question into his chest like a dagger.

"Your countess? However will you know her when you meet her?"

"I haven't given it much thought." Again his tone suggested that the subject was finished.

But oh, Lucy wasn't. "That is where most men fail in these sorts of things."

"Fail?"

"Yes, fail. Utterly. You men don't give enough consideration into the sort of woman you want to spend your life with. Instead you rather just sort of pick, like one might a racehorse."

"There is more to choosing a bride than that," he said, in a stuffy sort of manner.

"How so?" she asked innocently, as if such matters were well beyond her ken. Then again, he hadn't the least notion that she was leading him into a trap.

"Well, I suppose I will have to consider a lady's bloodlines," he told her, in such a pompous manner that Lucy almost wished Rusty and Sammy would arrive now and save her from this lofty lecture. "Her education should be impeccable, and I will have to examine her suitability, her countenance, the way she holds herself in public."

"Exactly as I said. Just as one chooses a racehorse," Lucy pointed out.

"Not at all the same thing."

She pulled to a stop. "By bloodlines, training and the turn of her lines. Isn't that what you said?"

His jaws worked together, his gaze fixed and narrowed on the road ahead. "Yes."

"Just like a racehorse, my lord." And with that, she tugged him back into the track in the road and they continued on in silence.

Apparently the earl didn't like being shown the shortcomings of his plans. Or the comparison of his future bride to an Arabian at Newmarket. "Miss Lucy, there is one difference you neglected to consider."

"What would that be?" she asked confident in her ingenious and disarming banter.

He glanced down at her, dark eyes smoldering with an intensity that sent a shiver of warning down her spine. He turned that devil-may-care smile on her, the one that suggested he was looking for something—or rather someone—to devour.

Passionately.

Lucy tried to ignore the tremor running down her spine. It wasn't guilt, or anger, or even fear. But something else. Something she didn't even want to know.

At least not with him. For when the Earl of Clifton looked at her that way, it reminded her that she was a woman, and that he was a very handsome man.

Too handsome.

"I've never been in love with a horse," he said. "But I will love my future countess. Without a doubt, I will not marry without love."

And this time Lucy stumbled.

MAD ABOUT THE DUKE

Object: Elinor Knolles Sterling must quickly find a husband so he can fend off her stepfather's plans to marry her younger sister off to an aging roué

Unlikely Hero: The Duke of Parkerton, who Elinor has mistaken for a solicitor and subsequently hired to find her the right duke to marry

In this scene, the Duke of Parkerton is here to recuse himself from her service as her solicitor, "Mr. St. Maur," in hopes of fending off what could become a big scandal. Before he can make his escape, Elinor gives him a list of likely dukes she wants him to investigate as marital prospects.

"Lady Standon—" he began.

Even as she said, "Mr. St. Maur—"

They both paused and smiled at each other.

"You first," he demurred, as only a gentleman should. He was still a gentleman. *He was.*

She nodded, then sat down, waving her hand at the chair to indicate that he should do the same.

He would have preferred to stand so he would be closer to the door and therefore able to bolt free at the first opportunity, but what else could he do?

James sat down, taking one last, wistful look over his shoulder at the door.

"I have prepared a list," she was saying.

"A wha-a-t?"

"A list. Of prospects." She pulled a slim volume from the pocket of her gown, and from that plucked out a folded piece of paper. She held it out to him. "These are the names I have determined are the most likely."

James stared at the paper. Husbands to be. A man to marry her. Rescue her. A man who would claim her devotion . . . and her love . . . and her body.

His teeth ground together.

"I've only included the ducal prospects," she continued. "At least for now."

The ducal prospects? Suddenly the dull, faded room brightened a bit.

She took his pause, as well as his reluctance to take the list from her hand, altogether wrong. "Yes, as my sister mentioned yesterday, it is my intention to marry well, a duke preferably."

He opened his mouth to say something. Something like *I am the most likely duke around*," but he knew that such an announcement at this moment, considering the circumstances, would hardly endear him to her.

Not that he wanted her regard. Not in the least.

Besides, she'd think him mad. As he was beginning to suspect was a legitimate conclusion.

"Yes, well, I have come up with a list of the only ducal candidates in London."

James nodded politely and took the paper, running through his own list of likely candidates, and other than himself, he couldn't think of one of his peers who was worthy of her. Unless she meant to go after one of the royal dukes.

Which would be madness in itself.

Making her the perfect wife for you.

James coughed. Where the devil had that thought come from? He wasn't in the market for a wife. He wasn't.

As he opened the paper, he considered what he should do next.

Oh, bother, just confess who you are, then declare your undying devotion, carry her off and be done with the matter.

And for one impetuous moment James came within a midge's wing of doing just that.

Until he unfolded the piece of paper and read the neatly penned names.

"I wasn't on the bloody list," James sputtered loudly as he entered the small dining room that was at the back of Parkerton House.

Jack and his wife, Miranda, glanced up from the luncheon they were enjoying.

"Pardon?" Jack asked, wiping his lips with his napkin.

James slapped the paper down on the table and marched away in a state of high dudgeons. "Her list," he declared, pointing at the offensive piece of paper. "Lady Standon's list of ducal candidates. I am not on it."

Jack scooted his chair back in hasty retreat, as if wanting to distance himself from this budding storm. Miranda, however, had no qualms about picking up the paper and reading it.

Short reading that it was.

Two names. Two bloody names and neither of which was his.

Where it should have read, *James Tremont, the 9th Duke of Parkerton,* there were two other names.

Whatever was wrong with him that she hadn't bothered to set his name to her wretched list?

He glanced over at Miranda. Demmit, whatever was she smiling about? This was hardly funny.

"What do you care, Parkerton?" Jack asked, having taken a peek over his wife's shoulder. "You've no regard for this woman and she's certainly not under your protection."

James set his jaw and paced a bit. There was the rub. She wasn't under his protection. Because if she was . . .

"Besides, what do you care? You've resigned."

James paced a few steps, not daring to glance over at his younger brother.

"Good God, tell me you've resigned," Jack insisted.

"How could I?" James said in his defense. "That foolish woman has Longford on her list. Longford, Jack!"

And not me.

ELIZABETH BOYLE

Memoirs of a Scandalous Red Dress • 978-0-06-137324-4
What if all you have are the memories of a rake . . . and the
scandalous red dress that nearly brought you to ruin?

Confessions of a Little Black Gown • 978-0-06-137323-7
She spied him in the shadows and in an instant
Thalia Langley knew the man before her was no saint.

Tempted by the Night • 978-0-06-137322-0
Lady Hermione Marlowe refuses to believe that the handsome
gentleman she's loved from afar for so long could be so wicked.

Love Letters From a Duke • 978-0-06-078403-4
Felicity Langley thought she knew what love was after years of
corresponding with the staid Duke of Hollindrake . . . until her
footman unlocked her passionate nature with his unlikely kiss.

His Mistress by Morning • 978-0-06-078402-7
An impudent wish—and a touch of magic—lands a very proper
Charlotte Wilmont where she always dreamed she'd be—in
Sebastian, Viscount Trent's bed . . . and in his heart. But not in the
way she had imagined it.

At Avon Books, we know your passion for romance—once you finish one of our novels, you find yourself wanting more.

May we tempt you with . . .

- **Excerpts** from our upcoming releases.

- Entertaining **extras**, including authors' personal photo albums and book lists.

- Behind-the-scenes **scoop** on your favorite characters and series.

- **Sweepstakes** for the chance to win free books, romantic getaways, and other fun prizes.

- Writing **tips** from our authors and editors.

- **Blog** with our authors and find out why they love to write romance.

- **Exclusive content** that's not contained within the pages of our novels.

Join us at
www.avonbooks.com

AVON

An Imprint of HarperCollins*Publishers*
www.avonromance.com

Available wherever books are sold or please call 1-800-331-3761 to order.

FTH 0708